CH00705507

MICHAEL S. JACKSON

Ringlander: The Path and the Way

Batch 3   6/17

John

Copyright © 2021 by Michael S. Jackson

All rights reserved. No part of this publication may be reproduced, stored or transmitted in any form or by any means, electronic, mechanical, photocopying, recording, scanning, or otherwise without written permission from the publisher. It is illegal to copy this book, post it to a website, or distribute it by any other means without permission.

This novel is entirely a work of fiction. The names, characters and incidents portrayed in it are the work of the author's imagination. Any resemblance to actual persons, living or dead, events or localities is entirely coincidental.

Michael S. Jackson asserts the moral right to be identified as the author of this work.

Cover illustration by John Anthony Di Giovanni

Cover layout and design by Michael S. Jackson

Maps by Michael S. Jackson

First edition

ISBN: 9798743109661

This book was professionally typeset on Reedsy. Find out more at reedsy.com

For Katie, Erin, Thomas and Player 3

Contents

Acknowledgement

For Katie, Erin and Thomas for not allowing me to sit for too long and for generally being absolutely incredible, and bright, and wonderful. My parents who set me on the course; you gave me my line. My brother, who probably without realising it, has always given me support and persuasion to set sail on my own. Helen for your unwavering support, editing skill and for putting up with my flights of fancy. My good friends Liam and Colin for the laughs, the fun times and for keeping me sane, I literally could not have got to the end without you.

I have to mention Imgur, Reddit and Scribophile, whose communities are some of the truest, most honest I have found, and an absolute gold mine of resource. If you're a writer, I'd recommend you check them out immediately.

Thank you to everyone who has supported me, financially, emotionally and professionally over the years. The world can be a tough place, but it is full of good people and you need to let them in. Embarking on a voyage like this one is hard enough without having a few cabin mates to nudge you back in the right direction along the way.

THE PATH AND THE WAY
RINGLANDER

MICHAEL S. JACKSON

mjackson.co.uk | @mikestepjack

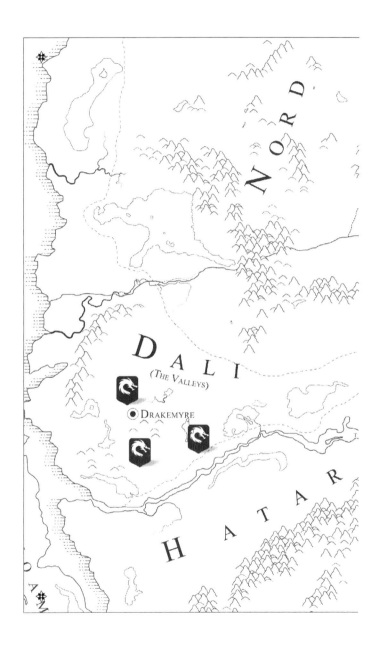

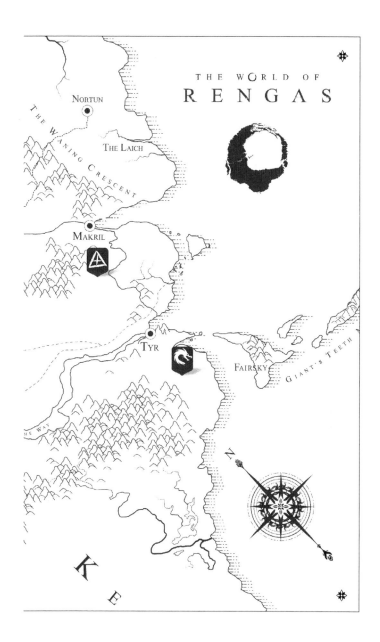

THE WORLD OF
RENGAS

NORTUN

THE LAICH

THE WANING CRESCENT

MAKRIL

TYR

FAIRSKY

GIANT'S TEETH

HE WAY

N

K E

Kyira

Kyira dragged her belt blade through the slaver's throat, acutely aware of each tendon and muscle tugging on the fine serrated edge. Warm blood burst out over her hand; she had taken the vein. A momentary flutter, but she clenched the bone handle and completed the movement, as though she were simply preparing a pig for the Feast of Moons.

Even as the slaver fell, another emerged from the mist, taller than the last by two heads and twice as wide. His minksin swirled behind him — a wide canvas larger than her sleeping mat. She set her feet as he barrelled towards her, spinning a two-handed ortaxe above his head with one arm. Kyira dove and slid into the plug of ice she had hauled out barely an hour before and sprang back to her feet.

"All he wanted to know was if you had any friends out here, girl," rasped the huge slaver. "The Kin would save you all. Might even let you go if you had a map or two." His deep-set eyes took her in. "I guess not. Still, that ain't no problem of mine. My reckonings tell me that you're out here all by yourself. There ain't no one what can save you."

"Get back!" snarled Kyira, swiping a nervous fish blade out in front.

"I don't think so, girl. Not me. You might be quick enough to catch old Okvik off guard, but not me, little one. Not Siskin."

Kyira shifted left, feigning an escape.

"Oh, no you don't!" The slaver rushed forward, realising too late that the ice hole lay between them. His feet slipped as he tried to fight his own momentum but he slid awkwardly in, coming to a stop with one arm and leg stretching out of the hole. "Curse you!" Guttural pants punctuated each word. "Forbringrs curse you!" His muscles shook as he struggled, searching for purchase on the sharp edges.

Kyira held her belt blade low but steady. The slaver's ortaxe sat just out his reach but it was heavy enough to rebalance him. He clearly had the same thought.

"Raaaa!" He thrust out his arm and clasped the weapon's handle, but the move shifted his weight the wrong way and he slid into the hole like a fat seal. She turned away.

No splash? "Shiach!"

She spun on her spot and peered into the ice hole. The slaver was holding his head a barely a finger's breadth from the slushy surface, the metal point of his ortaxe rammed into the wall, giving him enough tension to hold himself rigid against the inside. He was strong, but those great muscles were shaking, and he was holding his breath. It was silent again, but not the silence when useful things were being done. This was that special quiet that came before death, before the old ox was slaughtered, before the dog that had bitten its master was put down, before the pig…

Kyira side-stepped around the hole, away from the slaver's head and tapped the crook of his knee with her moccasin. The tension broke, his grip failed, and the slushy Laich swallowed him with barely a sound.

She stared at the gently bobbing ice, as though his wide mottled face might somehow emerge, angry and dripping, ready to exact hateful vengeance, but she knew better. His pig heart had beat its last.

She forced her gaze up, scanning the Laich. Mist was not unusual for this time of year, nor this time of day, but it had come on so quickly she had barely finished setting her fishing line when the hills had vanished behind a thick veil. At least she knew exactly where she was, as Pathwatchers always did.

The first slaver was sprawled a few paces away, surrounded by dark spatters. She collected her oil tin but didn't relight it. Slavers always travelled in twos, but there might be more out there yet. She rewound the wick and pressed it into the congealed mixture, then tucked it away in her waist bag.

She squatted over the slaver's corpse, holding her belt blade over his ruined neck. There was no coming back for this pig, but it never hurt to stay cautious. His face was black with Lines but there was no elegance to them, and they had no story to tell — nothing she could make out anyway. She touched her chin, feeling the raised patterns and following them to her cheeks. Each of the five Lines marked her cycles since becoming an adult, the beginning of her story, her aspirations, and her life. A Pathwatcher's life.

She blinked at the slaver. His Lines were those of a fishman, a chaser of sharks, and yet here he was inland, chasing down simple folk. The Sami had a name for those who ignored the Lines written into their skin: Culdè, and this man's aspirations looked as though they had been

3

forgotten many moons ago. Where his skin wasn't Lined, it was cracked and red. A Southerner, not used to the cold, dry winds of Nord, and judging by the beige patches on his breeches, he'd spent weeks, maybe months, in the saddle.

She rummaged through his pockets, ignoring the fleas crawling freely between his inner and outer garments: a dirty pipe made from a wood she had never seen before; some flint; some rolled smokeleaf; a chewstick; and a small pouch. She pulled the drawstrings and let the weight inside tip out onto her palm. There was no mistaking it, even in Nord babies sucked on the varnished wooden bulb to help them sleep. So, he *was* a man. A father. What sort of woman would have bred with you? Certainly no Sami, nor any other Nordun woman that Kyira had met.

A colony of dark specks crowded around a spot of blood on his furry hood, and she stood, feeling nauseous. Regardless of who he was, nobody who let themselves get in such a state lasted long out here, not least those who kept their guard down for so long. He had to have had a camp close by, she thought as she dragged him to the ice hole. The body slid along the edge, tipping in headfirst, just like his friend.

The ice plug came next, and it dropped neatly back into the hole, forcing a little water to gurgle up the sides. Pocketing the slaver's pouch, she dipped her hands in the water and scrubbed the blood from her skin, trying to picture which sort of fire would warm her up the quickest. It was a half day's walk from here on the Laich back to where Aki, her father, had camped and she would need to find somewhere along the way to sleep. There were a number of places: the cave upon the fourth sister above the Waning Crescent; a hidden alcove in the small waterfall a league beyond on the last sister — she might get wet, but at least she would be hidden. The cave would be best, and the fourth sister was a tall enough hill to spot anyone following.

The dark residue, colourless in the evening light, pooled with the quickly freezing water creating patterns.

She had not planned on being away from home for so long, but the new season's taimen living in the Laich were far too fat to just leave to the orca, and twilight was the best time to catch them. It was why she had spent most of the day cutting such a big hole through the ice. It was lucky it was not yet spring — things might have gone very differently if she had been fishing for eels.

A noise blew in from the north bank and her breath caught. A whicker. She stared into the darkening night, but the mist gave nothing away.

The belt blade slipped back into a sheath at her waist with a reassuring rasp, its bone handle still sticky with the slaver's blood; the rack of four taimens went over her back, the clasp hooking through the loop on her shoulder; and lastly, her fishing line, which she spun quickly around the gnarlnut shell, was thrust into her waist bag.

It was time to go.

She spared the mist a final glance and sped off over the ice towards the far bank. The frozen estuary was narrow, but she was closer to the northern side than the south. Hard ice crunched underfoot so loud she was sure someone would hear, but she pushed on, reaching the south bank's shoreline well within an hour. She slowed as she approached the rocky outcrops — if there were more slavers, they couldn't have guessed she could cross the Laich so quickly. In any case they were mounted and she was not.

5

Weaving deftly between the rocks, she leapt over the thinnest ice and onto the shore. The ground was permafrost all year round here along the Taegr — the line that marked the upper circle of the world — and was perfect for running. Only her brother Hasaan could match her stride, but not for long, a fact she used to enjoy teasing him with. The ground was a smear of colour beneath her as her feet carried her on, bounding lightly over and up the fat waist of the second sister, upon and around the ridge of the hill's back and onto the shoulder, the first of the two peaks.

Hopping over a decoy fork, Kyira carried on through into the rough grass until the slightest change of colour showed she had re-joined the ridge path. It was as clear to her as if it had been lain out with lines of oil and set alight. She stopped and turned back towards the Laich.

Three mounted slavers stood at the northern shore, black scratches on the pristine white of the Laich. Kyira ducked. They might not be Nordun but the horned nara they rode upon were, and they would catch her up and run her down before three hours had passed.

She took off, sprinting along the nape — it was slower but the rough ground would hide her shape. The line led her all the way to the shoulders of the third sister, a ridge that led to the highest hill on the Waning Crescent. She trudged carelessly through a large patch of snow as though she was heading down into the valley. Her pursuers would expect her to seek shelter in the vale before risking the ridges on a moonless night.

She raced along the ridge, trying to cover as much distance as she could before first dark. Panting, she dropped off the Waning Crescent and entered the second valley, a tree valley, named not for the trees, of which there were none, but for the multiple ways in and out. It was filled with glacial boulders and was a perfect place to rest and escape if she needed to.

She jumped down the few feet onto the first boulder and ran its length. Ten paces exactly. The next one, six, she thought, already in the air. She landed and rolled forward then again she was air-bound, springing over the stones with ease. The last rock was flat and although she couldn't see it, she knew it was five paces narrow and twenty-and-one-half paces long, with a short step to the grass. She hopped onto it, then jerked as her foot bumped into something that should not have been there, sending her spinning into the sharp edge of a split boulder. The ground barely had time to greet her before she was back up, staring at the dark lump. It was a grey glacial boulder ten paces wide and fifteen long, deposited many moons ago, and had lived at the bottom of this valley since then. Yet here it was, uphill.

"What are you doing up here?" she said, feeling along its edge. "You did not walk, and neither were you pushed. You are too fat for that." It had been split right down the middle. The ragged edge led to a face that was almost shiny, like the rock had spent a lifetime against a smith's forge. What force could split a rock in two?

Irrational panic bubbled in her breast, her heart pounded as though the slavers had somehow appeared before her. She drew a ragged breath, willing the shapes around her back into their still, stoic forms. She was alone.

Breathe.

Her skin tingled and her vision narrowed. The vale grew darker, but somehow clearer as a new focus settled upon her.

Breathe.

Her mother used to call it magic, but it was no such thing. It was just a way of tricking her body into listening. And feeling.

Breathe.

A sympathy with the world, from the crisp air to the frost at her feet.

Breathe.

A snowcrick chirruped on her right, looking for a male to fight. Another to the left. There must be a new nest nearby. She listened as they spoke to each other, imagining that she could understand their noises.

Breathe.

A soft wind bristled at the hairs on her face bringing a new smell.

Wood smoke. There was a fire close by. The vale was almost completely black now, but there... there was something...

Someone was breathing, and it was heavy and laboured. Kyira crept around the split boulder, and pursing her lips, whistled three short bursts, warbling the sound. There was a slight pause before the corresponding call floated in on the breeze.

The dim glow of the fire appeared from between the boulders, flickering shadows coming from the low wall of snow and rocks. A fire built in haste. Kyira stayed just outside of the light.

"Hasaan?" said a man.

"It's me, Aki." She manoeuvred into the hollow depression, skirted the fire, and knelt at her father's side. This was a well-chosen camp; they were well hidden here. "What happened? Why are you out here? It is not safe."

"You think I cannot handle myself?" asked her father, throwing his climbing stick clattering against the stones.

She reached over and moved the stick's leather wrapping away from the coals. "There are dangers. Aki, your skin is so pale."

He drew back. "Child, I am perfectly able—"

"Aki," said Kyira, pulling the taimen from her back and sitting them on the grass.

"Aki, Aki, Aki! Iqaluk is my name, Kyira! Aki is a name children use. You are Lined now. Act like it." He nodded back up the hill. "Where is your brother?"

"He is not with you?"

"He goes his own way. He always has." Even insensible, the words were meant to cut her. "He will be fine. He went climbing this morning."

"So, you are fighting again."

"That boy has much to learn!" snapped Iqaluk, grabbing the stick and shaking it at her. "As do you." He smoothed down his long grey beard.

"And what have I to learn exactly?"

"How to choose your own path for one!"

"I do that which makes me happy, Aki." Sickness rose in Kyira's stomach. "Besides, I know a Stormwing's call when I hear one." It was probably the most lame rebuke she could have chosen, but it was hardly the time to get into a debate on the course of her life.

"Even a Culdè knows the Stormwing, not least during mating season."

"A Culdè? You think I do not know myself!" Kyira spoke

before she could stop herself. "Well, I knew you were here, hiding, in this... hole. What if that stone rolled back down? What would you do then by yourself."

"Did you see it? No? I did. It is broken in two, girl! Cracked like an egg, as though there were nothing inside but... but yolk." The last word vanished into a bout of ragged coughs.

Kyira placed a tender hand on his forehead. Fever blood. Only the beginnings, but it would get worse. "Where are you hurt?"

Iqaluk tried to bend forward then after a second patted his thick skin jacket near his kidneys. Carefully, Kyira spread the coat, smelling the blood before she saw it. Her cold hands touched searing hot skin drawing a hiss between clenched teeth. She had never known her father to show pain. He was the strongest man she knew. She lifted his coat and shirt revealing angry red skin surrounding a puncture wound. She pulled the fishing line from her bag and knotted it around the jacket at his back to keep the wound exposed. "Don't move, Aki. I'll be back."

The low bushes and plants hid their medicines well this far north. Thorns and poisons kept all but the most determined animals at bay, but Kyira knew what to look for. Under the last rock and a few inches under the earth was a bulbous, woody weed: a type of inedible tuber root with soft red fur that was smooth one way but not the other. It was smaller than she would've liked but it would do. Heedless of the mud, she dug her hands beneath and gathered up a few wriggling grubs, before stuffing them in the pouch she'd taken from the slaver.

Back at the fire she peeled away the outer layers of the

10

tuber, and sliced along the root's length with her blade, careful not to touch the wet flesh. She waited until its distinctive smell permeated the air and then thrust it into a pile of snow. After a few minutes of preparation, the cold root and the grubs were infusing over the coals in her father's kettle.

Save the sound of bubbling liquid and crackling fire, a familiar silence hung in the air. It was the same quiet that usually followed their family meal, as they sat around tending to skins or sharpening knives, a time where no one spoke, and all felt at peace as their hands worked. Before she died, her mother would wind twine from sheep sinew, expertly weaving thin strands together, plaiting it over and over until it was tight and strong. Her deft fingers always moved so quickly.

Kyira wafted the sickly-sweet kettle steam then plucked out the red root with her knife and dropped it into the coals.

"Aki?" Iqaluk didn't move. "Aki?" He mumbled something. The fever blood was getting worse. "Iqaluk." His eyes opened at his name. "Iqaluk," she said, grabbing his head. "You must drink this." He sipped slowly, spilling some of the hot liquid over himself. By the time he finished he had only regained a little colour.

"Who did this to you?" She felt a fool for asking, seeing as she already knew the answer, but she had to keep him talking.

Iqaluk lay back, breathing deeply. "Slavers," he said, his voice high. "They were mounted."

"What did they want? What did they take?"

"Everything, child. Everything. They raided our supplies. The animals are all dead and burned. We have nothing left,

11

Kyira. Nothing."

"We will rebuild. We have done it before, Aki, and we shall do it again."

His hard stare softened. "Your words fill me with hope, but sometimes words can be as meaningless as the canvas upon which they are printed. You have to drive change and forge your path!"

Kyira nodded but couldn't stop herself taking a long breath. He had been talking like this more and more of late, imparting wisdom as though he might die in the night.

"Not every fight needs to be fought, Aki."

"I will not let these men get away with this! We will only find ourselves fighting more of them come spring. Let us kill this one at the seed." He propped himself up on a wobbling elbow. "Where is Vlada?"

Kyira worked her fingers. "I don't know. I sent him up to hunt, just before they came."

Iqaluk sat up. "Before who came?" Drops of sweat had appeared on his brow and beside his nose — the medicine was working.

"I was attacked."

Iqaluk's eyes widened, and he tried to get up. "By who?"

"No, please, Aki. Please. I am fine. I dealt with it."

"Good. Slavers care only for coin. They would sooner sneak into our camp in the dead of night and raid us in our sleep, only so they can attack the next day with the odds in their favour. That is if they didn't slit your throat while you dreamt. They are fools and cowards."

"They wanted maps."

"Maps," snorted Iqaluk, reeling like a drunkard. "Kyira, when the breathe of the Forbringrs carved the first paths,

12

it was the ways of the Kartta, the first of our people, that shaped the world."

He wasn't talking sense. "Shaped the world? Aki, please."

"Listen to me, Kyira! It is up to *us* to shape the world. The practice of documenting the paths was abandoned centuries ago, we must pass it down… as treasure to the next… next generation." He winced and his eyes rolled. "Even the slavers know… would know this."

"Aki, you must sleep."

"Yes, you are right. I will need my energy if I am to climb Hasaan's peak tonight."

Kyira's mouth opened in protest but was stilled as her father's hand rose to her cheek following the Lines on her skin.

"My daughter. You are as fierce as your mother ever was, and more. You will make a fine Pathwatcher. If only your brother were… if only… if…" He closed his eyes, and his chest began rising and falling with the heavy rhythm of sleep.

All for Show

The sun dropped behind the distant hills, casting the black and green plains on each side of the wagons into soft purples and reds. Even the odd gnarled tree poked out of the ground — an uncommon sight in Nord — its bark as black as scorched earth with fingers that reached upwards at the twilight sky. The plains gave way to high cliffs that rose up like city walls in the distance just begging to be climbed. Hasaan swallowed the lump in his throat as he realised this was the last time he would ever see them. Iqaluk would still climb them of course, but even he preferred to stay amongst the hilltops, it seemed that the flatter lands just enraged his fool of a father. Kyira was more calm at least, but still a bloody awful climber. He was sure she'd rather run for miles around the cliff face than attempt to climb it. He would have beaten her either way.

The trailer of the wagon had sweated pitch all over him, hands, tan boots and all, making the bumpy ride along the old road even less comfortable. The dense layers of his minksin offered plenty of protection against the cold, but not from ill-fitting slats nor rusted rivets digging into his rear. Besides, with all the other conscripts there was barely room for him to sit, let alone be comfortable, so he endured it quietly.

Cailaen sat crumpled next to him, head lolling back and forth while a line of drool snaked its way across his cheek. Cailaen was his brother, not by blood but by experience. No one had come close to being there for him as Cailaen had, whether it was seeing off the Dearg twins at the Nortun settlement when they were barely babes or being offered a hand at the right time on a challenging climb. They never spoke of the link, but it was there, and they both knew it. Cailaen snored and Hasaan rolled his eyes, looking straight up into the grimy face of a young girl across from him. She eyed him up and down openly through a flash of blonde hair hanging over her right eye. The rest of her hair was dyed black, which placed her from one of the Uigur clans, perhaps even the same clan Hasaan's mother had come from. He stared back, wondering if he would have to fight her. Maybe he might even have to kill her before they arrived in the capital city. He could do it. The damned earth, he would do it, if he had to. Iqaluk would disapprove of even just thinking such a thing, but then he disapproved of everything. The old man knew nothing about who Hasaan really was. Nobody did. He was vicious, powerful and perfectly capable of killing. If he had to.

The wagon crunched to a stop, and both lines of conscripts slid towards the front in a heap.

"Out!" cried the rider, swinging down from the nara pulling their wagon. The creature hissed and threw its sprawling antlers towards him. "Ya!" He fumbled at his side, and the animal quieted as a long leather whip unravelled to the road. "Yeah, you better flinch, if you know what's good for you!" He turned back to the conscripts and bared a gummy set of yellow teeth. "You lot, out!"

Each wagon in the caravan slowly emptied as their riders swore and shouted and threatened and whipped. They were all adorned in shimmering leathery skins from an animal Hasaan didn't know and while most of them had scars upon their faces only their rider had Lines. They were more crude than his own, colouring everything from nose to neck in black patchy ink. The rider caught his eye and pulled aside his iridescent coat to reveal a curved sword as long as his leg. "Git out!"

"It's all for show, Hassi," yawned Cailaen.

"I know," lied Hasaan. "By the way, thanks for leaving me alone with this lot."

Cailaen smirked. "Friend, I can talk small with the best of them. You, on the other hand, could do with the practice."

A whip cracked above their heads, and they both jumped up jostling with the rest out of the wagon into an untidy line.

"I swear," growled Hasaan, "if that thing hits me it'll be the last thing he ever does." He pushed at the boy in front. "Hurry up!" The boy turned and sneered as he stepped down off the trailer. "I don't remember being such a shit when I was that age." He added a sneer of his own and the boy turned away and dropped down from the wagon.

"Maybe they're a bit sore from being drafted into an army?" said Cailaen, dryly. "Wrong place, wrong time," said Hasaan.

They both jumped down and Cailaen tapped Hasaan on the chest proudly. "Or right place, right time."

The rider swished and flicked the sword as the conscripts formed a rough line. He looked capable with it, but Hasaan got the impression those flourishes wouldn't help in a real sword fight. He shared a glance with Cailaen. All for show.

Conscripts from other wagons were already scuttling back and forth with boxes, blankets and saddles by the time their rider finally lowered his sword

"For those that joined us in, whatever that last settlement was," he announced, "I am Gorm, First to Commander Lor." He paused to let the mighty words sink in. "We will be camping here this night, whereupon the commander himself will be joining us." He pushed his hand in between Hasaan and the Uigur girl making a show of separating the line into two. "In the meantime, you lot will set up canvas, and believe me when I say I want all groundsheets lashed tightly, because if I wake up one more morning on stingmoss I'll feed you to the fuckin nara!"

"Do they even eat meat?" whispered Cailaen.

Hasaan gave a snort. In truth he didn't know, but they were bigger than horses and those antlers were as thick as his arm. "We do. Maybe we should cut one down and cook it!"

"Yeah," said Cailaen. "Best I do it, though. Not sure you're ever going to be much use with a sword."

"Swords are only useful close up," said Hasaan, tapping the wrapping strapped to his back. "I prefer to keep my enemies at a distance."

Gorm moved the front of the line along, slapping the flat of his sword against any exposed skin that strayed too close. "That's right, off you go. And you lot…" he said, turning back to Hasaan and Cailaen's group. "The first to catch at least twelve squirrels eats tonight. I know when the other two riders get back they will be hungry. Now go." Cailaen rolled his eyes but set off with the remaining six conscripts towards the plain behind them. "Bear in mind I'll be taking half of them for myself," shouted Gorm after them.

"Can you not hunt for yourself?"

"What was that?"

Hasaan picked up a small round pebble the size of his thumb. "I said, can you not hunt for yourself?" He tossed the stone in the air and caught it. "I can catch a squirrel, any time of the day or night, even with this little stone, that is how good I am at hunting. But I would never ask someone else to catch one for me, let alone twelve." He stepped towards Gorm. "Then, I must assume that you cannot hunt."

Gorm moved to lift the sword, but it was too long and the space between them too short. "So, you're the one. The one with illusions of grandness. A Sami boy with barely three cycles since his Lines were drawn on by his mother."

Hasaan shook his head to hear such badly pronounced Nordun. This fool was a Southerner make no mistake. "Seven."

"What?"

"It has been seven cycles since my name day."

Gorm stepped back and pointed the sword at Hasaan's chest. "Really, now. You're younger than you look then. What's your name?"

Hasaan stretched to his full height. "Hasaan."

"And why are you here?"

"To fight."

"*You* have come to fight with the lord's army, and for the Bohr? What do you think you can offer the Bohr king?"

"My service."

"In that case, I suggest you listen to me. I have the ear of the commander, and I can tell you he does not take kindly to slackness," he pointed to a long scar behind his ear, "or candour. Unless you want to walk all the way to Tyr." The tip of his sword trailed down Hasaan's minksin and stopped at his feet. "Or at least as long as your legs hold out, then you'll be dragged until there is nothing left but a red smear." His sneer twisted into an ugly smile. "But we all deserve one infraction. A chance to learn and be taught. So, while I muse upon what I am to do with you why don't you catch us all something tasty and fat. Go on now. Fuck off."

* * *

It was the middle of night and still the conscripts rushed between orders, carrying packages, grooming nara, and prepping the animals for another day of solid walking. Other, more fortunate conscripts were sparring between themselves, using short swords and small knives under the watchful stare of one or two riders.

Hasaan took a pebble from a large pile and pressed it into the soggy earth next to two others. "And that's three," he said, with a sigh. "Do they really have to be in threes?"

A lanky conscript called Ander looked up and nodded. "Groups of three is what he said. Perfect groups of three."

"The death of me, Hassi," hissed Cailaen, from his left. "The death of me."

Ander leant in towards them both. "This ain't the half of it. Night before last he had two of the other lot searching for scrabs all night."

"Scrabs?" said Hasaan.

"Without lamps," added Ander.

Cailaen turned towards Hasaan. "An entire night chasing

19

beetles."

Hasaan ignored them and pressed another stone into the mud, trying not to think about the rumbling in his guts. He and Cailaen had eaten well before joining in Nortun, but that was well over a day ago, and while the smell of charred squirrel meat had long since left the air, his stomach remembered it vividly.

"An entire night," hissed Cailaen, thumping Hasaan's arm.

Ander leaned in again. "I heard two escaped earlier today."

Hasaan frowned. "Escaped? From what?"

Ander shrugged. "Not all joined willingly. You saw the lines of them in Makril—"

"Quiet!" spat Keene. "The lot of you! You want that idiot rider to come down again?"

Hasaan spared the girl a contemptuous look. Her face was even grimier now, but in the high moonlight she looked not too bad. Even pretty.

Cailaen caught his eye. "Nice, isn't she?" he whispered, eyebrows dancing.

"Mmm. You think she's an Uigur?"

"Could be," whispered Cailaen.

Hasaan stole another glance. Those who could shoot had a certain way about the way they moved. "They're said to be near unstoppable with a bow in the hand."

"Maybe she's Sami."

"She's not Sami."

"Why, because she knows how to rub pitch in her hair?" Cailaen's breath blew in over his ear. "She likes girls."

"What! How do you know?"

"Just a hunch," said Cailaen, making a spectacle of placing his stone just right. "I've seen her leering over them almost as much as you." Hasaan scrabbled the dirt around Cailaen's stones. "Oh no. Now, I'll have to begin again."

Hasaan's laugh blurted out before he could stop it, and Gorm's rickety form appeared over them. "I have some barrels needing broken down," he said. "And then put back together. Only after the stones have all been half-buried." He turned to walk away, then stopped and turned back. "And then dug back up." His laughter followed him until he was out of sight.

Keene stared at Hasaan. "You two will get us all kicked out before we've come close to being Earned! Either that or just hang us, and I'm far from being done!" She resumed burying the pebbles piled up beside her, punching them into the ground.

Hasaan sighed. Was this the reward for joining the lord's army? Eight hours a day performing menial tasks that served no purpose?

"You should probably at least pretend to care," said Cailaen, interrupting Hasaan's thoughts. "Seeing as you put us here."

"I've never known you to care about anything, Cailaen. What makes this life so different?"

"Keene is right. Once we're Earned everything changes. We'll be story makers of kings. Trust me!"

"Story makers?"

"We'll have whole squadrons of men under us who we can command. Men twice our age!"

"How?"

Cailaen looked bewildered. "Because we're First!"

Hasaan stared blankly at him.

"Come on, Hassi. Do you not listen to anything I say? The first of our bloodline. The first of any bloodline to serve in

21

the lord's army are almost guaranteed to become Earned. You remember Nevin? He left Nord after the Dearg twins jumped him one time too many. Story says he was one of the Kin and now he's Earned. Our age, and he's Earned! He's in charge of a squadron of nine men."

Hasaan could picture it: gleaming armour, a home in the most prosperous city in the world, a wife, children, fame and fortune. "I won't be able to climb in a city."

Cailaen's pressed his lips together. "You said to me not two days ago, that it doesn't matter where we end up. That this is a way out. Sure, my father might not be breathing down my neck as hard as yours, but I still have the exact same expectations on my shoulders. So, don't give me a story of how oppressed you are. We're all running from something."

Hasaan nodded at Keene. "Even her?"

"Maybe not her. I think she's here to make everyone's life difficult. But Ander is hiding from his two uncles. They want him to be a goat farmer."

"He does look like a goat farmer."

Cailaen nodded. "Exactly! You see what I'm saying, brother. We're the oldest here by at least two cycles."

Hasaan considered interrupting but settled for a loud sigh instead.

"Brother, we can own these people. All we have to do is stay the course. We are special. Unless you would prefer to just do what your father wants."

Hasaan shook his head slowly. "Watching paths."

"Maintaining a set of muddy trails through the wilderness. For the rest of your life."

"But this is all just so… pointless." Hasaan looked back at

his friend, then down at the small round pebble in his palm. He threw it over Keene's head into a stagnant pool behind her drawing sharp looks from her mucky face.

"She'll take your head off, Hassi! Don't push her."

"So, it's not just pitch in her hair then," said Hasaan, smiling. "Cail. Come on, fight me."

"What?"

"Fight me. Like we used to. Properly though or they won't believe it. I'm fed up and anything is better than this. Let's show them what we're made of." Hasaan brought the heel of his boot into the neat lines of pebbles in front of Cailaen, and dragged it back tearing out a long divot of turf. "Come on."

"After what I just said, you want to start a fight?"

Hasaan open handed Cailaen across the face, catching him perfectly. He rubbed his stinging fingertips. "Now?"

Cailaen's expression didn't change. His ability to take a punch was one of the things Hasaan loved about him. The Dearg twins couldn't touch the two of them, not with his quick hands and Cailaen's apparently dead nerves.

He flexed his hand and moved in for another but Cailaen sprung up right into Hasaan's guts and they both fell to the mud in a heap. A second later and they were circling each other, ignoring the protests of Ander and Keene as they trampled through their neat lines of stones.

Cailaen feigned right then switched left in an effort to unbalance him, the same move he always pulled, and as Hasaan threw his weight sideways, he left a leg out. Cailaen clipped it and ploughed into the other conscripts.

He pushed himself up, pulling bits of ground from his teeth. "That was a dirty move."

"Yeah well maybe you should—" Keene's hook caught Hasaan in the jaw, sending him to the dirt. It took a moment for the light to return fully, and when it did, he turned to see Ander swinging wildly at her. Cailaen sat grinning across from Hasaan, trying to stay out of the way. Then their eyes locked and they were back up and wrestling again. Cailaen was smaller but somehow still managed to grab Hasaan in a headlock, while behind them Keene was expertly jabbing someone who looked as though they had only been standing watching. Hasaan laughed, and grabbed Cailaen from behind, pulling him up at the waist and squeezing as tightly as he could.

"Argh!" shouted Cailaen, as Hasaan lifted him clear above his head.

"Haha!" roared Hasaan, but his elbow buckled and both of them tumbled to the wet earth. Hasaan dragged himself back up. "Again!" But Cailaen was staring back up at the road, along with Keene, Ander and the rest of them.

A pale nara trotted along the narrow road, expertly manoeuvring around the many potholes, and guided by a huge man; the biggest Hasaan had ever seen. A girl stumbled alongside, hands tied to the stirrup of the rider's saddle. The nara turned revealing a young man tied in the same way on the other side. They looked dishevelled and dirty as though they had been dragged along the ground. The nara stopped and a huddle of conscripts gathered around them.

"Come on," whispered Cailaen, clambering up the bank.

"I think he's the commander," whispered Hasaan, as they reached the back of the huddle. "He's huge."

"He's Bohr."

The rider was seven feet tall and bald but for a long

24

topknot that sprouted from the middle of his head and disappeared behind him. His jacket was stiff and grey, and flashed with red around the collar and cuffs while an aura of danger surrounded him likes waves of heat. Gorm walked over to meet the pale mount and held the nara's reins as the Commander swung smoothly down. His cold stare raked over each of them, and Hasaan felt his insides go cold.

"You are no one," said the commander in accented Sami, his voice like gravel in a tin. "Singularly you have no purpose. Only together do you exist now, and for those that make it, you will be one of thousands who will fight with you and for you. You will provide a necessary arm to the Bohr armies, providing resource and resupply to those in battle. You may even be chosen to fight in the lord's army." He scanned the circle. "Although only a few will ever see the inside of the barracks at Tyr."

"Resource and resupply?" hissed Hasaan, sideways at Cailaen. "I thought you said we were here to fight?"

Cailaen winked. "We'll beat them all, Hassi. The story makers of kings…" He nodded forward.

A hush had drawn over the conscripts. Gorm was freeing the boy and girl from the saddle.

"Until that time," continued the Commander, "you will have to prove that you belong. If you feel that this life is not for you then Gorm here will find other uses for you. His word is final."

Gorm pulled the boy and girl away from the nara and stood them to face the line of conscripts.

Hasaan's breath caught. They were brother and sister, except he had not seen them since they had left the town of Makril. They were young, and both had the same brown hair and bright eyes as the man who had offered them up for service.

Gorm lifted the girl's chin and moved close enough to kiss her.

She stared back defiantly, but her chin was wobbling.

"Deserter!" he shouted, spraying the girls face with spit.

Something about her reminded Hasaan of his sister, either the way she stood, or the way she held herself. Would Kyira have let herself be caught and corralled like an escaped goat? There was a scuffle of feet on earth and Gorm's fist crashed into her face breaking her nose. She crumpled to the ground, and the brother moved to intervene, but Gorm knocked him down with a heavy shoulder. The boy struggled up and Gorm smiled. Another punch, but this time the boy took it. Again, and again, and again, Gorm pummelled him until the sister clawed at Gorm's legs, pleading and crying and squealing, but her brother stayed standing, his face a bloodied pulp around red eyes that could surely barely see. Hot bile rose in Hasaan's throat as Gorm unsheathed that long sword from within his coat and paced back and forth spinning the blade in the space between the prisoners and the conscripts. The commander watched on silently, with no emotion.

Hasaan should have looked away — it was clear what was coming — but something held his gaze. His choices had led him here, and he would honour them, and hold to them because what else did you have but the choices you make?

"Pleash!" mumbled the sister, hauling herself up and standing in front of her brother. "Leave him!"

Hasaan's resolve broke. His heart hammered. His foot twitched. He had to do something, honour or no.

Cailaen's hand grabbed at his wrist. "Hassi. No. Don't."

Gorm taunted the deserters, pretending to cry and pout. Mocking them like the Dearg twins used to mock Cailaen. Hasaan had stopped them once that day he and Cailaen had become friends and brothers, and maybe he could stop this. He had to do something. He had to.

"What did they do?!"

"Deserters," snapped the commander.

Gorm nodded. "Ran away night before last, so they did. Now they got to pay the price."

Gorm turned to face the girl, and she spat blood into his face. He spun the sword, and cracked the hilt into the bridge of her broken nose. A killing blow. Stunned, her body held rigid, then she fell motionless to the rider's feet.

The brother dropped to his knees, feeling at her broken face while his own bled over her. "Rian! Rian!"

Gorm took the boy by the arm and lifted him to standing. "Come on," He didn't resist as Gorm led him to the middle of the circle, turning him just so to face Hasaan.

The boy just stood there as Gorm planted his feet. Hasaan wanted to cry out, but it was too late. The boy jerked as the sword pushed through, the tip of it flashing briefly through his chest. He staggered backwards as Gorm pulled the sword free, then fell upon the body of his sister.

Confusion washed over Hasaan, followed quickly by deep dread. He was aware of his body, but he couldn't feel anything. The world beyond that boy and girl didn't exist. It was only when the commander stepped forward that Hasaan realised that he had stepped out of line.

The Bohr's booming words were now only for him. "There will be stops along the way," he said, stepping over the

27

deserter's bodies, "and some of you will be asked to do questionable things. If you disregard anything that I or any other rider asks of you, your life is forfeit. If you try to leave, your life is forfeit. If you turn upon your own, your life is forfeit." The words were a sword, held to Hasaan's chest, directed at him and him alone. "You belong to the lord's army. You are the Kin."

The Gods Themselves

The tuber root was medicinal, but along with its fixing properties it sometimes created visions if left to stew. Nordun peddlers harvested the root for exactly that reason, drying and pounding it into powder to extend its life. They called it Tomha and used it to treat wounds and long nights alike. Kyira had never found a reason for carrying Tomha powder with her; there was always a fresh root to be had somewhere. She had removed the root from the kettle, well before it should have got to the stage where it caused visions, and yet her father was pulling himself up the cliff face as though he was a young man again. He was as high as a bird, and in more ways than one. The concoction had knocked him out for near half an hour, after which he had awoken and immediately insisted they find Hasaan. They had arrived shortly after at Hammer, one of the highest peaks around Nortun and indeed Nord itself — Hasaan's favourite climb.

"Ho!"

Kyira had just enough time to bring her hands over her face as Iqaluk's stepping rope whipped down in front of her. She reached out, feeling the fibres beneath her fingertips then squinted down into the darkness. An icy blast of wind slapped at her face, passing through her thick skin jacket like it was not there. There was no sign that they had already climbed half the mountain. They could have been but a few metres from the ground were it not for the misery gradually filling her stomach like rising tsampa bread. On top of everything, Vlada's absence gnawed at her. She longed for the feel of his weight upon her arm, and his powerful claws pinching her skin. Her fool brother would be fine, he always was. Hasaan would often disappear only to return a day or a week later. He was as stubborn as their father, which was most of their problem. Vlada, however, hadn't stayed away this long since first learning to fly, not that he would mind the freedom — he was probably gorging himself on deer or ox at this very moment. She inhaled and pursed her lips, catching the whistle before the sound blew out of her cheeks. No. She couldn't call him. Not when enemies might be nearby.

Breathe.

She jumped for the first knot, feeling a split second of panic as her weight fell and brought the knot in tight. The rope whipped out sideways, dangling her precariously over the sheer face.

"Open your eyes, child!" roared Iqaluk, over the wind.

"They are open, you fool!"

"Accept that you are in danger and open your eyes!"

Breathe.

Her over-zealous jump had taken her completely past the first knot and onto the second. The rope kicked out again, but this time she countered the movements, forcing her upper body as straight as she could, leaving her feet to hang loose, and slowing the rope to a gentle swing.

She squeezed the thin rope tightly between her thighs and shuffled up one knot at a time, shoving her foot into any part of the rock that would take it. The cliff face stretched up and over her head in a long overhang that looked like the head of a huge hammer bursting out from the side of the hillside, with her rope anchored off to the right of it. Why hadn't they just gone around?

"Aki! Where are you?"

"Ho!" came his voice, closer than she expected. His head appeared over the edge of a hidden alcove, imperceptible from the surrounding rock.

"Aki, I'm… it's too high. Help me!"

There was no reply.

She growled at the man's thick-headedness. Imagine bringing her up here in the first place. What a fool he was! She planted both feet on the rock to steady herself and walked up over the edge. "Why didn't you help me!" she shouted. "Are you hearing me? I almost fell!"

A red trail glistened on the pale lichen leading to her father where he sat. He said nothing, and just stared back out over the valley. "Even the Forbringrs could not have brewed such."

Illuminated from within by some unnatural light, a huge spherical cloud hung above a hill in the distance — the first sister of the Waning Crescent. The bruised sky jerked and pulsed like a heart still beating as it consumed the mist from the surrounding vales, drawing it up the hillsides like lifeblood in thick lines. The air was charged, electric like before a lightforks storm but within that cloud the forks held fast — the pulsing veins of the Gods themselves.

"I've heard tales of such things before," said Iqaluk, not

taking his eyes from it. "Clouds that spin so quickly as to suck up everything in their path, consuming entire cities within a heartbeat."

Kyira couldn't speak. The immensity of it shocked her. It was so big it could crush these hills flat.

"We need to find shelter," said Iqaluk.

The top of the Hammer was only a short climb away beyond their position, and the summit mostly flat, covered in grass and lichen. By the time they'd reached it, the cloud had flattened into a huge disc that stretched out towards them, its wispy fingers grasping and quivering at the centre of the disc, but with no more mist to consume leaving the drop down the Hammer's sheer face unnervingly present. The low cloud around the Waning Crescent began to shudder, gathering until all at once the whole sky itself dropped around them. Kyira fell to her knees, hands above her head as though she might somehow prop it up. She shouted, but her words were snatched by the whirling clouds around her. She couldn't move. Her frozen limbs were locked to the ground as though she were a metal plate stuck to a lodestone. A strange buzzing reverberated through her from the hill below, and suddenly she was part of the hillside. She was not Kyira of the Sami people, nor the daughter of Iqaluk and Thea, sister to Hasaan or master to Vlada, she was the land, the earth, a speck of life that could be rubbed out on the whim of the Gods.

A brilliant floating point of blue fire, bright against the clear night sky, hung above the eye of the storm now nestled in the valley below. Lightforks licked up to it from the spinning whirlwind, surrounding it in a net of crackling light and drawing it down. As soon as it touched the hillside,

32

it shrank into itself and grew so bright that the stars above vanished.

"Get down!" Iqaluk threw himself over her, but it did nothing to stop it.

Eyes screwed shut, Kyira held her ears and screamed as some force threw her against damp earth. Rocks bit into her side; dirt scraped her cheek. A shadow loomed above, and she was dragged upwards. The earth beneath had torn itself up and was sliding back towards the Hammer's overhang, with Kyira along with it, riding it like a sled. She scrambled for something to hold, snatching at the rope just out of reach, at the earth, at the air. The slab of earth teetered on the edge, snagging on the rocks, then rose upwards into the air away from the Hammer's summit, as some unknown force tore it away from the mountainside. Iqaluk's stick hovered in front and Kyira grabbed hold of it and as the earth slab lifted off the side of the mountain. The stick held firm, dragging her sideways to tumble back into the pit left by the missing earth.

Kyira looked up perplexed as more slabs of earth floated over them and the summit like raevens gliding on the wind.

"Daughter! Are you alright?"

Kyira sat up and threw her arms around him. "Aki!"

Iqaluk embraced her then pulled her away. "Look."

The sky was full of debris torn from the hilltops and pulled towards the Waning Crescent's peaks. Kyira and Iqaluk stood watching until the slabs slowed, then stopped a thousand paces above the vale, just hanging in the air. Then they fell. It was like a wave, the closest to the Waning Crescent falling first. One slab blew Kyira's braids back as it hurtled towards the earth along the sheer face. It smashed onto the great boulders below along with the sound of a hundred wet thwumps that echoed around the hills.

When the last echo had all but vanished, Kyira turned back to the Waning Crescent. The hillside around the first sister had fallen away completely, leaving a quarry of mud that stretched back to the valley floor. A needle spire of rock, too thin to be so tall stood above it all higher than the peak.

"Where did that come from?"

"I don't know," uttered Iqaluk, "whatever caused the Gods to be so angry." He turned toward her, eyes wide. "But we have to find Hasaan. We need to find him, at all cost."

Made from Sand

A sea breeze blew in through the window, rippling the purple hanging silk and bringing an unpleasant chill to Rathe's bare chest. With it came the reek of fish which was almost as intense up in the council apartments as it was in the square below. The Middle Sea winds blew the stench in from the docks so that no matter where abouts in Tyr you were, be it Terävä amongst the shanties or Vasen standing in the fresh green grass gardens of the upper class, the human upper class at least, you were sure to experience the odour of week-old fish. The Tyrians called the stink, *hav,* as though such a trivial thing deserved a special name. The dependency these humans had on animals from the sea was something Rathe would never get used to, not in a hundred lifetimes.

The last few stars winked out as the sun appeared over the distant hills — a rash of red that spread outwards burning away the sharp streaks of cloud that still clawed around the towers of the Forbringr's Domst, across the square. There were worse sights to behold. Indeed, it was rare to see the sun at all in this cold, forsaken city. The Kemen Empire's constant blue skies seemed a life away. His life, as it so happened to be — a two-decade exile to mediate between humans and Bohr so they may either kill each other or coexist, the former of which was winning out. He had been a fool for volunteering, but the draw of the second wealthiest city in Rengas had been too much for him to pass on. A fool's errand. Any money that existed here was controlled by the Bohr only, and being a Child of the Bohr, a mere half-blood meant his access to it was limited. Still, he had been fortunate enough to watch the western sun rise from many different points in the city, and from much lower than where he stood now. He had enough currency to his name to see him through another hundred cycles regardless of how this latest crisis turned out.

Bohr and human relations were always fraught with complications, as far back as when even his father lived — simpler times. There were fewer humans then, living as prey with the Bohr as predators. Since then the humans had multiplied, filling cities and fighting each other for as much land, currency and resource as they could get. Recent estimates said they now outnumbered the Bohr three to one. He shook his head. Three to one. A not-inconsiderable number.

Yet, regardless of the state of the world there was another more important problem bringing dread to his being.

"Kael?" came her sweet voice from behind. Her red hair was tousled with sleep and her brown eyes half-lidded and demure. She was one of the most beautiful creatures he had ever seen, north or south of the Kemens and as she slid through the thin birch doors and padded towards him, dragging his white satin bedsheets along with her, he yearned to hold her.

"You're up early," she said, stifling a yawn.

Every one of those sweet expressions, sighs and moans was a lie, the Kumpani were famed for it. Even so, she was damned good at it.

"Yes," he said, more stiffly than he intended. Still, a hot night need not turn into a hot morning. Not today. "Go back to bed, Fia. There's no need to be awake just because I am."

Her full lips drew into a pout. "If you're sure."

Another little lie. "I'm sure," said Rathe, stepping back.

She stepped into him and let the bedsheets fall to the black stone. Her breasts rose up with her, shimmering in the morning sun, then she scraped a fingernail along his neck and reached around to his bare buttock and gave it a sharp slap. "Don't be long."

There were not many humans who would dare treat a Child of the Bohr so, but that was precisely why he kept coming back to her. She padded back to the bedroom and the beams of sunlight highlighted the delicate Lines that followed her curves from ankle to shoulder. It was one of the more unusual customs of the north, colouring one's skin with ink, but he was coming round to it.

He moved to turn back to the window then stopped as his eye fell upon her folded hak. When had she done that? They had gone straight to bed after she arrived, and there they had stayed until now. She must have been up whilst he was asleep. The neatly folded bundle fell to the floor.

"A moonflower?" he said, with a snort. He picked up the bloom from within the delicate folds of her hak and held it in his palm. There was no reason for one of the Kumpani to wear the moonflower!

He turned to say something but Fia was already back in

his bedroom. No. Not today. He threw the moonflower out of the window, watching as it disappeared beyond the edge of his stone balcony towards the Domst Square. Enough distractions.

* * *

Rathe's footsteps rang on the blue tiles as he marched along the corridor that cut straight through the centre of the council chambers to his office in the east wing. It was a noise he knew well, far better than he should for a Child of only one hundred and eighty-nine cycles. The Justice Court was the name given to the entire set of buildings, not just the courts themselves where the councils convened — a common misconception from those across the Way channel in Terävä unlucky enough to be summoned there. He peered down into the oval chambers, where a human court was in session. A lonesome male hung by his neck above the dock. They must have started early this morning, unless they hadn't yet adjourned from the previous night. Either way, they had clearly decided on the defendant's case.

Rathe quickened his step. There was no time to be pulled into street affairs today. From here the corridor became narrow, twisting and turning around the central courts towards the offices. Polished hard-wood panels ran the full-length of the walls at waist height, above which hung portraits of Bohr leaders, generals and kaels all the way to the ceilings high above. He slowed as he approached the east wing station and the two Pan Guards turned to face him, blocking his way. They wore red as Pans often did, with cloaks that hung around a single slipknot, ready to release in a single move. Pans preferred a modest covering over the groin, if anything at all, but he had witnessed Pans in nothing but leather belts and a topknot. Battle ready.

"Kael Rathe," said the closest Pan, sniffing the air, "you smell prepared."

"So, you know," he replied.

The Pan's laugh sounded like a wounded elk. "Yes, Kael Rathe. We all do." He stepped forward. "And we await the outcome with a thirst that none of human blood could ever know."

They all tended to speak like this too. "As do I, Pan," said Rathe. He focused on his office door a hundred paces past the station, swallowing down the anger. Disrespect would do him no good here.

The Pan stood aside, and as Rathe passed him by the lead Pan spoke again. "Blessings upon your shadow, Kael Rathe."

Rathe stepped into his office and threw the door shut, then marched over to his wide desk. He had intended to tear it from its bolted feet and throw it through his bay window, but his anger, which had just been so palpable was already defused. He lent on the end of his desk breathing deeply.

An array of perfectly formed models sat upon the desk: three black charn dragonheads lay on their sides in the middle of the province Dali, or the valleys, as it was sometimes known, around the nondescript town of Drakemyre. A metal triangle with a cross within it stood proudly over them; the Tsiorc rebels. The victors.

South east was the black Domst spire of Tyr, its single elegant tower a perfect mimic of the real one outside his apartments, and between the wooden pegs that marked the coastal town of Makril sat a dragonhead standing for the

Kin. Rathe reached over and plucked the Tsiorc model from the Dali region. It was poorly made, but that didn't bother him. He'd come to enjoy looking at its hewn surface in the few cycles it had sat snaking its way around his table. It wasn't a shade on the beautiful dark charn models of the Bohr, but surely that was the point.

If someone had asked him a week ago about the contours carved into the redoak at his fingertips he would have told them that it was a perfect facsimile of the land itself. He might have gone on to talk about the men and women who had died to collect the information he had poured over for months, and the announcement that the map was the most detailed description of Rengas in existence. The Bohr lords who funded the army of the same name would swoon, congratulate, then boast to others at parties of how they had laid eyes upon it. He would not have mentioned that it was those initial surveys that had angered the locals and given birth to the rebellion. No. That piece he would have left out. Because why else would the Bohr take an interest in Nord — an otherwise empty mountainous wasteland? To mine it? To draft its peoples? To conquer it. The world was far too big to leave to the humans. Unchecked they would breed and breed and breed until there was nothing left of the Bohr but the memory. A memory of an empire.

There was a ruffling of material in the corner and Rathe's eyes darted up to meet those of a squat man with thick eyeglasses. The Altinda'har's chubby fingers clutched a leather-bound folder.

"Seb," said Rathe, doggedly. "Is it that time already?"

"Yes, Kael. I'm afraid so. It is not all bad news though."

"You know, Sebreth," began Rathe, waggling one of the

Tsiorc's models. "I asked the smiths to create three of these, each representing a thousand of the Tsiorc. They came back with some excuse about dwindling copper reserves." He shook his head. He had been so wrong. Three thousand? It was more like ten. Who would have guessed the rebels could amass such an army so quickly? This new captain was certainly cunning. He opened his fist to see his own blood colouring the metal.

Seb coughed. "The reserves are low, Kael, but there are plans for the mines to be pushed even deeper. We could even open up some up in Vasen."

"Vasen?" said Rathe. He placed the Tsiorc model back at Drakemyre and took a seat near Kemen Empire in the south. "No. They would never allow mines in Vasen. Who knows what secrets lay hidden beneath that part of Tyr."

Seb squeezed by the wide desk following Rathe to a section near the arched window. He removed his eyeglasses and breathed on them before wiping them against his greasy shirt.

Rathe pulled out a handkerchief from his drawer and wrapped it around his hand. "Well?"

"Yes," stuttered Seb, opening the folder. "We've had a few issues. Lots of… issues."

Rathe began rubbing his temples as the engineer listed the numerous problems affecting trade through the Way Bridge. Fishmen were worried over stock, port minders were unhappy at the length of time merchant ships were staying anchored in the bay, smuggling between the two halves of the city was on the rise. It was all so *routine*.

"What about the new coins?"

"Yes," twittered Seb. "The musta. They are not so much

41

coins anymore, Kael. We couldn't get them to stay circular, and we dare not use our precious charn, because—"

"It would be like gilding the latrines with gold."

Seb looked puzzled. "Yes, Kael. I've heard that only the mythical lands of Ge'Bat can afford to do such a thing."

Ge'Bat owned the shipping lines for almost the entire Eastern side of the world. Or so those who travelled west would say. Rathe snorted. "Well, who wouldn't want to shit on gold, Sebreth?"

"Indeed, Kael. So, we went with a coin, or *brick* made with an inferior charsand dug up from some farm outside of Dali." He produced a small flat brick, a quarter-inch thick and two inches long. "They're ready to be distributed any time. The merchants who trade within Tyr will soon come to know the face of the Kael very well." He turned the brick over to show an effigy of Rathe's face stamped on the rough surface.

"Can we use it to tempt some of the trade up from Kemen? What of my contacts?"

"Um," stammered Seb, "your contacts have not really been forthcoming to my requests."

Rathe felt the anger rising, and Seb flinched in expectation. "If Tyr will *ever* match Ge'Bat or Anqamor's prosperousness," said Rathe, trying to conquer the fire in his belly, "then we need more ships down the Way! The latest vessels from Anqamor are so fast they just don't need to travel the Way to get to the cities in the inner circle of Rengas, no ships means no taxes. Instead they spend years travelling down and around the South seas and the outer circle to deliver chits and chattels. We want their precious minerals and their bejewelled stones here, Sebreth!"

"I shall enquire again, Kael Rathe. At least the ships we

do have will soon be lining the docks waiting to spend their new currency."

"Because they cannot spend it anywhere else." Rathe crushed the brick in his hand. "At least a new currency gives me more control over the taxes that can be squeezed from the city itself. That should go some distance to topping up the coffers. Let us hope then that we can garner enough support." He rubbed his eyes, looking beyond his reflection to the square, and his apartments. Fia might be awake now. He could have stayed with her, should have stayed with her. "That last thing you mentioned. Something about smugglers?"

"Oh, yes, the blue-eyes."

"Blue-eyes? There are still Sulitarians getting into Tyr?"

"Oh yes," said Seb. "The dock patrols discovered a corpser tug that was hiding immigrants amongst the bodies. The captain kept complaining of unusual currents in the Way mouth."

"Why are you talking about currents?" said Rathe, getting impatient. "The Way tides havn't reversed for nigh on a millennia. What about the Sulitarians? How many got in?"

"The blue-eyes? By the state of the ship we guessed around two hundred who managed—"

"Two hundred!" Two hundred Sulitarians, roaming, stealing, begging.

"Yes, Kael." Seb stuttered. "We did capture one."

"Then let us meet this man!"

"A woman, Kael. I'm afraid she was despatched by the guards."

"Did you not think, Seb, that an immigrant from Sulitar might have some key information? Not least what is happening over there?" He tapped on the desk across the vast flat surface of wood that marked the Middle Sea. "An opportunity to perhaps gain some intel on the Outer Isles. A place no Bohr has set foot on since the Forbringrs walked Rengas."

Seb puffed his chest out. "Kael. You once said to me the job of an Altinda'har was to fix and figure and in choosing me you also got yourself an engineer, a scientist, a keen—"

"Seb."

"Yes," muttered Seb. "Yes, well, where others see chaos I see order. Science, chemistry and physics are my only thoughts. I care not for the political minutiae of..." Rathe stared at him. "You're right, of course," he said, eyes wide. "Sorry, Kael. I should have foreseen..."

"Not to mention that one of those peasants might actually know something of this mysterious rebel captain. The head cannot make decisions without information, Seb." Rathe grasped the man's stinking shirt in his fist. "Next time a blue-eyes comes in, legally or not, I want them brought to me to stand in front of the Justice Courts."

"Of course, Kael," stuttered Seb. "You need not worry. I shall see that the patrols are briefed accordingly."

"Good," said Rathe, satisfied. He brushed down Seb's shirt, then inspected his own fingertips for any dirt he might have picked up from the man.

"Kael, what did you mean when you said you still need support for musta? Musta is a new currency for the city of Tyr and there is a significant resource involved."

Rathe blew the air out of his nose and shook his head. It wouldn't matter whether Seb knew, but it still felt wrong to tell him. "As Kael there is not a single thing I can do about

Tyr's money problems. Any new tax or sanction I would vote into favour could and would be shouted down by the more numerous council leaders of Tyr."

"I thought the Kael's powers were unsurpassed...Sorry Kael. I do not wish to anger you. I see a problem, and I am compelled to fix it."

Rathe's hand wrapped gently around the engineer's head. He could crush it like an egg. Perhaps not today, though. "And don't ever change, Seb. There are others to whom I report. A Child of the Bohr may indeed reach heights no human ever could, and still fall short of the royal lines. I imagine some lords may even try and surpass me given the chance." Seb's expression shifted, as though the little man's loyalties had come suddenly into doubt. "Fear not though, Sebreth, for today it will all change, and you will be alive to see it happen."

Games

F ia waited until the door slammed shut before bounding over to the sliding doors bare feet squealing on the veinstone. "Rathe? Kael, are you there?"

Other than the distant sounds of prayer bells and breaking waves, all was silent. The hav hung heavily in the air, so the Teräväen docks across the Way had already begun work.

She'd barely managed to finish rummaging in Rathe's study during the wee hours before he had begun to stir, but she'd had all night to think about where to look next. The heavy cloth mural hanging along the chalk wall of the lounge, nothing; the drawers of the long table in the main dining room, just neatly folded silk shirts; even the glass lamps dangling from the high ceiling, which held nothing but new candles. It wasn't long before she was slumping back onto the mattress defeated.

She drummed on her stomach and it growled back at her like a rabid hound. It wasn't hunger, but rather the hollow uncomfortable feeling that followed a evening of over-indulgence. The night before had moved quickly, typical then that knowing that she would be staying with Rathe, she'd begun nervous eating early on. She belched, feeling a little better. Rathe didn't usually bring butterfly wings to her stomach, but robbing him blind certainly did.

"Get your head in the game, Atalfia!" She sat up. "Where would you hide it?" Maybe Janike had been wrong or had misunderstood the conversation she had apparently overheard. Janike was handy in a fight, but stealthy, elegant or subtle, she was not — just like her father. Her eyes fell upon the wall panels, and she leapt up. "It can't be." One of the panels was darker at the edge than the rest, like a scuff that been made at an unusual angle. Perhaps while standing open.

She gave the wooden panel a knock, rapping the white wood with her knuckles. Tap, tap, tap. Clunk. The edges were well machined, even more so than the rest of the wall. Her probing fingers found the slightest of indents along the top, and with a gentle pull the entire panel swung out, revealing a set of hidden shelves behind. Trinkets lined the shelves, some shiny, others made of materials she didn't recognise. Her eye flicked over the objects, judging the value of each until she reached the pile of papers at the end. The stock was heavy and the dragon head seal that held the papers together was broken roughly in two. She opened it, careful not to crack the green wax further, then scanned each one trying to translate the Bohr's written runes. She shook her head wishing she had spent more time learning them. Laeb had tried to teach her to his credit, but she was an awful student. It was only when she reached the last document that she recognised Rathe's name. She ran her finger over it.

The acoustic of the room changed as the main door opened an inch, and a voice muttered angrily in common

Tyrian with someone down the hall.

"You said it was done!"

"It was, he must have undone it."

"It is his room! He is allowed to undo it. Go and remake it."

Fia threw the documents back on the shelf, and a square parchment fell from between two sheets and dropped to her feet, but there was no time, she scooped it up, closed the panel then sprinted back into the bedroom. Before she had even pulled the covers over herself the main door shut and hard heels clopped around the lounge.

The eunuch walked into the room without knocking and dropped Fia's folded hak unceremoniously onto the bed and left, sliding the doors shut behind him. Fia slid out from under the covers and pulled on her shorts and shirt. The hak went over as tight as she could, adding a twist at the hips as was the fashion, with the excess tied in a knot above her navel. She tapped the spot where her moonflower should have been and shook her head. She'd have to buy another.

"Time to go, time to go, time to go," uttered the Eunuch in the tune of The Missing Queen.

"Alright, alright," said Fia, sleepily. The square parchment went into a hidden pocket within the hak. She ruffled her hair then made a show of tying it up in a bun as she nudged the doors open with her big toe.

"My shoes," she said in accented Kemenese.

The eunuch seemed to struggle with the window, then slammed it shut. His face a mask of thunder, he took up her sandals and bag, holding them out as though they had been dipped in clam oil. "Time to go."

"Of course," she said, slipping each shoe on. She followed

him to the main door, which he held open expectantly. "Do you know when he will be back?" she said, stepping out.

The eunuch's pale grey eyes creased in amusement. "No."

She made a motion to ask something else and the door slammed shut. Perfect.

* * *

The pale, wide stone steps of the council apartments spiralled downwards, seemingly forever — they were the killer of many a night of sexual want. The tall doors at the bottom stood above the towering steps up from Vasen Square, serving as a clear reminder of where Vasenfolk featured in the order of things. It filled her with unspeakable rage, the inequality of this accursed city, but only its people could ever change that. It was an annoying irony that in order to change the game, she first had to play it without breaking the rules.

The square was already bustling with activity, as a steady stream of them weaved between the Pillars of Time and on towards the Way Bridge. The long shadow cast by the central monument was half way between the fifth and sixth pillars, which would normally have been Ataeru, or prayer-time. It was usually a chance to see who knew who, but not today.

Fia set off across the square, ignoring the congregation and mingling with the thickening lines of bridge traffic. After the Bohr's recent defeat at Drakemyre there were new rules limiting passage at certain times between Terävä, where most Tyrfolk lived, and Vasen. — one city spread over two continents, barely a quarter league apart. It meant that those who wished to attend the best parties, rather than the most expensive ones, would have to cross the Way Bridge to Terävä early on and tonight was going to busy.

The chalk white walls of the council apartments grounds merged into those of the terraced embassy homes, their fenced gardens stretching away into long streets. The power of this city resided in Vasen, and of them only the richest lived this high, clinging to the council like a bad rash. Gardeners tended their empty gardens, devoid of children or animals, and the smell of new grass mingled with salty air. She took big gulps of it because it wouldn't be long before she was nose deep in street cooking, sweat and wine. After she had met with Janike of course.

A group of Domst monks overtook her, missionaries with loaded bags and heavy haks sweeping over the cobbles. The young one glanced in her direction, turning away when the elder next to him dug an elbow into his side, before nodding an apology. Fia nodded back — the Kumpani were revered, but that did not mean they had to be feared. A merchant barged by her, mumbling something incoherent as he weaved in and out of colourfully clad Vasenfolk making their way down to the Way Bridge for a whole day and night of dancing and debauchery.

Two Pan Guards stood either side of the bridge gates, watching the traffic flowing freely through. Fia manoeuvred herself into the middle of the stream of people and loosened the knots at her stomach. If she was good at anything it was not being noticed, and the huge guards barely registered her. It was a trait of the Bohr — as large and predatory as they were — that one human looked much like any other. The crowd of people spread out, giving Fia a chance to speed up, and she moved as quickly as she could to the next gate.

This close to the docks, it was almost impossible to navigate through Terävä in a straight line. Lose focus even for a second and you'd be dragged beneath the wheels of a fishcart or the feet of an ox. Fia had lost count of how many Kumpani girls had lost a limb or even a life to the streets down here, and that was before you considered the pirates, thieves, and slavers that prowled the side-streets. She wound her way through the crowd, hopping over holes and piles of dung until she reached the main street that led uphill to the market-square.

She skipped up the long staircase that divided the city into two halves, stealing glances inside the stilted shanties that followed the steep contour of the Teräväen mountainside. Bands of white monkeys leapt along with her jumping from razor rock to razor rock, until seeing she had no food, turned and followed someone else. Even the monkeys knew today was special — soon the streets would be teeming with drunken dancers eating and singing and screwing, and those monkeys would steal and eat and screw themselves until they were fat and satisfied. The thought made Fia smile.

The razor rocks became smooth walls that rose high above the street. Some women nodded as she passed by, then glared at their men for doing the same. Fia stopped at the third landing, and veered right, and turned into a colourful market square, thrumming with activity. Bright flags and canvases flapped in the morning wind as vendors moved between stalls, smelling fruits, comparing colourful cloths and inspecting the livestock that bleated from wooden cages. Veiled women spooned spice from the top of great cones, filling the air with intense aromas. Children watched and played amongst the stepped rooftops, daring each other to hang from flagpoles or jump the narrow gaps. Those not selling entertained, played violins, danced, sang, juggled, told jokes — anything to catch your attention. Anyone not carrying something was followed by merchants old and young, bellowing prices and promises after them. There was more activity filling the tiny square than the workers of both docks put together.

Fia stopped by a moontree and lowered one of the branches for a closer look. Like every other in Tyr, it had produced thousands of green buds overnight, and tonight at full-moon each bud would burst into flower. It marked the first day of spring and was called the Feast of Moons, the prospect of which filled Fia's empty stomach with wonder and excitement. Rarely, a tree might flower a day or two early, and like the bloom she had bought they were picked and sold at huge mark-up, even if it was usually tradition to give them. The first flowers usually got the best offers.

A waft of fried hog drifted in from somewhere and Fia's stomach growled. "Janike, you'll just have to wait."

Hopping down from the tree root Fia scoured the market-place for the source, and made a beeline to a stall where an entire pig was spit roasting.

"You are so pretty!" said a Makriliaen girl stepping in her way. "Your face is so beautiful."

"Oh, thank you," said Fia. She made to move by her, and the girl sidestepped too.

"Do you like my earrings?" said the girl, waggling her head.

Fia knew enough not to look too closely at the twinkling

pike scales jangling from her ears. She nodded and again tried to get by to the hog stall, her mouth rapidly filling with saliva.

"You are local, yes?" said the girl, barring her way.

Fia gritted her teeth. "Yes."

"Vasen?"

"Sometimes."

"Then you are far too pretty to be without a pair of these!" The girl lifted the long earrings out and held them toward Fia.

Before Fia could respond, an older man appeared out of nowhere and whacked the girl across the head.

"Idiot!" cried the man. "She is Kumpani! They do not buy from the likes of you!" He gestured to the gold bands at Fia's wrist and the gold leaf at her neck. "You see those don't you, Ferret? She could probably buy you if she so chose. Go on!" He booted the girl's behind, and she scampered away into the crowd. "Apologies," boomed the man. "She is yet young."

"It's fine, really." Fia motioned to pass, but this new obstacle was far wider than the last.

The old man held out his hand and motioned for her to do the same. She did, even though normally she would not have; merchants were as dastardly as the games they played. The man placed a moonflower in her palm. It was fresh, and the stalk already wrapped with a small clip to keep it that way.

"Even as the Festival of Life approaches this night," he said, softly, "it seems unfair that one as fair as you should be without a first flower, when so many other Tyrians have one."

"And what makes you think I'm single?"

53

"You are Kumpani."

She tied the bloom into her hair. "It seems your games are improving."

The man's busy blond eyebrows, flecked with grey, arched up with his warm smile. "Games are all we have, Kumpani. Although it is nice to meet another who plays."

Fia dipped into her hak pocket, feeling the rough parchment against the back of her hand and pulled out a bronze mark. She pressed it into the vendor's hand and said, "Thank you."

He waved a hand over the palm, and the coin was suddenly gone. "It's nice doing business with one who does business, Kumpani. Blessings. I hope your night is full of… games." He winked and walked off, leaving the path to the stall clear.

"Now…"

"Too easy, Fia. You need to watch your back." A figure stepped forward into the square of light and smiled a familiar gapped-toothed smile.

Fia batted away the blade resting on her shoulder and winced as it nicked her finger. "You spend your life sneaking up on people, Janike," she said, sucking on the cut. "And where has that got you?"

"Two cutlasses and one longknife."

"Must we?" said Fia, sighing at the growing queue forming at the hog stall. "I've had enough games today."

Janike's eyes widened. "I can't decide if our weekly meets mean I know you too well or if your lies are just getting worse. I have never known you to be sick of games. Now, there are three of them. Two have cutlasses and one a longknife. Oh, and *all* are bigger than you. Much bigger. What would you do?"

Fia glanced around, but no one was paying them any notice. "Fine. First, I would swipe out in a flat arc—"

"With what? Your hand?"

Fia stuck out her tongue. "And with my blade, take the first one's head off."

"Yes," said Janike. "With your *flat arc*. Yes. Then what?"

"Then, using the blade's momentum, I would twist, and crouch then cut through the knees of the beast advancing from behind."

"The ankles are weaker," said her friend. "And what about the last? His blade is able, and he's bigger than you by far."

Fia scowled as a few looks came their way. Maybe they thought they were entertainers too. "I would follow the curve up from the ankles of the second, bring the blade up between the legs of the final one, splitting him—"

Janike's eyebrows raised. "or…"

"Or her," continued Fia, "up the middle to stop firmly within the chest. Two seconds, maybe three. Start to finish."

Janike laughed cruelly, then poked Fia in the chest. "The chest? You certainly think a lot of yourself!" She touched the moonflower in Fia's hair. "But it would seem you do occasionally listen. Eoin will be surprised if you ever cross blades with him again."

"I've beaten him before," said Fia.

"Yes," said Janike, "but now you can do it on purpose, rather than relying on how much drink is in his belly." She took the flower and pushed it into her own hair above the ear. Janike never did anything with her hair other than let it cascade down her back, which was a shame because it was luxuriously thick and shiny. Fia had always been jealous of it, although jealous was perhaps the wrong word. The pale yellow of the moonflower against her dark hair and olive skin suited her more than Fia would ever say.

"Yet you still cannot beat your own father," said Fia, as sweetly as she could.

Janike's expression turned hard. "Kavik is an oaf whose only friends are horses."

"I assume by your mood you haven't paired up before the Feast of Moons tonight?"

Janike scoffed. "I hope you are not asking me, Kumpani. You are not my type. Your shape is all wrong."

"Wrong?" laughed Fia. "These hips hold only truth."

Janike stepped close and cupped Fia's breasts like she was weighing two lamb chops. "I prefer men, and most men do not have these."

"Most… men?"

"Stop stalling. Have you done it yet?"

"Not here," hissed Fia, taking her arm. "Come on." She pulled Janike into the street she had come from and turned on her. "No, I haven't done it yet."

Janike shook her head, letting her cowl drop around her shoulders. "I knew it! Fia, you are the worst spy I have ever met. You were tasked with disrupting the upper echelon of the lord's army, by killing none other than Kael Rathe himself, and what do you have to show for it? Nothing. Neither Laeb nor Dia'slar will be impressed."

"Dia'slar?" exclaimed Fia. "He is one of the Tsiorc?"

"Of course," frowned Janike. "You did not know?" Her eyes widened. "Wait, you did not… service him did you?"

"Damn that blue-eyes! Damn him!"

Janike threw her head back and cackled. "Oh, Fia. Did no one tell you that it was the enemy we must extract the information from! I hope he paid you well. Or at least put a babe in your belly."

"Be quiet, Janike."

"I hear that is exactly what happened to Lyla."

"Be quiet...Really? But she's a Captain!"

"So?" laughed Janike. "That does not mean they do not enjoy the pleasures of the flesh! They probably do more than even you!"

"How do you know?"

"I received a raeven from Nord a few days ago. Some of us are actually doing our jobs here, Fia."

Fia ignored the last comment. "Who is the father? Not Bryn? Tri?"

"Isak."

Fia's mouth dropped. "Isak. And I always thought he was so quiet. At least it wasn't Tri. That oaf. What beautiful skin that babe will have. A Nordun father and a Kemen mother."

Janike smirked. "Oh, the life of a captain of the Tsiorc. Leaving babes here and there like milk deliveries." She patted Fia's stomach. "At least you could give your bastard away. Vasen does have an orphanage."

Fia stuck out her tongue. "It doesn't actually. It shut ages ago. There were too many bastards to look after!" They both burst into fits of laughter and fell upon each other. Fia lost herself in the joy of it all, and it was a good few minutes before they had both regained enough composure to speak again. "Janike, listen, I think I have something even that detestable Dia'slar doesn't know."

Janike wiped her streaming eyes. "You lie."

"Rathe has been demoted, Janike. He no longer controls the lord's army."

"You are sure?"

"I found a stash of documents signed by a Lord Zuveri?" Janike shook her head in disbelief. "So, it is true."

"You know of him, then."

"By name alone," said Janike, pacing over to the wall and leaning on it. "He is a Bohr, with connections to the king."

Fia knew not to question how Janike gained such knowledge. They both had their own methods. A laughing couple walked around the corner speaking half in signs, half in Tyrian as was typical in Terävä. Teräväens had never really relaxed after the last occupation of Tyr, when the Bohr clans united, and the dynamic street language was born out of that mistrust. They were planning when to meet after the feast.

Janike waited for them to pass before speaking. "Did you find out anything about what happened at Drakemyre?"

"No, but Rathe told me that the reason they lost was due to the shape of the land."

"Pah!" said Janike, spitting. "He was outmatched, and Laeb beat him at his own game!" She turned away, mumbling curses.

Fia's fingers fell upon the rolled parchment in her pocket and she brought it out. The heavy words were brown, as though they had been written in blood, and scratched by a heavy hand and the heavy parchment wasn't parchment at all, but animal skin.

"What does it say?" asked Janike. "And where did you get it?"

"I took it from Rathe's rooms." An idea formed in Fia's head as she silently translated the roughly scrawled runes. "You know, maybe there's another way out of this."

58

Whims of the Mist

Kyira glared at the mist, absently weaving a length of twine around her fingers. Looking south there were three sisters hidden behind the cloud: the last sister of the Waning Crescent and then two more after that, and one of those was the highest ridge in Nord. A tall woman indeed. When had she began calling the hills her sisters? As long as she could remember. They were closer than friends, and she loved and knew them as much as she did her own family. After the ridge it was but a short walk to Makril. She sighed, hoping dearly she did not have to go as far south as that.

She twisted the twine. Most of the hills had names, true Sami names handed down by their ancestors, and map-makers, the Kartta. They who wrote the first laws that were supposed to govern Sami life. Hasaan had his own names and they were usually based on whatever the hill happened to look like. She shook her head and turned towards the north. He was somewhere out there pleasing himself as he always did, no doubt camped upon a ridge or stalking deer in the wide vales, unaware of the angst he brought upon his family.

The folds of mist melted together then separated, hiding

and revealing as though it were controlled by something larger. The tiny slither of Laich still visible appeared and disappeared on the whims of the mist, but there was no sign of her pursuers. What if they had found Hasaan? A deer upon his back, climbing that colossal spire that had grown out of the hill like a parasite. Maybe it drew the slavers there too. Where did it come from?

The twine snapped, biting the skin between her thumb and forefinger. "Shiach."

Never had she needed to think of so many things at once. She let the twine fall to the damp ground. At least Aki was safe. She had left him sweaty and delirious, lying in a cave not far from here, just below the summit of the fourth sister. He had to rest and let the remainder of that Tuber root leave his body if he was to be of any use at all.

"Damn, but I came up here to find that fool raeven, not mull upon the ills of the world." Kyira raised her chin and whistled high and loud, guiding the sound into the breeze with cupped hands. "Vlada, you fool. Where are you?"

She yanked a handful of long grass from ground, and began separating out the green from brown shoots, weaving them into a lattice. In all of the cycles she had been travelling Nord she had never seen such persistent mist. Perhaps it *was* that storm that had caused it all, but what had caused the storm? Mother of Baeivi only knew. She turned her attention to building the fire. The hole was ready, half as wide as her forearm and just as deep with the earth piled in a mound on the edge. The lattice went carefully around the inside, with the greenest grass woven into the top and the drier brown grass into the bottom to direct the heat downwards. It would burn hot and quick requiring only a thumbful of torv for fuel, and the sisters of the Waning Crescent had plenty of torv to spare. A second hole connected to the first would help reverse the upward draught of smoke, and pull it back into the flames, creating an almost smokeless fire that grew quickly then died down, perfect for brewing a cup of kaldi. She longed for a creamy cup of tsampa, simmered low and long with plenty of sugerleaf or perhaps honey, but all she had were kaldi nuts, and they would help keep her awake and bright. She pulled a flint from her pack and chipped it against a grey rock, and a handful of sparks flew against the lattice, catching immediately.

Before long the torv was glowing, melting down a lump of snow in her cup. She took her belt knife and scored several kaldi nuts, then dropped them into the bubbling water and waited.

Her blade was supposed to be a tool for cracking, splitting and paring, for skinning, carving and slicing. It had been forged by her great grandfather, and was strong enough even to chop wood, yet she had used it to kill. Iqaluk had given it to her on her naming day on her fourth cycle, as his father had to him. She ran the flint along its edge remembering his words that day:

A blade can decide your fortunes. Keep it close.

The brown and bubbling brew clung to the blade as she stirred, drawing the aroma up, then after wiping the excess brown liquid on her trouser leg and sheathing the knife, she lifted the cup to her mouth. The steam moistened her lips, drifting up around her nostrils. She drew the revitalising scent of kaldi into her body, savouring it, letting the fumes tickle the back of her throat, while her body practically squealed in anticipation for that hot mixture, for the wakefulness it would bring. It was the flint to the blade within herself, and it would sharpen her mind and senses just the same. Taking a long breath, she tipped the cup, and abruptly froze.

Three mounted nara had emerged from the mist not far along the ridge. The riders were talking quietly while the tall animals picked their way over the narrow walkway towards her summit. They hadn't seen her.

A fold of vapour drifted in between them, and they vanished from view. Kyira leapt up. The kaldi went into the fire, and as the smoke rose, she tipped the earth in to catch it. Already running, the cup, flint, and twine disappeared into her bag.

She pounded down the hillside, heedless of the noise she made — the slavers couldn't hear her, but if they saw her they would run her down within minutes. After a few moments the rise hid her descent, but she did not slow. She couldn't. There were only two routes off the fourth sister: along the ridge or down the long plains to the hill's back. The ridge would give her more time, but not much, and nara were as sure footed on precarious paths as they were on hard clay roads. She bounded down the open plains at the mercy of the mist.

Her feet slid on the mud as the plain gave way to a cliff, the rockface a blur on her right. She skidded to a stop at the cave entrance, straining to hear voices, footfalls, anything! The rocks dripped, babbling into tiny pools that collected in the cracks in the wall until they too overflowed. A snowcrick chirruped somewhere, and then a soft twitter of a blackback as it flew back and forth above, guarding a nest. It was silent, but something was wrong. Her eyes scanned the entrance — a cracked hole barely tall enough for a small child — and there, stomped into the mud were fresh footprints. Kyira pulled out her knife and scrambled in.

"Aki?" she whispered, from the entrance. "Aki, are you here?" The first cavern was empty. She swallowed hard. "Aki?" she said, louder this time.

She reached the cavern towards the very back of the cave and crawled in. The firestones were long cold. Three or four hours by her guess, and Iqaluk's mat had been slept in but was empty. His stick was still here. The strapped wood felt comforting to hold, but without the man it was just a stick. He would never have left it willingly. She lit her oil tin wick and followed the marks upon the cavern floor replaying the events.

Iqaluk had eaten all three of the taimen from his mat, then must have fallen asleep. At some point someone else. Wait, no. Two others had entered the cavern. Slowly, but not quietly. Iqaluk had awoken at the noise and hidden in the shadows to the left of the entrance. The prints there were only his and judging by the wetness he had stayed there unmoving as the pair of intruders walked around the cavern. As they had turned to leave one of them must have spotted him. Just off to the side was a large imprint where a heavyset person had come down hard — too heavy for Iqaluk. Had he tried to fight them? Not likely, but maybe the sleep had given him some strength back. Kyira moved the light around. Knee imprints. Rope fibres. Iqaluk had been bound. Someone had taken her father.

A Time and a Place

The bracken slid and crunched under Hasaan's bare feet, finding the gaps in between his toes with every step. At least the road had been mostly flat. This was the second day he had been without footwear, and even his hard-skinned feet were beginning to blister. He stopped and curled his toes, joints cracking in unison.

"The death of me, Hassi." Cailaen was red-faced and puffing from carrying so many saddle bags, but it didn't stop him scowling in Hasaan's direction any chance he got.

"At least they get lighter with each delivery," said Hasaan, with a shrug. Cailaen just stared at him.

A group of Kin jogged by each lugging a large black stone with them, and looking as tired as Cailaen did. Hasaan pulled Cailaen back, giving the runners and the nara behind plenty of room. "Keep going, Kin!" said Hasaan as they passed.

"Shhh!" wheezed Cailaen, turning his back on the parade. The rider frowned in their direction as she passed but said nothing. "Quiet! Or it'll be bloody me that has to pay for it!"

"Surely they would want us to support each other, Cail. Seriously. What use is a supply unit that don't talk to each other? Besides, I reckon there's not much else they can do to you." He cleared his throat. "To us."

"Hasaan, you are a fool if you think this is as bad as it gets. Trust me when I say that there is worse to come. I mean, look what happened to Rian and her brother. What of their father? Does he even know his two children were murdered the other day?"

Hasaan didn't need to be reminded of it. He had been part of the group tasked with burying their broken bodies. He doubted the father knew. How would he?

"There might be a way to get a message out," whispered Cailaen.

Hasaan shook his head in disbelief. "Three days in Cailaen, and already you're talking about mutiny. What happened to all that story makers of kings rubbish? Just keep your head down. Besides, I've only seen one messenger raeven and it belongs to Lor unless you want to go knocking on his door."

Through the trees, the runners were just passing by Gorm. The rider caught up with them and ran alongside a young boy, mocking him. When the group reached the bog, Gorm gave the boy a nudge. He teetered, trying not to drop the large stone, then his feet hit the wet mud and he went sprawling to the ground. Gorm jumped back, giggling in his sickeningly high voice. He had been strutting around more than usual since they had stopped in this forest — if you could call a handful of bare trees a forest.

"Shit," hissed Cailaen, as Kaleb strode out from behind a cart, mud and hay in his hair. "I swear Hassi, if he gives me more to do, I'll stick my knee in your guts."

The keeper of horses made straight for them. "Ah, there you are," he said, smiling, completely at odds to his permanent frown. The effect was the very reason the recruits had renamed him to Crazleb.

"Sorry, Cr…Kaleb," said Cailaen, straightening as much as he could. "I was just—"

"Are they for me?" said Kaleb, already lifting two of the saddle bags off Cailaen's back. The man's arms were huge while the rest of him was skinny, giving him an off-balance appearance. He looked like he had been moulded from mud by a child.

"No," blurted Cailaen. "No, these bags are all for the riders! Greyt root and sinew, for stewing."

Kaleb smiled again, and this time one eye opened too, and wide enough that Hasaan feared the eyeball might just fall out.

"Greyt? The girls love a bit of greyt. Here, let me lighten your load."

Cailaen shook his head vigorously. "Please, Kaleb. Gorm will take my balls if I lose any of these. I can't let you give them to the nara."

"My girls work hard," said Kaleb, "and they deserve something sweet. Tell you what, I'll just take one. Which will leave you a whole testicle all to yourself."

Hasaan placed his hand on Kaleb's forearm. "Kaleb, come on. You know what Gorm is like. Leave him be."

Kaleb stared at Hasaan's hand then up at him, his lined forehead crinkling up even more than it usually did. "Remember your place, conscript. I've been with the Kin for nigh on ten cycles, which was long before Lor decided to drag us up to the freezing wastelands of the north. I went through the same shit and came out the other side with my sanity. And with both balls mostly intact." He winked at Cailaen. "Gorm is all talk. Most of the time. But I wouldn't let that get in the way of a beautiful friendship now. Cailaen I'm taking the greyt. Hasaan, Lor wants a word, and from one friend to another, I'd suggest getting yourself to his tent before the messenger reaches you. Thanks be with you, friends!"

* * *

The smell of burning inside Lor's tent stung Hasaan's nostrils, so he breathed through his mouth. A hollow bone filled with powder sat smouldering upon a desk where the commander himself sat. The rest of the big tent was empty. There was no bed, or space for clothing, and the tent stood over twice Hasaan's height — height than any other on the camp. Even the commander's wide desk looked small with the Bohr leader hunched above it, brooding over a letter, like a vulture over prized carcass.

"Sir?"

Lor didn't acknowledge him, and Hasaan knew enough not to try again. Standing up to Kaleb was one thing, but a Bohr commander? He was learning quickly that there was a time and a place for speaking his mind, and here and now was most definitely neither.

Minutes passed, the only sound coming from the scratching of the commander's pen on the page. Unlike his father Hasaan hadn't learned to write, it didn't help with herding or hunting, and was a skill only the Kartta, the Pathwatchers of old, needed to learn, and Hasaan was no Pathwatcher.

Lor sat up and rolled his shoulders with a hideously loud crack. He was not like the Bohr that the stories described; this Bohr was more a man than the giants that

67

were mentioned in the stories passed around amongst settlers. The commander's Lines painted in white over his dark skin, were seemingly non-sensical, with no aspiration or stories written into them. They had the patterns of language, but none Hasaan had come across. He followed the shapes and runes down the Commander's wide neck and behind the single clutch of tied, matted locs.

"You took your time," rasped Lor, in accented Sami. He spared Hasaan the smallest of glances, flashing dead eyes, then returned to the paper.

Hasaan swallowed. "We are delivering food around the camp."

"Not every statement requires a retort," said Lor, not looking up.

"But every death requires a reason."

The scratching stopped. "You think the deaths of the deserters were unjustified?"

"Yes, I do."

The chair was suddenly catapulted across the tent and Lor rushed over to Hasaan. He looked down at him like Hasaan might stare down from a cliff top. "And there is your first mistake. You do not *think*. You haven't earned the right to talk to me about what you think. You are here to learn." The commander's teeth locked together like a wolf's might.

"I am not afraid of you," lied Hasaan.

Lor's snarl faded, but his dark stare stayed locked onto Hasaan. "What *are* you afraid of?"

"Obligation."

Lor's expression softened a hair. "Obligation? Obligation is nothing to be afraid of. Of those who join the Kin willingly there are two types, the ones who are running from someone and the ones who just wish to kill. From your ill-fated remarks," continued Lor, "I can assume it is not your wish to just kill." Lor's black eyes drifted over him. "The lord's army requires each of the Kin to follow orders, without question. Obligation is the cornerstone of what we are, without it, systems fail. Governments fall. Apathy reigns. The people need leadership, and their usefulness is directly proportional to their compliance. It is as simple as that. Obligation keeps the masses in line." There was a rustle and Hasaan looked over to see Gorm standing at the entrance of the tent. "A moment, Gorm," said Lor. The commander squatted down to Hasaan's height. "Obligation binds us together in harmony, it ensures victory." Lor bit into the last word as if it were a crisp apple. He turned and calmly sat back down, then took a new sheet of parchment from the shelf beneath and began writing. "Kin, I believe Kaleb requires your very unique skill set at the back of the caravan."

"Yes, sir," said Hasaan, his cheeks flushing. He turned to go then stopped as Lor coughed. The commander had crossed the few steps between them completely silently. He took one of Hasaan's biceps in his shovel-sized hand and squeezed it. "Hasaan, if you receive one more punishment for insubordination, Gorm will take your arm. Not all of it, but enough that you'll miss it."

Hasaan nodded, fighting every urge within to reply. He stared at Gorm.

"Go."

Hasaan hurried away from the commander's tent, still feeling Lor's touch. Two riders pushed by, leading a scruffy man with a bruised eye. A slaver, easily recognisable by his chapped face and heavy minksin. No matter how long the southerners spend in Nord they all came to look the same.

One of the riders hung back. "On your way, boy."

Hasaan nodded and left them behind him. A time and a place.

* * *

Lor felt nothing but hatred for those who would choose to sell someone for profit, and of course the irony wasn't lost on him. It was funny how quickly the game changed. A man whom he had never met before, had information so potentially dangerous that it might undo all of his work here in Nord. He read the letter again, already knowing that his brother would baulk at his rough hand. Satisfied, he rolled the parchment into a finger-sized metal sheath then stepped outside onto the grass.

"Commander," nodded Gorm.

The two riders either side of the entrance brought their fists to their chests as was proper, saying nothing in the presence of Gorm, who was Earned. Truth be told Lor would have placed a mongrel dog as leader of the Kin if it had been standing next to him that day, but Gorm happened to be in the right place at the right time. There were other more important reasons to be this far north and none of them involved training a band of children to carry sacks of grain and rice. Lor stalked over to the perch behind his tent, and the raeven clicked her beak excitedly beneath her head shroud.

"Fortuna, I need this in Kael Rathe's hands within two days."

After making sure the metal tube was fastened tightly to

the little raeven's leg, Lor slipped off the shroud and took a mouse from the bag hanging below the perch. The raeven extended her neck as far as it could, and with her short black beak gently plucked it from Lor's flat palm, swallowing it whole. Her wide leathery wings flapped outwards and steadied as though she were testing the air and she exploded upwards. Lor watched her until she disappeared into the clouds.

"Did he add anything else?"

"No more than you squeezed from him," said Gorm, with a sneer. He spat on his short sword and wiped the bloody blade on the slaver's heavy coat.

Lor approached the slaver's corpse. There wasn't an inch of his face not covered in cuts. Gorm might've been a mongrel, but sometimes that's what was needed to get things done. "Did you really have to nail him to one of the good carts? We are surrounded by trees."

Gorm shrugged. "One of them'll fix it," he gestured through the trees to the group of runners passing by in the distance. "What now though? Do we look into his claims?"

"No," said Lor. "We continue as planned." A thought occurred to him. It was always better to have a back-up plan. He knew Fortuna would not fail him, but whether his message landed in Rathe's hands unmolested after it arrived in Tyr was another matter entirely. "You will, however, go back north to see if this group of strangers the slaver spoke of are indeed real."

"They sound real," said Gorm. "I don't think I ever met a slaver that would lie after what you put him through."

"Good," said Lor. "Then you will go and find them. But before you go, find a reason to make the boy Hasaan a squad

71

leader."

Gorm looked bemused. "A squad leader? He's as loose as my Edda's last tooth! Why in all the eight kingdoms would I do that?"

"Because I fucking said so!" snapped Lor, punching a hole through the side of the cart and causing the slaver's head to roll forward. He pulled his hand away from the splintered wood and flexed his fingers. "The boy is not just Sami you idiot, he is of the Pathwatchers, and without knowledge of the paths through Nord the lord's army will fall like leaves in autumn the second they cross the Way channel. We need to know what awaits us in the wilderness. Our ancestors abandoned Nord, because they were afraid of it. We are the new generation and we will take and hold what they could not." Lor grinned. "Besides, that boy has a monster under his skin, and I mean to let it out."

The Box

The old meat house. Fifth level of Terävä. Upper quadrant.
Possibly guarded. Definitely hidden.

J anike's eyes moved slowly up from the tattered
parchment. "Did Rathe write this?"

"No." said Fia. "It's definitely not his hand."

"Does it lie?"

"It was well hidden, Janike. He didn't plant it."

"How could you possibly know that?"

Fia paced the width of the narrow street. "He's preoccupied with some meeting, and probably the demotion too."
She had watched him standing at the window of his rooms,
staring at nothing for some time before he had realised she
was there. Connecting so easily with people might have
been her gift, but it could be a curse and sometimes she
cared when she should not. Rathe was her target, but by
all the fish in the sea, she may as well enjoy herself while
she was at it. As a Bohr, sure Rathe was imposing, but he
was also the softest, most gentle lover she'd had the luck of
finding.

"Unless he knew you'd be searching for something."

Fia shook her head. "Which would mean he knows I am

73

spying for the Tsiorc, Janike. Think before you speak."

Janike's expression became intense. "Before I speak? Atalfia, perhaps you should announce to the world who you are!" she hissed. "Come, let us find that young merchant girl and we can tell her of Laeb's plans! We could paint the Tsiorc's position on a canvas and hang it in the market for all to see!"

"Now who's announcing it to the world? And don't call me that. Only my father called me that."

"Be quiet, Kumpani. You know him better than any other, so what is he hiding? Why does he not just—"

"Get it himself?" Fia nodded. "I thought of that too, and I have no answer. It might be a trap."

Janike shook her head. "Then why should *we* go up there? Can you not work your wiles on him?"

"Or maybe, just maybe, Rathe is one of the busiest men in Tyr, Janike. Maybe he can't afford to go running up hills looking for…" She flapped the parchment under Janike's nose. "Whatever the hell this is."

"He is no man."

"We're overdue some news, Janike. I want to actually report something for once. Laeb is waiting for us and we need to give him something." She rubbed her forehead, trying to banish the gremlins within. "If it is a trap, it is probably not for us."

"Probably. That's what you're giving me? Probably."

Fia shrugged. "Take it or leave, it's all we've got."

"Alright then," Janike smiled. She almost looked impressed. "The morning is running away, and we'll need to get going if we are to locate this meat house. The fifth level is mostly abandoned, it will take some time to find."

"Now?" scoffed Fia. "The Feast of Moons is tonight!"

"Which gives you at least six hours. And that reminds me." Janike reached into her skirt pocket and pulled out a large pale, dead insect as big as her palm. "Here, take this. It's about time you learned how to feed Prig."

"Uch. Really?"

"He doesn't bite like the other raevens," said Janike, carrying on as if she hadn't heard her. "And the smell of it will warm him to you." Fia took the awful leggy beast by one of its feelers and held it up, repulsed by its many black eyes. Janike took hold of Fia's chin, as though talking to a child. "Atalfia, you've been in Vasen so long you're practically a citizen! You've forgotten your roots. You would still be a serving girl batting away the probing fingers of whalers and fishmen, had I overlooked you that night."

Fia scowled deeply at the continued use of her full name, but Janike was right. Still, that didn't mean she had to know it. "I had plans, Janike, just like everyone else."

"Thieving is hardly worthy of being called a plan."

"And what are we doing now?" said Fia, getting angry.

"You have a cause now. You are not just lining your own pockets with the spoils of others."

Fia laughed and tapped the gold bands at her neck and wrist. "The only difference now is that we steal from those with more than us! Do not poison your actions with the stench of belief. Any plans I had died the day I became Kumpani."

"Any plans you had as a human let alone a thief would have soon been cut down by the Bohr. The new taxes are choking this city offering the Bohr a convenient legal way of killing who they wish while we stand by and nod. Their

75

plans to squeeze trade with this new *musta* currency is just another crank of the shackle. Soon the people will have no will left at all. That is why we fight."

Fia had joined the Tsiorc to get out, not to fight the Bohr, and anything she said in retort would only serve to prove Janike right. "What if there is nothing in this *meat house*? Or what if there is something? We have no idea what awaits us."

Janike shrugged. "We must all of us die sometime."

Fia scowled. "I disapprove."

"I know," said Janike, with another rare smile. "You always do. That is why we are so good together." She scanned the empty street and replaced her cowl. "Are you ready?"

"Yes," lied Fia. "Let's go."

* * *

It was hard to deny that there was beauty up on the fifth level of Terävä. The world below appeared close, yet also so far away should her eye stray beyond the shanties to the bay below. The lines of tiny ships moved slowly in from the Way channel, leaving wakes of hazy white behind them, so small she could almost pluck them from the sea like toys. There were only a few places where the currents allowed ships to travel in from the Middle Sea and it meant traffic built up along the cliffs either side. Although of late there had admittedly been fewer vessels spoiling for trade. The Teräväen docks were obscured by the shanties that ran down the side of the mountain but the Way Bridge was a clear line connecting Terävä to Vasen, where the great white wart that was the dome of the Forbringr's Domst was clearly visible.

The views were soon forgotten as the piles of human waste

and discarded animal remains that gave the slums of the fifth level of Terävä its distinctive odour hijacked Fia's senses.

"Is all *this* really necessary?" said Fia, motioning to Janike's shortsword.

"You never know when you may meet an enemy."

No sooner had the words escaped her lips, than an old man, frail and frigid stepped onto the narrow walkway. Janike pulled her blade out, pretending to inspect it in the sunlight.

Fia waited until the man had limped around them then spun on Janike. "The only danger around here is from you! Now put that away."

"Better safe than dead."

Janike jumped as a group of naked children ran towards her, chasing a baby goat, winding between them then vanished into the shadows between the tall wooden buildings, their joyful squeals swallowed up by the narrow streets.

"It certainly seems dangerous."

"Danger is everywhere," said Janike, sheathing the sword. "And don't be so dry, Fia. You are better than that." She skipped away before Fia could respond, up the last set of steps, stopping on the last landing. "Well, this is it. The top of the Teräväen stairs. I have never been up here."

Fia glanced sidelong. There was a good reason why none came up here. The vagrants that were inclined to come so high usually did not want to be bothered.

"There is a community to the east. But I think our meat house will be on the west side."

"West then," said Fia, stomach sinking. No people and no witnesses. She drew a ragged breath and followed after her.

The streets were so steep that even the footpaths were barely walkable. The few buildings there were had to be hinged to the mountain by a long wooden walkway that itself was only connected on one side with stilts on the other. Who knows how long they had been there. The slats between the thick sleepers creaked and bits of wood crumbled from the rotting underside. They carried on by some broken buildings until the ground levelled out. At least a fall here would mean a drop of forty paces, rather than a thousand.

"Look," said Janike, pointing ahead.

From the outside the long warehouse looked just like any other building they had passed, with its black slats, haphazardly nailed together over empty windows and doorframes, and all held up on the far side by narrow stilts. The only real difference was that the warehouse made use of the flatter land and was set back from the walkway by a short bridge of perhaps ten paces.

"One at a time," said Janike. "It may collapse if we go together. You first."

"Me?"

"You are lighter than me. I will keep an eye out around us."

"You have the sword, Janike!"

Janike stuttered. "I...I will make sure danger does not mean to trap us inside."

"You are afraid of heights!"

"Quiet! Just go!"

The short bridge was solid, or at least it didn't fall to pieces when she stepped across it. The outer walls of the warehouse were less so, and as Fia heaved open the misshapen door, the whole building shuddered.

The entrance landing had three boxy rooms which apart from the dust and mouse droppings were all empty.

Janike led the way through the short hallway which opened out into a main room. Screwed to the bare rafters beneath a bare, leaking roof were sets of rusted metal runners, with evil-looking brown hooks running the entire length. Bats flapped somewhere high above, their dust drifting down as bars of light through the partially shuttered windows. Janike manoeuvred past the piles of boxes stacked higher than their heads, peering in between. Fia shook her head at her friend's sudden loss of trepidation, but they were alone. The building was empty.

"There's nothing here, Fia. It seems your target is playing with you."

Fia swallowed. Maybe Rathe did know she was a spy — she had been so careful.

The door to the room at the far end hung ajar, and Fia peeked in. The wispy window shawl moved slowly with the wind. The room, more a cupboard, was as empty as the rest of the place.

Janike stepped in with her. "What if your Bohr friend has been here already?" She lifted an old canvas at her feet. "Maybe not."

Janike was right, the canvas was the only thing in this building not covered in dust. That and the box that was under it.

"Oh, wow." Fia reached out for it, and Janike let her take it.

The box was wonderful to hold — all bevelled and soft. It was clearly well-made. Intricate swirls and loops led to a cross in the centre which considering its age looked as sharp as it must have the day that it had been chiselled. She sat cross-legged with it on her lap and felt the carved indentations with her fingertips. The lid felt heavy, but when she applied pressure something clicked. The top opened and as it did, it revealed four words carved in script along its narrow edge.

Who Shape The World

"It's empty," said Janike, disappointed.

Fia looked up and her gaze flicked towards the door. A figure stood behind Janike, wider than any man had a right to be, and so tall the face was hidden above the doorframe.

Janike's eyes widened at Fia's expression. Then she was standing. Spinning. Stabbing and swiping. The Bohr moved like liquid in front of her, dodging away from each strike as though it were simply dancing with her.

Janike's stab went long, and the Bohr pulled a heavy sword. It struck past her, barely a hair her from neck and stretching almost to Fia herself. Janike ducked beneath, her shortsword like a child's toy against that brutish lump of metal. Steel flashed through beams of light until the Bohr's sword bit into the door. The Bohr yanked the door closed pulling Janike back into the main hall, and shutting Fia in the box room.

"Janike!" screamed Fia, pounding the box against the door. "Janike! Janike!"

"Fia… RUN!" Janike's breathless words were punctuated with grunts, and smashing wood, the house shuddering with each blow.

"GO!" came Janike's scream. "GO!"

Fia turned to the window and tore off the old window shawl, squinting into the bright mist. She pivoted onto the frame and swung her feet out onto a narrow plank shuffling as fast as she dared around to the corner of the warehouse. Around to the front. Over the bridge. To the old walkway. Running. Running. She didn't look back.

Fear

Kyira hesitated. The ridge between the fourth and fifth sister was deadly to those without experience, more so when you could barely see your feet or the bottom of your stick. She had followed this path once before, but over six cycles ago — avoiding the dead ends would be tricky in such thick mist.

The tracks she had been following stopped at the river, so the choice had been to take either the ridge, or the valley that led around to the coast. What else was she to do? Slavers behind, slavers in front, and her father, taken. Was he injured, tortured? Dead?

Breathe.

It wouldn't do her any good to think on what might be. She needed to find these people who had taken her father and she needed to kill them.

The folds of vapour drew apart revealing a precarious figure, hunched over. It turned to face her, flaunting a wide pair of wings that grew in size as it swooped in.

"Vlada!"

The great raeven hopped forward, his huge leathery wings spread out for balance and Kyira had just enough time to switch the stick to her other hand and thrust her arm out.

Vlada leapt up, landing gracefully on her forearm, black talons gripping the thickened arm of her skin coat. The raeven tucked in his wings and head-butted Kyira clumsily on the temple.

"Hello Vlada," whistled Kyira, in silbo — the language of the raevens.

The raeven clicked his beak, then whistled a reply. *"Greet."*

"Yes, I missed you too." Kyira smiled, running her a hand down Vlada's breast to his dense scales. "Oh, it is good to see you, you foolish raeven, but I'm afraid I have nothing to give you." Vlada gave a friendly chirp and stretched out his neck in consent. "Ah, but I see you've eaten already! Here." Kyira lifted her arm up and the raeven hopped neatly onto her shoulder and turned to scan the hillside behind, beak clicking contentedly. Hollow bones gave him a lightness that belied his size, with most of the weight coming from the leathery wings that allowed him to glide on even the weakest thermals, but, truth be told, Vlada was still very large for his kind, and a sensitive soul for so threatening.

"Have you seen Aki?" whistled Kyira.

"Yes."

Kyira's breath caught. "Where?"

"Warmth of sun," whistled the raeven.

South. "Was he with others? A group?" Vlada let out a series of excited screeches and clicks. She threw up her arm, and Vlada launched upwards into the sky. "Then lead me to him, Vlada, Go!"

* * *

It was dark, but there was still no way Kyira could pass by

the slavers without being seen. Vlada's beak clipped, then he whistled. *"Fear."* He was as afraid as she was.

She shook her head at him, then whistled low. *"Leave, Vlada. Fly."*

The raeven didn't hesitate; he spread his leathery wings out waiting until the next gust filled them and silently lifted up and away into the hidden clouds — a dark shape against the dark night.

With his absence the sudden pressures of the world came tumbling back. Fear for Hasaan, for Iqaluk, of what she had to do next.

Breathe.

The trick was not haste, but accuracy. One hit, one kill. A hunt.

They had come up the ridge, led along a different path that Iqaluk must have known, leaving her with no option but to attack in their faces. Iqaluk sat bound upon the other side of the fire, out of the light but she knew his shape. He was alive. There were others with him, dark shapes sitting quietly away from the fire and the food — that was the slaver way, to keep the food for themselves and leave the prisoners weak and subdued. More prisoners meant more complication but she would meet that maker once her father was out of danger.

The slavers were busying themselves in between, readying for a night of watch and meals. Kyira had chosen this point amongst all from the last three hours of watching, and now it was upon her.

Breathe.

Kyira followed the stench of fermented fish to the first slaver. The woman had made the mistake of loitering at the edge of the firelight where Kyira lay, rummaging in a sack.

Kyira crept forward on her belly like a firesnake, waiting for the slaver to glance away. She slid Iqaluk's stick forward, checking that the twine lashing around her belt blade tied to the end, was tight.

Breathe.

Kyira lunged the stick forward like a spear, taking the slaver in her throat. The woman gasped in silent shock, but Kyira was ready, and hopped up to catch her.

"Hurry it up, Mags!" said a gravelly voice. "You en't getting out of this cooking."

Kyira shuffled back into the dark, leaving the dead slaver and sprinted to a rock at the very edge of the ridge, praying that no one had seen her.

Breathe.

She unravelled the lashing and released the knife; a spear would do her no more good here. A bullock of a man with a blue plaited beard, stalked by the rock.

"Mags, you arsehole! It's your turn!"

Kyira allowed him a few steps then followed behind, padding low —there was still another in the mist near the fire that might see her.

As Bluebeard reached the body Kyira growled like a wild dog to make him turn. She thrust the blade between his ribs with little resistance, and he grunted. Another stab, higher, in the chest. The heart. Then again, higher, the neck. Red and blue mingling.

Breathe.

Using Bluebeard's weight she pushed away and spun to meet the last slaver, who was caught waiting. The red-faced oaf had barely time to protest before Kyira's blade vanished in through his eye. Footsteps rushed up behind. Fool! She had miscounted them! Kyira ducked with Redface as he stumbled forward then sped back towards the edge of the of the light, wind and blood rushing in her ears. She outflanked the last slaver, ran in and leapt upon his back. He was tall, and his wide minksin was finer than the others, but it didn't matter, his time had come. He would greet the earth, as his companions had.

Kyira growled, the noise deep and guttural. The slaver reached up awkwardly, but she threw herself left and right, grasping onto him with her thighs. Noise. Fear. Doubt. It all had to go. This was a hunt.

Breathe.

The darkness drew in until the only thing she saw was the flash of pale skin between the slaver's unkempt beard his fine padded collar. The blade saw it too, ducking beneath a wild jerk in her direction and connecting with his skin.

Breathe.

She gripped the handle and drew a deep line across that pale patch of skin, feeling the steel vanish into the man's neck. He held there, his body coming to terms with the truth of his death, then his muscles went limp and they fell to the ground as one.

Kyira jumped up, gasping for breath, but it was not tiredness. The pounding in her chest grew but it was not fear. The task was done. She had won, but something was wrong. Iqaluk ran towards her, clutching at her and throwing her off before crouching down at the slaver's side, feeling at the wound on his bloody neck as though trying to stop the bleeding.

Her father looked up at her with wide eyes. "Kyira. What have you done?"

"Aki, what are you doing? Leave him! Leave…"

The slaver's eyes darted back and forth; he looked up at her stricken and panicked with a face that was too young, with skin too smooth, with clothes too fine. He held up his bound hands to Kyira, choking on the blood pouring into his lungs.

Another captive pushed by. A woman, her hands were bound too. She fell to the slaver's side. Holding his face in her hands and crying, "Breathe, Isak. Breathe!"

"Aki!"

The slaver held his bound, shaking hands against the woman's round stomach, and the woman clawed uselessly at the bindings, as though she might set him free and undo all that had been done. The last slaver's mouth trembled with words unsaid, tears falling. He pushed the woman aside, holding an arm against her protecting her from Kyira. The man's eyes grew intense, then he gurgled once more and fell still.

The woman broke down and fell upon him, screaming his name over and over. "Isak! Please, no! Isak!"

Kyira's throat was dry, her head was empty. She wanted to drop the knife, let go of the still slick handle and never touch it again, but she couldn't let go. It was a part of her. She looked up Iqaluk, but he was already walking away.

Little Bird

Fia rushed into an empty side street alongside Vasen Square and fell breathless into an alcove, dropping the box from the meathouse to the cobbles. Her cheeks were hot, her windpipe constricted. She coughed, but the noise that came out was more a whimper squeezing past the lump in her throat. No! The Kumpani did not cry! They were steely, cold and calm. They were tough, beautiful, majestic and…

"You coward, Atalfia! Who are you? You are coward! That's who. A coward!"

She pressed her face in her hak, embarrassed as the tears flowed freely. It could only have been a Pan Guard waiting for them at that meathouse, and there were only a few who had the power to control Pans. What of Janike?

Fia's stomach was hard with guilt, but what else could she have done? It was not possible to fight a Pan and live! Taking down Eoin or Kavik was one thing but Janike could not win against a Pan at close quarters. No human could. She visualised that giant, thick sword cutting wood, brick, bone…

A noise made her jump, and she looked up to see a man walking away. The half-mark he had thrown into the box spun to a stop crown side up. If the Pan knew she and Janike were spies then so would Rathe, and she knew what kind of man he really was: a human ambassador with not a shred of humanity. She had to leave Tyr, but first, the Tsiorc had to know. Janike's father had to know. Fia scooped up the box, and made off down the alleyway.

A short while later she was slipping out of her flat leather shoes and into the entrance hallway of the Forbringr's Domst. It was as old as Tyr itself, so old that some said it was conjured up from the mantle by the Forbringr herself, the city merely growing like fungus around it. The Domst was usually an oasis of calm away from the bustling city, where people came to be more respectful and human but today it was just a building. The ushers in the lobby stood silently at the entrance of each corridor, barring anyone that strayed from the queue to the main prayer chamber. Fia stopped behind an older man with a babe at his shoulder. Salty tears found the lines of her lips and seeped into her mouth. Her chest bounced with fresh sobs, ready to burst out of her.

"Control yourself, Atalfia." You have a job to do.

The infant blinked large brown eyes at her, and she did her best to smile back. She took a long breath, enjoying the fresh smell of the place, the look of peace upon those waiting their turn to pray, the cool veinstone beneath her bare feet. She held out her hand as she approached the statue of Mother Baeivi and waited her turn to touch the breast, and as the father with the baby in front moved on, she touched her fingers to the worn stone and lingered there.

A Vasen man dressed in an evening hak, with long hoops dangling from each ear, tapped his foot behind her. "Speed

89

it up, Kumpani." He said in a thick Tyrian accent.

Fia took a long, deep breath and barged into the father's right side, then quickly sidestepped out of the line. The father turned and grabbed the Vasen man roaring obscenities at him over his screaming baby. As the man roared back Fia slipped behind the crowd and up the now unguarded staircase, as the ushers rushed around trying to restore order.

She bounded up the spiral steps two at a time, almost all the way to the top before stopping to put on her slippers. The great wooden door to the roofs creaked open, its once rusty hinges grinding. How long had it been since she had been up here?

Blinking in the daylight she squinted west. The dome roof of the Domst was barely a tenth of the height of the towers but you could still see it right across the Way, and beyond to the Giant's Teeth mountains standing tall past Fairsky. Fia leapt down the few steps to the low roof that ran along the perimeter, moving wide around the circular hole which fell to the Domst floor far below. Dry guano crunched underfoot, making her wince with every step but there was nothing to do but bear it, or fall to the alleyway far below.

The mew on the opposite side was split into smaller cages that housed the raevens in order of how swiftly they could deliver, and those faster creatures were up near the top underneath the tiny roof which was their only protection against the sun. The slower ones fluttered around in the smaller, more exposed cages below, which held as many dead as there were alive. She spiralled around to the little doors of the cages and opened one three down from the top.

The redback raeven that hung upside down from its perch, leather wings wrapped around its fuzzy little body, was Prig. It was the only raeven that Janike used and it was trained to sniff out another similarly pungent aviary in the Tsiore camp, but only when fed the correct food.

Steeling herself she reached in. "Ouch!" she said, jerking away. "You little bastard!" She reached into her pocket and, grimacing, pulled out the insect, dripping from her pocket. It must have been crushed somewhere between the fifth level and here. It smelled like a week-old latrine, but Prig gave an excited squeak.

"Not yet," she said, holding it away. "Not until you let me tie the message on."

Prig presented his pouch proudly, shaking in anticipation. Fia took the parchment she'd taken from Rathe's rooms and pressed it against the cage, scrawling her own message on the back with a piece of charcoal. After she had finished, she rolled it tightly and pulled a blunt pin from her hair and shoved it through the parchment. She looked at the items in her hands, insect and parchment, and with resignation placed the insect between her teeth by one of its disgusting spiked legs, so she could clip the parchment securely inside Prig's stomach pouch.

"Uch," said Fia, handing over the insect. She wiped her lips, resisting the urge to gag as the little raeven crunched it into pulp, head, legs and all until there was nothing left. When he had finished he squeaked and jumped out at her, then in a clap of wings swooped low over the roof edge and disappeared above the square.

Fia watched it until it was nothing more than a dot against the sky. "Well, Janike, let's hope you did not die for nothing."

"And what would a peasant want with the Forbringr's famed messengers?"

"A peasant?" said Fia, spinning around. "I hope you're referring to someone… else."

A man emerged from the shadow of an outbuilding. Most Tyrian men had battled at some point in their lives, especially the older ones, and they bore the scars of battles like prizes upon their bodies, tailoring their clothes to show them off, but not this man. His skin was smooth, and yet his eyes held the wisdom of one who had seen many fights — he moved with the sort of confidence that only those who had won did.

"I'm afraid they wouldn't be much use to you," he said, gesturing to the cages. "These particular raevens are having trouble navigating. Indeed, it seems there are only one or two that are immune to the effects of it."

"Immune to the effects of what?" stammered Fia.

The man looked at the sky then turned slowly towards her. "I forget that you humans have such dull senses. I wager you wouldn't feel it if it were burning down your homes and searing the skin from your bones."

"I don't… What do you mean?"

"Don't worry yourself with it." The man smiled. "You look as though you have enough of your own problems already. I do enjoy the moments of a first meeting though," he said, smoothly, "and I hear by your heartbeat that I do not need to make the effort of an introduction." His gaze slid over her chest, and she suddenly felt as if she were naked. "How your heart flutters so, as quick as a little bird." He brought his hands together in a loud clap. "So! That makes things easier. You know of me, yes? Of my kind?"

"Yes."

The man reached the mews and offered his hand. She took it without question and climbed down. It was cold.

"And what, may I ask, is it that you have heard?" he said.

"You are one of the Banémen," said Fia, pulling her hand away as soon as she could. "A slayer. They say you can change shape, take the forms of others."

"Yes!" he said, brightly, "Amongst other things. And you're right, some do refer to us as slayers, but you may call me Jagar. It's Fia, isn't it? I always prefer to be on first name terms. I would have used a title if your father had done enough to bestow one upon you." He took a step towards her and took some of her hair between his fingers. "You are very pretty. Pale skin, red hair and brown eyes — an oddity in Tyr. Although from your shape I would say you are local born, even if you do have some Kemen blood in you, and Dali, too. I should think. I imagine you have no problem in finding work."

"No," she said, staring back at him, her eyes darting to his wrist before she could stop herself.

"It's ok, Little Bird," said Jagar, holding up the talisman strapped to his wrist. "You can look. Most who get as close to my spark as you are do not generally live to tell of it, but today is not your day. That is, unless you wish it?"

Fia bowed her head. "No, thank you."

"So, who do you hope did not die for nothing?"

"No-one."

He skipped forward a little and smiled as Fia stumbled back. "Come now. We are friends, and you have nothing to hide. Tell me."

The last words were said plainly but they held danger,

and she knew her body would betray her if she lied. "My… partner was taken this morning." She kept her eyes low, hoping he had missed the hesitation.

"Partner? Oh. That is a shame. I assume it was in the line of duty?"

"It was."

"Oh dear, and during the blessed spring festival of moons no less. Perhaps the Forbringrs decided she had not fasted enough. Although, I'm quite certain you Kumpani all have a measure of sin about you." Jagar clapped his hands together again. "I would hope then for your sake that you stay dry for the month, and I don't just mean the booze. Bread and water and lots of prayer. Nothing more," he said, with a smirk. "I assume you've heard the story of the Forbringrs Baeivi and the Stallo, Little Bird?"

"Of course," croaked Fia.

"Baeivi was a plant giant. Some say Mother Nature herself, wandering the plains of existence forever until one day she encountered the Stallo, a fearsome sky demon, and they fought with each other for a millennia. Their fight swirled and spun and stretched the cosmos, pulling dust and rocks from every corner of the universe until it surged around them in a seething mass of liquid heat. Ages came and went as the fabric of existence ripped open around them, but eventually Baeivi began to tire." Jagar paused and turned toward Fia, making sure she was still paying attention. "The Stallo seized his moment, tearing a chunk of flesh from her back, a chunk that came to be Rengas. However, Baeivi had lured him into a trap, and while the Stallo exalted Baeivi tore off his head. The great yawning holes they had rent pulled his carcass away in pieces, and as Baeivi herself died, the head in her arms became our moon and she became the sun, and the black rain that fell was the blood of the Forbringrs."

"Every child knows this story, Jagar."

"The point, as always, lies between the lines, Little Bird."

Fia scowled at the Banéman. "Stories do not rule my life." She couldn't believe the tone that left her lips was her own, but the remorse of Janike's passing was quickly growing hot with impatience.

Jagar's eyes narrowed. "I see that. You don't seem the type to readily accept what you hear. An admirable trait." He looked her up and down. "Now, may I continue? Yes? Good. Through time and tale the story of Baeivi grew, its characters, its creatures and its world penetrating the lives of the people of Rengas, burrowing into their souls, urging them: follow me! And so they did."

"I don't understand," said Fia. "What has this to do..."

"Little Bird," said Jagar, stepping uncomfortably close. "My question for you, is this: do you stand in line, or do you challenge?"

It was a test, but she had to answer truthfully. "Challenge."

Jagar turned on the spot all the way around, flourishing his cloak to fan out around him. "That is why I like you, Fia. I like those who fight!" He bit into the last word, flashing perfect white teeth. "However, I am left with a conundrum, I would like to talk more with you, yet I know you are eager to be away. The very essence of your body is screaming for it. But do I let you leave? What else exactly is there to do with a Kumpani that breaks the rules so? But then I like those who break the rules. That is why rules exist, to be broken."

Fia shook her head, trying to follow him, wondering how

she might get away, if she would get away from this cat and mouse game. Suddenly Jagar's expression shifted, and Fia flinched.

"Go. Now."

A Trickle and a Torrent

T he blue tiles of the Justice Courts rang like little
bells under Jagar's feet as he reached the east
wing of the council chambers, where servants and
eunuchs pottered back and forth during the night hours. He
preferred this part of the council buildings for exactly that
reason. Peace. The Pans standing in the corridors bowed
low as Jagar passed by, clearly making an effort to keep their
noxious breaths quietly to themselves.

Jagar stopped at a pair of redoak doors and listened to the
shouting inside. Some rubbish about disturbing the Kael's
quiet time. Jagar turned to the wall, every inch of which
was plastered with tapestries and vases depicting scenes of
victory by the Bohr. Bohr killing the dragons, Bohr killing
humans, Bohr killing themselves. One particular vase had all
three, and was distinctly Kemen-made. It seemed as though
Rathe was trying hard to impress his Bohr cousins, but then
why furnish your nest with what could earn ten times as
much shipped across the Middle Sea? It was all so gaudy
too. The Kael certainly knew how to piss away a good fund.
Taxes or no.

He reached into his black hak and pulled a parchment
from within, unrolling it. The hand was neat and uniform,

much like the man who wrote it.

Brother,

There's a group of strangers scouting north of our location, the word of a slaver but I believe him. I've sent Gorm to investigate.

I trust in your Judgement.
Lor

Jagar closed the parchment over and replaced it just as the door opened. A young captain backed out of the room looking red-faced, which only became redder when he saw Jagar.

"Leave the door," ordered Jagar, standing smoothly. The captain made a show of backing off and presenting the door to him, which was both gratifying and hilarious.

Jagar took the door handles and burst in. "Good morning, Kael!"

"No. It isn't," muttered Rathe, barely looking up. "You found the time to come see me then?" He was holding a candle to a wax stick, and letting it drip onto an envelope on his desk. He threw the wax into a drawer and slammed his seal tamper onto the paper, splashing molten wax over the front of his dress cloak.

"They say winning a battle produces the most paperwork."

"*They* are wrong," said the Kael, as Jagar moved a chair by the bookcase to the desk. "We won't be long, Jagar. I have a pressing engagement."

Jagar liked to think that his line to cross was further than most, but already it was being trodden on. "From what I've heard, *pressing* is hardly a suitable adjective to describe your engagement, Kael."

Rathe added the envelope to a pile of others on his left, but the bundle shifted and slid into the chiselled Kacm'aor Sea — the Sea of the Dead. Jagar had actually been there, to the largest sea in Kemen, and the paltry representation illustrated bore no resemblance to how massive that body of water really was.

Rathe stared at the envelopes as though expecting them to jump back up into his inbox themselves. Defeated, he looked up. "I have a mission for you."

"A mission?" smirked Jagar. "You understand that—"

"Yes!" Rathe coughed and shifted in his chair. "Yes, brother," he went on, more quietly. "I understand this may be a little out of your current remit. You heard of our defeat at Drakemyre."

It wasn't a question. "I, and most of the city, yes," said Jagar. "They're already calling it the *Lost Battle*, or in some places the Battle that was not won, depending on their grasp of our graceful Tyrian language."

Rathe reached over and scooped up the scattered envelopes, stacking them on top of each other carefully, as if each one was a piece of his own patience ever so carefully reconstructed. "Then you know we have much to do."

"I have to ask," began Jagar. "Why did you only send a three-ton to Dali? Surely you didn't expect that would be enough to win? Even the lowliest rumours spoke of the strength of the Tsiorc army. One would only need to open a window and listen to the little birds to get such information."

"Jagar, we need to know what is out there before we move in with our full forces. Nord is a dangerous and wild..."

Rathe's hands gesticulated as he talked, as though he were trying to figure out what he was saying as he said it; it was a common human trait that did but speak of the disorganised mind, and was especially funny in the body of a Child of the Bohr. This half-breed, this…

Rathe got up suddenly, moving with the confident resolution of a man on the end of a decision. "We can't simply move into Nord without experience of the land. The elements would destroy our army. Not just a three-ton but a hundred-ton! We would perish in the cold." He looked down at the table, looking for more words.

"Go on, Kael," said Jagar, amused.

Rathe stood and paced in front of his wide desk then stopped as a new way of illustrating the same point came to his mind, as though Jagar was somehow ill-equipped to understand him. "I commissioned this map to help us understand our world, but it is incomplete."

"Yes, it is," said Jagar.

"We must have intel if the Bohr's plans to expand have any chance of success. It is as simple as that. Intel is everything."

Jagar stroked his chin. "Intel *is* important, but so is strategy, force and will. This just seems like you are waiting around while the rebels are knocking at your door."

"Don't call them that!"

And there was the line. Jagar stood and rounded the table towards Rathe. The Kael stood up, and moved away from his chair like they were a pair of duelling swordsman.

"They are not *rebels*," said Rathe, pleadingly. "They are farmhands and countrymen with pitchforks and torches. Splinters waiting… waiting to be torn from our skin."

Jagar's reached Rathe's chair and sat down. "And sending

three thousand men to their deaths in Drakemyre was simply a diversion tactic, to test the Tsiorc's capabilities?"

Rathe, now standing at the foot of his own table looked suddenly resigned. "They were better equipped than I was expecting."

"I'm not sure Nevis would see it that way."

"The Kael commands the lord's army!" roared Rathe, "And no one else! Not General Nevis, not Zuveri. ME!" He slammed his fist down on the desk scattering the envelopes. He stared at the mess, like a petulant child, regretting his foolish outburst. Brothers! This half-blood had more in common with a lame horse.

"Kael Rathe," began Jagar, "would you prefer the list of the ways I could end your life cut upon your flesh, or perhaps pinned to your noticeboard?" He glanced around at the walls. "You don't have a noticeboard." He scratched a fingernail through the Kemen plains, leaving a charred line of wood. "Because I can only assume that my presence here is not enough to remind you that a Child of the Bohr ranks below, far below, that of a Banéman. Indeed, there are things that could occur in this room that the Pans outside would hear and ignore." He said the words as simply as he could, so there would be no chance of rebuke. It was exhausting having to instruct those who should know better.

He restacked the envelopes and placed them over the top of the gently smoking table. "Perhaps it is best you get the rage out of your system before your *engagement* with Zuveri, but please do remember who you are talking to." He stared at Rathe until those blank eyes fell from his. "So, to move things along. This mission."

"The leader of the rebels is a man named Laeb," began

101

Rathe, quietly. "He tore through our three-ton's ranks with more organisation and skill than I've seen from any Ringlander. We took a few hundred of his soldiers, but that was it. He commanded the fight from the beginning. It seemed to me that even his losses were by design."

"Laeb?" said Jagar. "He is Sulitarian?"

"Yes," said Rathe. "A blue-eyes. Have you been there? To the Outer Isles?"

"Alas, no," said Jagar. "The treacherous waters make inward passage impossible, but I've heard some do trickle through."

"A trickle? The little I know of them comes from the torrents of fucking immigrants that fall upon our shores every week! They are a cancer eating away at our city."

"Courageous though," mused Jagar, "braving the Middle Sea. And if they are here anyway, why not just draft them?"

"Beggars, thieves and killers," growled Rathe. "They belong in their own country, not lining the streets of Tyr, or fighting in our wars."

Jagar laughed. "From what I hear, blue-eyes women are fierce and beautiful, and their men hard and lean. They would make a solid first wave in a battle. Even Sulitarian mothers will fight in battles with their infants strapped to their backs. Indeed, I wouldn't be surprised if the babes had knives hidden within the folds of their swaddles. I don't suppose there is anything more terrifying than facing down a protective mother. They might even present a challenge for the likes of you, Kael."

"No drafting, Jagar. Tyr's blood will remain pure."

Jagar shook his head in disgust. "Tyr's blood would do well to use such an influx of new life," he hissed. "It has grown weak and stagnant of late." Such a wonderfully potent insult should have lingered between them like a bad smell, but Rathe was clearly preoccupied. The fun was quickly waning from this meeting.

Jagar sighed. "So, you wish me to find this Sulitarian captain? This Captain Laeb."

Rathe looked up. "No. I *need* you to find him, Banéman. I have to meet him. This man who brought down three legions of the world's greatest army. Kill who you must but find him and bring him here." He paused. "If you would not mind."

"I know of someone," said Jagar. "He berths in our Way mouth every third month, this month no less, and he may be of use in reaching your captain."

"Thank you, Jagar."

"Oh," said Jagar, reaching into his pocket. "You might also like to know that you received a message. Fortuna."

Rathe looked up as Jagar flicked the parchment over the long table to roll into the Middle Sea basin. "You've opened it."

"Call it a privilege of my station, Kael."

Rathe's eyes moved slowly over the words, and after a long moment he held the paper over the candle, then dropped it smouldering into the Sea of the Dead. "Seeing as you've read it then, maybe you might consider this group Lor mentions as something else for you to investigate on your travels. I suggest you debrief Gorm fully when you catch up with him."

"As you say, Kael." Jagar stood and moved around the table, prompting Rathe to move back around the other way. Jagar stopped at the door. "By the by, I bumped into that Kumpani of yours."

Rathe blinked. "Fia? Where?"

"On the Domst roof," said Jagar. "She seemed upset about a friend."

"Where is she now?"

"Dead, I believe."

Rathe's expression contorted into one of pathetic concern. "Fia is dead?"

"Oh no," laughed Jagar. "Her partner, Janike befell some sort of tragic end."

"Oh," said Rathe. "Where is Fia now? Did she say why she was there?"

"Maybe she was just taking a walk. Getting some air. It is nice up there." Jagar reached the door and turned the brass handles. "I suppose we will never know." He stepped back, pulling the doors open. "Goodbye, Rathe."

Jagar marched down the corridor. The Kael might be a Child of the Bohr, but he was truly as blind as any other human. Indeed, some assume that half-bloods are exactly half of a Bohr, but no Bohr would have ever let something so obvious as two spies in his midst pass him by. Maybe the Kael was simply unable to think beyond the end of his cock. Either way it didn't matter to Jagar, the world would right itself soon enough.

The Fiskar

Fia clutched the box close, the coin still rattling around inside it. She adjusted her hak to keep herself casually hooded. It came naturally to a Kumpani, being the centre of attention, but it was an acquired feeling. In the beginning when she had been serving drunkards in the Fiskar, she would have jumped at a loud shout, but rarely were words said in jest meant to be malicious. Fia followed the crowd of dockers, finding comfort in the wall of bustling bodies that carried her towards the warehouses at the docks. For all anyone knew she was just a fishwoman, on her way to the Way mouth to spread her nets across the swarms of silverfish.

The stink of rotten kelp and rotten fish mingled with the odour of sweaty skin but none cared. Teräväens were doers, makers, and catchers. Gatherers, teachers and merchants. The city was only a vibrant jewel because of those people. They made the city what it was, and Fia soaked it all in, welcoming the distraction of their busy lives. Conversation drifted around the tightly packed lines, as they talked of their jobs, their family, their pay, their lovers, conquests and their grievances. One such pair walking behind spoke of their fear of losing their jetty spot to a blue-eyes vessel. Others chimed in, adding their own nods and murmurs of agreement, until soon almost the whole crowd were planning to work together to fish the luminous silverfish in a line, so blocking entry to any outsider merchant vessels awaiting to dock. As with all good things the experience soon ended as the crowd dispersed into the stock warehouses along the dock.

Allander stood outside the Fiskar leaning against the supporting pillar — his usual place — watching the first shifts as they struggled back and forth between fish stores and boats, hastily unloading their cargo before they handed over to the new shifts.

"Fia!" said Allander, flashing his usual charismatic, slanted smile. "Forbringr's Blood." He embraced her warmly, and she held him tight, holding back tears. "I never thought we'd see you down here again. Not after... Oh, eh... evening, Naylor." A bearded man with deep tanned skin and blood-stained hands grunted. He shook Allander's hand and whispered something.

"Moonsquid? On the Way? Isn't that a strange thing? I haven't seen a moonsquid this far in land. Swarms of them you say? I never thought I'd live to see a day when millions of moonsquid were eager to jump in our nets. Maybe the tides are turning!" Allander patted the man on the back. "The soup? No, my friend. I didn't make the soup. It's made from a fermented paste imported from Makril. Go and have yourself a seat and I'll get you a bowl. I'll see you fed and no doubt." Naylor disappeared in through the low doorway, and a powerful waft of fish followed him in. "Don't mind Naylor, Fia. He's probably just afraid you'll try and whisk him from his wife's side."

"Well, he need not worry," said Fia.

106

"Ah now," said Allander, throwing his grey locs behind a shoulder. "I know it's been a while but best not let the riff-raff hear your speak like that or it might be you next in line for the cuttin' table!" He put an arm around her and led her towards the Fiskar's entrance.

"And since when do you import from Makril?" asked Fia. Allander smiled. "I don't."

The damp stone walls of the Fiskar were as dank and horrid as Fia remembered. She took a deep breath of the familiar smells: fish, seaweed, and old needlcwood sap. Oh, whyever did she leave? Fresh cuts and gauges marked the wood all over and there seemed to be a considerable shortage of furniture, too. Allander squeezed by the five sitting at the long bar and tugged the door to the den shut to stop the reek of poppy smoke drifting into the bar. It immediately creaked open again.

"Nothing has changed," she said, taking the only seat left.

"You're still day-dreaming, I see," said Allander, moving back and forth behind the bar. "I thought you might have grown out of that."

Fia tried to make a face, but judging by Allander's confused expression it didn't quite come across. "What about the old guy who always used to ask for me?"

"Old Tomkin? Gotta be Fia. Always Fia. He's dead now. Bless his shadow. Onich? What was it that took old Tomkin?"

"Gut rot!" croaked the old man at Fia's side. He turned toward her and winked. "Alright Fia?"

Fia flashed a fake smile — she knew at least how to do that. "Wonderful, Onich, wonderful. And you?"

"Thing's is dire, Fia. Dire." Onich was the sort of old man

who saw Fia as just another person. He took a sip from his soup bowl, but kept it held by his lips as he spoke. "When I was young, I remember having free rein of Terävä. I even got to cross the bridge once. Not now, though... I wouldn't recommend such a thing to anyone. Not if they valued their life." He caught Allander's eye, and offered out his bowl. "Al, eggs, please."

Allander pulled a dried egg sack from a box beneath the bar and dropped it into Onich's bowl. The steaming liquid immediately dissolved the sac, and it opened like a flower, filling the dark green broth with tiny purple spheres. Onich lifted the bowl and took a long slurp.

"You crossed the bridge?" asked Allander, leaning forward. "How'd you manage that?"

"Pulling guard duty one night," said Onich. "We had to cross it to check a disturbance on the west side. Got to see how the others live."

"You're lucky," said Allander, dipping his hand into a murky glass jar full of old leaves. "Don't think I've ever heard of any fishmen crossing the bridge before."

"It's a sad day when even Teräväen guards can't cross," said Onich. "Just the Pans."

Allander rooted around the leaves then jerked. "Ha!" He pulled out a tiny lizard, which wriggled its head out through an opening in his clasp.

Naylor spoke up, hiding most of his face in his bowl. "It's the immigrants, Onich. There ain't space in the city for more than we have."

"The blue-eyes?" said Onich. "Can't say I've ever met one."

"They're everywhere," said Naylor. "I hear the slums are overrun with them. City can only take so much before—"

"Ah!" A squirt of flame burst from Allander's closed hand and he dropped the lizard with a curse. All five men chuckled as he scurried about the floor slamming his foot down after the tiny creature.

Even Fia couldn't help but laugh. "You know, they say that you shouldn't kill a firelizard. It's bad luck."

"Blasted... awful... smelly things! HA!" said Allander.

He bent low and scraped its flattened body off the sandy floor with his spoon then flicked it to the leashed raeven who took pleasure in ripping the broken lizard to pieces.

Somewhere outside a distant bell clanged, and all five tall chairs screeched back at once. Onich dropped a copper harkko brick upon the bar, then pulled a cap from his pocket and pulled it on his balding head. "Be well, Fia," he said, as the men behind him looked over his head, eager to get by.

Fia touched her palm to Onich's face, as was the Kumpani way, and the old fishman smiled warmly.

"By heavens it's good to see you."

"See you in a few hours, gentlemen," said Allander. He waited until the last had shuffled out into the mild evening air then slid a tray with two small pewter cups over towards Fia, tapping one with his iron soup spoon. "Go on. You look like you need it."

She drank down the syrupy concoction, shivering as its sweet heat oozed down into her belly. "Hot?" she said, fighting back a cough.

"You must allow an old man his old habits. I always drink seete hot these days. It's got more of a kick." He poured another from the delicate iron teapot and threw it back. "Besides, I'm surprised you would still drink with such lowlifes as us — from what I heard you've been bandying about with the best of them. Not that I'm complaining. I'd have you down every week, if not for your company, then for the business you bring in to my shady little establishment. Onich will no doubt sleep very well this night."

Allander's way was direct, but he was always friendly with it. He would be the first to tell you that you needed some mint leaves to chew after a long day and no food, then he would hand you some of his own.

"Allander, I'm starving."

"Ah, say no more." Allander was suddenly up and rummaging through the cupboards, and the ice well, and before long Fia had a plate of sliced raw fish, a cup of thin soup, and some crusted sour bread in front of her.

"Everything alright?"

Fia slurped the last of her soup down, and wiped her chin. "Fine. Why?"

His eyes narrowed. "No reason. Try the fish its…" Fia had swallowed all six fillets before Allander had finished talking. "Silverfish."

She knew he was watching her, but what did that matter? She had to eat something. Lots of things.

"You know, it's been some time since we had silverfish here. It's usually uncatchable."

"S'good." Fia went to sip from her seete and gestured for a refill.

She tore off a hunk of bread and wiped the soup cup with it. "Allander. Do you know, that is, are you aware of… any… boats leaving soon?"

"I knew it! Forbringr's blood, I knew it. What trouble are you in, Fia?"

"You don't want to know." She readjusted the box beneath

her hak.

Allander leant close. "Tell me, kumpani, or I swear I'll never offer you another bite, no matter how nervous you get! You'll not eat in this shack nor any other on the Tcräväen docks while I still have blood in my veins!"

Fia swallowed. "You have a life here, Allander. People who depend on you. I don't want to burden you with my troubles."

Allander's intense frown softened much quicker than it would have, even a couple of cycles ago. He placed down his seete. "It's no burden, and to be honest with you, Fia, I'd welcome the distraction. Things here have been slow. The merchants from the Outer Reaches are not stopping. They're paying their tolls and carrying on out to the Middle Sea. Most of the time they're not even leaving their ships. It's killing us. I'd give anything for some excitement. Some action."

"I saw boats coming in today," said Fia.

"Fishboats, aye. But that's it, and that's only when the currents allow them to approach the Way mouth, which has not been often. The tides down the channel are getting stronger to the point where some vessels are just carrying on. And who would blame them? Would you fight your way back in to pay a bloody tax?"

Fia shook her head. "Are the watches on the bridge not reporting the vessels who don't pay?"

Allander rolled the seete around his cup. "It's mostly Pans since Drakemyre, and they don't care. They're leaving us to rot."

"What about the council?"

They haven't met in months. I've put feelers out, but all I

get back are warnings from the guards for intervening. The people of Terävä need a voice in the Justice halls, a seat at the table, otherwise they will be walked all over. There is a new currency being distributed tomorrow, and still the council haven't summoned any councillors to discuss it. Not me for Terävä, nor even Sofek for Vasen. It's like marshal law has been dropped on both sides of the city without conferring with the people."

Fia sipped at her seete, licking the sweet flavour from her lips. "Musta." She put on her best Rathe impression. "We're imposing a token-based currency which will benefit the good people of this city and tax those who wish to travel the Way. Any merchant vessels who cannot pay in musta will be forced to sell their cargo in exchange for passage down the Way and for access to the southern cities." She spoke in her normal voice again. "The merchants won't like it, not one little bit, and the shipleaders that don't pay will have their ships impounded. Within a year Tyr will be penniless. No other country will ever trade with us again."

Allander baulked as the reality dawned on him. "And they have to moor here so they can spend their new currency in the only place it is accepted. What will that do to marks? And harkko bricks?"

"It will devalue them," said Fia.

Allander gave a slow nod. "It's begun! The major food vendors are already slowing production. Livestock and building materials are becoming too expensive to make a profit from." Allander lifted the harkko brick Onich had left. "This will soon be worth less than the copper it is pressed from." He tipped his seete down his neck. "Let us not try to change what cannot be changed. I will bring it up if I am ever summoned to council. Now, are you going to show me what's stowed in your hak or not?"

Fia started. "What do you mean?"

Allander smiled. "Come now, Fia, give me some credit. We worked together for three cycles, and much of that time was spent admiring your curves." It wasn't said in a lecherous way, but rather the way a mother might brag about her daughter. Regardless, the comment caught her off-guard. She stared at him, trying to find a response but none came, then she unravelled her bundled hak and released the wooden box.

Allander took it from her, examining it like he was about to suggest a price. "Shape the world? Well, the Nord's certainly know their craft."

Fia nodded and made a sound of agreement.

Allander glanced sidelong at her. "You've no idea what it is, do you?"

"It's a box."

"Is it?" He handed it back to her. "It's a map box." He turned to the pot of simmering soup and added some of the leaves from the jar the lizard had been squatting in.

"A map box? For keeping maps in?"

"The very same," he said, stepping over and plucking out the coin. "And said to hold the secrets of the land. Although it looks like you're a little late to the party. It's a nice box though. You could keep your necklace in it!" He flicked the coin up, but didn't even try to catch it and it fell spinning to the floor. He turned to her, looking suddenly afraid. "Fia. Tell me, from whom do you run?"

Fia couldn't look away. "Do you know Jagar?"

"Forbringr's Blood! The Banémen? That's the *trouble* your

113

dragging around with you?" He rushed out of the bar, past the den and dropped the dusty beads over the Fiskar's main entrance — there was no door, because the Fiskar never closed. He turned back, his face as pale as old coals. "Atalfia, you better tell me everything. Everything."

Relics

The Bohr king didn't exist. He was lore — a legend. A fake figurehead so the council could make their decisions about blood taxes, trade sanctions and war costs in relative peace. An unseen villain the public never saw. Unfathomable power and speed meant nothing when your name was myth. Humans needed an object with which to associate, and so did Rathe, in a way. Except, Rathe knew the Bohr king was real. There was no denying the Pan Guard, trussed up in gold plates and armour delivering a summons to his apartment doors and who waited with him to read it. It was why he had called Fia around, and why now, after an entire morning of distractions it took all Rathe had not to tremble in fear and run away.

"It is our choices that make us who we are," he said, approaching the king's gardens. "Not our thoughts." Which was lucky.

The bountiful gardens beyond the council buildings had been part of the Domst grounds for centuries, but their beauty had long since diminished, and as a result, nobody ventured near them, or the Pans that stood watch. Standing high above the rows of overgrown shrubs were sheer black cliffs that held within them thick white veins of charsalt that, like many of Tyr's riches, the Bohr king had taken claim of. But nestled in the shadow of those cliffs was a crumbling stadium the king called his home. It was as old as the Domst, but unlike the pristine white building in Vasen square the stadium actually looked its age. It was a relic of another time.

"I am summoned," growled Rathe to the first Pan Guard at the entrance.

"So you are, Kael Rathe," said the Pan. He blocked a huge wooden door, easily four times his height. "You have no sword."

"I am here on the King's request," said Rathe.

The Pan reached behind him and pulled a sword from a barrel. It looked like a dagger in his palm. "It's safer if you're armed, Kael Rathe."

"I assume the King is also armed?"

The Pan's face split in two. "Zuveri is not armed, Kael Rathe, and does not need to be." He waited for Rathe to accept the blade then leant against the old door which creaked open, flecks of rust dropping from the hinges. "You may enter, Kael Rathe."

Rathe entered and began walking through the warren of shadowed hallways within the walls of the Bohr king's domain. Not just anyone was permitted to be cut down by the Bohr king, let alone have the chance to fight him. He drew a long breath. "Hopefully it won't come to that." There was still much to do.

Shadowy figures reached out of the narrow tunnel walls, their moss-covered anguished faces cut from the stone. Rathe followed the fresher air until a faint light ahead took over, and he stepped out into the outer rim of the stadium.

It stretched a quarter league distant, and was lined by vast pillars becoming matchsticks in the hazy distance. A dank mist hung over the shabby overgrown shrubs and trees that littered the space within, too dense to see through. Perfectly smooth and spherical black boulders peeked out of the wildness with a dark globe of rock bigger than any other in the centre.

Rathe made his way inward winding this way and that around thorny bushes and dead trees until he stopped at one of the black rocks. He ran his fingers over the mossy surface, feeling the set of deep scores that in places had torn growth away. It was pure charn, the most refined form of charsand. He shook his head in disbelief. Here, the city was fighting over chits and chattels and within these gardens was a king's ransom of their most valuable mineral.

Something ran along his back and he jerked around, almost tripping. Nothing. He held the Pan's sword out in front; it felt unusual, but the memory of iron was one not quickly forgotten. He swung it expertly around him. "Show yourself!"

He fought the urge to duck low; he had to appear strong, but damn the blade was heavy. He glanced back the way he had come, and there was a rustle as something passed behind him. He felt a tickle at his back, as softly as if Fia were tracing a finger over his skin, and his dress jacket became awkward. He shifted his shoulders and it fell off his back to the ground as a pile of shredded cloth. His heart racing, he felt at his shirt, which was still as whole as when he'd pulled it on.

"Stop the games!" he shouted, as levelly as he could. "I am summoned here by the Bohr king and I intend to either speak or leave. Show yourself!"

A dark hulking shape double Rathe's height emerged from the underbrush, stalking towards him like a man with too many muscles. It had thick leather straps pulled taut around a pale chest and groin and nothing else. Its face was mostly hidden behind a cowl, but it reached up with a veiny forearm and lifted it smoothly off, brushing away long matted ropes of grey hair, and revealing a wide mouth, filled with pointed teeth.

Bright, golden eyes regarded him. "How you lie to yourself," said the king, in a deep rumble.

Rathe blinked at the ancient being. "You are female?"

"A female cannot be King?" rumbled the king, danger colouring her tone.

"Not truly," replied Rathe.

The king stepped forward and let out a thunderous laugh that boomed around the circular walls. She had a chunk of flesh missing from the cheek — an old wound that looked long since healed. She could be hurt. Rathe clenched the hilt as hard as he could.

Abruptly the king's laugh stopped, and she approached Rathe, standing over him like a mother to a child. "I know your fears, Kael Rathe, and your lies. You lie to yourself that you are ready when you are not. You worry I am going to kill you, before your time, before you have achieved greatness."

"Yes. I worry," said Rathe, "but I do not fear it."

"Your body says otherwise," snarled the king.

Rathe suddenly became aware of every fibre of his body, and he hated each and every one for betraying him. "Why am I summoned here?"

"You speak as if you have done nothing wrong."

There was a blur of movement as the hulk grew larger, then suddenly she was back standing where she had been, except now she held his sword in her hand. He'd barely felt the hilt tugging.

"Bohr blood is not the driving force it once was. It dilutes with every generation. The Bohr kill, and rape, and trap for sport because within their blood is a need to conquer having been bred for war so deeply that the hunt is all they know. Times are changing. As one, humans are of no match for us, but as many, they outnumber us a thousand to one, and in this world numbers are all that count. It is only a matter of time before they realise it."

"We can reduce the herd."

The king's expression became almost thoughtful. She shook her head, and her braided locs rattled against each other. "A cull will only hasten the end. Humans are so many that they will organise faster than we can stop them. We require more subtle methods. We have an obligation to expand, or our way of life will perish along with us. There will be nothing left for anyone."

The king, who had a moment ago seemed like an angry bull, was now as articulate as a scholar. He couldn't keep the frown away as he stared into those golden eyes. "Your plans are to dilute Bohrblood even further by conquering?"

"The plans that I speak of are central to preserving our way of life, but they are being stifled by your lack of ingenuity and intelligence. As ambassador to the Bohr, your actions reflect us." She stepped towards him, and it took all of his effort not to step back. "Yet even as your body awaits a painful death by your own sword, you remain true to your thoughts, Kael Rathe. You have much strength in you."

It was delivered as a fact not a compliment, but it helped bolster Rathe's confidence. Anything less than pure honesty would see him cleaved in half in a moment. "The Tsiorc have a new leader," said Rathe. "A blue-eyes named Captain Laeb."

"Is he Bohr?" asked the Bohr king.

Rathe could see the trap closing around him. "No."

"Then how did he best you?" snapped the king. The echo of her bark bounced around the stadium causing a flock of birds to burst out from within the high pillars.

"I will not excuse my actions," said Rathe. "Mistakes were made. The three-ton legion was intended to move north through Dali to secure the high lands, but the Tsiorc were waiting for us in the heart hills of Drakemyre. They left us but one escape route, forcing the men into a bottle neck."

"And their losses?"

"Minimal," replied Rathe. "Had circumstances been different—"

"You are the maker of ways, Kael Rathe," growled the King. "The failure is yours."

Sweat had poured down Rathe's back. "Yes, but we couldn't have known they would have had such great numbers."

"Your mistake has seen three legions of the lord's army destroyed. I am taking full control of the council," said the King.

"I beg you to reconsider, Zuveri." Her eyes widened at the use of her name. "You say that the younger Bohr crave power, and that the treaties between humans and Bohr are the tenuous lines that hold them. Then we must do all we can to maintain them! The council must continue as normal, otherwise to all humans within Tyr it will appear as though the Bohr are rising up. You said it yourself, the Bohr are outnumbered, and to prevent that tide from washing over us, we must maintain our control over the governed. Leave them enough slack to dispel the tensions, otherwise the trickle will become a torrent and the races will revert back to civil unrest unseen since the Dreki Wars."

"War is here and now!" roared the Bohr king. "War is everywhere. A Bohr would know that!"

"Yes, but fighting the right war is what is important," said Rathe. Hearing his own stoicism surprised him. "If we descend into war against all humans, there will be nothing left for anyone."

Using the king's own words against her was supposed to lend weight to his argument, but all he felt now was regret.

Her stance grew still, like a predator getting ready to pounce. Rathe waited for death. He would at least meet it proudly.

"You will end the rebellion," said the king. "It is your main priority."

Rathe swallowed the sigh of relief. "I need resource, Tyr is penniless. I need to ability to control the Council, and I shall end this rebellion so that we may expand."

"Kael Rathe, you are in the highest position a Child of the Bohr can be, yet your half-blood craves yet even more power?"

"No... I—"

"Then you shall have it." The king walked towards him. "Will you beg forgiveness and offer more excuse for your sins?"

"I will not," said Rathe, flatly. "My word is simple. We will not fail."

"No. You will not," said the king, stopping directly in front of him, the Pan's blade almost lost in her fist. She lifted the sword and placed its point on Rathe's forehead. "Your fifth father, was my cousin. He led an impressive life, surpassed only by his impressive death." Rathe ground his teeth as the sword's point poked through his skin and cut a mark into his flesh. "You have much to live up to."

The king stepped back, and pushed the sword into the solid black globe as if it were made of mud rather than stone.

"I mark you Kael Rathe as the Guardian of Tyr. You have full autonomy, and full control of the council. I leave it to you to end the rebellion." She pulled the sword slowly from the black boulder then held it out to Rathe in one huge hand. "Prove your blood, Guardian Rathe, and rise above it. This is your last chance." She stood straight and took a deep rumbling breath, before nodding back the way he had come. "Your summons have been fulfilled."

Rathe waited until he was back below the pillars before wiping the blood dripping down his face. The sun had already passed its zenith, but the cast shadows were still some way from leaving the stadium completely. The day was yet young.

The Mother, the Bear and the Wolf

Kyira blinked up at the grey morning sky, her warmth creating misted shapes that floated up into the chill air. Iqaluk lay asleep nearby, his breath still whistling, but he looked better than when she had left him in the cave.

A few feet away lay one of the slavers she had killed, covered from the waist up in his own minksin. She had opened his throat like she had the slaver upon the Laich, except of the four she had killed, this one was no slaver — he was barely a man. The blade lay next to her, looking more menacing than it ever had, and yet it had not changed. It was she that was different, and it had happened when the Mother, the Bear and the Wolf fell upon the corpse of their dead friend, crying for his life to be returned.

She had named them so, because that was what they were to her. The Mother, for the babe she carried, the Bear for his size, and the Wolf for his unforgiving eyes, and he was the one that worried her the most. Wolves were patient hunters, running through the night and harrying their prey until they collapsed from sheer exhaustion. If he had four legs, he would have been a wolf, she was sure of it, and as the leader he was the obvious choice to restore balance.

The Mother lying across the fire stirred. They would all be awake soon and Kyira needed to find peace before then — if the mounted slavers from the laich found them now she would be as helpless as her unborn babe. Kyira pulled her legs underneath her and closed her eyes, matching each breath to the beats of her heart, until they both slowed and synchronised. Her consciousness began to detach, stretching and painting its own pictures: an ox pulling a plough; her brother laughing with his friends; the Laich in winter, crisp and fine, full of shapes and wonder, as though time itself had stopped; Vlada high up in the sky with a flock of noisy terns somewhere between. Kyira was a tern too, flying, dipping and diving like a white arrow between the hilltops. The flock moved as one, trying to dodge Vlada's talons, not realising they were being herded by a much more clever predator. Vlada led them between the pines and over the summits, and around the vales, and then suddenly he was diving. The terns scattered and Vlada barrelled through them, taking three of them with him. Opening her eyes and giddy from Vlada's successful hunt Kyira stretched her body.

Squatting, she extended her left leg outwards, and using only the right she rose up, dropping her hands down to touch her bare feet as they came together, running up her legs, and stomach to her chest until she was standing fully, arms extended up towards the sky. The second form came easily and she let the pictures in her mind stretch with each shape, tearing up the dark spaces that clouded her senses. A sense of peace descended as inevitable as the plough, as strong as the ox, as nimble as the tern and as warm as a fur blanket.

When she opened her eyes the Wolf was staring at her.

The Mother's head was in his lap. She was weeping again, and he was stroking her hair as though they were lovers. His other hand sat upon the hilt of a sword, and judging by the triangle newly carved into the silver pommel and the large amber stone, it was no slaver's blade; it looked as though it had always belonged to him.

Iqaluk and the Bear had also awoken and moved. It shouldn't have surprised her — if anyone could have moved around without her hearing, it was Aki, but the Bear as well? A man of his size should not have been able to leave the camp without her noticing.

"Aki?"

"You sound rejuvenated," said her father, without looking up.

"As much as I can be. Why are you still bound?" asked Kyira, reaching for his hands.

Iqaluk snatched them away. "Leave them!"

"Aki."

"Kyira, I am your father, but if last night proved anything it is that you are a child no longer. My name is Iqaluk. I no longer wish you to call me Aki."

Kyira swallowed hard. "Alright." She nodded at the three captives. "Who are they?"

"Travellers. Like us."

Kyira scoffed. "The Bear is no Sami."

"No. He told me they were farmers." He cocked his head. "The Bear? What have you named the others?"

Kyira flushed. "The Wolf and the Mother."

"Apt." Iqaluk returned to the dirt, digging with renewed vigour.

Kyira began to dig too. The mud was not good, and there

125

was barely any torv to be found.

The Bear appeared out of the low cloud, and after checking the dead one he went and spoke to the Wolf and the Mother. The Bear seemed to make most of the decisions, but it was the Wolf that was in charge, if anything the Bear looked a little afraid of him. Kyira guessed it was all to protect the Mother, because every time Kyira moved the Wolf placed himself between them.

They all wore the triangle symbol somewhere upon their bodies, either stamped into leather or cut into metal. They were a part of the same outfit then.

"They are like no one I have ever met before."

Iqaluk looked up. "The Mother's skin is too dark to be of Nord or the borders of Határ. My guess is Kemenese."

Kyira shook her head. "I didn't mean that. Iqaluk, what do we do now?"

"We dig for fuel."

"No I mean—"

"I know what you mean, child." He studied his hands. "I have never left Nord in my life, but the longer Hasaan is away from us the more I think we need friends, and these three need us too. The winds have handed us a gift, and we must do all that we can to preserve this friendship. If we ever intend to see Hasaan again."

"We will see him again, Iqaluk."

Her father nodded to the hole. "For now, just keep digging."

* * *

Kyira lifted the last stone ready to place over the boy's face.

It would be the last time anyone saw the patchy growth on his cheeks, or sunlight reflected in his eyes. She couldn't have guessed at his age, but this was hardly the end he, or anyone, deserved. She might've cried — it would have gone some of the way to undoing what she had done, but no tears came.

The Wolf reached out and pulled the Mother close, pressing her round stomach against his side while sobs racked them both.

"We should say something," said Iqaluk, from Kyira's side.

"Like what?" growled the Wolf, his chin wobbling. "It is done."

Kyira pulled the knife from her belt and handed it to him handle first. "You will use this."

The Wolf shook his head, then motioned for the Bear to stand with the Mother. When the two had swapped places The Wolf rounded on Kyira. "For what?"

Kyira couldn't stop her lip quivering. "To bring balance." She took his hand and pointed the tip of the blade to her chest. "I will not try to stop you."

"To kill you?" The Wolf hissed. "To cut your throat open?" The Wolf nodded to Iqaluk. "And you? What would you do after I stab your daughter?"

Iqaluk's expression was as stone. He smoothed out his long beard. "Her life is her own."

Kyira couldn't help but stare at Iqaluk. What a thing to have to say.

The Wolf considered the steel in his hands. "You may have killed my friend, but you saved us from those men. We've been in their captivity for some time and…" He lowered his voice. "Isak was in the wrong place at the wrong time.

Lyla loved him, loves him, and may feel differently, but I will certainly not end your life after you saved ours." He reached out and cut Iqaluk's bindings, then let the knife fall to the grass. "You will need to find another way to repay your debts."

Kyira picked it up. "For what it is worth, I am sorry. I did not mean to kill him. I wish I could take it back, but this world is a dangerous place for a mother, and while you and your friend may have some experience, you will not last long without us. There may be more of them out there."

"What do you know?" The Mother and the Bear were also watching her, waiting.

Iqaluk placed a hand on her shoulder. "Daughter. Now is not a time to hide."

Kyira looked down. "There are three mounted slavers somewhere behind, looking for me. I've killed two of them already, and when I discovered Aki was missing… Iqaluk, was missing, and that you had him tied up, I assumed you were slavers also."

It was Iqaluk who spoke first. "Mounted slavers, Kyira? You are certain?"

"Last time I saw them, they were on the last ridge of the Waning Crescent."

Iqaluk turned towards the Wolf, and suddenly Kyira was aware of how frail her father looked against the Wolf's muscled frame. "If the slavers find you they will take you, and you will spend the rest of your days on the end of a chain. If they let you live. Which is unlikely."

"What's going on?" said the Mother, padding up to the Wolf's side. She had claimed a shirt from the female slaver, who apparently was much larger than she was.

The Wolf took a long breath. "There are more slavers out here in the hills. The three that took us were part of a bigger group. Could be they are the ones searching Nord for the Kin."

Iqaluk shared a look with her. Kyira felt it too — these people were no farmers. Kyira nodded at the Mother's stomach. "They would sooner cut the babe from you and feed it to the raevens—"

The Mother slapped Kyira hard across the cheek. "You dare to speak that way, after killing Isak. He was one of us! And who are you? A jumpy little shepherd's girls?" She spat at Kyira's feet, and turned away, muttering to her stomach.

Heat spread rapidly across Kyira's face, but it was not from the slap. "Iqaluk, we should go."

"There is a town a day or so from here," said the Wolf, glancing back at the mother. "You should come with us."

"No!" said the Mother. Something unseen passed between them.

"Lyla we need the help. Three mounted slavers—"

"No, Feykir. No. She killed Isak."

The Wolf stepped over to her and they spoke quietly. The Mother shook her head, and turned away.

"We're heading to a fishing town called Makril," said the Wolf, padding over. "You told me you were searching for something. Well, Makril may well provide answers for you, whatever it is you seek."

Iqaluk looked uncertain, farmers were one thing.

The Wolf's eyes found hers. "We are on the same path, I promise you. Join us."

Old Friends

J agar dabbed his watering eyes with a neckerchief as the wind began picking up. There was no use in grumbling, the Way Bridge's central point was almost two hundred paces above the water — higher than some hills in the Lowlands, though much smaller than some of the dunes he had scaled in the Cracked Wastes. How the locals could so covet huge piles of sand, he doubted he would ever know.

He folded the square cloth and slid it down into the inside pocket of his hak, casting his gaze over the edge. Even at this distance, he could clearly see the whaler, moving through the crowds on the bank like a shark gliding through a school of fish. That was the metaphor Forn would have used. It was no mean feat, catching sandsharks. Their thick skin was acidic, and whalers were often left unable to tie their shoes by the time they went grey — if they survived at all. Forn's not inconsiderable bulk reached the steps at the far end of the Way Bridge pausing only briefly at the wide iron Terävaen gates for the Pans to let him through. A short while later, he was dropping his heavy hood and standing unmoving in front of Jagar like an oak tree that had erupted from within the bridge.

"Hello, whaler," said Jagar. "And how are we today?"

Forn nodded a silent greeting, and salt crystals fell like snow from his bushy beard. "Good. Good."

The whaler tapped a huge finger on the palm of his blistered hand and pointed to the long line of vessels below, stretching for leagues along the edges of the Way mouth.

"Yes, yes, I see her," said Jagar. "The Ariathar. She's been through the wars, hasn't she? Not a terribly pretty thing." The whaler didn't react, which was a shame. "Yes, well, the Ariathar and her crew join the rest of these ships, as property of Tyr until its masters pay the toll." Forn's relaxed posture became suddenly tense, and he stood straight up. A lesser man might have flinched. "Ah, now I see I have your full attention!" said Jagar, with a smirk.

Forn marked out a few signs; measured questions. He wasn't a slow man. No, those blue eyes hid a sharp mind.

"We're not holding you to ransom," said Jagar, rolling his eyes. "I invited you here for a reason." He reached into his pocket and pulled out a black rectangular coin, which he flicked into Forn's palm. "Each musta coin represents a fraction of a brick of petrified black charsand, Tyr's most desirable export, which you can now spend anywhere within the city walls, though you might find you get more for your money in Terävä than in Vasen." He spread a hand over the evening bay before them. "You will join the ranks of all the other rich merchants who have been afforded the opportunity of fencing their valuable cargo to this wonderful city." Rathe's words were like ash in his mouth; in reality Jagar could not care less for this accursed piece of land. Forn tossed the coin over the edge, looking as though he might try to throw Jagar over with it. "However, you need not worry, Forn, for today is your lucky day. I have an offer for you. I require passage north."

"We're not taking passengers."

It seemed to Jagar that those quick hands may have dropped in a curse or two, but it was so hard to tell.

"I believe you are," said Jagar, "and not only will you be taking me, but there should be others on board, too. A routine transport into Makril. The Ariathar might not be pretty but I'd wager she is fast enough."

"No."

"Furthermore, I would like to employ your services across land, to recover a band of rebels who I would like captured."

"We are not for sale."

Jagar bared his teeth. He'd had his fill of games today. "Disappointing a government official is one thing, whaler, but a Banéman? You may be used to dealing with the bigger fish, but don't mistake a slight stature for weakness. I will burn you from the inside out right here upon this wretched bridge."

Forn's large face remained as hard as when he had first appeared, but his booming heart pulsed the air between them, as clear to Jagar as a stone dropped into water.

"How many?"

"That's more like it!" Jagar slapped the whaler's huge arm. He really was a huge man, ridiculous to think then that he had not a drop of Bohrblood within his veins. "Of the rebels? I would say, possibly only ten, potentially as many as thirty. Although, from what I hear those sorts of numbers shouldn't bother you. Or your partner. In fact, I am sure Astir would jump at the chance to round up a few rebels."

"When were they last seen?"

"Six days ago. Heading south, and not quickly. I would

start south of Makril, near the white coral beaches. After you've dropped off your passengers of course." Jagar's smirk vanished. "But understand this, the rebels are not to be killed. They are no use to me dead."

The whaler signed again.

"Why am I asking you? The mighty blue-eyes Forn and Astir were once feared across the Outer Isles and you are still more-or-less as strong now as you were then." The whaler's face remained passive, but the cogs were clearly turning behind those bright eyes. "You may feel that I'm forcing you in between the precipice and the cliff edge but trust me when I say that the Bohr will eventually reach Sulitar's shores and it might be worth having a few frie…" Forn didn't move. "Fine. A thousand musta."

Forn rolled his eyes.

"Marks then. A thousand marks," said Jagar, not really trying to haggle — he had no problem spending Rathe's money. "And free passage through the Way means you can sell your shark meat somewhere else. And probably for more money. I'd say that makes this quite a lucrative trip."

"Gold."

"Don't push it, Forn. Silver."

Forn paused, weighing his options, then reluctantly held out a shovel-sized hand. Jagar seized it and shook it vigorously, wincing at the man's rough skin.

"Excellent!" said Jagar, clapping his hands together. "We leave tomorrow at dawn. Now, tell me what you know of this Captain Laeb."

* * *

Fia padded barefoot down the worn wooden walkway that separated the two sides of the den and stopped at the first empty mat. Her eyes were already stinging from the haze of purple poppy smoke that drifted throughout, cutting shafts of light from the gaps in the blackened window. The place looked to her like that bloody meathouse, a place that she was trying very hard to forget.

There were patrons already smoking: a young woman sitting with a book in one hand and the orange glow of a pipe in the other; an old man with a very long white beard lying neatly coiled at his side; and a pale topless man with dark scraggly hair. All ignored her — they probably had no idea she stood mere feet away looking them up and down. Poppy smoke had that effect.

She turned to an empty mat and sat cross-legged enjoying the illusion of isolation provided by the dirty, semi-transparent veils hanging either side. The poppy pipe sat loaded and ready next to a burning candle on the stool but she thought better of lighting it. Trust no one and stay alert is what Janike would have said, besides she was sure Allander had only given her the thing to get her out of sight. Her story had shaken him badly, and while the man had always been of the flaky sort, she had never him seen him so afraid. She was safe for now at least; no one would find her here.

She dropped her head into the groove of the old pillow and cast her eyes over the spiderwebs that hung from the rafters — probably the same spiderwebs from before she had left to join the Tsiorc. They swam in front of her, warping and bending with the old rotting rafters, dripping with dust... and seaweed... and blood... Jagar was up there, his unremarkable features as clear as a crisp spring morning, eyes glowing with anger, sharp pointed teeth bared. His hand moved out towards her, fingers reaching, stretching around her like snakes. His features distorted like he was underwater, his voice the clip-clopping of footsteps on wood. The room was an ornate box, its wooden walls leant inwards, getting smaller, the lid coming down, the light going out. More knocking like footsteps, closer now. A sword longer than her whole body appeared from out of the shadows above, moving too slow to stop, too fast to deflect, she reached for her own sword but there was only a tiny fork. She held it up and the sword connected with it, drawing fire and sparks from the clashing metal. The heavy sword slammed into the stone beside her, the wind of it bringing gooseflesh. It missed! She shivered at the cold, and insects poured out of the crack, rushing towards her, crawling up her legs, biting her fingers, nibbling her, eating her, one piece at a time. Fia screamed but all that came out was a hoarse whisper; the air too thick, holding her back, holding her down, strangling her...

Fia jerked awake and grabbed the blade at her neck. Metal dug into her palm, but it didn't register as pain. Not yet. She swept herself up and ducked out of the way to meet her attacker.

"Fia!"

She knew that voice, but it couldn't be. The background of the den came into view, but the figure stayed where it was.

"Fia? It's me."

It couldn't be! "Janike! How are you here? How?" She threw her arms around her.

Janike wrapped her in a warm embrace. "Fia, you are a

135

fool. What of the advice I gave you? Yet I find you here in a poppy den, smoking." Her eyes drifted down to the pipe sitting next to her bedroll.

"I didn't light it," said Fia, wiping tears from her eyes. "It must be their smoke." Janike pressed a hand to her leg, wincing as she picked up her sword. "Are you hurt?" asked Fia, unsure of whether to touch her. "Tell me what happened." Two thirds of her blade was stained black, and twisted like a piece of scrap metal.

"I will live," she said. "And even a broken sword is still a sword."

Fia barely had a chance to reply before the Den door blew open. A huge man, almost the size of a Pan Guard, stormed along the walkway towards them. Fia's stomach flipped over.

Janike pulled her onto the mat and the man barrelled past them, veils wafting along after him. He all but tore open the door on the other side and disappeared into the Fiskar.

Janike grabbed Fia by the jaw and forced her head around. "Don't be so jumpy, you'll get us killed!"

"I... I don't feel well is all."

"We have to be careful, now," said Janike. "I stuck..." She glanced around at the unconscious patrons and lowered her voice. "I stuck that Bohr through like a pig, Fia."

"You killed a Pan? Allander was right, we have to leave."

Janike shook her head. "I didn't kill it."

"So, it's still out there?"

Janike shook her head and brushed a finger over Fia's cheekbone. "One human is the same as any another to the Pans. Even if it could walk with only one leg, it wouldn't be able to recognise me. And I don't think it has what it takes

136

to describe me to another."

Fia took Janike by the shoulders. "My dear friend, I cannot tell you how happy I am to see you again. I thought you had died."

Janike looked uncomfortable with Fia's unabashed emotion. She made a point of looking away and gestured to the box lying near the mat. "Is that what we risked our lives for?"

Fia nodded. "Allander thinks it might have had some value, though perhaps not any longer. Now that is empty." She frowned. "Janike, how did you find me?"

"Oh Fia, half of Tyr knows you're from the Fiskar. It was an obvious place to begin."

Fia grabbed the box, and dropped the poppypipe into it.

"Where are you going?"

"Leaving," said Fia. "If you can find me so easily, so could Jagar!"

"Jagar?" A look of slow realisation appeared on Janike's face. The Banémen? How in Baeivi's name—"

"I met him on the rooftop of the Domst, and something in my guts tells me he has a part in this. I keep seeing him in my waking dreams," she said, pacing. "I close my eyes, and his face is the one I see. He did something to me on that roof, he must have."

"Did he try to… touch you?"

Fia scoffed. "I'm not a girl, Janike! I can handle myself."

"I don't mean like that, you fool!" snapped Janike. "I mean did he touch you at all? Your hands, face, body? The Banémen have strange ways. They can control those who they touch directly, change their face at will, create fire without a spark." Janike stopped. "The Domst. You sent the message?"

Fia nodded. "Yes, I sent Prig."

Janike took a slow breath. "You wrote of my death."

Fia nodded, and tears prickled at her eyes.

"It will shock Kavik."

"Shock him? Shocked, Janike? I think he will be more than shocked! Your father loves you! He will be devastated!"

Janike raised an eyebrow. "Yes, well. There is no changing it now."

A strange silence hung between them, and Janike took Fia's hand. Fia looked up in surprise as Janike turned Fia's hand over and ran a finger up her palm, sending her nerves tingling.

"Prig bit you."

Janike was so close that Fia could smell her. Even after a fight with Bohr Pan Guard there was still a note of flowers. She drew a deep breath of it and her cheeks bloomed.

"Does he bite everyone?"

"Only those he likes," whispered Janike, holding up her own palm. White lines marked it all over, except for one that looked fairly new. "The real trick is getting him to purr. There is only one person I've met he did that with. He doesn't even purr for me." Fia reached out for Janike's hand, then pulled back as the Fiskar door burst open. Two men tumbled into the Den. It was the large man with the beard, and he was being pushed around by a much smaller man with only one eye.

"Maybe you should think before offering up what we don't have!" roared the one-eyed man. "You hear me, you fucking mute? You fucking hear me? Of course, you do. How dare you decide such a thing without first consulting me! We're partners!"

Allander appeared behind them. "Gentlemen, please! Astir, please not here. We're good people."

Astir continued cursing until the bearded man signed something in a language Fia had never seen, prompting Astir to wave his hand dismissively and turn away. Immediately his single eye fell upon Fia and Janike. "Allander," he growled. "Which one was it you asked me about?"

Allander looked out from behind the large one's bulk. "The Kumpani, uh, that is Fia. Her name is Fia."

Astir's eye leered over Fia. "Allander says you need a ride. That true?"

Fia nodded slowly, glancing between the man's empty eye socket and the scowl of the bearded man beyond. "Yes, I do."

"Good!" roared Astir, throwing his arms up at his bearded partner. "Because apparently we're a fucking bus boat now. To hell with sandsharks or moonsquid. Nah, let's be hauling people all around the Middle fucking Sea!"

"Her too."

Astir looked Janike up and down, and she raised her sword at him. He stepped closer and the twisted point pressed against the coarse wool of his jumper.

"Why the fuck not," he said, showing yellow teeth. "You two have my cabin, eh? I'll just sleep on the fucking deck, freezing my fucking nuts off." He turned so he was standing with them and spoke directly to his bearded partner. "We leave first thing for Makril. Payment up front!"

The Ariathar

The cabin aboard the Ariathar was as dark as it was outside, and the flickering candle by the porthole wasn't enough to banish the smell of vomit from the small space.

Janike sat on the narrow bed plank, knees up by her ears and hands entangled in her long dark hair. "Are we there yet?" she groaned.

"No," said Fia, from her side. "We've a day or two yet." Janike's face glowed even greener at the words. Her colourless lips quivered and Fia leant away. "You OK?"

Janike's hair fell over her hands, and Fia placed a tentative hand on the woman's head. "No. Please do not touch me," said Janike knocking it away.

"Sorry, I was just trying to…"

"Trying to what? Is there some other new threat, which I must uproot my entire life to run from?"

"I did not force you to come."

"No, you didn't. And now here I am about to die from… this."

"It's just seasickness, Janike. You'll get used to it. My first time out to sea was just as bad."

Janike groaned then spat on the floor. "This isn't my first

time at sea."

"Oh?"

"My fifth cycle, but I do not remember feeling like this. Can we sleep outside?"

Fia laughed. "With Forn and Astir? I wouldn't trust them to mind a dead fish. Besides one of us should stay in here at all times." The mirth left her in an instant as her gaze fell upon the box. It might be useless, but then it might not. Better not to let Forn or Astir get their fishy hands on it.

Janike jerked up and thrust her head out of the porthole. Fia considered holding her hair back, then thought better of it.

* * *

When Fia awoke it was still late evening, but the sea had calmed. She glanced over at the empty space beside her, and stretched out in a star shape on the cabin bed.

"It's a good bed, isn't it?"

"Astir?" she said, scrambling to pull the blanket over herself. "Can I help you?"

"I was just admiring your Lines. Legend has it only Nordun folk write stories upon their skin."

"Not true." Fia shuffled the blanket around wherever cold air found skin. "How long have you been there?"

"Long enough," he said, his eyes drifting from hers down to her feet still protruding from the bottom of her blanket. "What do they mean then?"

Fia tried leaning forward, and the blanket slid. The man's eyes darted to her exposed skin, and with a whip she threw the blanket up and grabbed the dangling rope near her head, pulling the door firmly shut.

Astir's laugh echoed through the thin walls as he walked back above deck. "We'll talk again, Kumpani, and maybe we can share stories. I've a few myself…"

"In your dreams," said Fia, under her breath. The porthole in their room might have been small, but she had become very good at squeezing out onto the ledge that ran the length of the Ariathar — anything that meant not having to take the exit through the galley where Forn and Astir ate. If she slipped she would find herself swimming for the nearest shore, but the danger of it excited her. Holding tight to the handrails, she dropped her bare feet into the water, allowing the deliciously cool water to rise up her legs. The troubles of Tyr could have been a world away, that is until Astir's drawl again cut through the peace.

"You let him aboard, Forn. It's your doing."

Fia stretched upwards and peeked over on to the deck. Forn was signing something back to Astir in furious gestures.

"No, I won't let it go," said Astir. "I might've if I thought he would help out on deck, or that the extra weight would be worth it, but it's not. He hasn't helped, damn him he's been locked up in there since we left."

There was someone hiding below deck? Another fugitive, like her?

"Great!" snapped Astir, after Forn had finished signing. "So what if he hasn't eaten anything? Well done. The only plus point to letting him aboard. Meanwhile I'm sleeping under the stars with my back as it is! I want my fucking cabin! I want my fucking bed! You hear me, you goddamned mute?"

Fia crawled along quietly towards the rear of the Ariathar to her space: a small platform that sat below the normal deck and in between the two hulls. There were dried fish guts stuck to the wood, but it was hidden from view and wide enough to sit down on, away from grumpy sailors and sick passengers. She rounded the corner and saw Janike leaning against the handrail and smiling, looking as healthy and vibrant as when she'd first met her.

"Janike?" said Fia. "You're feeling better?"

"Yes, Fia. Much better. It took a few hours but thank the Forbringrs, I seem to have gotten used to this forsaken vessel. I can even eat again! I had blue mussels for supper."

"Good," said Fia. "You smell better. A lot better."

"Sorry I left you sleeping, but you looked so peaceful. Fia. I slept out here. I don't know, just the cool air and, oh the stars, I have never seen so many stars. Never in my life."

Fia glanced sideways at her. "So, I guess it's my turn to..."

Janike coughed. "Yes. Right, it's my turn on the box watch. Fia, I'm sorry for what I said. I'm so grateful to be here with you. Thank you for looking after me."

Fia nodded. "We will look out for each other, dear friend."

Janike cheeks flushed, abashed, then she turned and skipped down towards the galley. She was happy and Fia couldn't help but get caught up in it. This was not the Janike Fia had known in Tyr, not even when they had first met. She was a brand-new person, and this was their new start. Their new life. Together.

Broken

Kyira walked out in front. Not to show the way, but so she could ignore those behind her. It had been a long time since she had seen anyone but her brother and father, and now she wished deeply to return to that life. Even if she could somehow, the conflict she felt would still be there. Just like the mist it was a vague cloud she couldn't focus on, let alone describe. How then do you fix something that may not even be broken, or that was broken in a way you could not see? Isak's death was a question of justice, and it had to be corrected, but whenever she approached, the Mother Lyla, she had ignored Kyira, and whipped her wide green cloak before stalking off to the back of the group to mutter at her bulging stomach.

The Bear had at least been more direct, implying that he might stick his knife in her should she try to talk to him again. That at least, was easy to understand even if she would rather keep herself from being poked with holes, and he was powerful to do it, moving smoothly for one so large. Then there were his hidden knives, of which Kyira had counted at least six so far, tucked into the many folds of his travelling breeks and skin coat. If knives were indeed the makers of fortunes, the Bear had given himself many chances indeed.

The Wolf she hadn't even bothered with — he had been devastatingly plain with her from the beginning. He was taller than the Bear, but not as wide. Still, he had a loping grace to the way he walked that reminded Kyira of a wolf, and like the bear Kyira was afraid of him. It seemed that she would have to find another way to repay her debt.

Iqaluk caught her eye as she looked back, and he nodded ahead. "Kyira, look."

Upon the brow of the hill, silhouetted against the twilight sky, stood a huge ice boulder. It looked like any other fat stone you might find upon the sisters of Nord except that it was cleaved completely in half.

Iqaluk stopped at her side. "There is no force that I know of that could do such a thing."

Kyira nodded slowly. She knew enough of Hasaan's climbs as to recognise which rocks were hard and which were soft. "It's an ice boulder. Only the Gods—"

"The Forbringrs do not walk upon our land," said Iqaluk.

"Then how do you account for what you saw three days ago?"

He placed a firm hand on her forearm. "There are things in this world that are beyond our minds. Things that we could not, and dare not, dream of. There is danger lurking, Kyira, and we must find Hasaan before…" He stopped as though he couldn't find the words.

"Before what?"

"Before *it* finds him."

"YA!"

Kyira's heart lurched at the Bear's shout. He ran in a circle chasing a rabbit that had evidently popped out of its burrow at the wrong time.

"Catch it!"

The white tail bounced away, then as the Bear jumped the rabbit bolted left towards Kyira. Panicked, it somehow found the gap between her legs and made up the hill away from them.

"Isak was our hunter, Sami!" shouted the Bear. "If you want to repay your debt then you can start by catching that damned rabbit!"

Without another thought Kyira turned and sprinted after it. Oh, it was good to be running again! She scooped up a rock, not taking her eyes from the rabbit's white tail which zigzagged left and right to evade her, showing that it had some experience with the chase, but never before had it met Kyira, Pathwatcher and hunter!

Kyira feigned right, and the rabbit threw itself left, just as she knew it would. She threw the stone, flicking it with her wrist to give it some spin, and the rabbit skipped right at the last second. Kyira resumed her pursuit, keeping up the pace and scanning the ground for another rock. There! She scooped it up and without stopping flicked it hard. The pebble flew true finding the gap between the rabbit's ears and sailed clean through it.

"Shiach!"

Her legs were burning but she powered on up the hill and put on a burst of speed. She owed them this! One. More. Stone...

Abruptly the ice boulder was upon her. The rabbit jumped in through the gap and bounded along the inside of the ragged, almost vertical ice boulder, leaving Kyira to stare up at it. Up close it was so large it could almost be called a cliff, had she been standing on top. The edge was sharp and smooth but what sort of force had the power to split an ice boulder?

"Some hunter you are, Sami," said the Bear, from behind. "I've seen children with better throwing arms."

Kyira shook her head. "Are you not able to see this? This should not be split." Even now as her fingertips traced the rough interior she could never have imagined she would see the inside of something so old and so pure.

"It's a bloody great big rock," said the Bear, pulling a dried berry from his pocket. He pulled the stalk with his teeth and spat it out, then threw the fruit into his mouth. "That's all it is."

Kyira frowned. "It's an ice boulder. It is no more a rock than you are."

Iqaluk appeared at her side. "This fat stone, stopped and rested here a thousand cycles ago until that one day in the far future it would be so small as to roll away as a pebble."

"Aye, added the Bear. "And maybe some other girl might pick it up and fling it between a rabbit's ears. Or she might hit the thing and not go hungry."

Kyira ignored the comment. "Ice-boulders are so hard we often call them Gods. Don't you see? Somewhere, there is a force with the power to kill a God."

The Bear spat out a seed. "Kill a God? What are you talking about? It's nonsense, the lot of it." His demeanour suddenly changed from uncaring and indifferent to pointed rage. "You and him, you're trying to unbalance us, me, with nara shit. Trying to distract us from the cold truth that you are a murderer. Plain and simple." He leaned towards her, growling. "But let me tell you, I will never forget what you did. Never!"

Kyira glared back at him. "I did not... I did..."

"Did not..." The Bear looked at her expectantly, his eyebrows raised. "What? Did not murder our friend? Did not slice open his throat and break him like this bloody great rock was broken? Tell me, Sami, what it is you did not do and let us explore that for one minute." His hand hovered over the lump at his hip. He should kill her. She deserved it.

The Wolf stalked up to the Bear's side and placed a hand on his shoulder. "Let us not open up healing wounds, Tri. Leave Lyla to grieve."

The Bear spat on the ground. "Ignorance does not equate to justice, Bryn. And what are we to do for food?"

Kyira blinked.

"I know that, Tri. Our mission is bigger than Isak's life. It was an accident." He glanced behind. "A very unfortunate accident. As for the food, we will be sure to eat when we get to Makril. The spring festival should be in full swing by now. We shall gorge ourselves."

"What's the problem?" The Mother waddled up the hill behind them taking them all in, her gaze lingering on Kyira.

The Wolf shook his head. "Nothing, Lyla."

"Nothing, that a broken *God* won't fix," said the Bear.

"Makril is still a day south," nodded the Wolf. "We'll need a place to sleep."

The Bear stalked off, pausing by the Mother. "Sorry Lyla, it seems we'll be eating naught but dry bread and berries tonight, but I think my stomach can hold out for some tender fried seaweed dough. Or some salt-fish."

The Mother looked back and forth between them and the two of them drifted away, talking animatedly of soups, fish and beer.

148

"Your father was right," said the Wolf, quietly. "There is a danger lurking here, but it is not what you think."

Regular, Familiar

The black ether swirled in front of Jagar's eyes like liquid night. He reached out for the millionth time, marvelling at how it still ignored his presence, passing through his fingers as though he were not there. Flecks of colour swam through the mixture creating an iridescent fluid like oil on water. Eddies flowed and ebbed, whirlpools formed and died in a fractal beauty too complex to follow. Jagar focused his thoughts and the swirling mass began to slow, the ethereal arms pulling closer and tighter together. Small points of light began twinkling within the structure, but they were not new, Jagar knew they had always been there, burning brightly. The heat increased as it slowed, blossoming on what he imagined was his face, and filling him with strength and the wonderfully peculiar desire to wield it against someone.

Then he heard something. Something outside of the vision. Something regular. Something familiar. He could discover its meaning in an instant, but it would mean leaving here, and there was still so much to see and feel. His hand closed around one of those points of light and the spinning disc glowed bright, consuming itself, its steady rotation speeding up faster and faster until the light was so strong it obscured everything. It exploded outwards in a fist of light, blowing forth, and turning all to brilliant daylight. White light suffused Jagar's being and then all was gone.

A blurry cabin came into view. A boat? What was it called again?

The Ariathar.

He was here to find someone. A blue-eyes. The one called Laeb. Then he felt it again. Something regular. Something familiar. A heartbeat. Little pulses in the air too small for any mere human to detect, but Jagar was no human.

He smiled to himself. Little bird? Now, that is interesting.

* * *

There were hundreds of tales of journeys across the Middle Sea that took entire cycles to pass, fighting strange waves, exotic sea creatures, and maelstroms that pulled even the biggest vessels down to the seabed below. Tonight those stories felt like they belonged in another world — the sea was like a sheet of crystal glass.

Janike stabbed an olive with the fork from the box between them and held it out to Fia. "The Kumpani will always remain a mystery to me."

Fia took the olive straight from the fork. "Not everything needs to be understood, Janike." She rolled it around, chewing the juicy flesh until she had only the olive pip between her teeth then took a deep breath and spat it out as far as she could, watching for the faint glow of the glowing algae reacting to the splash.

"Not bad," remarked Janike, her side feet dangling in the water. "Not good, but not bad."

"You do better," said Fia, scowling. "And what is so mysterious about Kumpani? I always thought I was very simple when it came down to it all."

"Just your ways, I guess." Janike took an olive from the box. "We are the same in so many ways."

Fia wondered where her friend was taking this line of thought, but decided to go with it. "We are. I've always told you that, Janike. Although I'm very glad that you've finally worked it out for yourself."

Janike nodded thoughtfully. "Yes, I think I have. However, it is also very clear to me that we are still very different. For example, I would not think to take an olive fork with me, when running for my life from a Bohr assassin bent on exposing me as a spy to the Kael of Tyr."

Fia laughed. "I wish I could say I'd had the foresight to pack only my best cutlery for this runaway trip, but I'm afraid you'll have to blame Forn and Astir. I found it in their galley."

Janike's eyes widened. "Perhaps their roughness is all a facade, a trick to throw people off when actually they are the world's most wonderful chefs, travelling the seas, creating only the best cuisines from the fruits of the sea! I bet they even have a set of those tiny cooking pots — the ones that are too small to cook anything in."

Fia shook her head but couldn't keep away the smile. "Janike! They will hear you."

"I don't think so," said Janike. "When I passed by the galley, I heard them both snoring like mating pigs. Even Astir was sleeping below deck." She smiled and pushed the olive pip between her teeth. "Ready?" As soon as it left her mouth Fia knew she'd lost. The little bloom of light was twice the distance her own pip had gone.

"You've clearly had more practice spitting than I," said Fia.

"Are you alright?" asked Janike, suddenly.

Fia paused, an olive halfway to her mouth. "Yes, why?"

"You have such a sour look on your face. It must have been a bad olive." She adjusted the moonflower woven into the braid above her ear. The clip had done its job well, it looked as bright as when the old man had given it to Fia in the market square.

Janike tapped her forearm. "Oh my, look at that!"

Fia squinted over at the distant hills just as lightning flashed outlining the mountains against the cloud. She had no idea what the mountains were called but knowing how far out the Ariathar was gave a hint at their scale. Everything was further apart out here. With the distant clouds came wind, and waves followed soon after, slapping against the Ariathar's hulls. A cold gust blew through Fia's hak and she trembled and sat around cross-legged, facing Janike. "Come on, Janike. I want my bed. There's still a few hours of sleep we can have before we arrive in Makril tomorrow."

"Alright, alright," said Janike, closing the lid on the rest of the olives. She pulled her feet from the water and turned around, placing the box away from the edge. "One more game. Let's say a group of armed soldiers surround you. They look armoured, and well trained. What do you do?"

"What do I have?"

"A shortsword, but not a broken one like mine."

Fia shook her head. "I'm sure they'll have smiths in Makril, Janike. Now, a shortsword. Against how many?"

"Doesn't matter. Assume there are too many to count."

"OK," said Fia. "I would bring my sword up in an arc

and—"

Janike coughed.

"Alright. I would wait until—"

"No. Fia, you are doing me a disservice here. What of all our time together training? Think."

Fia stifled a yawn. "Then what, Janike?"

"Fia, when one person attacks, the odds are split equally between the both of you. Any more than one and you can consider yourself outnumbered. Even if you are with someone, you cannot assume that you will be lucky. Real fighting is not like it is in stories, it is brutal, fast and too quick to understand. Even very skilled fighters cannot split their focus and rely solely on their ability — the mind is just not capable of processing information quickly enough. Remember it like this: when you are outnumbered, the odds are not just against you, but *stacked* against you."

"Right, so even swinging an arc to see how many are behind me would—"

"Most likely result in your death. Yes." She stared at Fia like a teacher to a pupil. "Those who stand behind value their lives as much as the ones standing in front, but their advantage is time. Time to know whether you are skilled or unskilled, whether you have ever fought more than once before, and ultimately whether you will leave this fight with your life. They can ponder on their attack while you, on the other hand, have a window of about one or two seconds on which to change the odds to your favour, and of all the fights I have fought and seen, the best way to use that time is to attack. Strike hard and strike fast. Attack the closest to you and cut them down. It will reduce their numbers, and the shock of it will delay those behind long enough so that you can escape."

"Escape?"

"As fast as you can," said Janike, her expression serious. "There will come a moment, in your life — although I truly hope it is later rather than sooner — when the Forbringrs of death will stand behind you, and you will feel their breath upon your neck. In that moment you have a choice to live or to die."

"Not all of us are offered a choice."

Janike shook her head. "Choice is the one thing we have, and Fia, you must escape. You must hide. You must live."

The heavy words settled upon Fia's stomach like a big meal. "Of all the games we have played Janike, you have never once told me to run."

Janike rounded her shoulders, looking suddenly uncomfortable. "How do you think I conquered the Pan Guard? Do you think me a heroine of myths who felled him down like a tree? I barely escaped, Fia, and even then, I left a piece of my leg behind. Before even the fight begins, you must know when you are beaten and when you have a chance. Very few in this world can stand outnumbered and know that they will be the one to leave with their life."

"Did you know you would beat the Pan?"

Janike smiled. "No, but sometimes where a good friend is concerned, you find that you have no choice but to take on the odds regardless."

"What has the sea done to you?" said Fia, with a chuckle.

Janike's glare hardened. "Nothing at all. I am as I was when I boarded this forsaken vessel."

"You are not."

Janike sprang up. "You know nothing of me, Kumpani!"

Fia jumped up herself. She couldn't tell if this was playful anymore. She took her friend's hand. "Janike, I'm sorry. I want nothing for you but good things. I care for you greatly."

Janike's serious expression melted away. "As I do you." Janike snatched her hand back. "Alright, alright you do not need to lay it on so thickly. I know your Kumpani ways by now."

This was getting tiresome. "Tell me of my Kumpani ways, Janike. Please."

"You are a flirt, Fia." Janike poked her in the chest lightly with the olive fork. "A flirt."

Fia couldn't stop the emotion from touching her words. "It is not a crime to feel for another, Janike! I'm not just a *Kumpani*. I am Atalfia. I love olives, and long mornings. I love flowers and tea, and good conversation. I love my friends, and yes, Janike, I love you. I love all that you are, and I know who you are so well, and yet you, in all of your stubbornness, you have no idea who I am." Fia licked her dry lips, and found them salty. Was it seawater or were they tears? By Forbringr she was hungry. She swallowed the lump in her throat and looked up into Janike's shining eyes. "I love you, Janike. More than anything else." Her friend looked uncomfortable, as well she should. "I count myself lucky every day to have you written upon the script of my life. Your magic permeates me and revitalises my soul so that just seeing you fills me with joy. Our games make me laugh, your moods make me smile and you move like you were put together for me alone to watch and observe and love." She took a deep breath. "I don't expect you to mirror my feelings, but Janike we must embrace the warmth when it comes, or we will spend our lives unhappy. Surely there can be nothing worse in this world than to die cold and grey and unloved. I can think of nothing more awful than that."

"You should listen to her."

Fia's head jerked up to the silhouetted figure standing over them. His face was hidden, but she knew in an instant who it was. Her heart began to hammer. "Jagar."

"The very same," said Jagar, stepping into the light. "No, please, Little Bird. Don't move. I'll come to you." He hopped down onto the little space making it suddenly feel very crowded. "It's a nice spot this. Very private. This would be your friend then?"

Fia's mouth went dry. "Yes. This is Janike."

Janike stood completely still, one hand behind her, the other squeezing the handle of the olive fork.

"Janike?" said Jagar, almost singing the words. "The friend that died." He looked Janike up and down. "You look well for a corpse, my dear." He turned back to Fia. "Come, Little Bird, let us sit."

He positioned himself cross-legged between them and made a slight sitting gesture. Janike sat immediately, stiff-backed and barely breathing, while Fia sat over the box like a mother hen protecting an egg. They were sitting in a triangle, meaning she could no longer see Janike's hidden hand — instead her friend just sat staring at her, beads of sweat forming under her eyes. Fia gave the Banéman a thin smile, and gazed up to the swaying deck behind him.

"Don't worry, Little Bird, we are alone," said Jagar. He tilted his head as though trying to hear more clearly. "Forn is dreaming of fishing and Astir is... well, let's just say he's occupied with himself at present. I tell you, you should have seen my face, when I realised you were here. I imagine it was something like yours when I appeared." He looked back and forth between them both. "I do hope I didn't interrupt. Your heart was fluttering so."

"We were just talking, Jagar."

"Say no more, Little Bird. Say no more." His eyes moved to her crossed legs. "May I?" he said, reaching towards her. His eyes were a misty white, the colour of them almost grey. Fia let him reach in and slide the box from between her legs, shuddering as his hands brushed against her bare thighs. "Thank you." He took one olive and tipped the rest into the choppy water. "I do wonder, though, why you are holding this as though it were your new-born child?" He turned it over in his hands and opened it. "It looks old, and Nordic. *Who Shape The World*. A quaint sentiment. A container for something important perhaps?"

Fia felt her insides curl up. "It's just a box, Jagar. I bought it from a young girl yesterday in Teräväen market—"

"People are killed for less important things," said Jagar, "but lie to me again and I will not only kill you, but your entire bloodline and anyone you have ever spoken to." He held her gaze until she looked away. When he spoke again it was sickeningly sweet. "Tell me, Janike, have you heard many stories of the Banémen?"

"Yes," said Janike, straining, and dripping with sweat.

"And what did you hear of us?"

"Nothing of consequence," croaked Janike.

"Consequence belongs to the beholder, dear Janike. So, tell me, from whom did you hear *nothing of consequence* about the Banémen?"

"My grandfather," uttered Janike.

"And he is…"

"Dead."

Jagar burst into a fit of laughter. "Lucky man." He gave the olive a sniff. "Euch, I don't know how you can eat these things. In fact, all of your so-called delicacies are like this, too much salt, smoked, cured, bitter, made for *acquired* tastes. You kill the flavour of things. I prefer my meats raw." He held out the olive, moving it around in front of Janike, and her eyes followed it placidly. "You know, my dear, you are very strong." He smirked and placed the olive between her lips. It fell out and bounced overboard. "But I suppose that was a given, considering the state of that Pan you left at the meat house."

Fia sat forward. "Janike? Are you alright? What's happening?" Her friend's eyes rolled with every blink, but her jaw was clenched tight, and the colour of her skin had turned ashen grey.

Jagar clicked his fingers and cleared his throat. "Little Bird, you remember our little chat at the Domst?"

"Of course," hissed Fia.

"Well, I talked with our mutual friend shortly after I let you go, and he seemed concerned about your presence on the Domst roof that day. Not as concerned as perhaps he should have been, although I'm guessing those loins of yours had much to do with that. I am, however, keen to know where you sent that little redback raeven."

Fia couldn't find an answer. She opened her mouth, but it was bone dry.

"Forgotten already?"

"What are you doing to her?"

"Fia, we are trying to have a conversation here. I thought the Kumpani were masters of small talk. Masters of the

159

intricacies of human interaction. I might not be human as such, but I do enjoy the back and forth of it all."

He was right, she was better than this. "Janike is not just my friend, Jagar. Please let her go. Stop whatever you're doing, and I'll tell you everything."

"That's more like it!" said Jagar. "Truth. However, I am afraid I can't let her go. Stopping now would be like... Oh, how to find an analogy that you will understand. I suppose it must be like stopping before reaching climax. Disappointing, frustrating, even painful. Some things need to run their course."

"What are you doing?" she whispered, as tears began to creep down Janike's cheeks. "Please Jagar."

"All you have to do is speak the truth, Little Bird."

"No, I... I can't. Please Jagar."

"Then say it!" A sick smile had formed on his face, arching his eyebrows in intense delight. "Sssssay it."

The dryness that had spread to her throat was a stark contrast to the sea slapping at the hulls, so wet and inviting, so cold.

"We are spies."

Jagar threw his head back, eyelids quivering. "Yesssss." On any other it might have looked an act, but Fia had the distinct feeling the words were bringing the man waves of actual pleasure. When he sat back up, his breath was shallow, his cheeks were flushed and his eyes were bright.

"Spies. For the Tsiorc." His skin radiated heat, and an aura of darkness began to surround him where he sat, growing thicker and stronger with each satisfied breath.

"Please," whispered Fia. "Please, let Janike go. She's all I have."

Jagar sniffed the air, then smiled. "Ah, but it is too late now. It cannot be undone."

Janike's twitching eyes stopped moving, and her jaw went slack. She sat up and held out her arm.

Jagar smiled at the olive fork held within her clenched fist. "You may, my dear."

He motioned with his hand and Janike stood up. Before Fia could stop her, she lifted the point of the olive fork to her temple and pushed it slowly in. Bone crunched and blood burst from the wound splashing onto the wood at Fia's feet, but Janike didn't flinch. The moonflower fell from her braid and dropped into the water.

"Janike, no!" said Fia, rushing forward. She threw her arms around her friend, but Janike just stood there, eyes forward as though there was nothing left inside. "Janike! Please. Wake up, please!" Her tears fell onto Janike's shirt, mixing with the colourless blood dripping down her friend's face. She touched Janike's cheek, and her friend blinked at her. "Fi... a."

"Janike, what is it? Speak please. Tell me."

"I... I... love you too."

Janike shunted Fia back, then kicked out, and all at once Fia was airborne. The world spun. Jagar's face flashed into view, his expression wrath itself, then cold water enveloped her, striking out everything, leaving only panic as she struggled against the sea. Fia dove deeper, throwing armfuls of water behind her, swimming as hard as she could, down below the algae until her lungs screamed in agony and the weight of the ocean pressed upon her. Explosions of light burst in her eyes, but she kept going. She had to escape. She had to hide. She had to live.

Makril

M akril was no town, it was a village, sitting nestled in a bay between stacks of black rock standing half as tall as the Waning Crescent. Aside from the handful of scattered homes tossed over the uneven ground there was a large building in the town's centre and even from halfway up the hill Kyira could see people filing in and out of it. A few small boats were anchored further out from a small stone harbour, but that was it. Nortun was bigger. Still, anything was better than sleeping in the shadow of a broken ice boulder.

Before long they were walking through the winding streets, passing by the communes where many people lived together, and other than the stone-built inn which had a circular painted sign of a woman smoking a pipe hanging outside, most houses were made from redwood, even if there was not a single tree to be seen in any direction.

The air buzzed with the din of bartering, the sound of howling dogs making it too hard to tell from which direction.

A man and a woman around Kyira's age, stepped onto the clay road. She had narrow eyes and jet-black hair pulled back in a bun, but more striking were the thin scars marking her face. Her tanned complexion hid them well, but up close they were unmistakable — they had been cut into her skin, leaving delicate white scars in swirling patterns over her cheeks and chin. The man had actual Lines, but they were no less intricate: dark lines spiralled around his shaved chin, vanishing into a full beard on his cheeks and neck, and they told Kyira he worked on the water.

Kyira's heart thumped as a mounted nara trotted around a corner behind the couple. The rider sitting nestled between the nara's pouch and hump, shot Kyira a look.

"You look as though you have never seen a nara before," said the Wolf.

"I have seen a nara before."

"You know, they hail from the Outer Isles."

"You are well travelled for a farmer."

"Tell me, Sami. Have your paths ever taken you further south than Makril? It is well known your paths do not stretch as far west as Dali, so I doubt then that you have—"

"I have been to Makril." It wasn't quite a lie, but neither was it the whole truth. The town looked very different from atop the ridge.

"The shape of our world," continued the Wolf, "used to be well known. It was taught to all when they were young, but that knowledge has been lost over the ages. Where once our ancestors were well-travelled now we seem to have *forgotten* our roots. The actual location of the Outer Isles: Sulitar, Hauwi, Taraunteen, is a mystery to Ringlanders. As descendants of the original map makers, the Kartta, you Sami may remember much of that knowledge, but most Ringlanders do not. They are governed. Controlled. Cowed. The Bohr are changing the circles of the world and there is not a thing that can stop them." When Kyira didn't respond he flashed a wide smile. "I smell food, look! The tallo is ahead."

"He is no farmer," said Iqaluk, when the man had walked on.

"No, he is not," said Kyira. "And he knows much of the Pathwatchers. What are we getting wound into?"

"I wish I knew, but the winds have led us this way and so we must make the best of it."

Kyira stopped. "So we must follow him blindly?"

"We are not blind. We are here to find Hasaan! Pathwatchers follow the winds, the natural ways of things. You know this." Iqaluk nodded at the trio, now ahead of them. "The Wolf, as you call him, he is Bryn, the Bear is Tri, and the Mother, Lyla."

"They are like no names I have heard before."

"No. They are not from Nord as they claim. Keep your wits about you, daughter."

The crowds passing them by on the narrow winding path had thickened and so had the stares, but it appeared to be the Mother who was the target.

Bryn, the Wolf, turned around. "The tallo is really just a townhall, it is where the town meet to discuss business, trade, and justice. But more importantly, during the spring festival it is where they, and we, shall eat!"

"Then what?" asked Kyira. "We are here to find Hasaan."

"After the tallo we'll find a free house. There'll be plenty of them here. We can stay there the night. It'll be safe — your slavers wouldn't dare enter the town."

"Fine," said Kyira, "but I want to get out of this place as soon as we can."

The road grew wider as the five of them approached the town's centre, opening out into a large circle filled with mewing animals and people bartering and exchanging all manner of items. Alamar walked back and forward freely between paths, blocking the way and nibbling at anything that looked like hay. Kyira watched in delight as the Bear tried to slap the rump of one to move it along, and the animal turned around and spat a wad of foamy mucus over his jacket and neck.

Kyira gave the alamar a friendly scratch behind the ear and it flapped its long lips at her. "Good girl!".

In the circle's centre stood the tallo — a hall, taller and longer than any other building and large enough to hold the entire town and their livestock with room to spare. Townspeople milled in and out, carrying nets, spears, skins, and racks of dried fish apparently oblivious to the howls of the caged dogs that ran along the building's length.

Two men walked towards their group, round bread loaves in their hands, each one hollowed out and filled with a steaming mixture of meat and greens.

"Dog meat," said the Wolf.

The Bear sniffed the air as they passed by. "Woof. They might be loud, but they smell delicious. I think they're getting it from inside."

The tallo was far busier and brighter on the inside. People were dressed up everywhere: colourful papers folded together like scales, dyed animal skins, and painted faces adorned almost every person, some as flowers, others as effigies of exotic birds and animals — Kyira had never imagined that there could be so many beautiful animals out there.

The pounding drums, interspersed with tuneful whistles and high sounds from some instrument, brought warmth to the chill night air. On closer inspection, though, it seemed there were two peoples here. The local Makriliaens and the Sulitarians, and as they entered, The Wolf, Mother and Bear were greeted amongst the Sulitarians as though they were life-long friends. The Sulitarians seemed in perpetual motion, moving in and out of the tallo, laughing, drinking, dancing and eating heedless of the waning light. Sharp spice and tang floated through the air as the smells of a hundred different meals mingled, creating new concoctions of their own, and each one making Kyira's stomach grumble.

A man walked by with fragments of mirror covering his entire naked body, reflecting the light from the lanterns hanging above.

"It would seem our friends are Sulitarians then," said Iqaluk, watching the mirrored man walk by.

Kyira agreed. The Wolf and the Bear's blond hair and blue-eyes were the same as the Sulitarians, who were prettier than the local Makriliaens — they seemed happier too.

A black man with a colourful arrangement of feathers piled high on his head turned to greet them. He danced around Kyira and away leaving her smiling as much as he had been.

Iqaluk placed a hand on hers. "Go and enjoy yourself, daughter. Times like these do not come often to us. I shall be wherever the rice wine is."

Kyira wandered through the tallo, taking it all in. Flags with strange markings hung from long ropes above exotic stalls stretching in long lines from the entrance to the far end of the market. The people moved methodically down the lines stuffing their cloth sacks and skins with strange looking fruits and vegetables, gesturing at leashed animals, hauling racks of fish, folded fabrics and stacks of dried hanging meats. More than one vendor was offering weapons, shining knives, cleavers, and axes but even those were decorated with multi-coloured feathers and paint. A cat rubbed at her legs before leaping away over a basket of white apples. A stall to the left offered nothing but coloured glass beads, with huge sacks full of them marking out the vendors' space rather than a table or hut like the others. Bright cushions and silks dominated the outer rows of stalls, and as Kyira looked on she could see that even those without stalls were trading, handing over armfuls of cloth in exchange for oiled bags of fish and meats.

Someone bellowed in her direction and she turned to see a topless Sulitarian man pointing and gesturing at a long table full of all sorts of dried fish. Lines marked his skin spiralling down from his bearded chin along his hairy chest and down to his navel.

Kyira jumped through a gap in the passing traffic as the seller took up a fillet of fish, rolled it into a ball, then dropped it into a pan of steaming oil. He plucked it out a minute later with a sharp stick and handed it over. Kyira barely sniffed it before stuffing it into her mouth. It was the most wonderful thing she had ever tasted, salt, smoke and heat, and still moist. She swallowed and looked up hopefully, but the seller had moved on to another group on the opposite side.

An intoxicating smell cut through the rest, seeking her out, and she pushed through the crowds to a wooden table where a leathery-skinned old man stood pouring a dark, steaming liquid between two clay jugs.

"One," said Kyira, hopefully.

The man nodded and pulled out a pewter cup with no handle and poured some of the hot liquid in. Kyira took the cup and sniffed, breathing in the heady fragrance.

"You and I, Kyira."

Kyira looked up from the cup to find the Wolf standing there. "Hello, Bryn."

"It's a customary greeting the Sulitarians use."

"Are you actually farmers, or was that a lie too?"

"I have good reasons for lying to you, Kyira. But now, I think, I can trust you." He nodded to the cup when she didn't respond. "I think it is called cofaidh." He gestured to the old man, and accepted a cup for himself. "I drink too much of it, but of late, I have had no choice."

Kyira suddenly wished to be alone again.

"It keeps you alert," said the Wolf.

"Yes," said Kyira. "It is similar to our kaldi." She took a long draught, relishing the bitter sweet taste. He didn't take his eyes off her, and Kyira felt powerless beneath them. She stood straighter.

"I saw you meditating. The morning after you killed Isak."

Sadness brought a lump to Kyira's throat. "Did he have a family?"

"Not exactly. We were his family. Does that make it easier for you?"

Kyira swirled the last of the cofaidh in her cup. "No." She drained the last of it, and handed the old man her cup. She wanted to say she wasn't a killer, a murderer, but that simply wasn't true. "There is nothing I can say that has not been said already."

"Wait," said the Wolf, as she turned to leave. "Please, Kyira.

Your meditation. I'd like to know what it was. I watched you, and perhaps I shouldn't have, but I did. And you changed in front my eyes, from a grief-stricken girl to a warrior. A soldier. What did you do?"

"It allows me to connect with myself."

"How?"

"By stretching my muscles and controlling my breathing to match my heart."

"Did Iqaluk teach it to you?"

"No," laughed Kyira. "He does not approve of such things. It is nothing, it helps me take control of myself, that is all. Iqaluk does not realise it, but he meditates too, as you call it, every time he climbs. It clears his mind and gives him peace. My brother does it also. It allows them to do things that otherwise…" She caught herself. "I do not want to talk about this, not with you."

The Wolf nodded, but whatever he had wanted to know he had obviously obtained it. She was halfway to thinking what it might be for when there came an angry shout from behind.

"Shaich!" Kyira turned, but Bryn was already rushing by her, shoving his way through the crowd. Kyira ran after him to the long bar at the end of the tallo. It looked like a quieter place, or it would have been were it not for Iqaluk standing above the Bear and yelling at the top of his lungs.

"Do not be obtuse, Tri!" snarled Iqaluk. "Where is my son?"

The Bear crossed his arms, bearing his teeth as though he were an actual bear. "I told you, old man! How should I know?"

"Let us sit, gentlemen," said the Wolf, suddenly between

them. "Let us sit and let us talk."

"Aki." Iqaluk snapped around towards her as she touched his shoulder. "Please, let's sit."

The patrons at the bar watched openly even after Iqaluk finally sat down. The Bear intentionally meeting the eye of anyone foolish enough to linger. There were two of those white apple cores sitting in front of him as though he had been sitting already. Iqaluk must have approached him.

"Where should we start?" asked the Wolf.

"With the truth, Bryn Feykir of the Tsiorc," snarled Iqaluk.

Kyira placed a hand on his forearm but he moved away.

"Now, Iqaluk," said the Wolf, in hushed tones. "As you've probably already guessed, we are not farmers. I don't mind telling you that while Nord is considered safe for us, we are still in hiding, so if I hear either of our names mentioned out loud again, this conversation and our partnership is ended."

Iqaluk bristled. "Partnership? We are not partners, Br…"

"Careful, Iqaluk," growled the Bear.

Kyira shook her head. "Who are the Tsiorc?"

The Wolf regarded her, speaking quietly. "The Tsiorc are an army of rebels who have come together under one banner to fight the Bohr."

Kyira couldn't believe her ears. "The Bohr. In Kemen?"

"The Bohr own Tyr," said the Wolf, making an effort to keep his voice low. "And have done for many cycles." He took a swig from the Bear's cup. "I envy your ignorance."

Kyira scoffed. "What has that got to do—"

"Everything," said the Wolf. "The Bohr have been sending out scouting parties of slavers to draft young men and women into joining their armies. I've heard the name *Kin* mentioned in many tongues."

Iqaluk leant forward, his knuckles white on the table. "Do not take me for a fool. I know when I'm being lied to."

"It wasn't a lie," said the Wolf.

"But it wasn't the whole truth, either."

The Wolf seemed to think on it, then glanced over at the Bear, who gave a slight nod. "The Kin supply the lord's army."

"Where is my son?" said Iqaluk.

Suddenly it all came together. Kyira's voice shook. "The Kin have taken Hasaan."

"The Kin have been seen moving around Nord of late, looking for young Sami males to draft into their ranks. The Tsiorc's tactician, Captain Laeb is unsure why, so he sent us to track their movements. Among other things."

Iqaluk's lip was trembling. "Where are they now?"

The Wolf passed the cup back to the Bear, who promptly emptied it. "A few days south of here," said the Bear.

Iqaluk got up and left the table in a scuffle of wooden chairs.

"You know," added the Bear, "your brother may have joined the Kin on his own."

"No!" said Kyira, incredulous. "He would never..."

Iqaluk stopped a short distance away, spoke over his shoulder. "My son would never have joined willingly. Never. I know him. He is my *blood*!" He turned and stalked through the crowds, which parted before him.

Kyira stood herself.

"Wait," said the Wolf. "Why not come and fight for us?"

"I do not fight."

The Wolf shook his head. "Everyone fights. I've seen you fight yourself and win. I've seen you protect those that you love, and win."

"I do not fight."

"Kyira, this battle will come to your door, and it will not knock. It will burst in and cut you down. The world needs those who choose to say no, who stand up to the oppression brought by the Bohr." The Wolf's cocky expression became serious. "If you leave here today knowing only one thing, let it be this. Never. Stop. Fighting." He extended his hand. "You and I, Sami."

Moment

*M*oments have meaning, dear Atalfia. They are like ships, and there are those who wait their whole lives for one to arrive, not realising they stand already upon a deck. Feel the wooden deck of every moment beneath your bare feet, Atalfia and savour every second of the journey, because as the destination draws ever closer, so do those moments float away in the cold.

Her father's words seemed to taunt Fia, but they were right. She wished he was with her, smiling, scratching at that dry patch of skin on his neck upon where his violin used to rest. She wished Janike was here, but all Fia could see was grey skin and eyes wide with panic. Both of them had spoken of moments, and here she was, within a moment, thinking of others. She needed to leave them behind, she needed to concentrate, to think, to let go, but she couldn't let go.

There will come a point, in your life when the Forbringr will stand behind you, and you feel her breath upon your neck. In that moment you have a choice, as we all would, to live or die. Wake up, Fia!

Fia forced open her eyes. The world was black and white — devoid of colour and life. Water lapped up against her cheek, and cold wind rolled over her. The black rock towered over her, a slash against the grey sky, while wave after wave pounded the slippery rock — hardly a fitting place for a Kumpani to die. How had Jagar found her? It didn't matter now.

Another wave broke, submerging her face and she spluttered painfully drawing in more of the salty water. A cough began to form, as her body sought to expel the water in her lungs. She tried to supress it, but it came and knocked her off balance. Her moment was upon her.

No. She dug her fingers in forcing the mussels that lined the rockface aside until her nails scraped the rock beneath. The shellfish sliced new wounds into her fingertips but she was winning. She hauled herself halfway onto the rock's narrow edge, and drew a ragged breath.

Fresh coughs immediately racked her body, hacking at her saturated lungs, and then she couldn't stop it, she couldn't fight it anymore, and she was reeling. Her jerking tore the clump of mussels free, and she fell sideways. Long, slippery fingers welcomed her into the water, clutching at her and pulling her down. Terrified, she kicked out, but the kelp held tight. She opened her mouth to breathe and water rushed in.

Sixes and Sevens

Kyira caught up with her father and took his shoulder. "He would not have joined the Kin! Not Hasaan."

"Not now, Kyira!" snapped Iqaluk.

"Well we cannot just leave!"

He spun towards, with such a look of thunder that Kyira flinched, but he was looking over her shoulder. "You!" He staggered past her and grabbed the Mother Lyla, who had seemingly been following them. "You are the reason for this—"

The Mother stood awkwardly as Kyira's father, clutched her coat. "Let go, Iqaluk." She dropped a canvas bag of clothes and dried meats to the road.

"You are a captain as well?" growled Iqaluk. "A liar! Just like them."

The Mother twisted smoothly, so her back was to Iqaluk and grabbed his wrist. She leant forward, and as Iqaluk's feet lifted off the road, the Mother let go, throwing him over her shoulder and down to the dirt. By the time Kyira had her blade out and ready, the Mother was behind her father's head, a multi-coloured tri-dagger held over his windpipe.

"Stop! No, please."

"I won't," said the Mother. "I don't want to ruin the paint work on my new knife quite so early, and I like these feathers."

"Where is my son!" roared Iqaluk.

"Tell him to calm himself, Kyira. Dying in the middle of a street is no way to go."

"You are a liar," hissed Iqaluk.

"I did not lie," said the Mother.

Kyira stepped forward. "Aki, please. Not here."

The Mother stood, leaving her father to himself. "Tri might have lied, but he is his own. As is Bryn. I am not their mother." The strange weapon disappeared up her baggy sleeve. "Although, I'll admit, sometimes it does feel like it."

"You are a captain," said Kyira, helping her father to his feet. "Which side do you fight on?"

"Your side," said the Mother. "The Tsiorc are people, like you. Sami, Uigur, Nordun, Daliaens. Even a few Tyrians. In fact it was the Tyrians that gave us much of our current intel about the city of Tyr. There is not much to go on though, and the place seems nigh on impossible to breach." She stopped. "Look. We are you. We fight the Bohr, and you are not the Bohr." She picked up her bag. "We are not your enemy. Now come on, the street is not the place for this discussion."

* * *

The Mother directed Iqaluk through the streets to a tired looking building with a caved-in thatched roof. The soft smell of pine was a welcome change to the constant odour of smoking fish, but unfortunately it didn't reflect the freshness of the lounge, which was empty except for one skinny boy with a large wine-coloured birthmark covering half of his face. He stood by the fireplace, gawping at them.

"Hello," said Kyira.

The Mother appeared from a dark hallway. "It's this way. We have two rooms: six and seven."

The timber door was already open when Kyira reached the end of the hall. The number seven had been burned into the wood behind a horseshoe knocker.

"This room for all of us?"

The Mother squeezed by. "All three and a half of us."

"Did you mean what you said?" asked Kyira. "About not being our enemies?"

"Of course. I do not lie."

"Then what about the Kin?"

The Mother looked conflicted, as though she had been waiting for the question. "Your brother might have joined the Kin, or he might have been drafted. There is no way to know. You need to talk to him. If you can find him." She stood aside as Iqaluk entered, then closed the door behind him.

"Lyla, I am sorry about Isak, I did not mean—"

"Don't." The finality of the Mother's words was plain. She paused at the key, then turned her back to the room. "I am not your friend, Kyira. I understand why you ended Isak's life, but I will never forgive it." She slid the tri-dagger out from her sleeve, and threw it on the mattress of the only bed along with her bag. "Never."

"You are sleeping here?" asked Iqaluk, spreading out his sleeping mat.

The Mother pressed her lips together. "I am."

"You should be with your captains."

177

The Mother brushed a strand of dark hair away from her brown eyes. "I am also a captain, Sami, and do not forget it. But to answer your question, no. I would prefer to have some peace away from those two. Besides, they have room six across the hall from us and they will be a few hours before tumbling in yet. I want sleep." She put her hand up to him as he moved to the door. "Where are you going?"

"To take a spot in the other room," said Iqaluk, blankly.

The Mother gave Iqaluk's beard a tug. "I may be pregnant, but do not think that I won't haul you to the floor and sit on you until you fall asleep. You cannot possibly think I would let you stay in the same room as Bryn and Tri? Typical men, thinking you can act the goat and get away with it. No, you will sleep here. As will you Kyira."

Kyira opened her mouth to protest, then stopped herself. She owed Lyla this, and much more besides, for killing Isak.

The Mother glared back at her as though she had heard Kyira's every thought. "That's right," she said. "Now, get cosy."

A Good Meal

The Smoking Wench's back lounge was certainly not uncomfortable, but it could hardly be described as welcoming. A long carpet led from the main public rooms through the door to the kitchens beyond, grey-beige and threadbare in the centre from cycles of shuffling feet. It continued around the lounge splitting only for the circular fire pit at the room's centre.

Jagar sat at the back of the empty parlour forcing the final mouthfuls of grey sandshark down his throat. This was apparently what constituted a delicacy out here in the north, but there was nothing to do but put up with it for now. His body needed energy after his interrupted vision aboard the Ariathar. It was a complex process to maintain, and indeed none other alive knew that he possessed the ability, which was unique even amongst the Banémen. It was impossible to describe then how intensely frustrating it was to have the vision so torn from his consciousness by the machinations of a single human. Still, their deaths went some way to make up for the loss.

Wren, the inn's cat, meowed from the other end of the table and Jagar flicked the last piece of flesh to her feet. The cat sniffed it once, and left it where it was. The animal

179

trotted over, arching her back under Jagar's hand.

"Ah, well. What do you do when even an animal turns its nose up at the food…" Wren sunk her teeth into Jagar's hand. "Ssss!" he hissed, backhanding her off the table. She landed softly on the floor and began grooming her silver tortoiseshell coat. Jagar couldn't help but grin. "Good girl."

The heavy oak door flung open. "Jagar!" blurted the greasy-haired innkeeper, slamming the door shut. "It's been too long!"

"Maell. A delight, as usual." Maell sat down in the chair beside Jagar, the smell of old sweat following after like a pack of baying mongrels. "How is business?"

"If I was honest, Jagar, I'd tell you I've had enough of these…" he lowered his voice, even though there was no one else around. "These tearing blue-eyes!"

"You must be the only Makriliaen who doesn't like them."

"I am not, Jagar, and let me tell you why…" Maell's breath smelled almost as bad as the rest of him, and it grew hotter as the innkeeper leant in.

Jagar placed a hand on Maell's chest and pushed him back. "I can hear you from there, Maell."

Maell nodded emphatically. "Right you are! Right you are! I know for a fact that the whole of Makril would prefer these blue-eyes to be away somewhere else. The cities perhaps. They just loiter here with their hedonistic ways, fighting, dancing in the streets. Coming in ere' disrupting customers and speaking and… generally being a nuisance. I can't tell you how many I've seen flogged."

"Yes, well," said Jagar, reaching down and scratching Wren's ear, "they've got to go somewhere, haven't they? I assume that is why there are no locals out tonight?"

"Aye, and that!" added Maell. "A night when the place would be bouncing, and there ain't a single bloody soul out there, save o'course, Morten and Cronli. That pair would walk through fire to be away from their wives. So, what about you, Jagar? Are you in Makril long?"

"Just tonight," said Jagar.

"Are you in need of a room?"

Jagar barely suppressed his sigh. "Yes. If you have one."

"I'll set you up with new sheets 'n' all."

"What a treat Maell, thank you."

"Of course! Of course! It'll give the boy something to do. Gurt!" Flecks of spit showered over Jagar's sleeve. Maell shouted again, oblivious of Jagar's glare. "GURRRT!"

"Maell, leave him," said Jagar. "I have no bags with me. I'll be fine."

"Right you are, Jagar. You tracking criminals again?" When Jagar didn't answer he took that to mean he should talk more — a common human failing. "We've two staying at the commune that might interest you. Barely in a night before they got into a shouting match in the tallo. Arguing about politics of the north with some Sami."

"Did they give names?"

"No," said Maell, scratching at a damp patch beneath his armpit and releasing another waft of body odour. "Just that they claim to be brothers."

Jagar stood, and Maell took the dismissal, with a nod. "Enjoy your stay, Jagar. It's always an honour to have you here."

Once the man had left, Jagar headed into the kitchens. The cooks ignored him, barely offering him a glance as he manoeuvred between the wooden worktops that lined the long aisles. Here he was, Banéman, assassin, slayer, as well-known as he was feared, walking unseen amongst those who wouldn't know him if they heard his name. It was the strange juxtaposition of his role. Even Maell was unsure who he really was. Someone important no doubt, but someone to fear?

Jagar stepped into the back lobby that led out to the harbour, then stopped as he reached the inn's outer door. "You almost had me that time," he said, hand on the door handle.

Behind him, a small boy appeared from out of the shadow of a window. A purple birthmark covered half of his dirty face, and his skin was so stretched the poor lad's bug eyes looked as though they might fall out at any time.

"I a'most ad you!" slurred the boy, with a grotesque grin.

"Hello, Gurt," said Jagar.

A line of drool dripped from his bulging lower lip. "Wheresh you off to?"

"I'm just off to see some friends, Gurt."

"Can you do me shome more magic?"

"Of course," said Jagar, brightly. "But first I need your help."

The shabby boy stood straight and proud. "Yesh! Anything!"

"Maell said that two men were arguing in the tallo tonight."

"Yesh!" shouted Gurt, with a squint smile. "I shaw them! Two angry men! They was arguing with a Shami man, and there was a Kemen woman with them."

Jagar felt a flush of excitement. "Really now. A Kemen woman in Nord? And are this little group still in town?"

The boy's stupid face slackened again. "I want to shee

182

magicsh."

Jagar brought his hands together on the boy's cheeks and smushed them together. "You've done so well Gurt! Just tell me one more thing and you shall see magic, I promise. What room are the two angry men in?"

"In the commune," said Gurt, waiting expectedly. "Room shix."

Jagar plucked a coin from his pocket and rolled it over his fingers from one to the next before flipping it into the air, where it vanished in a flash of flame.

The boy watched, spellbound. "It'sh gone!"

"Not really," said Jagar. "It's just moved somewhere else. Would you like to see it again? I need your help if we are to conjure this coin back. Here, hold your hands in a ball, that's right. Now, are you ready?"

Gurt nodded enthusiastically.

Jagar focused his mind on the coin. The shape, the colour, the weight. None of which were real. They didn't exist in that form anymore, but he could still access most of the parts. His senses kicked into gear suddenly, bring the taste of iron in his mouth, the feel of heat at his fingertips, the smell of sulphur, the thin whine of twisting metal. He pictured the inside of Gurt's clasped hands and immediately a glow began to emanate from within them. The object wasn't large, but Jagar had to concentrate, at least to maintain control otherwise he might burn the poor boy to cinders. A sudden bitter aftertaste indicated the process had finished.

"Open your hand."

Gurt spread his palm and gave a little squeal of delight at the small, perfectly formed iron model sitting there. "Itsh Wren! You made a cat!"

183

Jagar ruffled the boy's hair. "Those who help the Banémen are rewarded, and you are a good boy, Gurt."

"Itsh so beautiful," said Gurt. "I musht be careful with it!"

"You need not worry about that," said Jagar. "It will never break, nor rust. Indeed, it will likely outlive us all. Next time I see you I shall turn it into seasilver. Then after that, gold, but now I have to go. Make sure you stay alert tonight. Alright? Should anything happen, run for the hills."

"Wheresh you going?"

"To light a fire, dear Gurt."

The boy nodded and wandered away into the kitchens, cradling the lump of metal like it was a precious jewel.

* * *

The lock on room six was old and would click when Jagar pried it. The men had chosen one of the smallest rooms; their want of privacy would soon work against them.

It was too light to stand in the hallway — his shadow would be seen beneath the doors — but he didn't need to be right next to the door to hear them. He touched the horseshoe on the opposite door to stop it moving and slipped into room seven, turning the key gently behind him. Luck then, that of the three slumbering bodies lying in the dark, none had thought to lock the door. He turned back to the door and closed his eyes. The two heartbeats in room six resonated through the wall as clearly as if Jagar were listening ear to chest. They were military, which was easy to tell by the way the men were expertly holding themselves from panic, and experienced militia this far north meant only one thing. Captains. If not inebriated captains. He squinted. No, just one captain, but the other was just as fit judging from his resting heart, though perhaps not as self-assured. Either way they had been very easy to follow here from the town's tallo.

The door to room six opened and muffled footsteps stepped out into the hallway. Jagar stood silently on the other side of the door smiling as the wooden handle he had just locked turned gently in front of him. The footsteps disappeared back into room six and the door closed. The men resumed their conversation in hushed tones.

"All is well. Lyla and the other two must be asleep. Have you moved?"

"Yes, Bryn. It's your go."

There was the sound of pieces clinking on a board. It sounded like Chinaes, an ancient game of stone and strategy.

"Ah, sneaky. I see you, Bryn. I see you as plain as day. As plain as the ugliness of your face."

"Better ugly than fat. So Tri, you were talking of your unwavering support for Suilven?"

"I was doing no such thing, you dog-headed oaf! Suilven is an idiot."

"Ah, but he's our idiot. He needs us to mind his back out there. He needs support from his captains. The Dreki wars may have segregated the empire but there's no need to quibble over such things. We are past that now. We need a united front." Jagar listened as the speaker took a bite of an apple, and swallowed it down into his beer-swilled gullet.

"We need a strong leader. And that is *not* Suilven. Laeb has my vote, for what it is worth."

"Laeb? The Tactician?"

"He's some head on his shoulders. Without him Drakemyre would have been a disaster. The battle that was lost, and won!" He took another bite. "What about that girl?"

"The Sami?

"Aye. What was that speech about? You trying to bag yourself a Sami wife? I've heard these Nordun women might be more likely to tear your balls off than settle down."

"The Tsiorc need all the help they can get, Tri. I'm not one to cosy up to command, but I'm sure even your fabulous Laeb will be happy to hear we have enlisted some new blood."

"Not sure about the father. All that strange talk of his son. He looked strong though. Maybe even strong enough to beat Kavik."

"I doubt it, Tri. The only fight I ever saw Kavik lose was against a horse. And a big one at that. I'll talk to Kyira in the morning. Maybe I can persuade her to come with us."

Jagar turned back towards the sleeping bodies. So these were the ones Rathe was looking for? The strange group seen in Nord who the great Commander Lor had thought might threaten to overturn the Bohr occupation: a pregnant Kemen woman, an old Sami, and his daughter barely bleeding? He could see them now sprawled out on the floor, minksins wrapped tightly around the two Sami.

Jagar stepped towards the pregnant one on the bed. Even in sleep she clutched at the spawn within her, protecting it. He squatted down and placed the tips of his fingers lightly on her exposed stomach. It was female, and almost ready to hatch. She was breech though, which was why Jagar had not heard the heartbeat. He pressed his ear to the skin. There was something else… Something… The woman's stomach moved as the foetus inside pressed up against the womb. Jagar concentrated then stepped back. "There we are," he

186

whispered to himself. "That should help move things along now."

The two captains in room six moved suddenly — their heartbeats quickening.

"Here we go then." He touched a finger to the sleeping mother's stomach. "Boop. We'll meet again little one, but for now I'm afraid, duty calls." He padded back to the door and closed his eyes.

"It's a fire," said the apple eater, chewing noisily. By the sounds of their muted voices they were at the far end of the room, backs to the door.

Jagar stepped out of the dark room and back into the hallway. Blood coursed through him at the anticipation of what was about to transpire. These men would die by his hand, and they were completely unaware of the fact. They might be on alert, but that just added to the excitement. The folly of humans was believing that they were indestructible, and that death, a force they could neither comprehend nor imagine, would never find them while still so young and so powerful. He tapped the talisman wrapped tightly to his wrist and tested the wire wound within — it was as taut and ready as he was himself. He pulled a spoon-shaped pick from his coat pocket, gave it a liberal coating of spit and with a patient hand he felt around the inside of the keyhole.

There.

He applied the slightest lateral pressure and the old lock mechanism shifted around, emitting the softest of clicks. He pocketed the pick and stood back against the wall, deliberately avoiding the high crack where the door met the floor. The smell of burning wood was getting stronger as his fire took hold.

"Could it spread to us here?" came a voice from room six.

"Possibly. These buildings are old, but the night is cold. It should extinguish before long. We should stay here."

Jagar exploded into the tiny room. The captain standing at the window spun to meet him, sword already in hand. Apple eater, sitting on the end of the single narrow bed, dropped his snow apple and threw a knife at Jagar, which whistled by and thwacked into the door as it swung shut. The captain lunged forward, shortblade out in front as though expecting to skewer Jagar in one fluid motion. Ah, youth. Jagar stepped to the left and with a simple bend of the knee, sent him stumbling into the door. Jagar drew a loop of light wire from the talisman, guiding it down over the captain's blade, then the hilt, and coming to rest over the man's wrist. Apple eater rushed Jagar, stabbing frantically with another knife, reducing the space so that they were almost nose to nose. Each of the man's many muscles foretold the next move as though they were a written scroll Jagar happened to be reading. He dipped beneath the man's strokes as they moved about him, each lunge earning the assailant a loop of wire from the talisman. As Apple eater was getting ready to retreat, no doubt to catch a breath, Jagar flourished, tossing a final loop around the man's head, before delivering a swift elbow to his throat. Apple eater reeled back, catching the bed post, and tumbled to the floor. The captain reengaged, throwing expert slashes so delightfully skilful they almost pre-empted Jagar's responses.

"Excellent!" hissed Jagar to himself. Jagar added a few feigns and parries of his own, getting caught up in the excitement of it all. "Wonderful strike!" He did so love a good opponent. The captain moved back and Jagar let out a long haggard breath, as though he was tired, manoeuvring himself so he was sidelong to the captain.

The predictable riposte came, and Jagar bent forward as though he was simply leaning on his knees to catch his breath. The next wild lunge flew towards him, and this time Jagar waited, watching with satisfaction as the tip of the blade drove towards him. It was a well-timed, and well executed lunge, and on any other day and with any other opponent it might have even nicked Jagar. The corners of the captain's mouth rose in the beginnings of a smile.

Now.

Jagar bent backwards, almost in half — a move that would have snapped any normal man or Bohr's spine — and the lunge hit nothing but the air above Jagar's stretched stomach. Jagar brought his fist up into the captain's confused face, allowing the momentum of the strike to carry a loop of wire from the talisman, gently around the man's head. The sword pulled back and the captain with it, striking out randomly as though trying to swat a fly. The wire had begun to tighten, indicating that apple eater had arisen. A throwing knife whistled by and thwacked into the window frame. Jagar stepped back casually, anticipating the apple eater's imminent blow and the man flew past into his comrade against the door. Guided by the pressure on the talisman at his wrist, Jagar pivoted on his heel in a flourishing spin and came to a stop with his back to the two men facing the window.

The orange glow of the tallo fire reflected his own face back at him while tiny figures rushed around within his features, their shouts permeating the air along with the thick black smoke billowing from the hall.

"How did you find us?" said the captain, sounding surprisingly calm.

Jagar watched their reflections struggling in the window. "It's easy when you know who to ask."

"Killing us won't make a difference. We are many."

"Let us go, or—" began Apple eater.

"Or what?" Jagar turned, following the crisscrossing of wire holding the two men firmly together mid strike. He plucked at the nearest wire and both men's faces instantly contorted in pain. "You underestimate the reach of the Bohr," said Jagar.

The captain winced as the wire cut into his skin. A line of blood trickled down from his neck onto the collar of his shirt. "What is it you ask for, slayer? Money? I can pay a hundred times over whatever you have been promised."

"Aye," added Apple eater, straining. "Let us go and we'll speak no more of it."

Jagar threw his head back and roared in laughter. "Feykir, you are hardly in a position to question my motives. It is Feykir, isn't it?" The fighter's eyes widened. "Captain Bryn Feykir."

"You know my name."

"Yes," said Jagar. "Your actions at Drakemyre are well documented." Jagar smiled as the captain's expression grew sour. "And I know much more than that, Captain. I know that while you boast that the forces under your command ninety leagues south of here are tens of thousands strong, they are actually only around two thousand and half of them are farm boys. I also know that the raevens you send south to your friends are best eaten roasted and go particularly well with an aged firewine."

190

Captain Feykir grimaced. "We won't talk, slayer," he said, his tone as hard as that chiselled jawline.

"I didn't expect you to, and you'll notice I never asked." Jagar plucked at one of the wires connecting the two men to the talisman at his wrist. "You'll notice," raising his eyebrows towards Apple eater, "that your knives provided wonderful anchor for my little wires. Without them, I would have been forced to… well, we might not have been able to have this little chat."

The bear-sized apple eater growled. "We won't talk."

"Your loyalty to each other is commendable, even enviable, but is ultimately misplaced. I will find you all eventually. Even this amazing tactician Laeb."

"Swine!" hissed Apple eater.

"You are mistaken," said captain Feykir, calmly. "The army you talk of is not an army of conscripts barely old enough to fight, they are people, workers, fishers and yes, farmers. But they fight by choice, and that makes us twenty times as strong. Our two thousand is worth fifty thousand on the field. Those who choose to fight tyranny will always triumph over those who are forced. Our loyalty binds us and makes us strong."

"It is, unfortunately for you, my talisman that binds you, dear Feykir."

"You bastard…" growled Apple eater.

"Yes, I know," smirked Jagar. "Now, who wants to go first?" He pointed at Apple eater. "This one is a no-brainer I think."

"HELP! He… l…" Jagar tugged hard on one of the many strands of wire, and it wound tight against the handle of the blade, cutting into the door behind him. Apple eater's cries were strangled as the wire around his neck tightened.

Captain Feykir's struggles grew wild as his friend's face turned slowly purple. Clouds of red burst into the whites of his eyes and the veins around his neck and head grew hard and blue, almost bursting as he strained. It lasted barely two minutes, before he went still. Jagar let the wire go, and Apple eater's head flopped forward.

"Damn you," spat the captain.

Jagar snarled. "Know this, captain, because I'd like you to understand. I will bring down every single Captain in the Tsiorc. Every single one. And it will not be quick. Not like your friend here. No, they will experience much worse when I find them. You just think about that a moment." Jagar turned to the window. The reflections really were beautiful, mingling with the flames, and distorted by the poorly-made glass. The fierce heat from the burning tallo was beginning to radiate through the hazy box-room window, flashing in and out of his reflected features, as blurry shadows of Sulitarians and Makriliaens alike danced in front of the high flames, running back and forth with water, sand, or whatever else they could find to quench the fire.

Jagar placed two fingers on the top of the talisman. There was the barest hint of resistance before the entire length of wire snapped back to coil up into the mechanism.

Some might call it the human condition, the way that humans helped one another in times of strife, others might call it necessity. Perhaps it was the latter. Perhaps these creatures would immediately return to their former states of petty hatred and superficial discord as soon as the immediate danger was dealt with. Whatever the case, Captain Feykir would eventually be proved right. Humans would always be drawn together, heedless of breed or race because below the skin they are all the same, and that was where the danger lay. A danger that Rathe was unable to see. Jagar could see it though, as plain as new fire. He turned towards the remains of the two men and knelt down to where amongst the lumps of neatly carved flesh lay Captain Bryn Feykir's severed head.

He tilted the head towards him. "I wonder, Captain Feykir, if those eyes still comprehend. I like to think in these last seconds, as your mind comes to terms with what has just happened, that you are wholly aware of it. The thoughts of your associates still mingling with those memories of your life, flashing by. Fading away." The captain's pupils contracted, holding, locked on Jagar, before slowly dilating. "I wish you better in your next life, captain, should you get one." Jagar inhaled the coppery aroma of fresh meat mingling deliciously with woodsmoke. "Finally," he said, with a satisfied sigh. "A good meal."

Rage

"Teine! Teine!"

Kyira coughed, rubbing her itchy eyes. The room was still gloomy with dawn. She yawned, then coughed again. Smoke.

"Fire! Fire!" This time the Makriliaen words outside her window made more sense.

Kyira jumped up and kicked her father in the behind. "Wake up, Aki!"

Iqaluk opened his bleary eyes, and focused on her. "Fire?"

"Yes! Did you not hear the screaming from outside? Come on, we have to leave now." Kyira leapt over to the Mother, tugging off her blanket. "Come on. We have to…" The Mother's usual bronze skin was a deep sweaty grey — she looked on the brink of death. Kyira bent towards her. "Lyla? Are you alright?"

"I need water."

"No!" snapped Iqaluk, pulling himself up. "By the winds! Don't try to move her." He leapt off his sleeping mat to her side, and spread his palm over her exposed stomach. "It looks like she is in labour."

"She can't be," Kyira scoffed. "Not now!"

Iqaluk checked the Mother's pupils. "Your mother once

said, a babe will come whenever it damn well pleases. For Lyla, that time is now."

"Aki, she is not our responsibility! Leave her."

Iqaluk looked at her in disgust. "I will not. What might have happened if you had just left me in the hands of those slavers?"

"Fine, but we do not have very much time. This town is built like a stack of dry sticks." She felt at the Mother's stomach, then recoiled immediately. "It moves!"

"Yes," said Iqaluk, dabbing the Mother's forehead. "It is in distress."

"Aki, this is no calf. You are sure about—"

"Kyira! There is no time for Aki this, or Aki that. Go and get Bryn and Tri!"

Kyira turned on the spot and rushed out into the hall. She banged on door seven. "Open up! Wol...Bryn. Tri! There is a fire you drunken fools! Wake up!"

The door opened a crack and an old, wrinkled face appeared. "Who are you?" he said, in a shaky voice. "What do you want?"

Kyira shook her head. "Where are Bryn and Tri?"

The man's breath came in shuddered pants. "I'm sor... sorry," he muttered, trying to shut the door.

Kyira jammed her foot in the way. "No, not until you tell why you are in this room!"

"I took the room late on," said the man, from behind the door. "It was empty. There was nothing but a pile of upturned furniture when I arrived. Please leave me alone!"

Kyira forced the door open, pushing against the man's weight from the other side until it swung open. She gasped. The room was empty — just a dishevelled old man who had fallen asleep amongst a pile of old rags.

The old man stumbled back, slipping on some round stones, then grasped for a seete bottle from the bedside table. He held it out like a sword, his arm shaking with the weight. "Be…be gone!

Kyira shook her head. "You can't help me! But help yourself! There is a fire. Look!" The man turned, seemingly only just noticing the bright orange glow at the window, and the licks of flame perfectly clear through the glass. "Go, before it catches the commune." Kyira spun and headed back into her own room.

The Mother's eyes were rolling in her head, her stomach moving as the babe struggled within. She stared at the bulging belly, unable to look away.

"Kyira!" snapped Iqaluk, from between the Mother's legs. "Where are they?"

"They're gone." A door shut behind her, and the old man spared her a look from the hallway. He tried to peer in, dropping his coat and bottle in the process. Kyira shut the door on him. "The fire is coming."

"I don't know what is wrong! The babe is still so small. At least a month from being ready." His fearful stare met Kyira's. "They will die, both of them."

"Iqaluk, we must go!"

Her father shook his head. "We cannot, girl. Not yet. We need something to carry her with or we shall be going nowhere."

Kyira dropped to the Mother's other side. "She would have left you."

Iqaluk frowned at her. "Do you truly believe that, Kyira? After all she said? After all that you said you owe her."

Kyira's frustration burst out of her like a flame catching. "Fine! I am surrounded by fools! Stay here. I will find us a cart!"

* * *

Makril was lost. The long homes were already flaming when Kyira stepped outside. The rushing people outside her window had not been trying to put the fires out, they were escaping the town. She followed the route back from the night before, stopping at the tallo which had already been reduced to a black shell. The ground, which only hours ago had been bustling with colour and life was peppered with smouldering piles of ash — echoes of the humans that they had once been. Kyira gave the smoking shapes of people, animals, homes, a wide berth and turned down a narrow street, jerking to a halt. The street opened out onto an intersection, before the stone harbour she had seen from the hill. In the middle of the road a rope of swirling orange fire was snaking up from a pile of rubble up high beyond the rooftops into the dark clouds themselves. It leapt about, snapping this way and that, flicking between piles of ash, searching for something more to consume until it found the inn, the only untouched building. Immediately the rope thickened, as wide as the house itself, tearing through the roof, sucking everything up into a whirling maelstrom. Kyira covered her face as the wind grew hot. The windows and doors of the inn burst outwards then were sucked back into the swirling vortex of fire, great bulges moving up and down inside. Molten ejecta burst from the top a hundred feet above them turning the low clouds a deep orange. A droplet of oily rain splashed onto Kyira's cheek, and she rubbed it away, sniffing the sooty residue. Another drop, then another and another until soon a dark torrent fell around them, feeding the smaller fires and building them higher. The fiery base swelled as the tendrils of smaller fires joined it as glowing, twisting veins, each hungry for more.

A shrill cry blew in on the hot wind, growing louder and closer until a fiery figure stumbled out from the inn. The screaming man ran at her, towards the water, forcing Kyira back into a muddy ditch and tearing by, leaving a trail of heat and the smell of charred meat behind. He managed another ten paces before stumbling into a burning pile at the edge of the harbour.

Kyira rushed over, scanning the ground for anything that might douse the flames. Her eyes fell upon a small barrel. She side-stepped the burning man, vaulted the short fence, and prised off the top, almost vomiting at the smell. She hefted the barrel of slop and went to pour it over him.

"Don't touch the fire!" Kyira stepped back as a Sulitarian woman sprinted to her side. "Don't touch it!"

"I can't just let him die!"

The woman placed a sooty hand on the barrel, her long fingernails where red with blood. "I beg you not to. It is not normal fire. How many fires have you seen without smoke? Watch." Kyira let the woman take the barrel.

Unheeding of the smell, the woman dipped her hand into the muck and scooped out a handful and threw it over the flames. Before the slop had even landed tongues of fire leapt up towards them. The woman snapped her hand away and they both jumped back, letting the barrel fall, while the flames crept along the scorched earth like a blind snake searching. They found the barrel and attacked it, tentacles of flame shooting out from the burning man to consume the new source of nourishment.

Kyira stared in disbelief. "It moves like an animal!"

The Sulitarian woman wiped her hand on the earth. "There are two more burning bodies back there, people helping people, then suddenly needing helped themselves. I chased after this one in the vain hope I might stop the awful chain of death." The woman shook her head, backing off as tendrils of fire began creeping along the gaps in the cobbles towards them. "Don't let it touch you!"

The road rumbled beneath their feet. The mortar between the blackened cobbles cracking under the crawling fire, then the stones themselves were crumbling to pieces, pushing upwards in front of her. The ground bulged.

Kyira shuffled by it to the street side, pulling the woman with her. The woman snatched her hand away.

"Run!" screamed the woman. "Find a way out, before we are all lost!" She turned and dashed back around the corner.

The bulge cracked, as the red clay beneath burst through. Abruptly, a shard of shining rock broke through the street, growing taller than Kyira until it reached even the flaming rooftops, and beyond. Kyira backed off, watching from behind the ruined shell of a smoking cart. The vortex of fire leapt upon the shard of shining rock, crackling sparks and blue lightning, connecting like the new wick of her oil tin. Kyira remembered that night above the Waning Crescent, the danger, the power. It had destroyed most of the hill, left it in crumbling ruins, pulled down the very sky around her.

The road cracked and groaned as the shard grew taller, reaching the full width of the street and crumbling the walls of the stone inn, the swirling vortex of fire spinning from its jagged peak. The circular sign from the inn fell clattering to the road and rolled towards the burning man on the other side, the image of the smoking woman peeling and smoking from the heat. The flames from the burning man leapt over it, and in a few seconds it was nothing but charcoal.

Kyira turned and ran as fast as she could following after the woman, back to the commune where they had slept. There was no time for a cart. They had to get out of this town now! The heat burned her back as she ran. Wood splintered behind her, the sky bruised and bulged with orange flame. The Forbringr was here. The Forbr—

Kyira's toe clipped the edge of something and suddenly she was airborne. Hot air engulfed her and then there was nothing.

Messages

L aeb stopped and folded his arms, following the young Farram as he rushed towards him through the tents. He couldn't have been much older than eighteen, but still he managed to strut around like a new rooster. It was not an uncommon sight during times of war, to have messengers rushing notes back and forth between the field but the affinity the Ringlanders had for recognising status did nothing more than slow things down for everyone.

"What is it, Farram?" said Laeb, harder than he intended. "I want to get to my bunk."

"Message for you, sir." The young boy reached out with a soggy looking parchment then promptly slipped forward, falling knees first into mud that had been churned up and lived in by near two thousand men over six months. A few crumpled letters tipped out of his bag and the boy began frantically gathering them up.

Laeb hauled the boy up from under his arms. "Alright, son, this is no place to be taking a nap. Now start slow. Who sent you?"

"Kilier. I'm the new Farram."

"So I see." The boy's eyes widened, and he bent over and plucked a ruined brown parchment out from under Laeb's boot, almost slipping again.

Laeb smoothed out the parchment against his starched cuff. "Thank you. I would suggest a quick clean up before returning to *Consul* Kilier." The accent on the title was not lost on the young messenger.

"Absolutely, sir! Thank you... sir."

Laeb walked on and read to himself, ignoring the stains of mud.

Tactician Laeb,

I think it's time we discuss the next move for the regiments. I am eager to hear your opinion on how we move forward. Report to the Commander's tent at once.

Consul Kilier
On behalf of Commander Suilven

Laeb crumpled the note then tossed it absently into a fire where three boys sat roasting squirrel — a smell Laeb knew well. They were not quite as tasty as the rodents back home, but there wasn't much choice in Dali in the way of game. And what little they did have was about to be stretched even further as the hunt for replacement soldiers continued.

The boys stood and saluted.

"As you were," said Laeb.

"Leave him be!" roared a booming voice from behind. The Leader of Horses was as wide as he was tall, made even wider by the custom-made chest plate he insisted on wearing everywhere he went — the Tsiorc vigil painted proudly in white across it.

"Are you bothering the captain," roared Kavik.

The boys shook their heads. "No, sir," said the tallest of the three, barely level with the chest plate.

"Well get on it then! I will not have you sitting around when there is mucking out to be doing! Go on!"

Laeb shook his head as the boys hurried off. "There's no need, Kavik. It was I who interrupted them."

"Ah, but it is good to keep the riff-raff in check." A heavy frown grew on his face. "By the Good Lord Baeivi, why do you always look like you are pondering on the sorry state of the world?"

"Someone has to, Kavik."

"Ah, but you must laugh, friend. You cannot right the ills of this world as much as you can right the ills of the Forbringr herself! You do not hear me complaining about my boys, of how little they have to eat, or how many of them lay dying next to their mates."

Kavik had a habit of referring to his animals as though they were humans, although considering that the last thirty horses had all died in battle in Dali, Kavik's title should really have been Leader of Nara, of which there were only eight left. Laeb wondered quietly how long it might be before they were in the pot.

Kavik laughed and shook Laeb's shoulders, almost dislodging the discs in his back. "If you focus too hard on these things, they will eventually rot your mind and your body until there is nothing left! But then, perhaps that has already happened!"

"Where are you off to, Kavik?"

"Drinking, friend!" said Kavik, with another booming laugh.

203

"Then do not let me keep you from it," said Laeb.

"Ah! But we must take these moments of celebration when they come, or they will pass us by like ships in the night. Come drink with me."

"Kilier—"

"The Consul can wait."

Laeb let Kavik lead him through the myriad of tents and muddy paths to a small clearing where two men sat talking jovially. The remnants of roasted rodents lay upon the coals turning slowly to ash.

"Sit, captain," said the first, a thin man wearing nothing but his underwear. "You want some meat? We still have some left. Although it's mostly rat. Or squirrel." Before Laeb could answer the man reached into a tin and pulled a handful of greasy meat out, thrusting it into Laeb's bare hand.

Kavik, settled down beside Laeb. "Prank, pass me the skin."

"I don ave' it," said the thin man.

"You tearing fool!" snapped Kavik. "You took it when I went to shit!"

"Aye," said Prank, elbowing the young soldier next to him in the ribs. "And we all know how long you like to take up privvy hill! You probably fell into the lake!" Both of them broke into a fit of laughter.

"Don't make me get up…" growled Kavik.

Prank held out his hands. "Worry not, ya great big slobbering dog of a man! Here." He leaned over and lobbed a skin over the flames into Kavik's waiting hand.

"Lake?" enquired Laeb.

Kavik drank deeply from the skin, then wiped his great

forearm across his beard. "I didn't bloody fall in the tearing lake!"

"No, I mean, I didn't know there was a lake up there."

"Yes, well," said Kavik. "It is not big, but it is tearing deep!" Kavik slapped the waterskin into Laeb's open hand, forcing him to juggle his handful of steaming meat.

Laeb took a draught, immediately regretting it.

"Almost pure alcohol," said Kavik. "Not my best batch, admittedly, but still who cannot love the taste of wild Daliaen beets aged in rusty bloody barrels."

"Cooked over horse shit," added Prank, with a wink.

"Aged," croaked Laeb.

"Aye," said Kavik, "well, just long enough to get bad, then get good again."

Laeb was breathing through his nose to bypass the burning in his throat. "Good?" He took another swig and stuffed the last of the salty meat into this mouth. "No Kavik, it's not good. I've not had good for almost an entire cycle now."

Kavik nodded slow. "Aye, some nice aged firewine. I'd even take a seete these days, although I always thought it smelled better than it tasted."

Liquid warmth was quickly spreading through Laeb's guts. "I'd be surprised if you had tastebuds left, Kavik!"

"Aye! See, that's better!" Kavik turned to the two men across the fire. "You know, I knew a man once who had most of his head chopped off!"

"Really?" said the young soldier, earnestly. "Did he live?"

"Aye," said Kavik, "but only by the skin of his neck!" Kavik and the two men burst into fits of laughter. "No, no. In all seriousness. There's a sure-fire way to win any fight. Ankles, groin, and eyes."

205

The young soldier nodded as though the words were a gift. Perhaps they were. "Ankles, groin and—"

"And eyes," said Kavik. "Don't forget them eyes. First you cut em down, then you disable them, then you blind them. After that, if they're still alive... well, that choice is yours ain't it? Winning, losing. It doesn't mean anything. Surviving the game is all that we can do in the end."

A strange silence settled upon them. Not awkward, but not enjoyable either as each man's thoughts turned to their loved ones, their lives outside of this fire, and these tents. Life outside of this army. It was the reason they were here. The thing for which they fought, and ironically it was easy to forget when surrounded by the promise of death.

It was the young soldier who broke the silence first, clearly emboldened by the Kavik's moonshine. "What's your name then?"

Kavik leant forward, almost knocking Laeb from the old log. "You watch that tearing tone, youngling. This here is Captain Laeb, and he's the reason we beat them filthy Bohrbloods at Drakemyre. He's probably the only reason we're sitting here now. That, and this right hook!"

Kavik stood up in front of the fire, fighting an invisible intruder; uppercut, uppercut, jab left, jab right, lean back and haymaker. He yanked off his breastplate. "I used to be a fighter back at home," he said, in between jabs.

"Sit down, Kavik!" roared Prank. "You'll do yourself a damage! Haha. Or I will!"

"Try it, Batkeeper!"

The two men made a game of trying to slap each other over the high flames, and soon Laeb found himself laughing with them.

The night wore on in much the same fashion, until gradually Kavik's elixir began to knock them out. The young soldier went first, then Prank — there was barely any fat on the man anyway — leaving only Kavik and Laeb.

"These lot don't know what it is really like," slurred Kavik. "They have no idea the pains you go through… as… as a father. You hear me?"

"I hear you, Kavik. But I wouldn't know… I am still as free as the day I was born."

"Free?" laughed Kavik. "Ha. Only a father knows just how useless freedom is. It means nothing to those who have it and everything to those who do not. Belonging to something, creating something. Now that is what life is all about. That is life."

"Life is hard enough," said Laeb, beginning to sway, "without wishing for what you cannot have."

Kavik pressed him. "You lie, Tactician Laeb. Oh, great captain." He added a mocking tone to the last. "Captain, you need…" He paused to swallow, and gave an uncertain cough, then gave his great chest a whack. "Ah, there we are. Now, captain. If the stirring of your loins does not pull you towards becoming a father, then tell me of your dreams. Where would you be if you were not here?"

"Somewhere else, Kavik."

"That's enough, now. I mean it. Let's say you never came to aid the Tsiorc. Would you have left the Outer Isles?"

"I would have left," nodded Laeb. "I'd no doubt have a few rice paddies in the green hills of Dali. Bryn, Tri and Dia'slar would no doubt be there too, and we would each be married."

"Tactician Laeb, a farmer?" boomed Kavik. "What would

you grow?"

"Goosgrapes, barley. Anything really. Just me, my wife and good tilled earth."

Kavik's stare rolled around with his head, as though he couldn't focus. "Goosgrapes?"

"They're like very large blueberries. You can make wine with them or add them to rice ale for an extra kick."

"Well, I know rice ale!" laughed Kavik. "You'll get it, Laeb. What is for you, won't go by you... and we all need something to... Shoot for."

Kavik clutched his stomach and let out a tentative belch which smelled of moonshine and sausage. "I should not have drunk so much."

The big man swayed towards Laeb, his boots churning up the ground as he tried to stay balanced, before all at once he fell back off the old log and thudded into a heap.

* * *

Laeb picked his way through the slumbering camp, still enjoying the warmth that Kavik's words had stirred within him. A patrol marched by and he stiffened, trying to appear sober as they saluted in his direction. He kept his eyes down on the dark, squelching mess of a path in front. It did not do well to forget your feet amongst roads that were well used by reams of Farrams, delivery carts, and livestock. The main thoroughfares had become quagmires deep enough to suck a man's boots from his feet. Every week Laeb promised to do something about it, but truth be told, it was low down on his priority list. There was a stack of duties to oversee, even after a battle had been won.

While the temperature barely waned through the small hours, it was still much colder than Laeb was used to, and as he approached his tent he quietly thanked Kavik's suggestion to move further down the valley, where the warmer cross Paladino winds crashed into one another. It was funny how quick a soldier became used to the ceaseless flapping of canvas when a good night's sleep was there for the taking.

He stepped over the guides and stopped at the entrance to his tent. "Duga?"

A shrouded man stepped forward from the side, face in shadow, moving like someone who knew everything that was happening around him, which, of course, was why Laeb had chosen him as his second.

"Captain."

The lack of a formal greeting was enough to convey the tone. "What is it?" asked Laeb, the intoxication leaving him in an instant.

"The redback," said Duga, nodding to the tent.

"Then let us see what news awaits us." Inside the tent Prig hung quietly from a perch above their heads.

Duga reached up.

"Be careful," said Laeb, "he bites."

"Yes, I know." Duga let the redback crawl delicately from the perch into his palm, and it immediately began purring.

"It appears there is no end to your talents, Duga."

Duga rubbed the creature's stomach then pulled a rolled parchment from its pouch.

"Perhaps this is the balance to our recent good fortunes," said Laeb.

"I don't believe fortune has had any place within our recent successes, captain."

209

Laeb took the parchment and held it close to the oil lamp on his desk. It appeared hastily written.

L,

We are discovered. I am leaving Tyr as soon as I can to come join you. Janike is dead. Tell her father she died well.

F

The back of the leather parchment had been written on, but the words had been long rubbed off, by wind, rain or raeven piss. He read the words once more, hoping they might mean something else, then dropped it to the floor.

"Our fortunes have indeed changed, Duga, but not for good. It's from Fia."

Duga replaced the redback on its perch then lowered his cowl. He was wearing his usual grim expression, made worse by the scar that separated his bottom lip, giving him a permanent snarl. "They are discovered?"

"Yes. Fia is travelling here."

"You will be glad to see her," asked Duga. It wasn't really a question, but somehow he made it sound like one. Still, Laeb couldn't bring himself to answer. Fia — her hair, her pale skin, her wit, even the constant rebukes. He stared down at the parchment.

"Janike is dead."

Duga's expression didn't change. It never did, but perhaps there was a hint of sadness behind those cold eyes.

"Kavik ought to be told."

"In good time," said Laeb.

210

Laeb moved the papers around his desk to make some space for the parchment. He was not a fastidious man, but nor was he unclean. The state of his desk mimicked the state of his mind: ration tables, hand written scribbles, equations and diagrams marking every space of paper. He reached below and pulled out a circular playing board from beneath the desk. The series of squares, which were wide in the middle, and narrow at the edge, were perfect for playing Muta, or Chinaes as the Ringlanders called it. It was cut from the stoytree; when on the rare occasion one would die before its time, the dense wood was sawed into board like this one. He dropped it heavily on the desk then fished out the bag of character stones.

"Duga, my friend. You knew Janike?"

Duga stepped around Laeb and took the bag of stones, fingering the leather. "Well enough. More than most, less than others." His lop-sided expression grew stern. "I know your thoughts, captain. We cannot move yet. We need to replenish our men, and our supplies. Another engagement now would finish us. We are not ready."

Laeb scratched his head. The board really was beautiful, the way the rings created a perfect checked pattern, and incredible to be but a simple act of nature and not created in some magical forge. Still, without the pieces the playing board was useless. Was it the pieces that made it useful? Of course not. One without the other left them both lesser than the sum of their parts. If the playing board was Dali then the stones were the Tsiorc. If the board was Rengas, the stones were all of its citizens, Bohr and human alike. Maybe he and Fia were the character stones, making the board the fleeting landscape of their lives.

211

He ran a finger over the lacquered wood. "Our resources may be low but the element of surprise rides with us. The Bohr, and their lord's army believe that we are too wounded to strike again."

"We are," said Duga.

Laeb turned towards his second. "Underestimation is how you lose a war, Duga. Balance must be struck if victory is to be taken. We will strike hard, and strike first, and when I meet with the commander tomorrow, I will tell him that."

Duga gave a single nod of acquiescence. "Yes, captain."

Laeb took the bag from Duga. "Now, do you want red or blue?"

Resistance

The air in Commander Suilven's yurt hung like a wet blanket. Laeb twitched as droplets of sweat ran down his back, silently wishing for a stiff breeze to relieve the headache beginning to take hold. Sulitar was either hot or it was cold, but here on the mainland the weather was as inconsistent as its people.

"Well?" said the officer sitting across the iron table.

"I'm assuming you have an answer for your superiors, Tactician Laeb?" said Consul Kilier from the commander's side. "Or are we to sit here until you finish devising one from that famously prodigious mind of yours?"

Laeb ignored the titter that rolled around the table. "Gentlemen. Our recent successes were not teased from those unwilling to give us their time. Our men are not mercenaries. They fight for us because they believe in us. I didn't convince them to join our cause, it was they who convinced me to join theirs." Talking around an issue was the part of his role he was least competent in, but it seemed the only way to communicate with these men. The five leaders of the Tsiorc exchanged glances, passing them along until they reached Commander Suilven, a large lean man with a long grey beard and brown skin. His stony expression didn't change.

"Still," said Kilier, "I fail to see why that means we should just pack up and leave."

"The Tsiorc have achieved an important win," began Laeb, "but they have also seen their friends cut down. Their effectiveness as a fighting force has reached a peak. I see it in their eyes. They are not hardened soldiers, they are men and women, and they *feel*. We need to make use of what expertise they have and capitalise on our win at Drakemyre before apathy takes hold."

The commander opened his mouth to talk, but Kilier got there first. "An impassioned statement Tactician Laeb. Perhaps I might first just enquire as to your experience." Laeb turned smoothly to Consul Kilier at the lower end of the elliptical table, eyes flicking over his shallow forehead, high cheekbones and thick black eyebrows.

"My experience, Consul?" said Laeb. "I fail to see the relevance—"

"To lend some much-needed weight to your words. It has only been eleven months since you joined us, and yet you are more famous amongst the men than even I. So, then the relevance, captain, is that before we can believe wholeheartedly in your radical suggestions we deserve to at least get a picture of the man, so to speak." His fingers moved like a conductor's might, caressing each slippery word as it slithered from between his thin lips. "To provide context. That is, to better understand his plight, as it were."

Laeb felt his eye twitch. "I know what context means, consul."

"Good!" said Kilier, as though he were talking to a child. "Then tell us of your history. Where do you come from? With whom have you fought? How did you even come to be here, joining such noble causes." He finished with an empty smile.

The mood quieted. Even the commander's lean features seemed held in animated suspension.

"My radical suggestions, as you call them, are merely solutions to unusual problems." Kilier moved to speak but Laeb cut him off, talking louder. "For example, how does an army of inexperienced soldiers outflank an army composed of some of the strongest, best paid fighters in Rengas, trained by the Bohr and led by experienced commanders?"

Magister Firam spoke up, mistaking rhetoric for an actual question. "What we always do! Frontline charges to harry and pressure and then cavalry to punch through." He blustered over the words as though they were getting caught in his greying moustache on the way out.

"Cavalry?" came the smooth objection from an officer to his side. "You keep Cavalry for wide flanking manoeuvres, you don't send them into a mousetrap!" He smoothed his bald head. "First you create a distraction, say…with fire and pitch, and secondly attack from the opposite side. Third sends a full-frontal charge with all lines and SMASH!" He brought his fist down with a thump. "Easy."

Magister Firam shook his head. "Attacks from the side only dilute resource. You have to punch through the lines and force them into submission. I'd take a show of strength any day over flanking manoeuvres."

The third officer, a thin man with grey hair which probably had once been luscious blond, barked. "Ha! Experience trumps all," he said. He had a booming voice for one so small, which was probably the only reason the man could be called an officer. "Infiltrate the lines before the battle even begins. Sneak into their camps in the dead of night and cut the enemy's throats while they sleep."

"As you can see," said Kilier loudly, gliding over to Laeb's side, "we have a wealth of strategic talent and practiced veterans right here. So, humour us. Why should we trust the opinion of a man who has yet, from what I hear, to make a single kill. A fact as blue as your eyes."

Laeb backed away from the man's bony hands. "When I received a request to join your then small regiment of rebels, I informed Commander Suilven of my skills, but if you insist, Kilier, then I will repeat it again for your benefit."

Kilier's nostrils flared. "Consul Kilier. But please, continue."

"I hail from Sulitar, the largest of the islands located in the region you call the Outer Isles. It retains the largest overland defence force in the northern half—"

A cough sounded from behind and Laeb turned to face a Farram, too old for the junior stripes on his sleeves. "Apologies commander. You have an urgent message from the city."

Commander Suilven shook his head. "Enough of this. I don't think we need a history lesson today. Come back after breakfast Farram." The old Farram nodded and ushered out of the tent. "Captain Laeb" said the commander, rubbing his temples, "your advice is to pick up our army and do what exactly?"

"Attack Tyr," said Laeb.

The three officers burst out of their seats simultaneously.

"You can't be serious!"

"You're joking!"

"We can't commit those levels of forces! We'll all die in a

rain of fire!"

Laeb didn't wait for the men to stop shouting. "Two of my last Tyrian spies have stopped sending intel. We now have no idea what the Bohr king intends to do. I have my ideas, based off his past reactions to us, but they are guesses, and without first-hand information about the upper echelons of Tyr we will have no direction. Our resistance will be as lost as rain to the sea."

Kilier cleared his throat. "Your wonderful seafaring metaphors aside, captain, Tyr is a rabbit warren of narrow streets and dead ends. If we were somehow able to get into Tyr we would soon find our little resistance corralled as, how would you say it? A school of fish? A bait ball? Which would make the Bohr the sharks."

"We are the sharks, Kilier," said Laeb.

"You put too much focus on intel, captain," blustered Firam.

"Sit down, Firam," said Commander Suilven. "This is a meet, not open council. Talking over your opponent and finishing his sentences will not spontaneously give you power over him. I always hated that rule. Please, hear him out. Surely his recent accolades have earned him that."

Laeb felt new energy rush into him. "The Bohr stronghold of Tyr remains as untouched as when the Tsiorc began their rebellion. Eventually we have to meet them, and we must win. Imagine it. Imagine taking Tyr, and releasing the citizens within from a tyrannical dictatorship. As the Tsiorc, we would no longer be thought of as simple rebels, a band of unhappy farm folk to be swatted away, we would be an adversary. Us versus them. Tyr is a human city, it needs a human government. It needs us." He waited for the words to penetrate. "If we do nothing the Bohr occupation will roll over Rengas like a tidal wave. Only the Tsiorc can stand in their way. Only the Tsiorc can stop them." He pounded the table to drive the point home. Firam looked conflicted, but the officer at his side nodded.

Kilier saw that he was losing ground and pulled a smooth response out of thin air. "And what evidence is there for us to believe that you simply do not wish to go to Tyr, and are using our army as a means to get there?"

Laeb rounded on him. "What are you suggesting?"

"I'm *suggesting* that you may have other reasons for drawing our army into the taegr's den."

"I would not suggest mobilising eighteen hundred men and women to fight the Bohr at their own stronghold to satisfy a personal whim, consul. Despite anything you have heard to the contrary."

"Commander—" protested Kilier.

"Consul," snapped the commander. "Please do not sully these discussions with accusation unless you have proof." He glared at Kilier. "Well... do you?"

Kilier's greasy moustache twitched, as he battled to keep his mouth shut. "No. I do not have proof. I retract my statement. I still do not think we can commit resources to this escapade. This blue-eyes will see us all dead before the year is out! We cannot trust him."

Suilven stood. "Consul, the world is a different place now. You call him a blue-eyes, I call him a fellow human. Captain Laeb *is* an outsider, whose methods I find as unilaterally baffling as everyone else. But you cannot tell me they do not work. The win at Drakemyre was the most significant engagement the Tsiorc have had, and despite the heavy losses we still taught the lords a lesson they will never forget."

"No!"

"Commander, please consider..."

"You cannot expect us to..."

"Quiet!" growled Suilven, and the tent fell immediately silent. His glare landed upon Laeb, making him feel small even though he stood well above the man. "Captain, your accomplishments at Drakemyre were some of the finest manoeuvres I have ever seen. Ordering the horses to retreat, in order to initiate a charge from the lord's front lines was inspired."

"Thank you, Commander," said Laeb. "It was the beginning of the end for the Lords."

"Yes it was," said the Commander. "However, it was also reckless. Any number of things could have gone wrong. The horses themselves may have been spooked, they're not half as battle-ready as the animals the Bohr have at their disposal. The fact remains that if the Kael had considered our forces more or received better intel he may have chosen to better equip his outfits. As it happened, luck was on our side."

"I do not believe in luck," said Laeb.

"No," said Commander Suilven, his head tilting. "I see that, and it's an admirable trait for one charged with tactics. Still, while I find Consul Kilier's words a little hard, I agree with them. The battle could easily have gone the other way. The changeable weather, the earthquake, anything could have changed the fortunes that day, which is something that cannot happen. As you say, Captain, we may only have one more good fight left in us."

"We should be looking to the outlying towns for men," said Firam.

Consul Kilier nodded. "Drafting is our only option."

The Commander drew in a long breath. "Captain, you have, no doubt schemes and plots awaiting your scheming and plotting. I would suggest you get on with them. In the meantime, I would like to discuss the details of a conscription decree."

"Maybe we can borrow a template from the Kin," said Laeb, "or perhaps the Bohr."

Suilven's glare returned. "Never compare us to those creatures again, captain. We have made allowances for your ways, but do not forget where you are. This is our land, and our fight. Consul Kilier will inform you when I have made my decision."

"As you wish, sir," said Laeb.

* * *

The smell grew foul as Laeb neared the latrines, but it was the quickest way out of the camp. He kept his head down, for this was no place to slip. A mule waddled by him, ribs and spine clearly visible, dragging a cart behind and deepening the already treacherous mud. Someone had taken to branding them with the triangle from the Tsiorc vigil, which was wholly unnecessary. The outer lying towns had yet to sell a single animal to them.

"You and I, Captain Laeb," said Duga, appearing at Laeb's side.

"You and I, Duga."

"Are you busy?"

"I'm heading to the lake. Walk with me. Carefully."

Duga squelched alongside until the ground finally firmed

up, and their pace quickened. "How did you get on?"

"It seems we may still be here when Fia arrives, after all."

"That is good," said Duga, absently.

"No, it is not!" Laeb shook his head and stopped. "Friend, I apologise. You mean well, and I take it. Thank you."

"Do not dwell on it, captain. I can see that you miss her."

The walls fell away. "I want to see her, Duga, but I'm torn between the two forces in my life. If the Tsiorc wait here the Bohr will roll over us like a tidal wave; if I force Suilven's hand and mobilise, there is a good chance I will never see Fia again."

"And Suilven thinks you want to go to Tyr to see her? Did you tell them she is on her way here?"

"No. Thankfully, it seems there is some honour left within Kilier's dried up insides." He looked down, only then noticing Duga's black cloak. "Forgive me, Duga. You mourn for Janike."

Duga inclined his head. "We all have our problems, captain." It was about as much emotion as Laeb had ever seen him show.

The pair carried on through to the Northern sector, where uniforms became farmers and civilians, peddling skins, furs, meats, vegetables and ales where they could. Prices, which had once been fair, had inflated so much the camp suppliers were being forced to extremes.

"I heard this morning," began Duga, "that there is a new currency taking hold in Tyr. The caravans are all talking about it."

"Well, it won't matter soon enough. Suilven and Kilier are drafting a decree of compulsory ownership, meaning that the Tsiorc could take control of the surrounding lands and its assets without payment."

"Assets," said Duga. "A strange way of referring to one's people."

They carried on by the baying animals and onto the weapons field, where the weapons master strode back and forth between the platoons of sparring men. "It's amazing we're still here at all," said Laeb, adjusting his boot to stop it from being sucked from his foot.

"We're losing more every day. They're returning to their communities with tales of fighting and death. It is a rot that will eat away the Tsiorc from the inside out. If we are not careful, there will be only you and I left to face the Bohr in Tyr."

"If we get that far."

"There's always Kai. I've heard his ships are moored in a cove halfway up the Way."

Laeb shook his head. "No. Let us hope it doesn't come to that." He paused while the soldiers moved through a synchronised manoeuvre. "At least these ones look like they are improving. Although a few good Hauwi fighters would have had them carved from wood."

Duga pointed to the pair closest to them. "That one there. She seems good, and her partner, although perhaps not with that grip."

Laeb nodded. "Mihkil. He is good."

Duga shook his head. "Although he'll take his own scalp off with that thing. Mihkil! LIKE THIS, YOU IDIOT!" The young man turned towards them as Duga made strong jabbing motions, then promptly dropped his spear.

"Mihkil might be useless with the spear, Duga, but put a bow in his hands and even the great fear him. You have to focus strength, brother, not scatter it."

Duga didn't look impressed. "They need to be able to handle themselves in close combat, captain. A bow is no use when a Bohr is standing two feet in front of you. I fear the edge of the Tsiorc blade is dulling, captain. We have been here too long."

Laeb nodded, withholding a sigh. "Suilven will not listen. What else am I to do?"

"We need an infusion of fresh blood. What about the towns that refuse to trade with us? They're crawling with young men. Men that we can use. Perhaps a drafting is the answer we've been looking for."

"The methods of the lord's armies have no place here."

"So, we will take their food, but not their men?"

Laeb turned to his second. "Fuelling our men is one thing, snatching firstborns living their lives to fight in an army they've never heard of is another!" A few men around them looked up from their fires, their gazes drawn by sharp words. Sulitarian was a harsh sounding language at the best of times, or at least it was to the Ringlanders, but two men standing in the mud snapping at each other would catch anyone's attention.

"Duga, I appreciate your candidness. I rely on it, but I cannot always entertain it."

Duga placed a hand on Laeb's chest. "There might not be much choice left. Not if you want to win this war. These Ringlanders know not of the miracles a lowly Sulitarian can achieve. We are as mysterious as the wind, the ocean and sky. They even go as far as to use the colour of our eyes to describe something they are afraid of. Are your eyes blue? Such a thing dishonours us."

"Yes," said Laeb. "I've heard it."

"They understand nothing but taxes and blood," said Duga, "but we need their numbers, and I'd rather their blood than ours."

"Friend. Our focus shouldn't be so blindly on numbers, but on unity. The towns of Nord will not see what is on their doorstep until it is knocking down their door. It is up to us to transmit the right message, of what the Tsiorc stands for, if we wish to draw them into our fight. They don't just need a leader, they need comrades, they need friends like you. They need loyalty like yours."

Duga seemed to think on the words, then he wrapped an arm around Laeb's shoulder. "Your words light a fire within me, captain. I will take a small patrol and find you your men. I will talk to them, and I will ask them to come with me and follow the man who orchestrated the battle of Drakemyre. The battle that was won."

"And I am sure you will spread that message with conviction," said Laeb, "but I have been gifted a few hours, and I intend to spend them in the lake, if not just to get away from this humidity."

"By submerging yourself in it?" said Duga. "That still seems the strangest thing to me. What's wrong with a simple wholesome fire to burn away the wet air?"

"You might be the only blue-eyes who hates the water, Duga," said Laeb, with a friendly chuckle. "I'd make sure it doesn't get out."

"I am as I am," said Duga.

"And I wouldn't have it any other way. You and I, Duga."

"You and I, Captain."

Bygones

F ia frowned. How big a stone did you need to crack a man's skull? Not that one — if it was too heavy it would land on her foot, like it had the first time she'd had to protect herself, when that lord, like most men, had wanted more than he was allowed. The box might have been enough, if she still had it, but Jagar had taken it.

"You'll have to do," she hissed, scooping up a smaller lumpy rock just bigger than her fist and lighter than it looked. She rushed back over to the clutch of white trees. For once luck had been on her side. She had decided it best to wear an almost completely white hak before leaping into the tearing sea to escape Jagar's clutches, but now, hiding behind these white trees it all made sense. It was tempting to even consider that there was a pattern to it all, but the thought that this was all a game was about the most unjust thing she could think of.

She wiped the tears from her face and focused — these men would not play games. Astir and Forn's shining personalities were not to be trifled with. Their conversations aboard the Ariathar had been in signs, but it wasn't so different from Tyr's street signs that Fia couldn't see they were awful people with awful stories. Tyr. Oh she wished to never see that place ever again!

Astir's voice grew louder as they walked, the sounds taking on an odd quality amongst all of the trees. There were three of them, which gave her very little hope, but the game might yet bring her some luck. She shifted so the sun was behind her and held the stone high ignoring the pit of hunger in her stomach.

The rock cracked down upon Astir's head, breaking his skull open and spilling his brains. The gore shocked his fellows, but by that time Fia had slammed the rock back into Forn's stomach. The man bent over double and Fia relieved him of his belt knife before he fell to the ground. As quick as a flash the blade disappeared into the third man's chest, and as he bent over, Fia grabbed a handful of Forn's matted hair in her hand and rammed the knife in though his temple to finish him off as well. He collapsed forward to land on his friends never again to—

"What are you about way out here, hiding behind trees?" Astir leaned his axe against a tree and sauntered towards her.

Fia started, then gulped as she was slowly relieved of the black stone by Forn. He nodded at her, smiling as a parent might take away something from a naughty child.

"Surviving," she said, playfully. It wasn't playful. Her voice squeaked like a rusty hinge.

"Daydreaming more like," said the third man. He didn't look clever, but he had the same mean squint that Forn and Astir had. He probably had awful stories too.

"Be fucking quiet, Gorm," snapped Astir. "No one asked you to come along. If I want your opinion I'll fucking ask for it. Understand?" Gorm lowered his eyes immediately. "Any-

226

way. Our mutual friend kept us abreast of the happenings on deck. It was I who had the luck of cleaning up the mess. You did alright though, Fia. To escape from a Banéman is no small feat, let alone with all of your limbs still intact."

Fia's heart sank. "Luck is no friend of mine."

"Ain't that the truth," said Astir. "I reckon those who play games got to accept that they might lose."

This couldn't be how her game ended. Fia had much more to give than dying in a forest in the middle of nowhere, because at present that was the only path she could see in front of her. She knew it. Astir knew it. They all knew it.

"Astir. I survived a Banéman. Twice. I survived a swim in the Middle Sea." She motioned to her ruined hak. "Because I know how to play the game. All spies know how to play the game."

Astir gave a lop-sided frown. "You are a spy. For the Tsiorc?"

"The rebels, yes…" She had to be careful, and give them only enough to make it seem like it was their idea. "They are nearby, Astir. They will try and find me."

"No, they won't. My bet, is that while they might be expecting you, they would be thinking you'd be coming from Makril, not here from two leagues south."

Forn signed quickly at Astir, this time using a different language, but Fia still caught the word: *money.*

Astir nodded. "You see, Fia, we're here to find a mysterious group of strangers, bent on causing harm to the doings of the Bohr. I reckon you're worth a little bit of a detour though, wouldn't you say?" Explosions were going off behind his eyes, as each potential situation led to the next, and in all of which he was decidedly richer than what he was now.

"The Tsiorc might pay a lot to get you back," said Gorm. "But my guess is that the Kin would pay ten times over for the intel that you hold in your pretty head." He rapped on Fia's forehead like she was a door. "A very pretty penny. If the Banémen are after you then Commander Lor would walk through fire to get a hold of you."

Fia shook her head quickly. "No, the rebels—"

"Can wait," said Astir. "Gorm, where are the Kin now?"

"Two days hard ride south. I'm to meet up with them and Jagar near Határ before they reach Tyr."

"Is that so?" said Astir. For the first time the three men seemed completely aligned in their desires.

Panic took hold of Fia. "The Tsiorc… the rebels have much more resource. They have a huge army of archers and soldiers and…and…" She stopped. Gorm wore an expression more suited to wolf than man.

"Go on, girl," he said, smiling so wide he was showing gum. "Tell us, what else do the Tsiorc have?"

Old Enough to Bear, Old Enough to Kill

T he setting sun painted the underside of the high clouds with red, as though they had been dusted with the ruby earth from beneath Kyira's feet. The sparse canopies reached out, silhouetted against the twilight sky. Some stubborn twigs had already begun showing buds, flying in the face of the chill air.

It hadn't been difficult to locate the convoy of traffic streaming out of Makril — the piles of dung alone were enough to signal the direction — but progress was slow. Kyira's thoughts spun, gravitating towards anything that seemed important enough to draw them near, only to slide away again. She had been sleepless for longer than this, but the sheer number of things to process from the past few days had left her exhausted, and without an animal to carry the sick Mother they had carried her between them. It was only after a kind woman had offered her empty cart that Kyira had managed to stretch the aches away with some simple walking.

The occupants of Makril, dirty faced and homeless, walked with her. Some had been lucky enough to leave with carts, others, had only the shoes and clothes they happened to be wearing. There were almost no injured — the fire having killed all it touched. The Sulitarian losses were low because living as groups meant that they had escaped as so; the Makriliaens on the other hand were settlers and home-builders and they had been devastated. Mothers, fathers, daughters, sons, and friends, all gone.

The atmosphere amongst the carts was still not one of separation, but one of togetherness. People comforted one another, brown-skinned Makriliaens sat within the pale arms of Sulitarians and vice versa, like they had always been. The Sulitarian woman who had warned Kyira of the living fire nodded down at her — her face sooty and her red hair tied up in a hasty bun. She smiled and hummed a soft lullaby to Lyla's new-born babe who she cradled in her arms.

Even amongst so much death, there was still much to be thankful for. "Why are they heading for Tyr?" she asked her father.

Iqaluk looked up at her, seemingly he was trapped by his own thoughts too. "There are no more towns this far south. Tyr is the next stop."

Kyira couldn't help but feel anxious at the thought of a city. "What about Dali?"

Iqaluk shook his head. "The road is too long. Makril pays their taxes as any other trade town. They'll be welcomed, and rehomed."

"All of them?" When Iqaluk didn't respond, she changed the subject. "You did well to birth Lyla's babe on your own."

"It was the same as birthing a lamb, or a calf. It is in our nature to protect our own. As Vlada does for you. Wherever he may be."

A pang of guilt filled Kyira's stomach like she'd swallowed

a weight of lead.

"He is more than capable of looking after himself," said Iqaluk. "He is powerful. He will do fine."

"You are right, Aki," She let it out before she could stop herself, and looked up, embarrassed. "Are you thinking on Tri's words?"

"He is an oaf," said Iqaluk. "If there is any good left in this world, he died in that fire."

Kyira gasped. "You cannot say such things! He was an oaf, but also a captain! Like Lyla. The rebels fight for good."

"As long as there are wars, there will always be rebels, Kyira. They are faceless and nameless. What is their symbol? A triangle? A square? Perhaps a smiling face, or a drawing of a dog. None of it matters. War is pointless."

"War is not pointless," said Kyira, doubting the words even as she said them. She kicked a stone. "Not when there is so much at risk. Not just a way of life, but actual lives. Imagine if the Bohr—"

"Imagine if they what? Invaded us? What do you know about them? Perhaps your life will be better under their rule."

Kyira scoffed. "You side with them?"

"Of course not," he said, more softly. "My point is that a rebel's fight is not your fight Kyira. There will always be wars, but the Sami do not involve themselves. We stand above it all, on the highest peaks, in the clouds protecting what is important. You've seen what is happening to our world, Kyira. It tears. It's people are fighting, and now even the Gods are fighting. The petty machinations of people will mean nothing, nothing under the vengeance of a broken world, and that is all we stand to gain. A broken world. The

231

best we can do is stand aside and let those who fight, die."

"So," said Kyira, disgusted. "That is why you are so worried for Hasaan? Because he does not do what you wish him to do. I understand now why he left. He wants something greater."

Her father kept his eyes forward, apparently transfixed on the colourful cart up head. The painted mural showed an young woman with the tail of a fish leaping from a deep blue sea. The Sulitarians certainly had a flair for the creative.

Iqaluk turned to her, and for a heartbeat Kyira thought she had gone too far, but she held her ground and stared back. If he was no longer *Aki* to her, then she was no longer *daughter* to him. "No son of mine could do such a thing."

How could her father be so closed-minded? She had to change tact. "Things are different now. There are other ways of life available to the Sami and Hasaan could do any of them. He is strong like you."

"All the more reason that you should both follow the ways of your people."

"Iqaluk—"

"The Sami are blessed in the arts of finding and being found, all the way back to when the first paths were written by the first of us. The Kartta's hot blood runs through our veins as a torrent, telling us to keep the paths in our hearts. It cannot just be picked up and dropped at a moment's notice, it is life."

Kyira placed a hand on Iqaluk's arm. "I will choose to follow and mind the paths because that is the pattern of my life, but Hasaan—"

"Is what?" snapped Iqaluk. "Different. Special? What Kyira? What makes Hasaan so above the rest of his people that he feels that he can abandon us to fight against his own people, burning them from their homes, and killing their sons and daughters, all in the name of the Bohr?" He stopped and rounded on Kyira, traffic passing either side of them. "No son of mine would ever do such a thing."

"Watch it!"

Two huge oxen bore down on them, the hulking animals throwing their heads from side to side, pulling against their reins and rattling the saddles of their two riders. Kyira pushed Iqaluk out of the way, only to find another cart trundling towards them; before she could think, she had pushed her father completely off the road and onto the grass verge amongst the trees. He reached out and grabbed her, hauling her out of the road and the cart carried on regardless.

When she turned back towards her father, there were tears in his eyes. "I have failed you."

Kyira swallowed. "You have not failed me, nor Hasaan."

Iqaluk shook his head. "I have failed you both. The world is hard, and those who face too many hardships can easily become like those two slavers who attacked you on the Laich. Those who value nothing, who see nothing but what they stand to gain. They were once as us, with parents who loved them, children, running and playing, until one day a poor choice goes unnoticed, which leads to another and another until they become the men you met on the ice. My mistake was allowing the same to happen to Hasaan. I did not protect you well enough."

Kyira pushed her father again, but this time much harder. "You treat me like a child! Yet I am old enough to bear and I am old enough to fight. Those two slavers will never bother me, or any other again, because of me! I killed them, and they deserved that and more. I am no child." She was pacing back and forth in front of him. "And neither is Hasaan. To treat us as such is an insult." Her face felt flushed, but the words were as true as was possible to be. Some part of her wanted to take them back, but it was too late — they were said.

Iqaluk was no longer just her father. He was a man, he was strong, powerful even, but she was Kyira. Nordun. Pathwatcher. A fighter.

"Then I can only offer you one more piece of advice," said Iqaluk. "When this broken world gets hard, and when you are lost, look within. You will discover that your blood is primed to guide you as it did my father, and his." Iqaluk's eyes blazed. "But know this, you and Hasaan are Sami, and will always be Sami. You are both mine. And I will snatch Hasaan out from under the Bohr's noses and march him home if I have to walk all the way to Tyr myself. Do you hear me?" He stalked off, melting back into the traffic and leaving Kyira alone in the grass.

A Shark in the Shallows

The lake sat nestled in the hills above the camp. Thousands of years of rains trapped between the soft peaks — completely unlike anything in Sulitar, where the summits were hard and high. But it was cold and it was wet, which was as close as Laeb would probably get to the sea for a long time.

From up on the hill the symmetry of the army camped below was beautiful. It looked powerful, massive and mobile — a shark in the shallows. The unfortunate truth was that it was becoming more like harmless flotsam, drifting apart and sinking below the waves one piece at a time. The feeling that they could be overrun at any time niggled at the back of Laeb's mind. Sure, the hills provided some level of cover, but they would soon find the muddy grounds of Dali's vales working against them. The bruised sky echoed the disturbances of his mind.

Laeb turned back to the shimmering lake, a hazy oasis of calm and cool protected from the winds. It wasn't the biggest he'd seen, far from it — he could have swam from one bank to the other and back again in less than an hour — but it was still a rare thing to find a lake so high up. The peaks were barely a hundred paces from the surface of the water. He unstrapped his jacket, unhooked his breeches, and all but ran to the bank, slowing on the slate shoreline so not to cut his bare feet to ribbons. The water smelled like freshness itself: clean and rejuvenating. What a way to wash away the cobwebs! Seawater would always be his first choice, but he would never turn down the opportunity of submersing himself in water, whatever the source. He held his foot above the water, relishing the moment, from dry to wet, dusty to clean, scabs to—

"Captain!" The Farram that had brought him the message strolled towards him, splashing through the lake. "It's Glynn. I served you yesterday."

Laeb let out a long sigh. "Yes, I remember. What can I do for you, Farram Glynn."

"Just came up for a dip is all. Took your advice about getting cleaned up." Laeb silently wished he had just sent the Farram back home. The boy stumbled to a stop in front of him. "Are you going in, Captain? The water is wonderfully warm. Hot even! So hot in places I had to get out."

"Hot?"

What Laeb had mistaken for haze was actually steam, sitting on the glassy surface like dry ice. "There has to be a hundred thousand gallons here. What power could heat so much water?" He scanned the opposite bank, and shook his head incredulous. hundreds of dead fish floated shimmering upon the surface. Cooked alive. "What—"

The land flashed around them. Laeb waited for thunder, but instead there was another flash, then another, crackling above them through the thick cloud.

"We should go before—"

Another flash struck down beyond the hill's summit, but

this time it held, connecting the land and sky as a vein of pure light. The ground vibrated, the grass, the stones, the very air thrummed with invisible fire, sending pulses over Laeb's skin. It flickered, then faded into nothingness.

"Do you feel that?" breathed Glynn.

"Yes. I feel it." Laeb pulled on his breeks. "Come, let's go see it." He made for the hill's summit with Glynn in tow, towards where the lightning had struck. He had to know what could be so powerful as to heat an entire lake. Soon they were standing upon the peak looking down at the lake.

The sky flashed again, and a fork of lightning struck the surface, so bright that the lakebed, the boulders, the shape of the valley were all visible beneath the green water. The water began boiling like soup in a billy.

The air around Laeb shimmered, and pressure pushed against him from all sides, threatening to pop his eyes from their sockets. He fought the urge to shut his eyes. He had to know! He had to see what could produce such power. A vortex of cloud spun above them, gyrating around the frozen lightning bolt. Blue forks flickered over the grassy hillsides, reflected on the surface of the swirling lake, now a whirlpool with an eye at its centre.

An orb of solid glass that Laeb couldn't focus on rose up from the depths of the lakebed in the centre of the maelstrom, its influence pulling the surface of the lake into a shining mountain of water until it was higher than the surrounding hilltops.

"We have to leave!" shouted Glynn.

"No," roared Laeb. "I have to know!"

The surface of the water continued to stretch upwards, its peak drawn into the clouds behind the orb like an anchor on a chain, until with an immense burst of pressure, the entire lake lifted up from the ground to surround the orb like a great watery moon, rotating before them. Waves broke around it, crashing together and leaving the great ball of water entirely. Clumps of ground bigger than an army ripped clear from the hilltops, sailing upwards to vanish into the tempest. Slate from what remained of the shore, flew through the air like cannon fire, so fast it would have cut them both to pieces had they stayed down there. The lightning bolt and orb merged, their combined light as intense as the sun, casting long shadows over the exposed lakebed.

Then silence.

An eerie equilibrium settled upon the world — a second that lasted for a thousand ages as the immense powers were held in perfect balance.

"Captain?" Glynn's words distorted in the air, echoing around them, becoming louder and louder, echoing around the valley. "Captain, CAPTAIN, CAAAAPPPPP…" The equilibrium ended as the sound hit the clouds, the glowing orb vanished into an infinite point, and exploded outwards.

"Captain!" roared Glynn, stepping in front of Laeb.

Fire rained down upon the valley, upon the hill, their hill. Laeb dropped to his knees and pried at a flat rock, which graciously gave way. He wrenched the slate from the ground, and wrapped his arms around Glynn, holding the slate as a shield in front of them both. The shockwave struck, the slate shattered and they were thrown from the summit.

The bright world became a mess of tumbling colours. Laeb thrust out his arm, but it smacked painfully against the stony ground. He tried again, twisting his body to slow his descent back down the hill of slippery slate. Glynn's ankle dropped into his outstretched palm. He closed his fingers and held on. The colours separated, becoming objects: grass, dirt, rocks, sky. Their momentum slowed, and they skidded to a stop. Laeb's head was thick, and his mouth scratched and sore. There was salt blood in his mouth. He lifted himself up. He had to know. But it was too late. They were two hundred paces further downhill. The summit of the hill was gone, the orb too, was gone, swallowed by the burgeoning clouds. It had ended.

* * *

Terrified shouts panned left and right, while ghostly apparitions faded in and out of view. Livestock, roaming free added their panicked calls adding to the cacophony of noise. On top of everything, it was snowing!

"Where are we?" shouted Glynn.

"We've come around by the front gates!" said Laeb, his bare feet slipping in the sludge. "We need to get to the officer's quadrant! If we're close to the paddocks we should take the main road in!"

"The main road will be chaos!" roared Glynn. "Come on, I know a better way."

Glynn pulled Laeb along through the pitched tents, keeping to the sides of the paths to avoid the disorientated men that crossed back and forth — the last thing he needed was to be attacked by some panicked soldier.

The clamour grew louder as they approached the central square — the main junction point for the camp. Laeb and Glynn stood at its edge trying to make sense of the chaos

239

mere feet away.

The sound of hooves came from behind, and there wasn't even time to shout. Laeb threw himself into the square and yanked Glynn with him as ox and cart came snorting and barrelling through the swirling mist. Laeb's feet slid and despite his best efforts he fell forward into the mud. The cold began seeping in through his breeches.

"Glynn!"

"Captain?"

"Glynn?" said Laeb, into the mist. "Over here!"

A dark shape materialised in front of him, arms out-stretched. "Captain? I... I can't see you!"

"Over here, Farram!" shouted Laeb. He grasped at the dark shape and pulled him in front. "Glynn! Listen, get yourself to the paddocks. Kavik will need all the help he can get rounding up the animals. We cannot lose our nara! Do you hear me?"

Glynn nodded, then his eyes grew wide. "Captain!" Glynn's hands thrust into Laeb's chest, and suddenly he was airborne again. He stumbled back across the muddy junction, as a cart crashed through the spot where they had been standing.

"Glynn?" shouted Laeb, at a large spinning wheel. "Can you hear me?"

"I'm fine, Captain," shouted Glynn. "You're on the right side! The officer's quadrant is just down the hill. Just keep going!"

* * *

"The Bohr have clearly harnessed the breath of the Forbringr and can unleash it at will!" snapped Kilier.

"For the last time!" roared Firam. "It. Is. Not. A. Weapon!"

Laeb stepped forward in between the sparring men. "Gentlemen. Please, whatever this is, I don't think it was directed at us."

"What proof have you?" said Kilier, stepping up to Laeb.

"And why do you look like you've been trampled by a herd of oxen?" added Firam.

"Because I almost was."

"Captain—" began Kilier.

Laeb held up a finger. "My proof, consul, is that I saw it with my own eyes. I was caught in the middle of it. There was lightning, but no ordinary lightning, magister. I saw what could only be described as the end of days from a peak that now no longer exists. The Farram and I were lucky to leave with all of our pieces intact." Laeb described exactly what he had seen, then walked over to a silver washbowl, and began washing the drying muck from his hands.

"And this Farram," said Kilier, "where is he now? He will attest to this story?"

Laeb laughed. "You don't believe me? I should have known!" He threw the silk towel back into the bowl. "Has your hatred for my people really poisoned your outlook so that even when the evidence is surrounding you, you deny the truth, purely because it came from a *blue-eyes*?"

A wry smile grew on Kilier's narrow mouth, highlighting his triangular chin. Laeb replayed his words. Had he just walked into a trap?

"We must mobilise," said Laeb, turning to Firam. "It is time we left Dali."

Firam sighed. "I'll take it to the commander." He unhooked

his skin coat from the antlers near the flaps, pulled it on, and disappeared out into the mist.

"Where can this Farram be found?" asked Kilier. "I'd like to just confirm some of the details of your story."

"I told him to go to the smithy," said Laeb.

"The smithy?" Kilier made a noise in his throat. "Captain."

"Consul."

"You're no fond of the man," said Kavik, after the tent flaps had fallen closed.

Laeb sighed. "An understatement, Kavik."

"Aye. Well. What are we to do then?"

"Have you seen any other officers?"

"They'll be hiding if they have any tearing sense about them, until this mist lifts." Kavik's words lingered between them. "What weapon have the Bohr now? Is this the work of their Banémen?

"It's no weapon, Kavik, it's something else, something much more dangerous."

Kavik's hand grasped him warmly on the shoulder. "Friend, you need not justify it to me. I believe you."

Laeb tapped Kavik's hand. "It was… unbelievable. I've never seen such raw power, not even in Taraunteen, where the hurricanes of this world are born. Whatever it was, it felt unnatural. It had a core, which is where I think its power was wrought, but it must have been immense to cause this aftermath." He held the tent flaps high up for Kavik to duck through, and they both stepped out into the mist.

Kavik looked troubled as he spoke. "I never thought I would ever live through the sky falling, captain."

"And I never thought I would ever describe such a thing as the sky falling as an aftermath. Something brews, Kavik.

Something we have yet to see."

"Then we better get about it!" The big man cricked his neck. "Oh, and I heard that you was needing me."

Laeb gave Kavik's chest a thump. "It can wait, friend. Come, we have much to do."

A Day of Court

The court chairs were not hard, but angled just so as to make the sitter uncomfortable after a few minutes. Rathe knew it was his human side that ached for the comfort of a hay cushion, but today he was able to ignore it. The wound on his forehead, throbbing with the memory of the meeting with the Bohr king was as big a distraction as he could possibly have asked for.

Incense tickled at his nasal passages, filling the justice rooms with a pleasant blue haze. It added an ethereal ambience that helped mystify proceedings, which made it harder for those lucky enough to get in to quantify their experience. The rooms were not as grand as the Domst Hall, but they were adequate for dealing with general public grievances, or at least the ones that had been deemed worthy of the Guardian's ear. There were a few rows of councillors in, which wasn't unusual — anything to justify a day's work. He nodded to the closest one, a dark-haired Kemen man named Dia'slar, and the man nodded back. He at least had some Bohrblood in him although he had only had the post for barely a cycle. Still, he would get the measure of him today.

The Pan Guard sitting on Rathe's left shifted noisily. "Are

these the only seats available, Guardian Rathe? I would ask for a Bohr's throne if I thought one would appear."

"The room not to your liking?"

"No, Guardian Rathe. These chairs are unsuitable for a Bohr as wide as me."

"Perhaps you should work on that then," said Rathe, deadpan. "I like the chairs. Don't you, Seb?"

Seb jerked around, and his glasses fell down his face. "Umm sorry what was that?"

"The chairs, Seb."

"Ah yes. Horrible, absolutely horrible. The ground would be comfier."

Rathe screwed his eyes shut, and took a deep breath.

The Pan shuffled in his seats. "So, what do you make of my suggestion, Guardian Rathe?"

"This is hardly the place for it. We are not here to discuss the movements of the lord's army. We are here to…"

"Yes," snarled the Pan, "of course. You are here to look after the human populace."

Populace? Where did he learn that word? "I was planning on actioning your suggestion anyway. Dia'slar, will you, as per the Pan Guard's *request*, make immediate arrangements for General Nevis to recall the lord's army to Tyr."

Dia'slar frowned. "Um…"

"Oh, come now," said Rathe. "The Justice rooms are but a medium to the grievances of this fine city." He glanced at the Pan. "Of the populace. And as one of its protectors you have more a right than many. Spit it out."

Dia'slar's deep brow furrowed some more. "Well, sir. It seems to me that bringing the army back to Tyr might… provoke the very war we are trying to avoid."

"A typical human response," growled the Pan, standing up from his chair and pacing back and forth in front of them. "Is fear all you know? After your failures at Drakemyre we find ourselves in need of new legions. We need to replenish our forces before pushing north. The army is of no use south of the city."

"Indeed," said Rathe.

Dia'slar consulted a large spread map of Tyr, easily identifiable by its winding streets and, of course, the Way Channel splitting Terävä and Vasen. "But where would they settle?"

"I don't care about the details!" growled the Pan, kicking the panelling on the far wall. The echo bounced around the circular room.

It was a rookie mistake, addressing the Pan. Rathe lowered his voice. "Have General Nevis settle the army outside Terävä's gates."

Seb looked up from his notebooks and whispered, "Why is he here?"

"Adjudication," said Rathe. "Apparently, the Bohr king has no trust in her new Guardian." He cleared his throat then clapped his hands to the guard by the door. "Let them in."

Seb lowered his voice to a croaking whisper. "I need to talk to you after this. Somewhere quiet."

"Fine." Rathe sighed as a Kemen fellow sauntered in through the open doors. He was six foot, with a face as smooth as any woman. He radiated a confidence of his own, but still jumped when Seb slammed the census tome onto the bench.

"Name, please?" barked Dia'slar, with feigned confidence.

The man stepped forward then spoke in a voice too high for his barrel chest. "Erdal."

246

Dia'slar folded the maps with great trouble, drawing murmurs from the councillors behind. "Your, um, request... has been advanced to the desk of the justice rooms at the behest of the community council, by um..." He flipped through a leather book, and ran a finger down a list of names. "Councillor Allander of the Fiskar. Alright, Erdal, you have precisely one minute to present." He turned the sand timer and set it down on a table now overflowing with loose papers.

Erdal cleared his throat. "I am in receipt of an offer to send my three daughters to learn under the wing of a Professor Arnus in the University of Vasen."

"Three daughters?" said Rathe. "You realise that it's illegal for Terävaen humans to have more than one child?"

"They were triplets," said Erdal.

"I see," said Rathe. "That is unlucky. I assume one of your family had to aid in the cost for this mishap?"

"Yes, Guardian," said Erdal. "My brother."

"Alright," said Rathe. "So, you wish to send your daughters to learn from this Professor, and I assume your blood status doesn't cover the cost?"

"No, Guardian," said Erdal. "I can afford only one."

"Well, let's see what we can do. Dia'slar, would they take him in the patrols?"

"He has the build," said the councillor. "And there is definitely space. Our patrol squadrons are very low. Maybe he would do better in officer training."

"I would never hold intelligence against a man, Dia'slar."

"Erdal," began Rathe. "It appears this office is able to provide assistance with your daughters."

Erdal visibly loosened. "Thank you, Guardian!"

247

Rathe took the scroll Dia'slar was offering him and traced the spidery lettering. "According to this census, you are of Kemen descent?"

Erdal nodded, "On my grandmother's side."

"It says here, you work as a shepherd. Is that accurate?"

"That's right," said Erdal. "Underpaid and undervalued mind you."

"Aren't we all," chuckled Rathe. The Pan paced back and forth in front of the two men looking anxious about something. Rathe eyed him, then returned to the scroll. "And your spouse, she died eleven cycles ago?"

"Yes," said Erdal. "I have raised my daughters myself; I am all they have. But they are strong and independent. True leaders. Eris, my eldest, wishes to be a councillor one day."

"Really," said Rathe. "Well, perhaps Dia'slar here could accommodate her. Councillor?"

Dia'slar frowned again, Rathe was beginning to wonder if the man had any other expression. It made him hard to read. "Yes. I'd be delighted. Eris?"

Erdal nodded. "That's her."

Dia'slar scratched something into his book finishing with a full stop that surely must have torn through the parchment. "Alright, Erdal," he said. "If you'd just like to approach the bench and make your mark, here... and here. This first one represents the change to your Blood Status, and the loan from Office. Your mark here ensures that your daughters will each receive one third of that loan, the payment from which will be fulfilled by you on their behalf."

Erdal signed both spots and handed back the pen. "Will I ever see them again?"

Rathe frowned. "Of course, Erdal. We are not here

to dismantle your life! We are here to ensure fairness under doctrine." He placed a hand on the top of the tome. "Which in this case will see you working in the Guard under General…" Rathe gestured to Dia'slar. "General…"

Dia'slar's finger moved down the list of names and stopped. "Oh, um. General Nevis?"

"Nevis, yes. A dragon of a man if ever I met one. He'll keep you straight, providing you give all you have to the service."

Erdal looked hopeful, optimistic even. "I am so very grateful! My daughters will be very happy with the Guardian's decision. I thank you. And I shall send Eris along to—"

The noise of the Pan's scimitar unsheathing silenced the room. The Bohr stepped towards the bench, tapping the curved sword against his huge palm. "Erdal. You are property of the state, your blood belongs to the Bohr and is ours to do with what we choose. Guard, offer him your sword."

"You can't," said Rathe, standing up. "Not here."

The Pan's snout wrinkled into a vicious snarl. "I can. The Guardian's power may go no higher for humans, but to the Bohr you are an underling. Guard, give your sword to the human."

The guard's human eyes flicked towards Rathe, then he unsheathed his shortsword and thrust it into Erdal's hand. Erdal stared down at it. It looked strange on him.

The Pan let fly a swipe of his long blade. The tip found Erdal's chest, leaving a line of blood visible through his white shirt. The rows of councillors shuffled in their seats as the Pan walked back and forth behind the gate, like a bull waiting for a command to charge.

"What is he doing?" whispered Seb.

Rathe shook his head. "Exercising his *rights*," whispered Rathe. "Say no more."

Erdal paced back and forth doing his best to stay opposite the Bohr towering over him.

Then it came.

Erdal tripped over his own feet, stumbling enough to shorten the gap between the two. The Pan's scimitar met his short sword and slid up it, making a sound that Rathe had heard many times before. The heavy ortaxe followed the line of Erdal's sword, ran off the end, and sliced the top of Erdal's head off from the bridge of his nose up. Erdal stood rigid for a second, his remaining eye twitching, before he collapsed to the floor.

Apparently satisfied, the Pan walked up towards the upper exit, leaving a line of pale councillors cowering in his wake. The upper doors opened and slammed shut, the sound echoing around the room.

"Dia'slar," snapped Rathe. The councillor turned towards him. He looked amused.

"Guardian."

"Inform the rest that we're done for the day. And might I trouble you to find someone to clean up this mess?"

"Guardian," said Seb.

"What!" roared Rathe. He breathed long and hard then began anew. "What is it Sebreth."

Seb waited for the last of the councillors to rush out before sliding a small sheet of paper over the bench towards Rathe. "It's from the Banéman."

"You know, Seb, you can call him Jagar."

Seb quailed as though the words did him physical harm. "I'd rather not if it's all the same." He nodded to the parchment. "There's been an incident in Makril."

"The fishing town," said Rathe. "In the north. What of it?"

"It's gone, Guardian. Burned. But the fire—"

"And they were always so prompt with their taxes."

"Yes. Um. The fire…"

"Spit it out!" Seb cowered as he opened another parchment that had been clutched in his sweaty fist. "Give it here." Rathe examined the drawing. "Is this to scale?"

"According to reports. One of Lor's men also witnessed it. Jagar has ordered him to Tyr. He should arrive sometime tomorrow."

"Not Gorm?"

"Yes, sir."

"I hate that idiot." Rathe glanced back down at the image. It was a beautifully drawn view of Makril, showing the distinctive homes and smokies of the residents, all dwarfed by the dark scribble of rising flame that struck up from the paper's centre all the way to the heavily shaded clouds at the top. Thick lines of lightning had been scratched along the fiery column. "Well, Jagar can certainly draw, but tell me, what exactly am I looking at here?"

"There were once tales of something similar in the south, but reports are sketchy. A fishman saw shimmering air above the water, shortly before a huge pillar of seawater reached up from the sea to a stormy sky." Seb's fingers rubbed up and down the drawing as he spoke, smearing it. "When the lightning did finally strike the sea, the clouds fell to earth, smothering Fairsky in mist for days."

"So, what is it?"

"You know how the old stories go," began Seb. "When the Forbringrs of old fought each other in the Beginning, they

251

destroyed and created worlds around them. Baeivi fought the Stallo—"

Rathe stormed out of the chambers and Seb hurried along beside him.

"This is relevant, I promise. As one Stallo died another would replace it, and their great battles distorted the cosmos, stretching all things: the earth, the stars, the moons above, until finally reality began to thin and tear like an old blanket. Holes appeared." He was gesticulating wildly. "Well, I think there is some truth to those old myths. There were holes rent by the Gods, holes, between *realities*. Holes that may allow things to travel from one reality to another."

Rathe scoffed. "More than one reality, Seb? I accept that your scientific nature breeds curiosity of all things, but I do not have the time to humour—"

"There are theories," began Seb, "particularly by Hallam and his research with precious metals, that suggest infinite realities, in infinite variety, and indeed when one considers that one reality can exist, the door opens, so to speak, to many more. My interpretation of those theories is that whenever a reality reaches the end of its life, it disintegrates, just like that old blanket, and as it tears it pulls on other realities around it. The point is that these dying realities pass on their last remaining energy into the realities surrounding it. Godblood, moving between worlds. Just like the old myths would suggest. Mother Baeivi and the Stallo literally tearing reality apart like a threadbare blanket in order to create the cosmos."

"Seb," said Rathe, his footsteps ringing against the tiles. "You are mistaken. You told me once that all energy was finite. That it couldn't be created or destroyed. How then does a reality *pass on* its energies?"

"Correct, Guardian. Energy is finite, but the death of a reality doesn't seem to break those laws because each reality has its own finite energy resource." He raised his hand to his chest like a depth marker. "Each reality's laws stay intact until their death upon which their energy, their matter, leaks out into the adjacent worlds. To think as well that while our reality has this level another reality may have energy of this level! Or of a different consistency, or at a different frequency, or—

Rathe raised his own hand to quiet the excited engineer. "I'm afraid to ask. What has this to do with the fire in Makril?"

"Everything, Guardian, everything," panted Seb. "The effects of a tear opening would be catastrophic. The topological stresses alone could render the immediate area unliveable. We're talking macro, Guardian. Multiple, if not hundreds of pressure systems fighting for control of our ecosystem. Clouds that fall from the sky, Explosions with enough energy to level a city! It would be the fight to end all fights, a war of the Forbringrs." He held out a hand and pulled Rathe to a stop, and stepped so close Rathe could smell the smears of oil on his ill-fitting jacket. "Some of the residents in the Fairsky reported seeing a translucent sphere within the water. A hole."

"A hole? You just said it was spherical."

"Yes, in three dimensions a hole might appear as a sphere, but it would be a tear in reality. *If* such a thing existed, which I believe it does, Guardian."

Rathe glanced back and forth behind them to make sure they were truly alone. "So, wherever a hole exists," he whispered, "the weather will be severely affected?"

"It all adds up."

"The water at Fairsky…"

"The fire spiral at Makril," added Seb. "Guardian, Hallam's work on chaos theory states that for every occurrence of an event, any event, there will be many more unobserved. It is my belief that it is now only a matter of time before we see one here. And if there were to be a hole that somehow opened near Tyr, it would bring with it all the anger and malice of the Forbringrs. The city would fall and there is nothing we could do to stop it."

Rathe snapped. "Nothing? You underestimate the power of this city, Seb. Not even a Stallo itself could penetrate these walls. We are Keepers of the Way." All at once a thought occurred to Rathe like a candle flickering into life on a dark night. "Do you think a person could travel through one of these holes?"

"Of course," began Seb, "It's feasible to imagine people could travel through these holes, they are matter as much as the stars, the earth, the sea…" A look of understanding fell upon Seb's face. "You wish to go through one?"

"Think of it as a plan B." Rathe let go of Seb's shoulders and dusted them off. "Seb. Look for more news of strange weather, would you? Let me know immediately if you find it."

Twine

Kyira's group sat together with a small circle of refugees around a new fire. The space was barely thirty paces from the road and had a clear way in and out so they could get ahead of the main glut of traffic, that was if they managed to leave before dawn.

Kyira squatted by the Mother's head. Her breathing was shallow, her expression tight with pain. "Quiet now. Save your breaths and rest."

"She can't hear you," said the Sulitarian woman who had saved Kyira from the fire. The babe still sat nestled quietly in her arms wrapped in a bundle of charred rags. "There's no helping her."

Kyira looked up. "Why not?"

The woman flashed a wise smile. "It's alright, you don't need to whisper. The babe won't awaken tonight. She's had enough ox milk to feed a village." She nodded over to two oxen on the other side of the camp.

Kyira recognised the two men and the animals as the ones that had almost run her down. "You think Lyla will die?" said Kyira, still whispering.

"I didn't say that. I said there's no helping her." The woman unravelled a length of twine from beneath her leather skirts.

"The fates own her now, it is not for us to say or not say whether she will survive. I am still hopeful, of course. My sister, she, how do you Ringlanders say it, *met the earth* in much the same way. The child lived, though, thank the fates." She measured a few arm lengths of twine and looped a ballknot so that each strand hung from it, then anchored the ball between her muddy toes and began plaiting the lengths together.

Kyira frowned. "I do not believe in fates. What would happen to the world if we all left our decisions to the fates. Nothing would get done."

The woman paused, looking at Kyira as if she were able to see right inside her. "You are correct, in a way. But also you are wrong. The fates may not seem to care for the little things, but it is those little things that decide the futures of us all." She resumed plaiting, and the motion created a gentle rocking.

If the fates were real, then they had a lot to answer for. "You are good at that," she said, changing the subject.

"I should be, I have been doing it since I was but a quarter of your age, Kyira."

The babe let out a long, sweet sigh.

"What happened to the babe — your sister's babe?"

"He might have become mine had I not six of my own, so he was mostly cared for by the town." She smiled again. "We call those children without parents the Avere. The whole town cares for them, feeds them, clothes them. Sometimes they live in this house, sometimes that house. They usually grow up fat." The corners of her mouth creased, and Kyira felt herself smiling along with her.

"You children, were they in Makril? Did they…"

256

The woman frowned. "Die? Oh no. They left home many moons ago to follow their own ways. Long before I settled here in Nord." The woman smiled at Kyira's frown. "I was young when I had them."

"I saw a boy with you on the cart."

The woman shrugged, but didn't look away from the twine. "Gurt. He needed someone. We all need someone. Even if they only appear in our lives for a brief moment, we still need them. They appear, they impart, and they leave. It is the way." She held out the coiled length of twine. "You had better take this, child. There is a distinct lack of cooking smells upon the air, and a forest full of rabbits awaiting you."

* * *

Of rabbits, there were none. In fact, for all of the trees there seemed to be only finches and sunwings, flittering around in the dusk before the bats came out to take full advantage of the moths already descending from the empty canopies.

Fires blinked through the trees as figures busied themselves with supper, but Kyira stuck to the darker areas. She was not afraid of whatever may be lurking in the dark; indeed, whatever was out here rustling through the dry grasses should be more afraid of her, if there was anything to be had at all. The twilight land stayed flat, until the sparse white-barked trees began to give way to taller, more dense needlepines.

She wound the twine back and forth over her fingers, tying and untying it. Everything was easier when you were by yourself, away from the incessant crying of the babe. Her thoughts turned to Lyla, squirming by the fire, her skin grey and dank...Who was she? And where were her companions? They could not have just vanished. She doubted the Bryn the Wolf would leave Lyla. Nor even Tri, the Bear. Something had happened to them, which was altogether a terrifying thought.

The chill evening air should have cleansed her, but everything felt wrong. It was all moving so slow! On top of it all, her father's single-mindedness in finding Hasaan was blinding him to everything else. There was so much more happening. The fire, these refugees, the Mother. Kyira wished she knew whether this was normal. It couldn't be. People were good. They didn't set out to hurt or fight one another, and yet she was being drawn deeper and deeper into a world that was not hers. This was the farthest she had walked from Nord's shadow.

"Shiach!" She pulled her knife and threw it hard, and it thwacked into the thick powdery bark of a nearby needlepine. Sighing she pulled it from the wood, and the bark crumbled away. It looked like it would make good tinder, she was always on the lookout for...

She froze.

Dog.

She could smell it.

Closing her eyes she listened, but there was no sound. She may have thrown the blade in frustration, but it had barely made a noise when it hit the tree.

She sniffed again. It was coming from downwind. The trees were shaped for clearings, so there were likely more than one. The tree she had taken the bark from had scratch marks all up it, and fur. How could she have missed that? She ducked down and began moving with the soft gusts of wind. At second glance the trees were not as healthy as she had thought. There were too many lying broken heaped upon each other like a fallen fire stack. A new smell. Fresh. She bent down to a steaming pile of dung at her feet. There, in the clearing.

Kyira moved silently over the bracken to where the two dogs lay sleeping, curled up together on a bed of brown leaves and needles. They were young and skinny, but they had enough meat between them to feed her, Aki and the Mother.

There was a rustle from behind and Kyira spun, ready to plunge her blade into the dog that had snuck up on her. A man stood there. A man she had seen before.

"Hello," he croaked.

Kyira gritted her teeth and padded backwards until she was level with him. She grabbed the old man by the collar, and dragged him away from the clearing. "I am trying to hunt!" she said, masking her surprise that he had managed to sneak up on her.

"Hunting? Then I can help!" He raised his eyebrows at Kyira's hard stare. "I am Jaem! You have not heard of me?"

"No," she hissed, "I have not."

The man beamed. "Well, I am Jaem, and I sell the finest wares in all of Rengas. I remember you from the commune. You tried to break into my room."

"I did no such thing," replied Kyira. "I was looking for someone. The previous occupants."

His eyes screwed up revealing deep smile lines. "I am sure they will turn up somewhere, my dear. If they were lucky enough to escape the flames, of course. Did you see the fire? Those people. Those flames. They were—"

"Be quiet. And yes I saw them." She could still see the shapes of the bodies as though they were burned into grass. "I am glad, at least that you made it out."

He beamed. "Yes, yes. But alas, I am lost. Are you camped nearby? Are you with people?" He looked around hopefully. "I have only my bag here to my name. I need help from people like you."

"Jaem?"

"Yes?"

Kyira's irritation reached a fine point. "Jaem. I. Am. Hunting."

"Yes, yes. You're right. First things first." There was suddenly a sharp wooden stake in his hand." He held it out. "This will be much more useful than a little twine snare, my dear."

Kyira nodded despite herself. There was something wholly unlikeable about this man, but she could not place it. "You must stay downwind."

"Downwind. Of course, of course."

"Come then, Jaem. There are two dogs lying asleep in the clearing. I shall take the big one. You circle around and create a distraction, but wait for me."

Jaem nodded. "Yes, of course."

They split up, and Kyira crept around the right of the clearing, carefully avoiding the mounds of dry bark and debris littering the base of each trunk. She stopped and waited behind a prickly bush and Jaem did the same on the opposite side.

The closest dog scratched sleepily at a bald patch on its neck, and even from here Kyira could see the swarming skinticks. They would need to fire the skins if they intended to eat these animals. She glanced down and frowned as the scent of more dung wafted by her. There was much more here than these two pups could be responsible for.

She called the greyfinch — a warning — but it was too late. Jaem stepped out from his hiding place, brandishing the stake like he had with the seete bottle back at the commune. Kyira tightened her grip on the knife and stepped into the clearing herself. The dog licked its mouth, ready to yawn; all dogs were the same when their bellies were full.

The pup opened its eyes, but she was already diving towards it. She landed on top of it, and rammed her knife in under the jaw and up into its skull. The other pup managed a single bark before Jaem's weight bore it down from above. He stepped up from the dogs broken body, the sharpened stake dripping blood onto the dead animal's grey fur.

"You are a fool!" snapped Kyira. "Do you not know a greyfinch means wait!"

Jaem shrugged and picked up his dog by its back legs, then held it out towards her, grinning stupidly. A white mass of fur slammed into his side, knocking him back. He threw it off, but the dog recovered quickly and reared back, snarling and snapping between them. Jaem strode towards the animal, waving the stake mockingly, but a growl sounded from somewhere behind, then another, and another, and suddenly the fool man was no longer smiling.

It wasn't a clearing. It was a den.

Dark shapes moved on all sides, stalking between the needlepines. The white dog jumped, and Jaem sidestepped out of the way, stabbing at its belly as it flew by. It landed at Kyira's feet with a squelch. Another jumped out of the darkness, but this time Jaem only caught the leg. The dog limped away into the underbrush, and another replaced it immediately. The forest was alive with noise and movement.

Jaem launched forward, kicking one savagely in the face, and stabbing furiously at the other. Kyira spun around as one leapt at her, and the animal died upon her knife, its bared teeth still snapping at the air between them. It fell awkwardly off her taking her knife with it. Another two dogs jumped into the clearing — there was no pretence now, and each one attacked immediately, biting and snapping. Kyira threw herself left, barely managing to keep away from slavering jaws, stumbling from one space to the next as the bodies piled up around them.

Jaem twisted, dancing between them and bearing down upon them ferociously, stabbing, punching and kicking.

Kyira lunged towards another, stabbing until her fist met fur, fresh warm blood running down her forearm.

Jaem, having no animals left to fight, had taken to throwing the corpses out to land in amongst their circling companions, roaring like a taegr. Two dogs burst out of the trees biting at every swing of his weapon, and then a third, surrounding him. Kyira slipped in through a gap and placed her back against his so that they faced the snarling animals together.

Their fetid, smoking breath pressed them in against each other with each snarl and bark. Jaem locked an arm around hers, and they were one, spinning on the spot to meet each animal as it leapt towards them. A patchy brown thing with a diseased eye took Kyira's moccasin, and her balance faltered. She kicked out, but its feet stayed firmly planted, teeth locked around her foot. Jaem dragged her and the dog around and took over, stabbing the bloody, wooden stake through the hound's remaining eye, leaving it to a yelping retreat. Kyira let go of Jaem and jumped into the spot ready to meet the final two, but he just moved out of their way, almost casually stepping aside, stabbing with incredible accuracy and power, until both dogs were full of holes.

Jaem jerked back towards her, and Kyira flinched at those fierce, inhuman eyes set upon his blood-soaked face. She would be next, poked full of holes and left to rot amongst the stinking corpses of these dogs.

He flashed her a bright smile. "Well then. It looks like we won't be going hungry after all!"

Fever

Kyira stepped into the firelight and dropped two dogs at Iqaluk's feet. "What are they doing?"

"Who?"

"There." Kyira nodded towards the oxen owners.

"Lyla took a turn while you were away, and they decided they could both help."

"They were watching? Waiting until I left?"

"She was screaming, Kyira. Most of the townspeople came to see. You didn't hear?"

"I was busy."

Iqaluk slapped the leg of the dog closest to him and shook his head. "They look a bit old. We might have to stew them. They have skinticks too. We will have to fire the skins."

One of the two oxen owners turned, revealing Lyla's babe nestled comfortably in his thickly muscled arms.

"He is Makriliaen?"

"Yes. He is Tor, I think. Are you going to tell me about this man? He is no townsperson. A drunk, if ever I saw one."

Jaem was talking to the Sulitarian woman, and she seemed to like him. Perhaps she wasn't so wise after all. "He claims to be a peddler," said Kyira, "but don't let him fool you. He is savage."

"Savage?"

"That is what I said." Her stomach gurgled. "There are another ten of these in a clearing north from here."

"Ten?"

"The pack was easily fifty strong, Iqaluk."

"Well," he said, standing up. "There's no use letting them go to waste. We'll hand them out to some of the families."

Kyira grabbed the closest dog and, starting at a puncture wound on the neck, tore the skin and yanked it down past the legs. Her nails dug into the bloody folds between and soon it had been completely skinned. She ripped off a slim chunk of fat and swallowed it without chewing, then rubbed her hands with a little dirt, and grabbed the next one. It wasn't long before the chill air was warm with the smell of roasting meat. Iqaluk could stew his all he wanted, but she wanted to tear these things to pieces. Just like they had almost done to her.

The oxen owners danced silently around with each other, each taking turns with the babe, while the other tried to keep the Mother comfortable: soaking the rag, dabbing her forehead and stroking her hair. As darkness drew in, the firelight began to fill up at the promise of a hot meal, but it wasn't until Jaem appeared that Kyira got up to leave. The dry bones of her supper went back into the flames and she turned to find a spot to lie down.

"The blue-eyes suggested I talk to you. Your friend is very sick."

Kyira stopped at Tor's vast bulk. "She is no friend of mine."

The man's bushy eyebrows drew together. "I don't care who she is to you, but she suggested you were charged with Lyla's care." He paused, but Kyira didn't respond. This man had no claim to her loyalties. "Alright then," he said, continuing. "The cold is in Lyla's bones, and if that doesn't kill her, the blood fever absolutely will. She has at best, a day and night before she dines with her ancestors." He turned to walk away.

"And what care can I offer her exactly?"

Tor spoke over his shoulder. "You do not care if she lives or dies?"

"My obligations to Lyla are none of your concern."

Tor rounded on her. "No, they're not. But the life of this little one hangs in the balance." He shook his head. "Kyira, understand, I do not care about the past, only for the future of this child and her mother. If you do not care I shall leave you be."

Kyira opened her mouth to rebuke the fool man, only to be cut off by Jaem, appearing out of nowhere. "You are fooling no one, Sami. Your father just told me of your debts to this woman and by the sounds of it, you owe her much. Much more than you could ever repay."

"Iqaluk would never speak of such a thing. Not to you."

Jaem flashed a smile. "I find I have the sort of face people like to open up to." He held up a finger. "But worry not, I actually came over here to help. You are worried about the mother's fever? Why not burn it out of her?"

Kyira suppressed the urge to slap the man. "What do you mean?"

"These bodies are fickle," shrugged Jaem. "They draw in dangers as much as they draw in the good things of this world. However, often the fire within can burn away badness when it comes. I've seen it done many times and in many towns. In fact. I remember once a witch doctor—"

266

"It can work," said Tor, folding his arms beneath his barrel chest. "I've seen it cure calves. The mother oxen will all gather around a sick calf and lie with it all night. Their combined heat burns the fever from the sick animal. It's something we can try. If you care, that is. I'm sure Lars and I could take care of her."

Guilt filled Kyira's stomach like hot bread. "Just tell me what I need to do."

"We build the father of all fires and stoke it all the night. Or should I say, you stoke it all the night." Tor nodded to the two oxen standing just outside the firelight. "That's Penni on the left and Cimi on the right. We'll set them both behind Lyla and let the fates handle the rest."

Lars stood watching them quietly, the babe rocking gently in his arms. Kyira swallowed. "What about the child, if Lyla dies?"

Tor seemed to grow suddenly uncomfortable. "Lars said he... We could take her."

"What makes you think you could take on a child?" asked Kyira. "She is not your own, and she is certainly no ox."

Jaem nodded. "There is no substitute for a real mother. Or at least so I've heard."

"No?" said Tor. "Lars and I have raised two children from womb to watch. Can you say the same?"

"I can," said Iqaluk, walking over. "And this is one of them," he said, gesturing to Kyira. Her father thrust his hand out, then barked his name, as men often did.

"Tor."

"You and Lars are brothers?" asked Iqaluk.

Tor's teeth flashed a smile under the thick brown bristles of his moustache. "I hope not."

Iqaluk nodded slowly. "I see. Well, do you think you can save Lyla?"

Tor sighed. "She's no ox, but as Jaem says, the same hurts affect us all. It's worth a try."

"Then I shall get the last of the dogs," said Iqaluk.

Tor laid his hand on Iqaluk's shoulder. "I can help, if you need it. Lars can handle the fire, but Penni will need to walk. She gets restless around so many people." He glanced around at the townsfolks milling around them in the dark. "As do I."

"Good. Then let us get going, before the morning arrives and we find ourselves having to walk again."

"Peddler," said Tor. "You have a cart? Or supplies nearby?"

Jaem nodded emphatically. "Oh, yes! Of course, of course."

"Medicine?" asked Tor.

"Yes. Yes, I imagine so."

"Good," said Tor. "Then get yourself ready. You are coming too."

Supplies and Demands

The moonlight shone bright and clear now that most of the small cookfires had been extinguished, and Kyira and Jaem passed more carts and camps than she could count, each with families, children and livestock. Gradually the soft noises of people sleeping were replaced with rustling grass and keening branches.

"They are very alike," said Jaem, breaking the peace.

"Who?"

"Tor and your father," said Jaem, gesturing over his shoulder. "Tilled from the same earth."

Kyira glanced behind at Iqaluk and Tor. They walked in silence with the ox, staring at their feet. "I suspect there are many thick-headed men out there who you could say the same about."

"Indeed," coughed Jaem. "And this Mother. You said her name was…"

"Lyla."

"Lyla?" said Jaem, sounding it out. "Your father mentioned she was with a group?"

Kyira frowned. "Why do you ask?"

"She looks like a Kemen if ever I saw one."

"You know much for a peddler," said Kyira.

Jaem beamed. "We peddlers see much of the world. There," he said, pointing. "Just behind those bushes."

Between the trees was Jaem's cart. It was small, but well kept. Kyira stepped into the clearing and moved to lift the tarp.

"I'll tell you what I have for sale, girl!" snapped Jaem, batting her hand away. His expression shifted so quickly she almost didn't see the malice there.

"Is it all for sale?" asked Kyira.

"Most of it, I'd wager," said Jaem, clearly trying to add lightness to his tone. "You'll just have to wait and see now, won't you?"

"What do you have for the mother and babe…"

"The babe?" asked Jaem.

"It doesn't sleep."

Jaem nodded. "I see. Well, I believe we may have some…" He leant through the back of the cart, disappearing under the tarp. Stacked items fell inside as he rummaged around. "Well, it's actually mostly just…" he reappeared, holding an armful of netting. "Fishing nets."

Kyira took some of the netting. It was made of good quality twine. "We need medicines, not fish nets."

"Yes. Right. There must be some… just give me a moment."

"Where do you keep your medicines?" she said, stepping over to the back of the cart. "Every peddler I have ever met carried some Tomha somewhere."

"Tomha." Jaem muttered something in another language Kyira didn't recognise, not helped by the muffling of thick canvas. "Tomha means 'dose'. They… We use it for… visions?"

Tor and Iqaluk stopped behind them with the ox. "What

have we got then?" said Iqaluk.

Kyira held up the nets. "Fish nets. And apparently this peddler has never heard of Tomha."

Jaem took a nervous step back. "I'm afraid not. It looks as though I'm all out."

"Alright then," said Iqaluk. "Tor, will Penni pull this cart back to camp?"

Jaem rushed forward as Tor jumped down and began attaching the cart-reigns to the ox's yoke. "What? No! You can't just take it!"

"You'll not be needing it," said Iqaluk. "We have a new mother to carry, and we can't rely on the kindness of strangers, not when we have a cart available, and they already have so much to carry."

"Available," laughed Jaem, but in a heartbeat his expression grew dangerous again. "This cart is my livelihood! You will not take it. It's not yours."

"It's not yours either," said Kyira.

Jaem stopped, a hurt look on his face. "What do you mean?"

Kyira jabbed him in the chest with a finger. "This isn't your cart, Jaem. Any merchant worth their wares knows exactly what they have and where. Especially their medicines. I knew there was something off about you. You are a thief. Do you even know what a tuber root is?" She grabbed the straps of Jaem's bag. "Perhaps you have it here, no?"

Jaem snatched back the bag and held it close. "No, I don't know what a tuber root is. Does that makes me a criminal? That makes it acceptable for you to rob me?"

"Rob?" snapped Kyira. "It is not robbing when you take from thieves!" The comment lingered between them like salty mist. "Come back with us if you want, but we're taking the cart."

* * *

The fringes of dawn had begun to lighten the sky when Penni and the cart trundled back into their camp. Mother and babe were asleep, wrapped up tightly in front of a crackling fire. Cimi's huge bulk lay behind her like a wall, that focused the heat down. Lars jumped up and embraced Tor, leaving Kyira and Iqaluk to unpack the cart in silence. Other than the bundle Jaem had removed, there was nothing but a few fish nets and empty boxes.

Kyira watched as Iqaluk checked the axles. "Aki, I..."

"Daughter, I am still not ready to talk to you."

Kyira drew a long breath. She had been expecting it, but it was still hard to hear. "Aki, I am sorry."

"Sorry?" Iqaluk looked surprised. "That is not a word I hear much from you, Kyira. If you asked me when I heard it last, I could not answer."

"I do not like to say it, so enjoy it. I will not say it again."

Iqaluk suppressed a smile. "I shall, daughter. Like I did the last time. You remember the firesnake?"

Kyira covered her mouth. "Oh no! I had forgotten about that." She pictured Hasaan waking up to find his boots aflame and had to suppress a giggle herself.

"I still maintain that he deserved it," whispered Iqaluk.

She found herself smiling with him, until suddenly it slipped from his face. "This world is a hungry animal, with no remorse and no love. It would not hesitate to take my children from me if it could."

272

Kyira wanted to touch him. Help him, but something had changed between them. She took a deep breath. "No animal, person, or world controls my life, but me. My life is my own. I have you to thank for such stoic resolution, and father... Hasaan is just as forthright. Whatever decisions he has made, take solace in the fact that you gave him enough of the world beneath his feet to make them. He is you, as I am you."

Iqaluk's expression was as firm as stone, and Kyira wondered if her words had been wrong. When her father spoke his voice was cracked, like breaking granite.

"It heartens me to hear you say it, dear Kyira, but life will always have the last say." He cleared his throat. "Always."

Tor appeared at Iqaluk's side smiling and content, until the realisation he had interrupted something. "Did you find anything in the cart?"

"Nothing but spiderwebs," replied Iqaluk.

"Well, Lars secured a dose of Tomha from a group of Makriliaens, even if they had to be talked into parting with it. No one else would part with theirs."

"And...?" said Kyira suddenly hopeful. "Did it work?"

"It was very old, so I guess not."

Iqaluk nodded. "We are too far south for the root to grow. I wouldn't give it away either. Especially for some Kemen."

Kyira held up the fish netting. "We could spread this out for her. It might make her more comfortable when we are moving."

"If she lasts the night," said Iqaluk.

Kyira let the nets fall. "Then I will stay with her." Iqaluk didn't even look at her.

Tor tried to cough away the awkwardness. "Then I will mind Lars," he said, nodding to himself. "He's not slept in two days. Cimi will keep Lyla's body warm, but, Kyira you must keep her head cool to fool her body into thinking all is well, or the heat will overcome her and her heart will give out."

The Mother's chest rose and fell, and a new silence blossomed between the three of them. It was the same quiet from after she had cut open Isak's neck, and after the Slaver had vanished beneath the water of the Laich. A quiet upon the world where once there had been emotion and life. It was the sound of death.

Beetle

The new day arrived far slower than it should have, and Kyira felt it keenly as she took in lungfuls of damp air. She moved through each of her positions, stretching and reaching in the hope that it might invigorate her, but she was left tired and out of breath. Even so, her mind was sharper, so when a faint rustle came from behind the fire she knew it was no ox.

"It's just me, I'm afraid," said Jaem, appearing from behind the cart. The ill-fitting rough wool of his breeches and jacket looked crumpled.

"Did you sleep in your clothes?"

"I have nothing but my bag now that you have the cart," said Jaem, sighing.

"Well, seeing as it wasn't yours to begin with, I'd say that balance was restored." All at once Kyira's heart leapt. "You're awake!"

Lyla gave a thin smile as she approached. "Thank you. I'm still very tired. She looked down at the babe in her arms. "And a little bemused."

"I am so very glad you are here still, Lyla. The night was long."

"And I thank you, Kyira, and your father, for saving our

lives."

Kyira swallowed. "I did only what I thought was right…"

Lyla stepped forward, and her red-rimmed eyes locked on to Kyira. "You murdered Isak, my love, my partner, the father of my child. I will never trust you, nor forgive you for it."

Kyira's lip trembled. Would Lyla bear an excuse if she offered it? Iqaluk had once told her to exercise caution in what she said to these people, but now something told her to do the opposite, and be completely honest.

Tears filled her eyes. "I wish I could take it back, Lyla." The words stuck in her throat, as though they were all eager to escape at once. "I had been attacked by two men. Two men that would not have thought twice about killing me. I was lucky to get away from them, but when I discovered my father missing I had to do something, I had to find him and punish them, before they hurt someone else." She took to studying the dried blood beneath her nails. "Not a second passes where I do not think of Isak, and not a second passes where I do not regret my haste. The only option I see before me is to ask you to rebalance." Kyira removed her belt blade and held it out across her palms. "I will accept your justice."

Lyla took the blade and held it by the handle. "Isak had a plan to escape from the slavers the day after you killed him. Perhaps things might have gone another way if we had acted more quickly." She examined the steel of Kyira's belt blade, flicking the edge with her thumb. "The day we first met, Isak told me that he loved me. I laughed at him for being such a boy, and kept him at arm's length. But he persisted, and soon I believed him. He trusted and followed and protected me as I did him. His persistence got us in trouble many times, but it didn't stop me from falling in love with him. When we were taken by the slavers, Isak was searching for cotton plants to make a softer bed for me, and when he returned he found himself outnumbered. He fought them, but they took him down. When you appeared he knew straight away that you were not like them, and he was able to stand up despite his bindings. I imagine that to you, from afar, the scene must have looked very different, but he wanted to *help* you, Kyira, and you repaid him by slitting his throat." Lyla pressed her lips together. "You're right, a debt must be paid." She pointed the knife at Kyira's chest. "And as Isak had his life cut short, you must bear the weight of your actions for the rest of yours." She slipped Kyira's blade beneath a fold in the babe's blanket. "He will live on as a part of you, forever changing all that you are and all that you do, that is at least something, some small relief to me and his daughter. The blade I will keep."

Kyira watched as the Mother turned and walked back towards Lars and the oxen. The debt might have been paid, but the hole in Kyira's heart was as ever present as it had been since the moment after she had taken Isak's life.

* * *

As soon as Lyla had been helped onto the padded cart, they left. Their haste took them near the front of the convoy of townspeople, and while the cart was small, they were able to rotate positions, so all had a chance to sit for a spell. Kyira ran alongside, relishing in the action and movement of her body. She had new energy, and it felt good to be going somewhere.

"Kyira," said Jaem, from the back of the cart. "You've been running all morning, come and sit. I didn't see you sleep a single wink last night."

"I'm fine," said Kyira, between breaths.

"Please, you look tired."

Kyira reluctantly jumped in beside him, letting her feet dangle out the back. "There. Are you happy?"

"You run well," said Jaem, shuffling around. "I mean, that is... Even for a Sami. It's a thing lost on those from the city. Such an act is pointless, when there are carts and horses and oxen to carry you and your things from place to place. Especially one as large and with as many hills as Tyr. There are places in the far east where machines carry people around, if you can believe such a—"

"Are you from Tyr?" asked Kyira.

"No," said Jaem. "I am from Dali, but I once lived in Rengas's greatest city. You have been? I expect not."

"No," said Kyira, looking back to her feet. "And I have no desire to."

"Then why do you travel there?" said Jaem. "This road leads to many towns, but ultimately it ends in Tyr. Surely there are better ways to spend your time than going somewhere you don't wish to go?"

"I search for someone," said Kyira.

"I see," said Jaem. "We all search for something." He smiled at her, and she stared back at him. He cleared his throat. "Well, I hope you find whatever it is you are looking for."

She wished quietly she could jump back down and run, and avoid this man, but the carts were too close together now. The wheels were constantly shifting to avoid the holes and ruts in the road, and their pace was swift. It would do her no good to be dragged under a cart.

"Have you ever fished?" asked Jaem.

She looked at him. Perhaps losing an arm to a spinning cartwheel was preferable after all. "Of course."

"The woman," he said, quietly, "who left me this cart, was waiting for her husband on the outskirts of Makril. That is why I have it, you see. He went searching for his two boys at the docks, and never came back. She went after him, and when I saw the firespiral I knew they must have perished." His pupils seemed to grow in size. "You do believe me, don't you?"

Her stomach twisted. What had she seen in this man? He had all but saved her life, but there was something about him that unnerved her. "Yes. I believe you."

"Good! I'm glad." he leaned in closer. "I overheard you and your father before. He was right about the world being a vicious animal."

"Do you listen in on everyone's conversations?"

Jaem shrugged. "As a peddler of goods, I find it a useful way of knowing who is buying and who is really buying. We all must play the game to some extent." He leant back behind the sleeping Lyla and pulled a cabbage from a canvas bag then prised open a leaf. "Look, see there. That little creature? That little thing?"

In between the two leaves was a beetle, its iridescent shell covered in mottled green spots.

"It is a beetle," said Kyira.

"A greenbeetle," nodded Jaem, "and it has probably lived within these leaves for its entire life. It emerges from a cocoon and spends its short life eating its way through this one cabbage. Do you see?"

Kyira frowned. "See what?"

"Until just now, this greenbeetle had no idea that we existed, nor this cart, the caravan, the road, nor the world beyond it." He let the insect onto his finger. "Worlds within worlds, all behaving as they see fit, acting as though they are Gods. But what of Beaivi you might say, what of her, Jaem. What of the Mother of all creation, standing above us all, pointing and judging and proselytizing. The cunt. Then I would say, no, dear Sami. Beaivi is powerless and weak. A figment of the human mind." He closed his fist around the beetle and crushed it tight. "It is a war. Us versus them."

Kyira stiffened up; he was frightening her. "A war, like the Bohr—"

"No!" snapped Jaem. "Men, women and Bohr alike are but side effects of a larger war, a war to end all wars. The worlds fight for prominence as the trees fight for light, and below the humans fight for their irrelevant freedoms like insects. None of it matters. Do you hear me Kyira? Baeivi and the Stallo fight ever more and realities fall like stacked Chinaes stones around them. None of it matters!"

The cart skidded to a stop, and Kyira pulled her legs up as the Cimi and Penni rushed towards them. The animals came to a halt as Lars and Tor battled with the reins.

A band of men and women wearing uniforms of green and brown, stood in the middle of the road in front of the caravan.

"Eight," whispered Iqaluk, appearing from around the cart, "and four unseen."

Kyira hastily scanned the surrounding trees. "I see five."

"There are six in the trees," murmured Jaem. "Not five."

The front rider heeled his dark horse and came to a stop

in front of the lead cart. "In the name of the commander of the Tsiorc you are hereby ordered to redirect!"

His Makriliaen was heavily accented, and he looked built from stone with shoulders that would have supported the horse should he fancy it, but for Kyira it was his bright blue eyes that stood out most, and her cheeks reddened as his gaze fell briefly upon her. "The road ahead is held by the Tsiorc. You have to turn back." The riders behind him leaned on their mounts, as though relishing the opportunity to rest.

"We cannot turn back!" came a shout from the cart beside them.

"We have nowhere to go!"

"From where have you travelled?" asked the lead rider, peering down the lines.

"Makril!"

"What's going on?"

"Who are you?"

"Get out of the way!"

Townspeople began threading through the gaps between carts and animals as they made their way to the front of the caravan. A wide man with a bushy beard and red face marched past Kyira, a long blade in his hands. He reached the lead rider and stopped in front of his horse. The other riders were suddenly alert again, mounted a few steps behind him, while the bearded man's own followers grew in numbers. Soon the riders were outnumbered by townspeople, standing nose-to-nose in front of them brandishing tools, hammers and even a rake.

The riders behind glanced back and forth between themselves, whereas the lead rider and his horse stayed as motionless as the rock from which he was hewn.

"Let us through," growled the bearded man, pointing his long sword at the horse's chest.

"Get him Eoin!" came a cry from behind. The bearded man held up a fist to silence them.

"I say again," said Eoin. "Let us through."

One of the riders, who had a cowl covering the lower half of his face, trotted to the lead rider's side. After the lead rider nodded, the cowled rider retreated, taking the other riders with him. They all turned as one and dismounted.

The lead rider stepped down himself, and ambled towards Eoin, only stopping when the point of Eoin's sword rested upon his chest. "What happened in Makril?" he asked.

"Fire," said Eoin.

"Fire?" said the lead rider. "The entire town?" The cowled rider leaned forward and whispered again.

"There is no need for this," said the lead rider. "Come with us, and we will help you." With the slightest wave of his hand the cowled man pushed his curved sword back into its sheath.

The point of the Eoin's longsword dropped as well, and the lead rider bowed his head. "Please, the Tsiorc don't have much in the way of supplies, but I'm sure we can rustle up something to see you through to wherever you are going. What do they call you?"

"Eoin. And who might you be, rider?"

"I am Captain Laeb, and we are the Tsiorc."

Lessons

"That's it," said Hasaan. "Just a little lower…" The cadet was a bit younger than he was, but he'd seen her make this shot before. He ignored the loose hairs blowing into his face and watched as the target appeared above her shaking hand. He closed his left eye, making every effort not to touch her or her bow. "That's it. Now, when you're ready, draw the bowstring back with your breath, and release it when you exhale."

Her arm lost its lock, the bowstring broke through the nock and the shaft fell uselessly to her feet.

"No!" said the cadet, "I was so close that time!"

Hasaan's eyes rolled towards Cailaen before he could stop himself.

"It can be hard," said Cailaen, patting her shoulder, "but don't worry, it'll come to you. You can't expect to pick it up as fast as those who have been shooting their whole lives." He gestured to Hasaan, implying he should add something, but Hasaan's mind had gone as blank as the cloudless sky.

"Yes," he said, slowly. "That's right. There are many… other things to do on camp. We need cooks, and suppliers, and runners."

Her eyes became glassy. "I want to shoot!"

Hasaan laid a hand on her shoulder as Cailaen had done, but for some reason it felt awkward. "Just… just keep at it." He smiled and shuffled along behind the narrow shooting line towards the next cadet.

"Really?" said Cailaen, under his breath. "Runners?"

"Lor said that a soldier is only as effective as the runner who delivers his messages."

Cailaen rolled his eyes. "Lor said this, Lor said that. You ever wondered why no one else is getting the attention you seem to be getting? What about the rest of us, stuck teaching children how to shoot straw men?"

Hasaan grinned. "Those who can't do, teach."

Cailaen's lips pressed so tight they all but disappeared. "I can shoot you under the canopies any day of the week!"

Hasaan cleared his throat. "And who do we have here, Team Cadet Cailaen?"

The young cadet stood proudly, looking confident.

"Fudil," said Cailaen, through his teeth, "show the Squad Leader what we've been working on."

The cadet brought the bowstring up effortlessly and began humming quietly. He held the string firmly and released it smoothly. The arrow left true, barely wobbling, and thwacked into the stomach of the mannequin standing thirty paces down the line.

"Deep," said Hasaan.

"And well placed," said Cailaen.

"Well done," said Hasaan, "but what about the humming?"

The young cadet scratched at the light growth on his chin. "Sorry, Squad Leader. It's the only way I can do it without losing concentration."

"A little humming never hurt anyone yet," said Hasaan,

patting the Cadet's back. "I'd say we've found our dark horse." Hasaan glanced over at the first girl who stood watching, tears rolling down her cheeks. "Leave her, Cail. She needs to learn."

"Is that an order, Squad Leader?"

Hasaan shook his head, "Let's not—"

"Fudil," said Cailaen, loudly. "Give Freya some pointers would you? Natural ability is one thing, but that doesn't mean you can't *teach* those eager to learn."

"He's good," whispered Hasaan, as Fudil walked away.

"I said as much," replied Cailaen, "He's already better than you were at his age. Up here then."

"I could shoot a Flyfish from a hundred paces by my seventh cycle. He must be at least sixteen."

"Did you ever actually do that, Hassi?"

"Of course," said Hasaan. He couldn't remember the day in question, but he would never forget that feeling of accomplishment when that poor fish leapt out of the water only to be skewered by his arrow. It was a shot in a thousand. He turned to Cail to say as much but someone caught his eye. He sidestepped over to the next cadet. "Keene? I didn't know you could shoot."

"Seems you don't know a lot of things, squad leader," she said, flicking her head to get the hair out of her eyes.

Cailaen suppressed a smile, and Hasaan was suddenly aware that he was standing in the centre of an arranged meeting. "Go ahead, Keene," said Cailaen. "Show the squad leader what you can do."

Keene gave Hasaan an unreadable look, then turned towards the target and took two arrows from the cluster in the ground at her feet, carefully balancing them both on the top of her glove for nocking. With barely any effort she drew and let loose, whipping her hand sideways as she did. From the thwap sound alone Hasaan would have said there was not enough power, but both arrows left true, flying side by side until they disappeared into the mannequin, the fletchings protruding from the hay filled head like red eyes.

"Lands," said Hasaan. "Who taught you that?"

"I taught me that," replied Keene.

"No, I mean that hand flick thing?"

Keene brushed the hair from her eyes, then shrugged. "Just my style. As soon as I feel the bite, I flick it back and release."

"And the two arrows?" said Hasaan, itching to try this new style of shooting.

"Sometimes the wild pigs I hunt need two shots, but I'm slow with loading." Keene held out her bow. "I don't have many enemies to shoot."

"Gaining enemies is not a life skill," said Cailaen.

"Oh, I wouldn't say that, team cadet Cailaen," said Lor, floating towards them. "It's good to have enemies." Everyone stiffened. "Otherwise, who would we fight?" He walked so silently for someone who towered over everyone else on camp, yet Hasaan noticed how his footfalls barely left a mark in the mud. "They look better, squad leader. You have done good work."

Cailaen stood taller. "Sir, they are. We were just discussing—"

"Squad leader," hissed Lor, "tell me, how do they progress?"

Hasaan gestured towards the straw man. "Cadet Keene, please show the Commander what you just showed us."

Keene nodded, but her stance was awkward, and the confidence Hasaan had seen a minute ago was gone. She was afraid, as all in their right minds would be. Lor's pale complexion and deep-set, dark eyes were enough to make anyone quail, but the commander had an aura about him that drew fear, and he clearly liked to use it.

Keene pulled two arrows from the mud. Her tendons took the strain, but there was no time to think on it further. Her hand snapped out exactly as it had done before, and the arrows left the bowstring and thwacked into the mannequin's mouth.

"Impressive," said Lor. "Now all we need is an enemy to point you at."

"Yes, sir," said Keene, her voice wavering.

"Cadet," said Lor, turning to Fudil. "Stand in front of the mannequin."

The colour drained from Fudil's face. "Sir?"

"Now."

A silence grew like new mist as Fudil propped his bow against his cluster of arrows and walked slowly to the end of the shooting line. He reached the mannequin's side and turned to face Keene. Hasaan wanted to stop it but found he couldn't move. Keene looked up uncertainly as she reached for the arrow, but Lor's eyes found her first. She took two arrows between the fingers on one hand and nocked them. Hasaan opened his mouth to speak, then Keene drew.

Thwap. The sound was louder than before, and her wrist flicked, but this time a hair less. She had used more power, and the shafts glided further apart with each foot. They each sailed by either side of Fudil's head with barely an inch to spare, and out into the trees behind.

"Squad leader. I know you saw the difference. You see how one minor detail altered the course of this man's life? Now imagine he was the enemy and his squad's success hinged on this lucky man's fate. Now imagine that the success of that enemy's legion was contingent on the success of that lucky man's squad, and the army to that legion. Whole battles are decided by single acts and choices. A fight won here, but lost there." He stepped close to Keene. "All because you *missed* one archer. Multiply that by every life you save, and watch victory trickle through your fingers. An entire war decided on the flight of an arrow."

Lor's cloak flared as his arm struck out; spinning metal gleaming in the sunlight for the briefest of moments before, whatever it was hit the cadet in the chest and threw him onto his back.

Hasaan's legs twitched, but something stopped him from running to Fudil and calling out his name, roaring for help, stemming the blood. He rounded on Lor, but the commander was already walking away.

"Squad leader," said Lor, "report to Kaleb at the guard tents at once. And take your team leader with you."

* * *

Hasaan turned the metal plate over in his hands, marvelling at its symmetry and fingering each of its six dagger-like points.

"It was made to kill," said Cailaen.

"Then why didn't it?" said Hasaan.

"He missed."

Hasaan shook his head. "A man like Lor doesn't miss, Cail."

"He is no man," whispered Cailaen. "Not as we know them anyway. He almost killed Fudil, Hassi. What was he trying to do if he wasn't…" His sentence dwindled into mumbles as an officer marched towards them.

Once the man was safely out of earshot Hasaan rounded upon his friend, pulling him back from the parked carts. "Blessed Winds! Tell the whole camp why don't you? He was teaching them, Cail. It was a lesson."

Cailaen pushed Hasaan away. "A lesson? I can't believe you're defending him!"

"He's a commander! He can teach us any way, any how!"

"And that means killing recruits? To prove a point?"

Hasaan skipped in behind a cart of dirty-faced cadets as it trundled by them. "If it keeps them in line," he said, as Cailaen caught up with him. The youngsters on the back were drafted from the most recent town the riders had visited. He wondered if he looked as bewildered when reached the camp — a time that felt an age ago. He lowered his voice. "Fudil will live. The point to take away, Cail is that if we don't abide by the rules, we'll never make it to the top. We'll find ourselves on the frontlines as fodder for the enemy to trample."

"The enemy," said Cailaen with a snort. "The more I hear of these Tsiorc the more intrigued I am. Why won't the riders tell us where they are? Or who they are? This mysterious fighting force."

"Because none of that is important! They're rebels who oppose the Bohr's rule, and that's all we need to know!"

Cailaen looked taken aback. "Hassi?"

Hasaan took a deep breath. "We can either ride the tide or drown beneath it." Cailaen's mouth had fallen agape. He managed a few blinks, then shook his head. "Look," said Hasaan, "we're here. That's Kaleb's nara. Let's forget this for now." Rather than wait for his friend to respond, Hasaan nodded to the two guards and stepped into the wide tent.

Kaleb stood just inside the entrance, talking quietly with three men, a bearded man who looked almost as tall as Lor, a skinny man about Hasaan's size with only one eye, and the rider Gorm.

A woman lay on the trampled grass at their feet. Her wrists were tied to a rope that ran from her ankles to her neck, so if she moved her limbs the rope would cut into her windpipe. Judging by the bruising on her soft pale skin, it had taken her some time to figure that out. Her white hak was torn at the stomach, revealing pretty Lines beneath.

"How many are there?" Kaleb asked Gorm.

Gorm wiped his eye and inspected his fingertip with a thoughtful air. "The spires? Oh, all over, so I've heard. They're popping up everywhere. One in Makril, another out in the Middle Sea and one in Dali. As tall as mountains but narrow from the base to their tips. People are already calling them *Shards*."

Kaleb scratched his chin. "Shards?"

"The towns are alive with rumours of devils, demons and spirits ready to punish those that…" Gorm stopped as his gaze fell upon Hasaan. "You have a guest."

"Where have you been?" said Kaleb, rushing towards him. "You think that because you have been promoted that you can leave me to wait around while you please yourself?"

"Promoted?" scoffed Gorm. "You are a team leader?"

Hasaan pulled himself higher. "Squad Leader. Which just about makes me level with you, Gorm. Doesn't it? I'll be Shieldless next with a whole hand of riders like you beneath me."

Gorm's face contorted into a full sneer. "We shall see about that!" He stormed out towards the entrance, bumping into Cailaen on the way.

Cailaen stepped aside as the other two guests followed Gorm out. "Oh dear," he said to Hasaan. "In trouble already?" He stopped, aghast. "Who's this?"

"First off," said Kaleb. "Tell me why you took so long to get here?"

Hasaan held out his hands, "We were just—"

"Attending a fallen Cadet," finished Cailaen.

The Horsekeeper squinted at them. "I see. Let us talk no more on it." He turned towards the chained woman. "Now, are you ready to try and get some answers from this piece of nara shit? Then perhaps I can get back to doing some actual work. Not this nonsense." He kicked the chained woman in the leg and a thick line of angry curses exploded forth.

"Now, now," said Kaleb. "Cailaen. You can talk Tyrian, can't you."

"A little," said Cailaen, looking bemused.

"Well, it's not too dissimilar to Samian. Good luck, cadet." He said winking at Hasaan. "Scuse' me. Squad leader."

Hasaan grabbed Kaleb's arm as he tried to leave. "Kaleb. Who is she?"

Kaleb stared down at Hasaan hand's until he removed it from his woollen jacket. "She is a spy." His gaze fell back upon the prisoner. "And she knows the captains of the Tsiorc."

"So…" said Hasaan, incredulous. "What do you want *us* to do?"

"Get her to talk." He stepped out into the cool afternoon light, but held the entrance flaps open. "She'll lie, but think of

291

this as practice until Lor gets his hands on her because if she ain't bleating like a goat by then…" He raised his eyebrows and let the flaps fall.

Reunited

Cimi's sharp shoulders rolled uncomfortably beneath Kyira's thighs, almost dislodging her for the hundredth time. She doubted the crowds marching alongside would even notice her falling off the fool ox, judging by the excited conversations taking place all around.

"But who is this Laeb?"

"A captain of what?"

"What does he want?"

"Can we trust him?"

Only Jaem was quiet. He sat perched on the cart wall behind staring at Kyira, while Tor sat with his back to her. Lyla had taken to riding with the Sulitarian woman, and was a few carts back.

Cimi shook her head, sending the crowd shuffling awkwardly away from her horns.

"I said stay there, child!" growled Iqaluk, as Kyira made to jump down. "We are on the border of Határ and Dali being led around by foreign soldiers. It is a place you have never been, and I myself have been only twice, so just sit where I can see you! These people will have their own agendas like everyone else, so just make sure you don't lose sight of yours. If we get separated, find your brother. Find him." He stalked away.

Kyira ground her teeth. How dare he talk in such a way?

"He's just looking out for you." Lars smiled at her.

"He's a fool, like every other man."

"*He* is your father," said Lars. "Parenting is hard. Perhaps the hardest thing you might ever do. Our children have left, sure, but Cimi and Penni more than fill the gap. Isn't that right, girl?" The ox snorted happily, and threw her head, scattering the crowd.

Kyira shook her head, welcoming the change of subject. "How old is she?"

"Cimi? She's in her fourth and is as sweet as they come. As you know from drinking her milk yesterday!" The other ox snorted and threw its head back along the yoke catching Kyira's calf with the side of her horn.

Lars whipped his cane. "Penni! Don't be so grumpy! Kyira, are you alright?"

"Fine," said Kyira. "It isn't sore."

"Penni is almost in her tenth, and an absolute pain in the rump!" He leaned forward and slapped her for good measure. When he sat back up his head took on a sympathetic tilt. "Your father will come around. Just give him time. It's hard to let them go. Trust me. Tor and I cried for a month straight when our two left."

"How did you—"

"Oh, they weren't ours," laughed Lars. "Such a thing wouldn't be possible without intervention from the Forbringr Mother Baeivi, blessed be her shadow! No, they were the children of Tor's sister, but she passed when they were only three and four, and so they became ours. We taught them, clothed them and fed them. Maybe one day you will have one of your own and you will know what it means to care for something more than you care for yourself."

"Where are they now?"

Lars gestured to the thick needlepines on their right. "Over the hills, in Dali. We will see them again, of that I am sure. They both have families of their own now, but once Tor and I have enough money we will travel the Wayroad to Dali and finally meet our grandchildren. Where are you headed, Kyira?"

Kyira told their story so far, and Lars's hand came up to his mouth.

"Oh Kyira, I'm so sorry. No wonder you are down. I wish I could help, but you're sitting on one half of all we have left." Penni grunted again. "Yes! You are the other half, you smelly ox!"

Kyira leant over and gave Cimi a friendly slap and the beast leaned into her in thanks.

"Here," said Lars. "Take this. It's not much, but it might bring you some luck." He tossed her a small leather pouch, then held a finger to his mouth. "Tor gave it to me long ago for my naming day, but…" He glanced to the back of the cart where Tor sat sewing. "In truth, I never really liked it."

Inside was a lead figurine of a man chopping wood. She ran a finger over his face marvelling at the intricate detail.

"I thought it looked like your father."

"It does," said Kyira. "Thank you, Lars."

"Just do me one thing," he said. "Look after our people, Kyira. The residents of Makril, be they Makriliaen to the bone or Sulitarian, they have no home and nothing to call their own. The firespiral obliterated everything, the seaweed crop, the winter stock, the fish. They need someone like you to watch over them. Promise me."

Kyira could not promise such a thing, the troubles of an entire town of people was not hers to mind. She laid a hand over his. "I will keep them right."

"You are good people, Kyira," said Lars, "and good people should stick together. There is much evil in this world."

A commotion drew Kyira's eye forward and the convoy slowed. The riders at the front were directing them off the road into a bank of trees, and as Penni and Cimi approached the tight corner she took the chance to study them. The closest, a woman in well-worn tight, leather armour looked tired and hollow cheeked. Kyira knew the look well. Those too inexperienced to survive in Nord were treated poorly by the lands and quickly found themselves dying of hunger. Now that she saw it, they all had the distinct look of malnourishment.

The lines of carts and people continued on through a thick forest, splitting amongst the trees until they began to thin. The last few trunks sat upon a mound, and as the oxen plodded up the hill Kyira soon found herself looking down the length of a short valley flanked by slanting hills on all sides. At the bottom sat a sprawling sea of tents and yurts almost a quarter league in each direction, bigger even than Makril. Kyira had never seen so much life in one place. Even at this distance she could see the horses, nara, sheep and oxen being shepherded from pens near the fringes to a makeshift entrance.

The riders led them down into a long area of trampled mud near a set of gates. Hard looking soldiers, stiff-backed and high booted with long dark jackets splashed with droplets of brown, watched the convoy closely as it trundled by, hands hovering around their belts even after nods from their fellows. They each had the same drabness and weathered expressions.

The caravan moved deeper into the camp where men and women too old and young to fight, milled about their tents busying themselves preparing food or polishing spears, swords and painting shields. The same triangle as had adorned the Wolf, Bear and Mother's clothes marked flags and shields alike. This was the rebel camp. A bearded man walked by with two heavy plates of iron tied to his chest and back, the white triangle on the front. A strong waft of horse drifting up from him as he passed. The caravan shuddered to a halt along the road and Eoin shouted in the man's direction. The soldier stopped and the two ran towards each other, slamming together and locking each other in a rough embrace, cursing and berating each other like men often did. Fools.

"You see?" Kyira jerked around to find Captain Laeb offering a hand up to her.

She ignored his hand, and instead hopped smoothly down to his side, relishing the feel of ground under her feet. "I see what?"

The captain studied her, his blue eyes bright and clear. "We are you. Men and women from homes likes yours. Families like yours."

"They are friends?" asked Kyira.

"Kavik and Eoin are brothers," said Laeb.

"One of your captains is with us," said Kyira, pointing down the lines of carts. "Lyla."

Captain Laeb looked surprised. "Lyla is here? That is good

news. Is she well."

"More or less," said Kyira. "She was with—"

Before she could say any more Iqaluk appeared at Kyira's side. "So, Captain Laeb who is it you fight?"

Captain Laeb scratched his head. "Sami, the Bohr are expanding into the Outer Ring and have been for months. Dali, Határ, Nord…"

"What do you know of these conscripts out of Makril?"

"Conscripts?" came a voice from behind. The captain's man appeared behind them. "What conscripts?"

"So, you are not as well informed as your makeshift army suggests," said Iqaluk. The air thickened between the three men.

"You do us a disservice, Sami," said Laeb. "This army has beaten back the lord's army twice already. These men may not look much, but they are free. They come and they fight for their lands, and for their families, and are bound to no one, but I will not lie, Iqaluk. We need your people as the Nightwhale needs blood."

Iqaluk's jaw set, as Kyira had seen it do a hundred times before. "We are Sami. We mind the paths. That is our purpose."

"Then why do you travel with these townspeople?" asked Duga.

Eoin stepped up to the group, still jubilant. "What are you talking of?" His eye fell upon Duga and he threw a massive arm over the slight man's shoulders. "Is that you, Duga?" Eoin pulled down Duga's cowl, revealing a pock marked face. It looked like a pox of some sort, probably as a child. The scars on top told a different story.

Duga stepped back. "You know it is, Eoin."

"Well, I never," said Eoin. "I'd heard you had joined some band of rebels."

Duga looked coy, but Kyira didn't believe he was. He was dangerous, and he scared her.

"These *rebels* may be the only chance Nord has left. How is it you are here, leading a town into the heart of an army? I heard one of your townspeople talking of a fire?"

Eoin's expression shifted quickly from irritation to sadness, and when he spoke of Makril's fate the words were hollow. When he had finished, his voice had become a croak. "We have lost many, Duga. More than I could account for. I did the only thing I could, and rounded up all we had left and made for the city."

"Then you did the right thing, Eoin." Duga turned towards Captain Laeb. "This could only have been the Bohr. It sounds very much like what you saw, captain."

"You saw a firespiral?" asked Eoin.

"Something similar, yes," said Captain Laeb, shooting a look at Duga "A few days ago I found myself at the top of a hill watching as an entire lake rose up from the ground, moments before the hill exploded into rubble. The hand of God came down with fingers of lightforks, wind, rain and fire."

Iqaluk caught Kyira's eye, echoing the feeling of dread quickly filling her stomach. "And you think it was the Bohr?" asked Kyira. "But how?"

"I've seen first-hand the magic that their Banémen can wield," said Duga, with absolute conviction. "There could be no bounds to the power they possess. That is what we are fighting."

"It sounds ridiculous," said Captain Laeb, shaking his head. "But it is what I saw. The camp was shrouded in cloud for days, as though the sky fell down. We were just fortunate that no one was badly hurt."

Duga nodded. "Some of the men have begun to talk of the return of the Stallo."

"Sky demons?" scoffed Eoin. "I'm not sure that—"

"Were you alone?" asked Iqaluk.

Kyira quailed to think at how such a question might be taken — implying the captain of any army was out of his mind would see them banished, or worse.

"You're not the first to doubt me," said Captain Laeb. "I was with another — a young Farram named Glynn."

"A messenger?" said Iqaluk. "And he survived too?"

"He did," said Captain Laeb. "Just."

Eoin nodded slowly. "If the Bohr did this then we must fight back. They have taken our home from us."

Duga nodded. "Are you able to talk for your town?"

"I am," said Eoin. "None of the rest of our council made it out of the fire. It was by sheer luck that my mare decided to give birth the morning our council was due to meet. I was late, and they died in flames." He looked down. "All of them."

Duga tapped Eoin on his broad shoulder. "You are here now though, where you can join your brother and fight with us and take back what was taken from you. You will tip the scales in our favour, Makriliaen"

Eoin seemed to grow bolder with each word. He nodded and knelt down at Captain Laeb's feet. "I pledge the peoples of Makril to your army."

Captain Laeb looked tense as he held out a hand to Eoin.

"Welcome to the Tsiorc."

Duga shook Eoin's hand warmly. "I see that there are Sulitarians with you."

Eoin nodded. "They landed a few months back from across the Middle Sea. The town was united against them at first, but since the fire they have supported and cared for us. They are as much Makriliaen as my father and grandfather ever were."

Jaem appeared out of nowhere and thrust a hand into the circle. "Jaem!"

"Captain Laeb."

"A captain?" said Jaem, with a grin. "I never thought I'd meet an actual captain!"

Captain Laeb spared Jaem a fleeting look. "Well, you are welcome to stay here as long you need. An offer that extends to all of your people. Kyira." He took her hand. "Let us talk more on these conscripts. The last thing I need is more surprises."

Jaem's face suddenly brightened up. "Conscripts? You mean the Kin?"

Captain Laeb turned towards him. "The Kin?"

Jaem adjusted the shoulder strap of his bag, clearly enjoying knowing something someone else did not. "The roads are alight with news, Captain Laeb. One simply has to know where to put one's ear. Perhaps we should have a meet."

Kyira suddenly became aware of the captain's guarded stance, and the hilt strapped to his side — a sinuous blade, curved to match the contours of his body. Duga, too, seemed to have tensed up.

"Alright," said the captain. "I am eager to hear what you have to say…"

Jaem's lips bared into something resembling a smile. "As I said, Captain Laeb, you may call me Jaem."

"Well, Jaem, it is time to eat. We'll arrange a meet after our meal."

Kyira stepped back quietly as the group split. She had seen troubled men like Captain Laeb before. Those who bore the weight of the world upon them yet were unwilling to admit the fact. It was both admirable and foolish in equal measure — they were dangerous and unpredictable.

Eoin joined his brother Kavik, who was standing talking with Tor by the two oxen. She couldn't hear them, but the conversation was easy enough to follow as Eoin revealed that they would be fighting together. Kavik picked Eoin up and threw him over his shoulder, running in circles as though Eoin weighed no more than a child. Two brothers, reunited. Kyira wanted to smile and laugh along with them as Lars and Tor were doing. It would have been so easy, but something dark stopped her.

Shadows

"What do you have to say for yourself?" growled Laeb.

Duga might've stepped back from the captain's glare, except there was nowhere else to go. "I have nothing to say."

"Nothing to say? You set up a trap and they walked straight into it! You have just made my life extremely difficult." Laeb turned towards his desk and idly rearranged the written leaves scattered upon it.

"Your life has been made more difficult, because we've signed up an entire town's worth of soldiers? I think we can afford the time to enlist these new men, captain."

Laeb rounded on him, a vicious glint in his eye. "And women, and children. Don't forget them, Duga. Don't forget the families you just drew into this army. You manipulated those people into a battle that is not theirs."

"Captain, the events you witnessed—"

Laeb slammed his fist down on the desk. "Have nothing to do with the Bohr! I took you up that hill, and you saw the huge stone spire where once there was a lake. It is only luck that the clouds refuse to leave the surrounding hills. If the camp was to see that shard of rock they would have every right to panic and leave."

Duga couldn't believe his ears. "That is what you are afraid of? A spire of rock?"

"No power the Bohr possess could have drawn rock from the very ground, let alone to stand as a tower. There is nothing in the fables of Banémen with whom the power of the worlds lie, who could do such a thing. Those beings who could wield the elements like they were pulling on a shirt, and yet here it is! And you seek to blame it on the Bohr?"

"We need men…"

"You lied to those people, Duga. LIED."

Duga sighed. "It could have been the Bohr." Laeb turned away. "Did you see the spire form, captain? Did you see the rock grow out of the ground into a tower?"

"You know I did not."

"When even you, who stood upon the peak and experienced the event, can't explain what you saw, then you cannot categorically say it was not the Bohr."

Laeb shook his head in disbelief, although Duga had prepared himself for a worse reaction. "You're right, Duga. I cannot categorically say that the event I witnessed was not some masterful illusion of the Bohr, in the same way I cannot say my own mother wasn't the wielder of all that power! No. This is larger than us all. The power of it Duga, you have no idea. It could have scrubbed me, you and the entire Tsiorc army from existence on a whim, and if it can happen here, it can happen anywhere. You know what, I can't… Duga. I just… Leave. Now."

Duga turned around and left without salute. It wouldn't have made a difference anyway — his betrayal would eclipse any misdemeanour for some time. Still, he had to prove to

304

the captain that acquiring the townspeople, however illicitly gained, was a worthy investment.

He drew his cowl and crossed through the camp, steering clear of the roads and populated parts where soldiers congregated. The night had become fine and drizzly, with a breeze that drew in the soft scents of the sea. But this was not the time to think of Sulitar, however much he missed his home.

He hurried along, moving from between the shadows until he reached the northern quarter where the townspeople were camped. He stopped behind a half-unpacked cart and extended his spyglass. Most of the town had come together around a large bonfire, and there were some good fighters amongst them. Big men and women, some Sulitarian and some Makriliaen, but all weathered and well bred. The Sulitarians would just need a sword and a direction to go in, whereas the Makriliaens might need persuading. The old, young, and pregnant would no doubt be useful in one way or another.

Behind the fire, by some stacked logs the Sami girl and her father stood talking heatedly. She seemed to be pleading with him, but the father was having none of it, and after a few moments he snapped at her and walked off. She swore loudly and stormed away towards the camp. The Sami were well-known navigators, so maybe they would be of use.

The two brothers Eoin and Kavik were talking jovially and already half-cut, swaying back and forth through the people, as Eoin introduced them all to Kavik. Eoin had always been strong, but he was no longer the farmer Duga remembered from his stay in Makril so long ago. The pair were met with smiling faces and warm embraces at each turn. Glasses clinked, meat was shared, and Makriliaen and Sulitarian alike hung off of Eoin's every word.

Eoin was both saviour and protector of Makril, but for Duga it was the fact that he was the only council member left that interested him — a full council would have done nothing but argue and disagree for months, causing delays — a single town representative would be a useful ally once trained and directed.

He glanced down at the fire, and his breath caught. The man Jaem was staring right at him. There was no way the peddler could see him through this netting, not at such a distance. Duga ducked lower checking that he was still shrouded and the spyglass got caught, and tumbled into a canvas bag full of cabbages.

"Shit." A second later he had the glass back out but Jaem was gone. He flicked it back over the fire, glancing at each face but there was no sign of him.

"You are an inquisitive one."

Duga jerked back as a blurry face took up the whole viewport.

"Jaem." Duga schooled his face to stillness, ignoring the hammering in his chest. "I like to watch."

"Don't worry," said Jaem. "All is well. I just caught the glint from your looking glass there, and thought I would investigate. I assume you are just checking to see we are settled in for the night?"

"You assume correctly. I am charged with protection. You move quickly for one who is so... inquisitive."

"Ah, but we are all inquisitive, Duga. As humans, it is in our *nature*."

Duga nodded down at the bag hanging from Jaem's

shoulder. "You mind if I take a look?"

"Of course, of course," said Jaem. "Just as soon you empty your pockets for me."

Duga frowned. "You are denying me?"

"You assume correctly."

There was a whicker from behind. Duga knew what the noise was and even which horse had made it, but for reasons he couldn't fathom he turned to look anyway. The animal standing by the front gates blinked at him. Duga stared back entranced, and the animal stomped a foot then returned to its saltlick. It was one of Kavik's beasts — a beautiful dappled thoroughbred but by the all-damned sea Duga could not remember its name. He jerked around to the cart, but Jaem was gone.

Tyr

Wakefulness lingered in Fia's peripherals, but it was panic that rushed in first clutching at her insides with icy fingers, grasping for the surface, gulping for air.

The cart bumped, and Fia's head banged against the sticky black floor.

"Nice sleep?" asked the rider in his heavily accented tone. His name was Gorm and he was a cruel, scrawny man with legs too tall for his body and a face that looked as though it had been flattened by an iron.

"Not really," she said, blinking at the late afternoon light. She shuffled herself up, working around the wrist shackles that were bolted to the cart floor. "How long this time?"

"Twenty-four hours," said Gorm, perched on the side of the cart, peeling a plumfruit. He pulled one of the purple segments out and popped it into his mouth.

"Twenty-four?" repeated Fia.

"Euch! Sour!" He threw the plumfruit to the ground and the cart behind crushed it into pulp. "It's like there's a fucking plague eating up the good things of the world. Why do only bad things happen to me?"

Fia struggled to comprehend. "I've been out for a whole

day?"

"Aye," said Gorm, smacking his lips distastefully. "Like a broken oil lamp." He leant in towards her. "And next time it'll be two days, then three, then after that who knows, you might never wake up."

Fia slunk backwards away from him. Her cart was the third in a line of six being pulled by two nara — each pair of animals were roped to the cart in front so the riders could trot alongside. Behind, there was another thirty carts, all filled with young soldiers, calling themselves the Kin, and each cluster of them was directed by men like Gorm, dressed in long jackets made from what looked like crocodile skin.

"Where are we?" asked Fia. Stars exploded in her eyes, and the shackles snapped taught.

Gorm squeezed her cheeks hard. "We are not friends, bitch, so do not talk to me like we are." He pushed her away. "Forn and Astir sold you to Lor, I work for Lor so that means you belong to me now."

Fia worked her jaw. "I thought we had already established that smacking the hell out of me was not helpful."

Gorm's hand reached out again then stopped in mid-air when Fia didn't flinch. Instead he pointed at her nose. "Maybe you had. I like destroying beautiful things. If you ask me there's not much else to gain after you've seen them once." He looked thoughtful for a moment then hopped down from the moving cart, tumbling over in the process. The youngsters in front all looked his way, but he picked himself up, dusted himself off and stared them down.

Fia had only seen a handful of people who were older than her and they all appeared to be riders. The Kin were not the veterans Rathe had made out, and what's more the

Tsiorc knew nothing of them. Most of them were Norduns or perhaps Daliaens, from their weathered skin and narrow eyes, and training younglings like this gave a hint at how long the Bohr thought the process of conquering Nord would take. Laeb had to be told somehow.

Fia's eye was drawn to the high banks around the road as the sight of a familiar spire grew from between the low hills.

"Oh, good," she said. "I really thought I was done with this place."

* * *

Hasaan leapt down from the cart as it slowed, admiring the dark steel gates wrought into twisted designs of creatures fighting, so detailed that it was almost impossible to see through. The shining white veinstone of the city entrance walls closed in, revealing more twisted figures carved into the rock and when the tunnel opened out into a street the convoy was met with guards dressed in pristine cloaks and iron vests, standing between each building.

So, this was a city! A thick smell of smoke and rotting fish caught in his nostrils. Did they all smell this bad?

The veneer of affluence was strong, but the mood was sombre as the Kin moved deeper into Vasen. Hasaan marched by a scorched tree, with many more lining the road ahead, the scent of char suddenly all around. There were more townspeople milling around too, their colourful silk gowns held down by new leather armour, but no one looked further than their own feet, let alone at a convoy of soldiers marching by their homes.

The walls were daubed with hastily painted blocks, covering messages in red that had been scrawled onto the white brick. A gap opened up between the buildings revealing a message that had yet to meet a brush:

For Erdal. In his name!

Erdal? Before Hasaan could think any more on it the scene was stolen away. The Kin trundled on by through the tight alleyways, the right-angles of Vasen's roads a stark contrast to the beautiful, organic lines of the favelas that appeared like painted canvas between buildings whenever the road changed direction — apparently there was not a single straight road anywhere in Tyr. The dock at the base of the mountain ran the entire length of the city, but looked largely empty of ships. In fact, there were barely any ships floating anywhere on the rough white water of the Way channel. Smoke was rising from a section of the favela. Squinting, Hasaan saw a fire near the base where the masses of shanties were most numerous and it was swarming with bodies.

"Why do they fire their homes?" said Keene, appearing at Hasaan's side.

"They are rioting."

Keene spat. "What have they to riot about? Look at the size of this place. There are more roads and homes than I have ever seen in one place. Surely they have everything they would ever need, and within arm's reach?"

"Maybe all you see is not all that is going on!" snapped Hasaan.

Keene glared at him, then jogged ahead, leaping onto a cart with Fudil and Ander.

Amidst the thickening smoke people ran towards the flames from all directions. Even at this distance Hasaan could make out a group of people fighting, silhouetted in front of the flames, moving around upon the roofs of the shanties.

The road changed to a peculiar tarred gravel as the downslope steepened, and all at once the street opened out into a square. The Kin jerked to a stop in front of a huge dome atop a hill of stone steps. The building was made from bricks as large as a house with veins of bright colours running through each one that made the it shimmer.

But it was the obelisk standing in the centre of the square with twelve smaller towers surrounding it that caught Hasaan's attention. Smooth and white it was clearly made by people, but it was so tall! How did you build something so tall without it just falling over?

"Have you never seen a sun clock before?"

* * *

The Kin turned and scowled at Fia. "A sun clock?"

"You do know what a clock is — or do they not have those in Nord?" she said, as coolly as she could. The Kin stared at her. "It tells the time."

"I know how clocks work."

"Good. So then, is it time we continue our little dance? It has been a whole day since you last beat me." She despised being so hateful, but if anyone deserved it...

The Kin leaned in closer, and Fia waited for the stars. "I had to do it," he said, quietly.

Fia exhaled loudly. "You had to pummel me over and over

312

until my eyes were blackened and my lips were split? You *had* to?"

He leaned in closer. "I had to make it look real. Please forgive me. I would never have…" He stopped and shook his head. "Lor would have done much worse to you."

Fia snarled. "You are pathetic." She sat back, disgusted with him, the situation, the world. Herself. His friend had stood by that first time, silently watching as she bore the brunt of his cruelty. She touched her half-healed lip tenderly, wishing not for the first time that her mother had given her more curves. Janike had such wonderful curves and she had been so much stronger for it. She could have borne this bastard's brunt with much more self-respect.

"I told you things," said Fia. "You asked me for information and I gave it to you, and still you beat me. You are a coward!"

The Kin looked down. "Your information might save hundreds of us. Hundreds of people like me. The ranks and layouts of the rebels—"

"You lied to me." Fia lowered her eyes like a disappointed mother. She may have told him things, but it was the same story Janike had helped her fabricate should they ever get caught. It would do this Kin and his army absolutely no good at all; indeed she wished she had been clever enough to tell a story that could have somehow tipped the advantages towards the Tsiorc. It seemed like an empty wish though now Janike was gone.

Guilt washed over the Kin's stupid face. "The Tsiorc ranks and layouts you described will help the lord's army defend itself if an attack is launched. The Kin will aid in their fight and as long as both sides remain true to each other then all will be well. There doesn't have to be death—"

"You are scum," hissed Fia. How dare he try to justify it! She went to spit at him then stopped herself. "You are not worth even the saliva of a Kumpani."

But the Kin wasn't listening. His green eyes flicked up and back, and Fia followed his gaze along the line of carts. A Child of the Bohr was swooping down the lines, a cloak of dark silk flapping, and of course Gorm scurrying behind like a little pet dog. The Kin's eyes dropped to the cart floor, and Fia felt herself following suit as the Child passed them by. He was their commander, and there was something very familiar about him. "Who is that?" uttered Fia.

"Lor," said the Kin. "Commander Lor."

And it all fell into place. Lor was Rathe's brother. Fia pulled at her shackles like a cat on a leash. "I need to talk to him!" She wrapped the chain around itself and tried to introduce a kink as Janike had once taught her to do.

The Kin grabbed her hands. "No! He will kill you!"

"I need to talk to him!" she growled. If she had claws they would be fully extended right now. "Gorm! I need to—" Gorm slapped her hard, and she stumbled back to the cart floor.

"Are you having trouble with your prisoner, squad leader?"

Fia sat up, tasting blood. "No... It's fine."

"She speaks for you too!" He smirked and sauntered away, clearly pleased at his own wit. "Oh, Hasaan," he added. "Come with me, boy. You're needed."

"What about her?" said the Kin.

Gorm gestured to Fia as though she were a sack of potatoes. "Keene will look after her for now. Maybe she can be your Shieldless, Cadet Keene? Eh?" He elbowed the girl as he might a drunken fellow in a tavern, and where

Fia expected to see annoyance from those sharp eyes, she instead saw satisfaction, and a sneer blossomed across cadet Keene's pale cheeks like a moonflower at midnight.

"You, however" said Gorm, poking Hasaan in the chest, "have bigger things to worry about. The council meets soon, and as squad leader you are *naturally* invited. I hear good things may happen this night. And good things for Lor, means good things for us."

The Fire Within

It was almost dusk when Iqaluk and Kyira were finally summoned to see Captain Laeb. Jaem tagged along beside them, making awkward conversation. Kyira had not known many awkward types — there wasn't much time for socialising in the towns of Nord when supplies needed to be bought and trades finalised — but the ones she had met were never malicious people, they were just made differently. Jaem, on the other hand, was something else. He would watch her whether she was looking in his direction or not. She was thankful even for her father's sullen company when they eventually reached the officers quadrant and ducked into the captain's tent.

Kavik stood in the centre where it was highest, with Eoin beside him. Even side by side she couldn't tell they were brothers. Kavik was tall and broad — easily the largest of them here — while Eoin was squat and hard. The captain and Duga stood talking quietly until they entered, then Duga pushed by Kyira to stand outside. She frowned at him through the gap in the canvas. "Fool."

"Kyira." Iqaluk gestured to the desk table and nodded again for her to sit down.

In the tent, Laeb's sleeping arrangements were much like

the man seemed himself: simple and practical. There was a low mattress and a desk, most of which had some amount of raeven dung on it. It was a sleeping tent, rather than a yurt or ghoati, but still large enough to fit them all comfortably.

"How long have you been stationed here?" asked Jaem, as Kyira sat. She peered around him, to watch the captain's response.

"Too long," said Laeb, removing his long dark jacket.

"Indeed," muttered Jaem, "And all of the Tsiorc are based here?"

"For now."

"Ah," said Jaem. "Drakemyre. The Battle that was Lost. Or at least for the lords, that is!"

"You seem well versed in Bohr affairs," said Laeb.

"Oh!" laughed Jaem. "I am but a simple trader, and like all good traders I keep my ears open and my eyes to the ground." The air had again grown thick with awkwardness, as was typical whenever Jaem happened to be around.

"Tell me more of these Kin you spoke of," added Captain Laeb. "I assume they are not related to you."

Jaem crossed his arms. "Alas, I know little. Just that they exist and are led by a fearsome commander. A Child of the Bohr."

"Lor," said Kavik, his voice as rough as a bristle brush.

"You know him?" beamed Jaem.

"By reputation alone," said Kavik. "He may be a Child, but he appears to be the most pure-bred Child I have heard walk Rengas. He is vicious."

Kyira frowned. "He's a child?"

"Ah the folly of youth!" laughed Jaem.

"The Children of the Bohr," said Laeb. "Bohr-human

317

hybrids bred for war."

"Bred to kill," added Jaem.

Laeb turned to Iqaluk. "What about you, Sami?"

"What about me, captain?"

"You seem guarded."

"You would be, too," replied Iqaluk, stiffly, "if you stood in the wolf's den, with your own children to protect."

Laeb waited patiently, but her father gave nothing away. "I understand, Iqaluk. You have your own pack to protect, as do I."

"Is that why we are in your own tent rather than the officer's tent?"

Laeb's expression hardened. "You are keen, Sami. Yes, I am unsure of your intentions. And not just you, but your daughter's, and the people that ride with you. It is my job to be suspicious of all that is new."

Iqaluk visibly stiffened at the mention of Kyira, and shuffled quietly in front of her, blocking Laeb from view. "The townspeople of Makril—"

"Are an unknown factor," snapped captain Laeb. "And unknown factors have a way of sprouting problems like roots."

Iqaluk's jaw set. "They ride with us, captain. I trust them, and I do not give out my trust so easily."

The two men stared at one another. Were they stags, they would be butting heads. "We all ride with one another, Iqaluk," said Laeb, finally. He pulled his shirt from his breeks and started to unbutton his waistcoat. "What must I do to convince you that I mean you no harm?" The waistcoat came off, then the shirt, and his belt and sword. Suddenly the captain of the Tsiorc was standing half naked, palms out in front of them. "No armour, no weapon, no tricks."

He was tall and well defined, but with not a single scar, which made him either an exceptional fighter, or a liar. Kyira noticed Duga watching her and she looked away — she hadn't seen him enter.

Kavik stepped in and placed a friendly arm around the captain's shoulder. "Laeb, you've been surrounded by soldiers too long. It is natural for a citizen to be wary in a circumstance such as this one. Give the man his space."

Laeb's expression soured, but he did not shrug off Kavik's arm. "You do indeed swim in the shark's shallows. So, it is more important than ever, that these sharks know if you are food or friend."

"We can be neither, captain." Kyira's tone sounded stronger than she felt.

Laeb's gaze flicked towards her, then back to her father. "Tell me what side you fight for, Iqaluk."

"We do not fight," said Kyira. "We live."

Iqaluk gestured softly to her. "Kyira is only partially correct — we fight when we need to." Laeb frowned, then took a clean shirt from the back of the chair and pulled it on. "You have a queer way of gaining people's trust, captain. Besides, we all have secrets. Your man here, for example, has to be one of the least trusting I have ever met."

Duga bristled, but predictably it was Laeb who replied. "You speak plainly Iqaluk, which I appreciate. The people and practices of my homeland in Sulitar are unusual to Ringlanders. Our cultures differ, but I am a man like you." His gaze fell upon Kyira. "And we all have families to mind."

Iqaluk stayed as still as the mountainside before the wind.

"Fine," said Laeb. "Fine. We are waiting in this valley for

our scouts to return. Good scouts are too hard to come by to just abandon, even if they are yet to bring us anything newsworthy. I also have a number of captains who seem to have vanished from existence." He stopped as Duga stepped between them, whispering something. The captain shook his head. "I think we can trust them, Duga. Someone has to take the first leap."

"Why do you need scouts?" asked Eoin.

"Our scouts map the lands because we need to know the best way in."

"In?" asked Eoin.

"To Tyr," said Laeb, casually.

The whites of Eoin's eyes were bright against his red face. "You intend to launch an assault on Tyr? That is not what I signed up for!"

"The Bohr already control everything south of Tyr," said Laeb, "and they have used that power to toll the Way itself — our lifeline to the Outer Reaches. An effect that is already being felt in Nord. The new Tyrian currency — *musta*, they're calling it — is forcing trade to remain within the walls of Tyr, and nothing is getting out."

Duga sighed, reluctant. "And before we breach Tyr's walls, we require intel on the layout of the place. It is a mess of tangled roads and narrow paths. That is the plan."

Laeb pulled on a leather waistcoat. "At least it was the plan," said Laeb. "But the Commander of the Tsiorc has since pulled his support for the idea. If it were up to them, and I fear it is, then they'll start building houses here in Dali. We've been here so long now that I'm starting to think that they might never want to leave, even if by some miracle we find a way in to Tyr."

"Can you not place spies into the city?" said Jaem, suddenly.

"We have spies, but they have…" Laeb glanced at Kavik. "Gone silent."

Eoin shook his head. "There is something far more sinister at work here, captain. The fire spiral in Makril took the lives of a thousand families. If it was the Bohr, as you claim, then perhaps the answer is not to fight but to rebuild. How do you expect to take the city if they can wield that sort of power?" He shook his head in disbelief. "I still have no clue what could have caused such a thing. If the Bohr are behind it then they have magic and strength that your people cannot resist. What do you hope to gain against such a force?"

There was no denying Eoin's logic was sound, and Kyira found herself nodding along with him.

Duga grimaced and stepped towards Eoin. "You committed yourselves to us. To the Tsiorc. Pulling out now is a dishonour to your people."

"Honour is for the dead," said Iqaluk. "Invading Tyr would be like kicking a nest of fire ants."

"Ants?" snapped Duga. "Left unchecked, the Bohr will spread upon the land, and consume and destroy the human race! Besides, the decision has been made, so if you don't stand with us, you stand against us."

Iqaluk shook his head. "The Sami stick to Nord away from the affairs of the cities. It is true that our ancestors roamed beyond the central borders into Kemen, but those days are far beyond us now."

"Then go back there, Sami!"

Iqaluk bowed his head, then took Kyira's hand. "I'm afraid whatever your fight is, captain, it will be without us. Now,

Kyira, let us leave these people to their games."

"Oh dear!" interrupted Jaem. "And so our intrepid explorers go their separate ways." Kyira turned towards him. He was holding a wooden box the length of his forearm in Iqaluk's path. "Maybe this will be of some help."

"What is it?" asked Laeb.

"Your miracle, captain."

Iqaluk's eyes grew wide with wonder. "Where did you get that?" He took the deep red wooden box, and lightly caressed the strange patterns adorning each of its sides.

"From Tyr, of course." said Jaem, smiling. Jaem leaned in. "You recognise it, don't you, Iqaluk."

"Yes. Do you?"

"I have an idea…" muttered Jaem.

Duga lowered his hood revealing a mane of black hair tied up in a tight bun. "Iqaluk, do not open it," but it was too late. The bottom swung open, and Duga drew his sword.

"It's empty?" said Laeb, hand on his own hilt.

"Of course, it's empty," said Iqaluk. "It's a Maelta."

Jaem let out a single laugh. "*Maelta.* To deceive? That's what it means?"

"Yes," said Iqaluk. "That's what it means. Though I have only ever seen one." Iqaluk turned the box to reveal the inside, which was just as intricately patterned. His fingers felt over the shapes, searching until stopping an inch from the edge. He dug his nail into a gap and the top sprang open. Kyira gasped as the box unfolded. "And now," continued Iqaluk, "we close it." He reformed the box, now inside out.

Laeb pushed by Duga and took the box from Iqaluk, holding it as gently as a mother holding her babe. "Is this what I think it is?"

"I need some parchment and ink."

The captain handed the box back to Iqaluk and reached below the desk to a hidden compartment and produced a sheet of blank parchment, a wide brush, and an ink well, and laid it out in front of Kyira.

Iqaluk dipped the brush in the ink and lightly painted the black shapes carved in the wood and placed the painted side gently onto the parchment. Laeb surveyed the process like a hawk watching a foal, and by the heavy breathing behind her Eoin and Kavik's interest had also piqued.

"Gently!" said Captain Laeb, as Iqaluk lifted the ink-sticky box from the paper.

The parchment fell gently to the desk, revealing an intricate pattern. Seeing the negative space become positive changed the design completely.

"It's a map," gasped Kyira, following the narrow streets, roads, paths and even individual buildings.

"There it is," said Iqaluk, finally pulling in some air. "A piece of Tyr." He stepped back as Duga and Laeb muscled in, studying the printed section on the parchment with a low candle.

"Amazing," said Laeb. "What part of Tyr is it?"

"The map does not reveal itself until the end. They were created by the Kartta, the first generation of Sami, who lived and travelled Rengas before it was even called so. They were used instead of documents to retain knowledge and were overlooked as simple containers that held spices or twine. When the eldest child grew of age, the knowledge was memorised and passed down. It was the job of the Sami, to protect those secrets, to forge and mind the paths our ancestors walked. We keep no such trinkets now, but I had heard that there were still some Maelta boxes in existence."

Laeb held the parchment up to the lamp. "Finish this map, Iqaluk, and you may just win us this war. Jaem, how did you come by this?"

Jaem cleared his throat as everyone turned towards him. "I took it." He looked different. Was it the light? No. His face was now someone else's, and his features had become smooth and ageless. Even the way he moved had changed. "I took it," he said, sneering, "from the hands of a spy before she fell from a ship into the Middle Sea. She was using it to carry olives. More important though was how the spy Fia came by it."

Laeb's stony expression broke. "Fia?" He unsheathed his sword and held the curved blade out in front, the point stopping barely a foot from Jaem's chest. "Where is she?"

Kyira felt suddenly claustrophobic, and Duga was padding along the side of the narrow tent away from them. Waves of motion seemed to emanate from Jaem through the thick air.

The man drew a deep breath, and the whites of his eyes shone bright. "I am Jagar. Banéman to the Bohr King herself, destroyer of souls, and I have come here to kill you captain Laeb, like I ended Tri Ordeus and Bryn Feykir."

Iqaluk stepped in front of Kyira. "Jaem was a lie."

"Oh no," said Jagar, "the peddler was absolutely real. I took his name after his death. One day I may even use your name, Sami."

Laeb stepped forward, pushing the point of his blade onto Jagar's chest. "Where is Fia?"

"If she is not currently at the bottom of the Middle Sea," said Jagar, "like what remains of her associate Janike, then I guess she will be in the hands of two of the worst smelling fishmen I have ever met."

"What?" Kavik's face dropped. "Janike? My daughter is… dead?"

"The father is here?" said Jagar. "What a happy coincidence."

"And her uncle," growled Eoin, balling his fists.

"Well, now," said Jagar. "A chance to eradicate another impure bloodline from the face of Rengas." He turned to face Laeb. "I expect you'll want to do something about that now, captain? Shall we?"

Jagar closed his eyes and all five men moved at once. Flashes of steel sailed through the air, slicing canvas and cloth alike, but Jagar twisted away almost lazily into gaps that looked too small for a man to move through. Laeb and Duga took turns to swipe their swords while Eoin and Kavik bludgeoned from the other side, but Jagar had yet to be touched. Eoin roared in frustration and stepped in, and Jagar planted an elbow into Eoin's windpipe knocking him back. Laeb advanced from behind, but his sword sang through nothing but air.

Jagar returned to a neutral stance: hands clasped at his front, eyes closed, like he was asleep and unaware of all that was taking place before him. Kavik reached around and grabbed the seat of the chair Kyira had been sitting in, and brought it crashing down over Jagar. Wood smashed in all directions, but the man was as rock. Kavik leapt upon Jagar's back, and Jagar twisted, flicking Kavik's full weight crashing to Kyira's feet. Before Jagar could turn back Eoin pushed between Laeb and Duga's swords and grabbed Jagar around the neck, drawing him into a headlock.

His massive biceps bulged around the small man's neck.

"You're mine, slayer!" he roared. "Nobody breaks out of Eoin's lock!"

"Finish him, Eoin!" croaked Kavik, trying to push himself up. "Finish that tearing fucker!"

Jagar's eyes snapped open, and they were misty white. The redness of Eoin's cheeks turned a sickly grey, and his own eyes shifted from brown to ice white like Jagar's. They were linked somehow, and Eoin was clearly the one being controlled. Laeb and Duga stepped away, but Eoin held firm, twitching as a mysterious force ravaged his body. He coughed and blue veins snaked their way up from his chest and up to his neck and face. His white eyes burst red as blood exploded within, and with a strangled gasp his grip failed, and he slid off.

"A weak heart for a man his size," said Jagar, stepping away from Eoin's twitching body.

"I'll kill you!" roared Kavik, hurtling towards him. Iqaluk spun around and wrapped his arms around Kyira as Kavik and Jagar smashed into one another.

"Let… go!" screamed Kyira.

When she looked back, Kavik lay motionless in the far corner, next to Eoin. There was no time to consider what to do as the sound of steel on steel rang around them. Laeb and Duga parried furiously as again Jagar seemed to move casually out of the way from moves that would have cut any other man to ribbons. Duga pushed the sword clumsily out to the left, and Jagar dipped right to avoid it, just as a knife slid out of Duga's sleeve. Duga jabbed out, and his blade met skin.

"You are faster than these Ringlanders give you credit for, islander," said Jagar touching his cheek lightly. "It has been too long since I saw my own blood." He licked his fingertip.

"You talk too much," said Duga, panting.

Jagar cricked his neck, "Alright, then. Let us finish."

The fight continued, the parries and retreats an orchestrated dance of sinuous beauty. Even so, Laeb was beginning to flag, as his returns slowed. Jagar struck a fist out into an impossible gap and caught Laeb on the nose. Laeb reeled back, then blindly rushed forward attacking from Duga's side, swinging out his sword in a wide arc and forcing Jagar to duck. With unbelievable speed, Duga ducked under Laeb's advance with barely a hair between his head and Laeb's blade, and with his back to Jagar pulled his sword in a devastating high arc, and as Jagar batted away Laeb's attack, Duga's sword struck through the only gap it could have, straight down into Jagar's neck.

There was an explosion of light and everyone was blown away from Jagar. Droplets of fire showered across the tent, falling to the ground and solidifying as tiny pools of shining liquid metal. The hilt of Duga's sword cartwheeled to a stop at Kyira's feet, the remaining shard of white metal hissing upon the grass.

The light vanished, and there stood Jagar, more whole than he should have been, a smudge of soot upon his neck the only sign of any contact at all. A spark crackled from Jagar's wrist, and a flame grew from his arm, twisting around it like a snake. Duga and captain Laeb picked themselves up but were both without their weapons. Duga, cradling his arm, stood and faced Jagar, as stubborn a man as she had ever seen.

Jagar pointed at him, and the fire burst forth and engulfed Duga. Kyira shielded herself from the intense heat as Duga's shape was outlined with a torrent of fire. He fought it, leaning against the flames like a salmon fighting the stream, as pieces of him were blasted away. The hazy figure buckled and fell to the ground as a burning pile beside Eoin's still corpse.

Jagar brushed at his patchwork jacket and turned towards Kyira and Iqaluk. "Now," he said, adjusting his still smouldering sleeve. "The two Sami." Iqaluk stretched across Kyira and wrapped his body around hers. She could smell his breath, his skin, even feel his thumping heart as he held her close, dropping to his knees with her and encasing her like a set of raeven wings. Kyira screwed her eyes shut and waited for the fire.

There was the sound of more struggling as Kavik grabbed Jagar and lifted him off the floor, one arm around the man's neck and the other covering his face. They teetered together back and forth, tipping between the smouldering remains of Duga, while fire leapt hungrily about the tent canvas.

"The entrance, Kyira!" hissed Iqaluk. "Go!"

Kyira burst up and sped towards the entrance of the tent, towards the cool air flowing in, but shouts and movement came from behind. She turned towards Kavik. His face was the same ashen grey as his brothers... She couldn't let it happen. She had to make a choice. She could stop this. Iqaluk grasped at her, but she pulled away and took up Duga's blackened sword hilt. She could see Jagar's face, his misted eyes. He was evil. His name was evil, and she would restore balance.

The ease with which the still glowing shard slipped into the Banéman's temple shocked her. His head jerked with the force of her lunge, even as the top of the hilt stood still an

328

inch from the side of Jagar's face. Kavik fell back, and Jagar landed upon the mud. Kyira fell with him, holding the hilt as tightly as she could, twisting it, forcing the metal deeper into the Banéman's head.

Jagar's rolling eyes focused on her for a second. "Little Bird?" he said, softly. "Is that you?" His expression contorted into malice itself. "I WILL BURN YOU—"

Kyira slammed her palm into the pommel, driving the shard deep into Jagar's head. Cracks of light appeared in his face, growing wide and bright. He bucked this way and that, as the fire within burned him from the inside.

Iqaluk appeared from behind and pulled Kyira up bodily, dragging her away from the flaming Banéman.

Jagar's eyes glowed as the cracks converged and he let out an inhuman wail. "NOOO!"

Heat pulsed off of him in waves. His face buckled and tore, then caved in, and a plume of white fire erupted from his ruined head.

A Father's Prerogative

Cool air filled Kyira's lungs. Flickering orange was replaced with an expanse of vivid indigo. Blurry figures grew details: leather straps, buckles, hair on skin, wooden pails, splashes of water that hung suspended in the air before falling onto trampled grass. Above it all the smell of fire and burning meat.

Jagar was gone, but his fire remained, leaping hungrily from tent to tent, eager to consume the camp. It was fire, but not the same as Makril's fire. Those living snake tongues that crept along the ground searching like an animal. This was the same fire she knew, the same fire that she had grown up with, respecting, cultivating. The warmth of it bringing life, sustaining her and her family. The same fire that had just torn her family apart.

She looked over at Iqaluk lying silently beside her. A tickle in the back of her mind beckoned her to look lower, and she fought it — knowing what was there — but again and again it came. Below her father's chin, his chest lay open and burned almost all of the way through. No blood. His eyes stared open and glassy up at the starry sky. Numbness spread through Kyira's body like the time she fell into an ice pit, water engulfing her, claiming each limb until she couldn't move. The same feeling the slaver no doubt felt before the cold took him. The feeling lasted barely a second, before vomit filled her mouth. She rolled onto her side and let it come, wishing desperately for grief to release her.

"Leave it!" roared a familiar voice. "Concentrate on the spread!"

The world moved again, and a dark shape blocked out the indigo canvas above. Rough fingers probed her ears, mouth and eyes, and wiped her face, then lifted her, taking her weight, before placing her back down. She coughed; her throat felt like she'd swallowed a jug of dry needlepines.

"You did good," came a gruff voice.

"Kavik? You're alive?"

"Because of you, Kyira," said Kavik, his lips puffy and bleeding. "Your father…" Tears fell from his eyes, lost on the wet ground. "I'm sorry I couldn't save him. I'm sorry I couldn't save… her…" He broke down and collapsed to the grass in a fit of sobs.

Kyira's thoughts hardened in an instant. "Eoin."

"My brother dines with the Forbringrs now," said Kavik, tilting his head towards the evening sky. "And my daughter. My Janike."

Captain Laeb appeared from within a cloud of smoke, his face blackened with soot, and knelt beside her. "Are you hurt?" he asked, tenderly.

Kyira dragged the reply up from the depths. "Fine."

"You are not fine, Kyira, and pretending otherwise would do the dead a disservice."

"I don't see how it makes a difference."

Laeb stood and offered her a hand. "Come with me."

She couldn't bring herself to take it.

331

"It wasn't your fault," he said. "I saw what Iqaluk did. He saved you."

"He shouldn't have bothered. Both of my parents are dead by my hand. My mother, during birth, and now my father... at the hands of the demon Jagar."

"Do not speak his name," growled Laeb. "The Slayer was no demon. Come with me, Kyira. Please. I need you."

Kyira looked up at him. He was a beautiful man. His strong features reminded her of the earth, of her brother, of Aki. Before she could stop herself, she threw her arms around him and cried.

"It should have been me!" The walls came crashing down, and she sobbed and screamed and bellowed her father's name, and she could do nothing but let it wash over her like a wave. Her father was dead. She buried her head into Laeb's chest, feeling his warmth leach into her. Minutes passed before she pulled away, leaving the imprint of tears on his shirt.

He wiped her eyes. "It is a father's prerogative to give his life for his children," he said. "Perhaps one day you might even be lucky enough to do the same. Now come with me. Please Kyira. Please."

She looked back at Kavik who was sitting up, head on his knees.

"Don't worry about him," whispered Laeb. "We all grieve in our own way, and Kavik needs space."

Laeb guided her over patches of blackened grass and smouldering piles of ash. She could sense figures staring at them, but she didn't bother to look back. Instead she let Laeb lead her to the southern quadrants. The grass was muddy, and it was windier than down in the valley but there were still tents here, which was a vast improvement. They walked into the thick of them and stopped at one in the middle.

The tent had been recently vacated by its previous occupant, judging by the smell of candle smoke, the ruffled bedding and the half-corset hanging from below the main lamp flame.

"What about you?" asked Kyira. "What about Duga?"

Laeb's expression was flat, as though he were trying to keep it that way. She had lived around men long enough to know that often they just didn't know how they should feel. It was one of their peculiarities that she wished she could have had for herself.

"Duga… was… he always wanted a fighter's death, and he got it."

"He was so fast," said Kyira. "Faster even than… whatever it was."

"Jagar was a Slayer," whispered Laeb. He started moving around the tent, collecting things and dropping them in a corner. "His kind are inbred over hundreds of generations, folding traits within traits in an effort to create the perfect combination of warrior and mage. Some hunger for power, some for manflesh, but all are formidable."

"Mage?" croaked Kyira.

"It is said in legend," began Laeb, sitting on the edge of the bed, "that there were once men and women who lived away from the towns and cities, following strange religions. Religions that allowed them to take control of the world around them with only a thought. But I must confess I had never seen it used until… He used it."

"Edda used to tell us stories," said Kyira. "Baeivi and the Stallo. The Gods of the Lands. But I never imagined… They were nothing like what Jag... what he did. Twisting fire like that. He could control it."

"But he couldn't make it," said Laeb. "That is important. They have ways, but so do we all. Did you see the contraption at his wrist? It was a flint. Without that flint he has no spark, and no fire. Don't let their *magic* fool you. Magic is false. They are the same as you and I."

Kyira shook her head. "But he moved so fast."

"Not fast enough," said Laeb.

A strange silence settled upon them, and after a moment Laeb took her hand. "What will you do now? Do you have other family?"

Kyira breathed a heavy sigh and wiped the wetness from her cheeks. "My brother fights with these Kin... he spoke of."

If Laeb had been an animal, she might have seen his ears prick up at those words. "I see. And you are searching for him?"

Kyira sat upright. "Hasaan is gentle at heart, as his father is. Was." She paused. "If he fights, it is not by his own will."

"Can you tell me any more about them?" said Laeb.

"What, so you can find them, and kill them?" She pulled away.

Laeb shuffled closer to her, "You know, I can still hear Duga's voice telling me to hold my tongue, even now as I try to speak of things I shouldn't." His eyes glazed over. "His mother will miss him, and his wife and four sons. They'll need told..." Abruptly, he seemed to become aware of Kyira's stare. "I have heard reports of men moving through Nord and the Outer Circles, drafting young men into a secret army."

334

"The Kin?"

Laeb nodded. "Many of whom were tricked into joining."

"Hasaan left because of Iqaluk," said Kyira. "They were fighting the night before, and the next day he left. I've not seen him since." She had no tears left, but their echoes still racked at her. Laeb laid his arm around her, and drew her in. She fought it for the briefest of moments before giving in to his warmth.

He knelt down in front of her. "I need your help, Kyira. Iqaluk's death will change you. He guided you and helped you forge a path through this life and his presence will leave a mark on your soul. A mark that you will carry with you as a badge of honour. You have the same fire within you. But the only way to move forward is to leave something behind. You must take up his mantle."

"I will," sobbed Kyira. "I will find Hasaan."

Laeb paused. "I will not offend you by lying or excusing my reasons. The map your father made was destroyed in the fire. It shows the way into the Bohr stronghold that is Tyr, and more importantly, the way out. Without that map, the Tsiorc will be cut down in foreign streets. I need you to remake it."

"How?"

"You watched him make it," said Laeb.

She closed her eyes, and bone-deep fatigue settled upon her. "I can't. You'll use it to hurt Hasaan."

"You mistake our intentions. Our aim is to bring peace to these lands, not war. Speak to any one of those soldiers outside, each of whom are worth ten of the lord's army. Why? Because they fight for themselves. They fight for their homes, their land, and their families." He let go of her. "That

335

is why I am here. That was why Duga was here, and Eoin, and Tri, and Bryn. They gave their lives to protect those they loved." He stood and turned to leave.

"Wait," said Kyira. "You can't leave me here. What am I supposed to do?"

Laeb turned. "This is your tent, Kyira, not mine. Glynn!"

A young man, a little younger than Kyira herself, entered the tent and stood stiffly. His hair was the colour of honey-tsampa. Smudges of soot marked him from forehead to below the neckline of his messenger coat.

His eyes flicked towards her then back to Laeb. "Captain?"

Laeb tapped the boy on the shoulder. "This is Glynn, and no matter how hard I try, your Gods keep bringing him back to me!" Glynn smirked. "This Farram has saved my life twice already, and now I charge him with helping you. He will get you anything you need." He stepped towards Kyira and took her by the shoulders. "We need you, Kyira." There was a flash of something unreadable on his face, before he turned away. "Glynn, look after her."

A Change of Fortunes

I t hadn't taken long for Glynn to fall asleep. He had
been in the midst of the action, carrying water, moving
tents to stop the spread and even saving people. Or at
least that's what he had said. Kyira crept past him. There
was still an hour before dusk, which should give her more
than enough time to put a few leagues between her and the
Tsiorc. Her feet twitched at the prospect of running along
the road back up into the sisters of Nord.

From the elevated southern quadrant and with dawn's
early light, it was easy to see that all of the tents down in
the valley were gone. The grass was black all the way to the
muddy road where they had first entered only the day before,
which looked to be roughly a tenth of the camp. Lines of
bodies were laid out along each road, the winds dragging at
their makeshift coverings.

Avoiding the roads, she crossed at a particularly muddy
junction, which had wide wooden boards stretched across
it, then wound her way through the camp towards the gates.

A topless man stood watching her as she approached the
aviary, raevens hanging off every inch of him, and each
one apparently fast asleep by the little jerks and soft keens
emanating from his general direction. She nodded as she

passed, and he winked a pair of eyes too large for any normal man.

It wasn't long before she reached the carts and camps of the townspeople, still where they had stopped the previous day. Nothing moved, and nothing shone. It seemed even the fires had been extinguished. Something poked her in the back and she jumped.

"Penni!" The ox nuzzled into Kyira as gently as a calf. She grasped one of the horns and the animal lifted her smoothly onto its back. "You are a beautiful animal. You deserve better than being pulled into a war. You should be home, where it is cool and fine." Almost idly she retrieved the figurine Lars had given her from her waist bag. Now that she looked at it, she saw the likeness with Iqaluk that Lars had spoken of. The way the figurine seemed to be mid-movement. She tied it to Penni's yoke and let it dangle there.

"She likes you," said a voice, from the shadows. "And if she could talk she would tell me she always has. How are you, Kyira?"

"Tor. I'm fine."

"News of Iqaluk's death came to us soon after the fire," said Tor. "I am sorry. He was a good man."

Grief clutched at Kyira's heart as though he had somehow reached in and physically grabbed it. "You were kind to him," she said, the words drying up in her throat, "and me. But I must go. I cannot stay here. I have… I must…"

Tor opened his mouth to speak then stopped as his gaze fell upon Penni's yoke. He fingered the figurine. "I made this for Lars, and it was his to give, yet when I learned he had given it away I was upset. First, he said it had been lost, then that he had traded it for food, then that some blue-eyes

338

took it, then eventually he told me the truth. He had given it to you. To keep you." He unhooked it and studied it. "It is my father, caught forever in the space of my strongest memory of him. He was the strongest man I ever knew, and he made me who I am, as Iqaluk did you." An owl hooted softly somewhere behind them, and Kyira swallowed down her pain, grateful for the bird's distraction. Still, she couldn't bring herself to speak. Tor, however, stood proudly, wearing his tears like a coat of armour. He held her gaze, still as a mountain. "I give this back to you now. To keep you, as Lars keeps me."

Kyira took the figurine and held it in both hands. Its weight felt reassuring. "Thank you."

Tor nodded once. "We all need someone to watch over us, Kyira." He stood to the side revealing the faint glow of a fire behind.

"I thought everyone was asleep."

"Not everyone."

Kyira swung her leg over and slid from Penni's back, offering her a long stroke down her nose. She padded towards Tor and leaned past him, looking along the parked carts, where a small flame still burned, shining on the faces of Lars, Lyla, and her babe.

"She's been asking for you. Come." Tor led Kyira into the light and they all looked up as she and Tor approached.

"Kyira," said Lyla, smiling warmly. "Sit."

Lars, who sat poking at the fire as though he had never seen one before, looked up as Lyla tapped his leg. "You found her?"

"Penni found her," said Tor, taking a seat. "She's leaving."

"Oh no," said Lars, but Tor shook his head, silencing him.

Lars resumed his fire-poking.

"Sorry about your father, Kyira," said Lyla.

Kyira nodded back to her, her eyes falling to the babe bundled in her lap. "She is as beautiful as you, Lyla."

"She has Isak's eyes, so she will break many hearts."

Kyira's stomach felt like it had shrunk to the size of a pine nut. "Have you chosen a name?"

"Abika. It means *Forbringr's Gift*. Which is something that should make my parents happy. Baeivi knows they didn't approve of anything else I chose to do." She handed over a strip of blackened, dried meat. "Lars smoked some of the dog meat. It's a little bitter, but it's better than it was."

Kyira took it and nodded gratefully to Lars who was doing his best to pretend he was invisible. "Where are they? Your parents…"

"Dead." Lyla stared through her. "Killed by the Bohr south of Tyr many moons ago. When I sought out answers to their deaths I was met only with excuses. I followed the rules of society, and tried to bring those who had killed them to justice. I approached the courts, the council and even requested an audience with the Kael himself."

Kyira held the meat tighter. "And what happened?"

Lyla shook her head. "The Bohr do not care about the lives of humans. They must manage us, because they know that if they do not, we would quickly overrun them. All else is ignored."

"So, that is why you joined the rebels."

"The Tsiorc are not rebels, Kyira. They are humans. Swimming in the shallow waters of a deep sea filled with possibility. Rengas is so big, yet the Bohr want it all. They want to control kingdoms, passage, taxes, trade. They would take the sea for themselves, if they could. Only the Tsiorc can stop them."

Kyira tilted her chin. "You see these? My Lines define who I am. They are a map of my life, laid out on my skin. They keep me true and tell me where I am to go. Those who stray from their Lines are Culdè, and they will go through their lives never knowing who they are, or what they need to do. Better dead, than Culdè."

Lyla tilted her head in sympathy. "And what of your brother?"

"He does not need me."

"Iqaluk spoke of Hasaan often during the quiet times of that first day, when the slavers took him, after he realised that like him, we were travellers who had been snatched from our lives. He spoke fondly of you, also. It was clear that he loved you both." Lyla smiled warmly. "Perhaps you should find Hasaan. He may need you."

Kyira shook her head. "He doesn't need me. He never has. Besides, he chose to leave us, and he must pay the consequences."

"It sounds like you are punishing him because of how he made you feel, Kyira. And I understand that, but he made his choices." Abika gurgled and Lyla stroked the babe's fine dark hair. "In the end, we cannot define ourselves. We look to those around us to see our reflections, and it is those who are closest to our hearts that give us the clearest picture. We are nothing without family."

"He fights for...someone else."

Tor leaned towards her. "Kyira, everyone needs something to believe in." He lifted his shirt sleeve revealing a familiar belt blade that had been slid into the top of his fresh bandages. He pulled out Iqaluk's knife and held it by the steel. "There are few I respect in this world, and your father was one of them. You are like him, but that is not why I respect you." He took a breath, as though unsure what to say next. "This morning he handed me his own knife, and asked me to give it to you whenever you needed it. I think that time is now. He said it might change your fortunes."

Kyira's chest felt like it might explode from all the emotions contained therein. She had never before felt so much at one time. With huge effort she swallowed it down. "Thank you, Tor."

The steel was warm where it had been pressed up against Tor's skin, and the faint imprint of his arm hair was still visible on the metal. The hilt was very much like her own knife that she had given to Lyla — bone, inlaid with carvings and worn shiny on the inside where Iqaluk would press the hardest. She ran a finger along it, and could almost feel the memory of her father's skin there, working and moving with the knife like a tool. Its weight felt reassuring in her hand, even more than her own blade had.

"You see," said Lyla. "We are all just people. Whichever world we happen to be born into." Kyira stroked Abika's head, and then Lyla stroked hers.

She looked into the woman's eyes, which even against her dark skin were hollow and tired. She returned her warm smile and said, "Guma slàn dhut," and then more awkwardly in Tyrian, "Fare Well."

"Good luck, Kyira," said Lyla. "All is said. Go and do what you must."

Kyira turned her back the group and began making her way back towards the camp. When she reached the edge of the last cart, she stopped, feeling the layers of chipped paint beneath her fingers. The fresh scent of new blooms blew in on the dawn wind, and there came the sound of geese high above. It was time to follow her path.

Straw Men

Rathe had barely managed to sit down on the padded seat before the cart jolted into action.

Lor motioned to the clad ceiling. "You have some good men here."

"The driver?" replied Rathe. "You know I don't think I've ever actually asked him twice for anything, although perhaps he needs another lesson on how long to wait before I take my seat."

"Loyal *and* hard-working? Are you sure he's not a spy?"

Rathe pulled down the door shutter for a bit of privacy, loyal or no, some news was best kept for those who needed to hear it. "Not everyone is out to get you, Lor."

Lor sat lazily, although he was anything but. He nodded to Rathe's cap. "Show me the mark."

Rathe lifted the cap up from his forehead just enough to reveal the newly healed scar beneath.

"The Bohr king marking a Child of the Bohr," said Lor. "I never thought I would see such a thing."

"Times change, brother. The old creeds will soon die out, and we will be all that are left." Rathe peered out through the slats at the Vasen streets trundling by picturing what they might look like under his rule: cleaner, flowing gold, and charn, Vasen dock the new envy of the Inner Circle of Rengas, with not even Ge'Bat able to match—

"Times change, but people do not," Lor considered his own words. "Humans do not."

Rathe flicked open the armrest of his chair, revealing an inner storage tray, filled with morsels of various dried meat and fruit. "You are at war, Lor. It is as clear to me as this mark is to everyone else. Even now, sitting in the carriage of the Guardian of Tyr, you cannot relax. You are at war."

"*We* are at war," replied Lor. "For as long as there are enemies of the state. But I catch your meaning. Drafting children into the lord's army is neither difficult nor rewarding. A lesser blade might dull."

"Are you implying that my blade is blunting, commander?"

The white of Lor's filed teeth flashed. "Of course not, Guardian. I live to serve." He reached over and skewered the entire stack of dried venison from the tray with a knife that appeared from nowhere then swallowed it with barely a chew. "Now, your messenger was very eager to find me. Are you going tell me what you are intending at this meet or are you leaving me to guess?"

"There will be a vote," said Rathe, frustrated to leave the previous subject so unresolved. "A vote that should place you in a station more…fitting to a Child."

Lor took the news blankly, absorbing it and processing it like one of Seb's calculating machines. "A vote? And who is it that holds within their hands the course of my life?"

"The council."

Lor scoffed. "The council are a useless legacy of our forebears which should be cut from our lives like an infected limb. Why allow them a forum at all?"

Rathe glared at his brother. "Our heritage is a gift, Lor. What we lack in parentage we make up for in ambition. It is what sets us apart. By allowing the humans to meet, we take away the need for violence." The words were out before he could stop them.

Lor seized. "The need for violence. Any Guardian worth the mark would step out onto the streets occasionally, dear brother. And if you did, you would see that violence sits beneath the skin of all that walk them. Lurking and waiting to be set free."

"Yes, well. My reach, as universally omnipotent as it seems, is still subject to the will of the king. Still, there is much we need to do, that you need to do."

"You speak of the army?" He pulled a large chunk of meat from his molar and studied it.

"Even as Kael, I had control of the army," Rathe sighed. "To an extent. But the time for games is over. We need the army to do more for us. Now is our time, *dear brother.*"

Lor's eyes narrowed, his calculating mind already putting the pieces together. "That privilege belongs to the Bohr King. And then the *great* Nevis himself."

"Great? Perhaps in name, but General Nevis has never been great. Not like you would be."

The sound of cobbles changed suddenly to smooth stone and Rathe closed the food tray. "Well dear brother, we are here. Let us see how Nevis takes this news."

The doors opened and Rathe stepped out into an afternoon too dark for this time of year. "Have we a full house, porter?"

The porter nodded enthusiastically, her brown braid jumping. "Yes, Guardian Rathe. A full house."

"And the Kin?"

"Sitting in the Whisper Gallery," said the porter.

Rathe reached out and took hold of the two door handles. "Ready?"

"Get on with it, Guardian."

Rathe lingered for a spell and pulled both doors open. The party was already in full swing. Kaliste, the leader of the Banémen, was here. General Nevis too. The lords, the Kin — the chamber was full and already alive with heated debate.

"Let me begin," boomed Rathe. His voice echoed around the circular hall, amplified by his position at the foot of the dome. He made the appropriate welcomes and introductions, and all the while General Nevis's hawk-like eyes watched him. He was a slight man at only a little over six- and one-half feet, but what he lacked in stance he made up for in viciousness. None of it mattered, of course, but it helped to have the measure of a man before hanging him upon the noose.

"Kaliste," boomed Rathe, "while there are items on our agenda impatiently waiting to be discussed…" He took a moment to acknowledge the lords in the high seats. "I would ask first if any of you have heard from Jagar?"

"No." The leader of the Banémen's voice was almost as soft as Fia's, but dripped with the same ugly arrogance that every Banéman seemed to possess. She held a sad expression on her angular face. "Jagar's light has gone out."

"If you mean he's dead," barked the general, "then say it! The Hall of Council is a platform to speak plainly!"

Kaliste's eye twitched. "Dead, as you call it, is too simple a word to describe such a transition. Maybe it suits the battlefield—"

347

"It does," snapped General Nevis. "Life has no force. No magic. Life is cheap."

Kaliste sneered. "As you say."

"We all smell the same as a corpse," spat the general. "Much the same as the corpses lining the streets presently. What has happened to Tyr in the ten moons the lord's army has been away? It has become a midden. A shit heap!"

"Perhaps the new Guardian can answer that question," said Kaliste.

Rathe's breath caught as both figures stared down at him accusingly. "A midden? The city of Tyr flourishes!"

"What about the riots?" came a shout from across the room. Rathe glared up at the councillors. Councillor Sofek stood, looking ready to fight.

The porter stepped forward and whispered, "Councillor Sofek, Guardian—"

"I know who he is!" growled Rathe. The porter shrank back and Rathe snapped back towards the murmuring babble. "You refer to the new tolls…"

Councillor Allander's voice rang out like a bell. "The citizens of Terävä do not riot. They are upstanding people." Grumbles immediately wafted up from the back bench behind Sofek but Allander carried on, his clear tones cutting through the cacophony. "There are a few who have taken to expressing their anger with current conditions. Crops are failing, animals are dying. It is not helped by the economy. A loaf of bread, which last month cost a docker's wage for the day, now costs ten times as much! And what of the missing shepherd Erdal…"

* * *

Hasaan glanced to the sides, but the other Kin ignored him, too fearful to consider looking up from the white marble floors.

The room reminded him of a stoning quarry — a huge hole in the ground with levels at regular steps. On the second such step stood the source of most of the noise. His name was Nevis, and he was clearly high-ranking, broad and wore a dark leather coat held tight with a blue belt. He also had more scars than skin.

"You have taken this too far, Rathe!" roared Nevis. "What do you expect Commander Lor to bring to the lord's army that I cannot myself?" His voice rang around the chamber all the way to the rostrum at the very bottom where two Bohr stood.

"I am the Guardian of Tyr." Rathe removed his cap to reveal a long coil of braided black hair, which fell down his back. Upon his head was a red cross; a scar that had been cut into his skin. "Do not forget it."

The general's face turned crimson. Even from up near the roof Hasaan could see the man's bluster had run out. "Well, there it is. I am being ousted from my post after fifteen cycles, because I am not Bohr! Guardian, your handling of this is as shoddy and shameful as your handling of the sanctions upon the Way." The words shouldn't have been audible so far away, but the room amplified them somehow.

Kaliste, a tall thin woman, who looked ancient despite her ageless face replied in a thin whine. "You talk of incompetence having lost yet another battle."

"You speak of Drakemyre?" snapped Nevis.

"The battle that was lost, yes." replied Kaliste, flatly.

Nevis scoffed. "Then you speak of what you do not know."

"Then general," continued Kaliste, "you said earlier that the lord's army is camped on Mount Terävä?"

"Yes," said the General, through his teeth.

"And what good is an army stationed outside of its city?"

The general's slanted stare became a confused frown. "They are outside the front gates, Kaliste."

"I am aware of the Mount's location, General."

"Then what are you suggesting? That Tyr and its high walls will somehow be breached without the lord's army realising? There are over one hundred legions camped outside the city barely an hour away from this building, with thirty on the Mount itself. If you think that…" he stopped himself. "You know, actually, let's assume that the Tsiorc make it into Tyr, passing by one hundred and thirty legions, and crossing the Way Bridge and the Panguards guarding it. They'll be met with Tyr's winding narrow streets, which will break up any large force not intimately familiar with them; not mentioning the resilience of a people with Bohrblood running deep through their veins." He turned to the audience, watching from above his position. "I would pity any fool to make such an attempt. You Banéman, so full of useful advice. Do you think that we are somehow at risk here? Tyr is a fortress."

"In my experience—"

"In your experience," repeated Nevis, stabbing the air as though his hands were weapons. "Have you lived all the lives that can be lived?"

"The Banémen have been here before," said Kaliste calmly. "But not in any way that your human mind would understand."

"No city is invulnerable to attack," said Lor, suddenly. "Not

350

even Tyr."

The general aimed his scowl at Lor. "And what would a commander of supply boys know of controlling an army?"

A heavy voice boomed around the hall, but it came from Hasaan's left, not from the floor. "More than you, General Nevis."

A creature unlike any Hasaan had seen stood across the gallery at the doors. It had arms and legs like a man, and its reversed ankles and hulking back made it look something like a Bohr, only much larger — so large that its tied locs brushed the ceiling above. Its eyes, which were as big as plates, scanned the room, lingering on the Kin. There was a pause then it spoke again. "But less than a Bohr king."

"The Halls of Council recognise the Bohr king in accordance with the Bohr's Right of Entry."

"You may call me Zuveri, Guardian Rathe," said the Bohr king, looking down upon the hall.

Rathe nodded slowly. "Zuveri."

The Bohr King stepped over the barrier and scaled the steep stairs one landing at a time. "Three thousand soldiers," it said, in time with its footsteps, "two hundred horses, countless resources to fight an enemy borne from your own people, directed by a man." Zuveri stopped at the general's level and loomed over him, a full five times taller. "A man. Like you."

"War… is… never simple, Master Zuveri," stuttered Nevis.

"No?" said Zuveri, squatting right down, its head still above the general's.

"We… mistook our enemy," muttered Nevis.

"Yes," growled Zuveri. "You did." It gave a low-pitched growl, so deep that it stirred the hairs on Hasaan's face. He felt his heart speed up, as though the growl were directed at him. No one breathed. No one moved. There was a faint sound of trickling water as the general pissed himself.

"The Bohr will leave a legacy that no world has ever known, only if our enemies are destroyed. If we allow them to breed, they will no longer come to fear us. There are those who slip through the cracks, those who appear less than they are." Hasaan cowered under the thing's gaze as it raked around the hall. "Those who move unseen in the shadows. Those who do not crave power or strength or money. They are the true danger, and their only weakness is not knowing it." Its dark gaze lingered, and Hasaan stared back unable to look away, then, with teeth bared, Zuveri leapt up from the stands, hanging in the air before landing softly where Rathe and Lor stood.

"Rathe, I afforded you the opportunity to make good after the events of Drakemyre, but your actions have only caused dissension in a city that was once pure Bohrblood. As of this moment, I, Zuveri, king of all Bohr, take command of the lord's army and this council for now, and ever more."

The Path

Kyira cradled the redback in her palm, enjoying the purrs vibrating through its little body. What a wondrous thing it must be to feel so protected, to have so much power wrapped around you. It was said that raevens were ancestors of dragons, but like all myths, there was barely any truth to them. She ran a finger over its head, and it yawned contentedly.

"He's a Domst redback," said Glynn. "Or so Captain Laeb tells me. I took him back to the aviary, but he escaped. I came back after orientation one morning to find him back here." He held out his hand to take the creature away. "I think Captain Laeb would expect that we finish this quickly, Kyira."

"I don't care what Captain Laeb wants."

Glynn lifted the charred box from the paper-strewn desk and tapped it. "Fine, but we should try again. The map is too important—"

She batted the box away and it flew from his hand onto the mattress. "We? There is no we! I have to do this. Besides, nothing has changed. We've been here for hours. I cannot do it."

Glynn frowned. She was still getting used to seeing blond

hair on a man. It looked ridiculous. He was ridiculous. "Do you not have somewhere else to be?"

"No, actually."

"Then what do you do here other than pester anyone who comes too close?"

"Anything I'm told to," shrugged Glynn, pulling dried ink from his fingers. "Mostly carrying messages between the officers. They say I'm too young to fight."

"I've seen younger than you fighting."

Glynn ran a hand through his thick hair. "Well, I've never killed anyone, so I don't know what they expect me to do when we reach Tyr." Glynn moved to take the redback from her.

"Leave him!" The raeven hissed then flapped onto the bed and crawled under the blanket. "You fool! Look what you did!" She would not be pushed around by this youngling! "Now what am I to do? What exactly should I do now?" Her voice sounded like Kyira's, daughter to Iqaluk and Thea sister to Hasaan, the Sami girl from Nord who hated climbing, and loved cooking, and hunting and…but it was not her. She was detached from herself, observing everything that Kyira did and said as someone else.

Glynn stepped back awkwardly, fumbling with the opening to the tent. "I'll… give you a moment."

She watched as the fool boy left, irrational anger bubbling up inside her like rising tsampa bread. She stormed over to the desk and leant against it. Why was she so angry? It wasn't Glynn's fault. Her head was stuffed full of thoughts that she could not unscramble, her father, her brother, her life, the map, Laeb.

She opened her eyes and tears fell freely, rolling down onto the parchment and cutting through the six inked squares she had painstakingly pressed into the paper. The designs from the charred Maelta box were beautifully intricate, in their own way, except only two lined up. The floor was littered with her crumpled attempts to find ways of making the shapes work, but it was clear that the curved streets just didn't go together — they were completely misaligned.

"Shiach!" With a growl, she pushed the papers onto the floor. "I cannot do it!" She kicked the leg of the table, and annoyingly, it barely moved. There it was, she was simply not strong enough. Not like Iqaluk. "I hate you," she whispered.

The words broke her.

She fell back into the chair and dropped her head into her arms. What could she possibly do without him? How was she supposed to live by herself, without Aki to guide her? She turned towards the box; a relic of an age long gone.

"What am I to do? The answer is here, and I cannot see it!"

The redback let out another tiny yawn, it's needle teeth flashing, and Kyira found herself smiling down at the creature. It stretched its wings out so far they shook, then drew them back, encasing himself within. If this little redback could survive, living in the midst of an army, against the odds, against countless predators, then so would she. She would survive.

Breathe.

Standing straight, she reached down and touched the tips of her moccasins, bending the knee just enough to allow her right leg to stretch out to the side.

"I am alone."

355

Her ankle clicked as she bent it back and caught it behind her, drawing it up past her buttocks.

Breathe.

Her hip popped as she switched to the other foot.

Hasaan was missing.

She arched her back and pulled her ankle up until her toes touched her hair.

"I am Sami."

Breathe.

Iqaluk's words appeared like morning flowers in her mind's eye:

"Look within and you will discover that your very make up is primed to guide you. The answer lies within our blood, as it always has and always will. You are Sami."

She rushed over to the desk where the parchment lay, tracing one of the printed squares which had been split down the middle by her tears. "They are the same size!" Dropping to her knees, she rooted through the crumpled pieces of their discarded attempts, looking for a side print of the Maelta box. She found it and flattened it out comparing it against the one her tears had ruined. "The side of the box is exactly half the length." That had to mean something. Grabbing the Maelta box from the mattress, she used her fingers to roughly measure and they matched up. "It is a grid."

She flipped the parchment to the blank side and grabbed the inkwell and brush from the floor, but before she could paint her eyes fell upon the narrow edge. Along the strip at the edge there were words carved into the wood.

Who Shape The World

Something tickled at her mind, but she let it go, and brushed the top face of the closed box. She printed the block, and gently pulled it up, the carved swirls of the Maelta leaving tiny snaking lines woven together up to the edge where they cut off. The streets of Tyr.

Next, she painted the top, back, bottom, and front faces and printed those too, laying the four faces vertically with two at the sides, as if the box had been flattened out into two dimensions. The back and bottom faces in the middle of the layout aligned perfectly, forming a square, but no other face fit together, so none of the twists and turns of Tyr's winding streets connected beyond the edges. They had tried already matching the sides which too where misaligned.

"That is how you keep your secrets hidden," she said, shaking her head in disbelief. "The outside faces are not meant to match up." Maelta. *Deceive*.

This box was a puzzle, and Kyira stood at the beginning. The inside of the box had shallow grooves like the outside, but there was no way she could print the inside of the box. Even the lid refused to lay fully flat. Why had she had not paid more attention? She thought back to the tent, when Iqaluk was working. She had been watching Laeb dressing — his chiselled features, the lines of his body... "Concentrate!" She muttered to herself.

She pulled Iqaluk's blade from her sheathe. The blade was well worn, but well kept, and she pushed the tip into the corner of the box, searching for something. Anything. The sharp, thin steel caught on something between the two faces. Was it a nail? She applied a little pressure and the Maelta box clicked. Its tight corners fell loose, and the edges dropped apart, hanging together from tiny hinges. She laughed, as the box flapped about, now completely laid out, in the same pattern as she had printed on the parchment. What's more, the inside faces were now accessible.

They were carved as beautifully as the outside faces on the other side, and when she moved to reform the box, now inside-out, the motion drew out tiny metal teeth from in between the layers on both sides. The teeth had hooked ends, so the Maelta could be closed back into a new box shape.

"So that's how you're held together," she said, running a finger along the metal. On the top face one of the hooks was sticking out. She pushed it in, and the carved patterns rotated in front of her eyes, revealing new, uncharred wood. New streets.

"Glynn!"

"What did you do?" said Glynn, rushing in. He had obviously been standing outside the whole time.

She pushed the metal tooth on the opposite side just as Glynn reached her side.

"Holy Gods!" he said, as the pattern moved back to its original state.

"Watch. This pattern is new," she said, her breaths shallow with excitement. She pushed at another hooked tooth, and the box pattern shifted back into another new pattern, the ink blackened parts disappearing almost completely. "Iqaluk only printed the outside and inside of the box, but these patterns are new. I think what my father printed was only half of the map."

Glynn gasped. "Half? Tyr is split up into Quadrants, Kyira.

So, if this is half of the map, and these two central squares match…"

"We will have a complete map of Tyr," said Kyira.

"But there's still a piece miss…"

Kyira held up a finger. "I know, Glynn. Be quiet." She worked methodically, as Iqaluk had done, printing only the two central squares of each side. She pushed the tooth back in on the first side bringing the box layout into its second state. The patterns rotated and she gave it another coat of ink and printed the same two faces from each side. "One side of the unlatched box per quadrant, and the extra state makes another two. Four quadrants of Tyr. We have a map."

Pierce the Skin

L aeb's face was one of sheer fascination as he stood over the parchments laid out on the floor, pouring over each street, river and home of Tyr. Minutes passed before he looked back at Kyira and Glynn. "I don't know what to say. Catacombs?"

"Catacombs," said Glynn, winking at Kyira.

"And this all came from that little box?" said the captain. "You are truly a Pathwatcher's daughter, Kyira!"

Kyira flushed. "The Maelta showed me the way. Literally." She pointed to a dark printed strip that ran the full length of the quadrants of Tyr, and the sentence that had been left bare on the parchment from the carvings on the box.

The Ways — Of Those — Who Shape The World — Shape Us All

After she had brought the printed squares from each side together the message had revealed itself. A strange feeling of peace had settled upon her soon after, and she knew exactly what she had to do.

Glynn nodded. "She figured it out, captain. It was amazing. She is a gift."

"This message is the mantra of the Kartta, the first Sami.

Its meaning is two-fold. Those who know the Lands control the Lands. Those who control the Lands, control all."

Laeb stared incredulous. "If the Bohr come to know the lands, they will control them. They cannot get their hands on these boxes. Or the knowledge contained therein."

"There may be more out there," warned Kyira.

Laeb nodded. "Well, thank you, Kyira. The Tsiorc owe you more than can be repaid."

"Glynn, too," said Kyira, nodding to the Farram. "If it had not been for him, we would not have discovered that the other faces fit around the four quadrants." She pointed beneath the hatched section of rice paddies, outside the thick black line marking Tyr's walls. "And we would not have discovered the catacombs beneath Tyr, and your way in."

Laeb's hand shook as he held a finger over the tiny gap. "If I'm reading this right, this is a hole in the middle of a field, and its barely a metre wide, Kyira. It would take hours to filter a thousand men through there. The paddies are flat too. There's no cover."

"There is another way."

"Where?" said Laeb, scanning the thousands of delicate lines etched upon the parchment.

"Before I tell you," continued Kyira, "I want something."

"Name it."

Kyira took a deep breath. "I want to fight."

Laeb's keen eyes jumped up, scanning her face as though looking for something that might give her away. He would find no such thing. "No."

"Then you had better find another way into Tyr," she said. "These maps and this box belong to me." She took up the glowing oil lamp and held it above her head.

Laeb held out his hands. "No! Wait. Kyira, why do you wish to join us? To kill? To get revenge?"

Kyira shook her head slowly. "I do not seek revenge, Captain Laeb, I intend to find my brother, and free him. If I choose to kill anyone it will be more of the Banémen, but only if they get in my way." Silence hung between them, but she didn't break eye contact. The only movement came from the whites of Glynn's eyes as they bounced back and forth between them.

"I could take these from you," said Laeb, his tone sharp.

With her other hand Kyira pulled the knife Iqaluk had given her and held it out in front. "You could try, captain. But even if you killed me, it wouldn't stop me from burning this map, this tent, and the box. Then you would be down a map-reader, and a Pathwatcher at the same time. If you did not die in the flames."

"Have you ever killed someone?" asked Laeb.

"Yes."

"How?"

Kyira held up the knife, motioning to her own neck. "Like this."

Laeb stared at her, unmoving. His expression was almost unreadable, but she swore she could see sadness behind those clear blue eyes. She tightened her grip on the blade handle.

"Alright," he said. "Alright. You fight for the Tsiorc."

She lowered the lamp and sheathed her blade. "And you have a map-reader, and a way into Tyr."

* * *

Laeb poured over the map Kyira had left with him. He traced his finger through the main street, along the primary causeway and off down an impossibly narrow alleyway. He stopped at a little circular symbol within a square — a terraced house — then followed the straight double lines that led away into the hatched catacombs barely wide enough for his fingernail.

"There it is," he said to himself. "The tiny drain that will be the downfall of the biggest city in Rengas. The needle that punctures the hide. Pierce the skin and look within…"

"Sir?"

Laeb turned to the old guard standing at the entrance of his tent. "Just talking to myself. What is it?"

The guard coughed. "Sir, Consul Kilier and Commander Suilven await you."

"What, now? Where?"

"Yes, sir," said the guard. "Outside."

Laeb exhaled. "Alright. Send them in."

The tent flaps whipped open and Kilier burst in. Commander Suilven strolled in behind him wearing an odd expression.

"Good morning, Captain Laeb!" blurted out Kilier. He was already garbed in full riding gear, with his dark hair knotted around itself in a tight bun. "I see preparations are proceeding as planned."

Laeb greeted them with a nod. "Commander. Consul. We'll be fully mobilised within the hour."

"Thank you, Kilier," said the commander. "I can take it from here."

"Sir?"

"You heard me."

"Yes," nodded Kilier. "Right. Let me know if you need anything."

Laeb watched Kilier slink out of the tent, and the commander peered down at the map. "You think this map is truly as accurate as can be?" he said, tracing the words along the bottom.

The mysterious expression suddenly revealed itself. It was excitement, and it looked good on him.

"Yes, sir. Our new map-reader's knowledge is unrivalled. We need her."

"That's not what I mean, Laeb," smiled Suilven. "How accurate is the map, for today?"

It was a good question, but one Laeb was prepared for. "From the intelligence we've gained from the map we now know that the city was built in a very specific way, with Vasen sitting over the top of what looks like a huge magma chamber. I believe the rock to be composed of very hard obsidian which has forced itself into hundreds of sub-chambers. As you can see it looks something like a beehive."

"Which is why Tyr still stands."

"Yes, exactly," said Laeb, pointing to a collection of squares arranged in a hexagon. "You can see here that most of the buildings follow this pattern, to maintain that structure above ground, also meaning the alleyways sit on the waylines of the catacombs in between."

The commander stepped back. "So you're saying that city hasn't changed because of the age of the structure beneath it."

"Partly, yes," said Laeb. "We can't assume that there has been absolutely no development to the city since the map-box came into existence. But if we have a pattern, then we can at least predict the layout."

"And the ships that will take us there?"

"Awaiting us, sir," said Laeb. "Kai has a fleet on the Way. I've sent a redback ahead, so he knows to expect us."

The commander looked impressed. "You obviously have things in order, captain. Which I am appreciative of."

"It is why I am here," said Laeb. "But I must pass some of the credit on to Kyira. Without a Pathwatcher to help us, none of this would be possible. She's the one to thank."

"Then I shall do that," said the commander, stepping towards the tent flaps. "Once we have won."

Passage

The oiled oars broke the still water, leaving a wake of silt behind. The silt was black because most of the earth around the inner ring of Rengas was black, but that did not help ease the pit in Kyira's stomach as it swirled beneath the surface. It wasn't much better out beyond their little row boat, with the tall ships bobbing up ahead, growing larger with every pull and the rushing, choppy water of the Way beyond the bay ready to drown them.

"What are you doing here?" muttered Kyira, to herself.

"Concentrate on the oars," said Laeb, rowing steadily. He offered her the right oar, tilting it so it didn't drag in the water. "That's it. Use the resistance of the water. Match my strokes."

She sniffed, then pulled the long oar hard. It twisted, the tension broke and before she could stop it she was lying on her back with her legs in the air.

Laeb helped her up, barely suppressing a lop-sided smirk. "Most people fall, Kyira. Here, try not to twist it when you pull—"

She snatched the oar away. "Give me that!"

The old sailor sitting at the bow coughed and tapped away the dead weed in his pipe against the boat's side. "By the

366

grace of God's children! I should have done this myself and that's the truth. Give it here." He sat forward and tried to muscle in and take Kyira's oar, but she held it away from him.

"I'll do it!"

"Then hurry," said the sailor, sitting back down. "I en't got all day."

"What could you possibly have to do?" said Laeb, frowning.

The man's eye twitched, then he mumbled and pulled a fresh pinch of weed from an old leather purse before stuffing it into his pipe.

"He doesn't like me," whispered Kyira.

"I don't think he likes anyone," said Laeb, loudly. "And don't worry, Kyira. Not many Ringlanders take to the water so easily."

Such a thing might have angered her had it come from someone else, but Laeb confused her. Was it a compliment or just an observation? Perhaps she was just too simple to know, or perhaps he was just too good at hiding his feelings. Men were such fools.

Below the thunderheads, the snow-capped hills of Határ moved and rocked with her. Along the dim shore spots of light had begun to appear like twinkling stars as the Tsiorc army moved along the beach, bedding down, building fires, sharpening weapons, cooking meals of fish, shellfish and sulphur clams, fighting, sparring — all in preparation for the fight to end all fights. An assault on Tyr.

"How many soldiers are there?" she said, between strokes.

"Fifteen squads," said Laeb. "Each with a hundred men, plus smiths, cooks, farmers, tanners…"

"I've never seen so many people."

Laeb shrugged. "There are ten, even twenty times that who live in Tyr. Humans, like you and I, oppressed and cowed by the Bohr. Living out their lives, unaware that they outnumber their masters." He stared into the middle distance. "My hope is that we will be the tinder to their flame." The beach gradually panned away from them and she realised she had fallen out of rhythm. Laeb took the oar. "Here, let me. We'll need to be careful manoeuvring around these ships."

Kyira turned and gasped as the tall side of a ship suddenly loomed over her. It had not looked so big when she had been facing the other way.

The rowboat jerked as the sailor pulled a long pole from the side of the rowboat and pushed it against the ship's hull. "Not this one," he said. "We're still a couple out."

Their little boat moved slowly between the bows of the moored ships like a thief unseen. "Why are they so big?" asked Kyira, dragging her fingers across the shells of one hull as it drew near.

"They are load carriers," said Laeb. "Carrying cargo between the main cities."

"How do they not sink?"

"They displace the water, which is why they're so wide. All will become clear when you're standing on one. You'll have other questions on your mind after you meet Kai."

"Shipleader Kai," gruffed the old sailor, without turning.

"*Shipleader Kai* is an unusual sort."

This time the old sailor turned towards them, his expression hard. "Shipleader Kai is a gracious and powerful explorer who has tamed a hundred seas. No other has travelled as far and lived to speak of it."

"Maybe on the sea," said Kyira, staring back at him. "The Sami have walked the lands for a thousand generations."

"Well," said the sailor, wrapping his thin lips around the pipe. "Death does not await should you fall from your sleeping bag in the night or reach in from the shadows ready to pull you to the depths when you take a piss."

"No?" said Kyira. "Then it seems you have never strayed further than a beach in your long life, sailor."

"Alright, alright," said Laeb. "The sea is dangerous, and the land is dangerous. Let's leave it at that."

The old sailor leaned forward and pulled his pipe from his mouth. "Lessons take many forms, Sami. Let this be one for you. Do not underestimate the water. She laps, she dithers, she waits, and then the second your cares flutter away on the wind like a gull she takes all you have without mercy and hesitation, and that's the truth. If you ever listened to a voice, let it be mine, and let it be now." He held there over Laeb's lap, ash dropping onto the captain's starched breeches.

"Thank you for the warning, sailor," said Kyira, "but I think I will be fine."

"I do not doubt, Sami, that you might fare better than most, but hold your respect with you at all times, like it were your mother's love, your belt knife, or your pipegreen." He accented the last to show it was more important than any other, then with a flourish more suited to a circus announcer said, "Welcome to the Celsathar!"

The shipleader's vessel was impressive. Red and green banners hung over the railing of the Celsathar's vast hull, which had no visible planks. It was wider than any other ship they had floated past, and the wood looked almost new.

369

"It's the treatment," said the sailor, standing too close. He took her hand and pressed it against the shining hull. "You see? No seaweed can stick to it, and no barnacles may rest upon it." He stroked the wood himself, caressing it like it were the head of his first born. "The mixture is called wallow, but you'll not see it on any other ship. Oh, how I remember the smell of that awful stuff. Acrid enough to burn the nose right off you!"

"You were there at the ceremony?" asked Laeb, surprised.

"I was," said the old sailor. "I met my first wife at the Berthing Festival, dark hair as black as oilcoal, tanned skin and eyes like sparkling pools of lopal. I am one of the very few who can admit to being older than the ship they navigate. I tell you, the sound that tree made when it fell could have awoken Pantheon himself, and that's the truth!"

Kyira gasped. "The ship is carved from one tree? You lie. There are no trees so wide."

"Not here no, but on the Outer Isles, they can reach hundreds of feet up and are wide enough to be lived in by an entire clan."

A rope ladder unravelled against the ship's side, and without another word the old sailor hopped on and scurried up and over the edge.

"You first," said Laeb, standing.

Kyira lifted her rolled animal skin from the bottom of the rowboat and threw the tie around her head, so it sat snugly upon her back. Her cold fingers took hold of the first rung, but she couldn't bring herself to leave the rowing boat. Visions of the cliffside rushed back.

"Kyira, can you swim?"

"Of course."

"Then you'll be fine."

Kyira clambered up, countering the whip as her body weight flicked the ladder this way and that. She gripped the railing and scrambled over, only breathing when her feet landed upon the deck.

Colour was everywhere. Vibrant blue and green light illuminated the deck, changing the hue of the sails on each of the three masts, with each breath of wind. They were held together with ropes that ran in all directions to painted bulges and rings that stood out against the deep red of the wooden deck. Huge cracks spilt the wood, wide enough to fall in if it weren't for the shining yellow gold that filled them, sanded flush so that other than the slight change in resonance beneath her feet, there was no telling it was there at all.

Laeb landed beside her. "It's something, isn't it?"

"It's beautiful," gasped Kyira. "Are all ships like this?"

"Not all. In fact, not even Outer Isle ships dress themselves like this one. Kai is a lover all things dramatic, which is something to bear in mind when you meet him."

"Alright," said Kyira, uncertainly.

Laeb marched down the deck and Kyira followed not far behind, unable to stop herself from peering into the open doorways and windows along the way. The ship seemed largely empty, devoid of the sort of activity she would expect there to be on such a magnificent vessel. A few sailors moved lethargically around the decks, their clothes, which looked once colourful, now faded. Laeb walked confidently ahead, but his hand had dropped to his side, giving his gait an awkward swagger. She had seen him fight, so she knew that he was more than capable with that tailored blade strapped to his thigh, yet he seemed uncomfortable. The contrast with Duga was striking. Duga, who had struck a blow to a Banéman in open combat, moved as though the blade were a limb on his body. While Laeb and his sword were clearly old friends, they had met one another later on in life.

"I meant to ask you," said Kyira, catching up. "Where did you learn to fight?"

The question caught Laeb off guard, but he recovered quickly. "Don't mistake wariness with incompetence, map-reader." The abruptness in his tone took her by surprise. "Here we are." They reached the back of the ship, and came back on themselves, climbing a wide set of steps stretching almost from one side of the vessel to the other.

"Laeb!" A clean-shaven man with long dark hair and tanned skin stood barefoot along the top deck. From his position he must have been watching them from the second they came aboard. The man turned from the railing and rushed forward to meet Laeb, and the two men thumped their welcomes against each other's backs. His bright blue-eyes flickered, taking her in from over Laeb's shoulder.

"Ah! Shty mur assaillt!" said the shipleader.

"You first, Kai!" replied Laeb, still holding the man tightly. "Ru'deaerv mucanst!" laughed Kai.

Laeb chuckled as he bear-hugged the man and lifted him clear of the floor. "Awkward for a captain? Better a captain than a lackey ferrying treasures for the rich!" Laeb dropped the man with an exaggerated flourish.

"Haha! Well now. Who'd have thought it," said Kai. "A blue-eyes, commanding an army."

"I'm a tactician, Kai."

"A captain, so I hear." Kai's expression shifted faster than

372

a gust of wind. "Your commander didn't think me worth the trouble then?"

"Etiquette, Kai," said Laeb. "Otherwise they'd be here. You should know by now how this game is played."

"Indeed, I do!" said Kai. His smile returned, no less bright. He rounded upon Kyira. "And who is this that does not understand Takiagh — the language of the sea. A Ringlander?"

"I am Kyira," she said, taking the man's hand.

Kai looked her up and down, then spoke in perfect Samian. "And what do you have against Takiagh?"

"You speak Samian well," replied Kyira, "for a Sulitarian."

"Really?" said Kai. "Tur dalla mur fin ma de'a?" He stood waiting for a response. "Ah, so you don't know Kemenese. Alright, how about Redula then? Thäehiänmernin dräwh mært'lerr?" Strange clicks came from his lips between each word.

"I do not—"

"No," said Kai, coming closer. "You do not know. If you had, you would have hit me. Those noises are called thripla, and they change the meaning of the words preceding them. Sometimes drastically. Much like Sami can be changed with hand movements." He moved his hands into the Samian shapes *"Do you always follow great men around like a sheep?"* whilst simultaneously speaking the words, "It is good to welcome you here into my home."

She clenched a fist, then opened it, and brushed her open palms together: the standard objection. *"I am no sheep."*

"So, you know shapes," replied Kai, "as all my helmsman do. There are, of course, subtle differences between Samian and Takiaghian shapes, but none so that we cannot converse.

373

Is that all you speak?"

Kyira pursed her lips and whistled. *"I follow no one. The paths I walk are mine and mine alone."*

"What was that?" asked Kai, clearly impressed.

Kyira flushed, despite herself. "It seems you have yet to fully grasp Silbo then. Some of the Sami tribes use it to talk to raevens, nara and even orca."

"You can talk to animals? Now that is impressive." Kai turned to Laeb. "Tactician or no, captain, I'm glad you still have the time to be picking up Sami girls along your way. And clever ones at that." Kai took Kyira by the waist. "Kyira, we must spend more time together. I'd like to learn this Silbo."

Laeb stepped in front of him. "Time is against us, Kai. The Tsiorc sit upon the bank, tired and hungry after two days solid marching."

Kai nodded, still holding Kyira tightly. "Then you'd better say what you came here to say." He let Kyira go, offering a sorry look, then sauntered away along the deck with Laeb in tow.

Kyira moved to follow then stopped. A pair of yellow eyes stared up at her from the floor. Its body was almost invisible against the rich red wood. She pulled her knife out, and it hissed a long, forked tongue.

"Draiko!" shouted Kai, from half way down the deck. "Heel!"

The animal shivered, and changed colour right in front of her, revealing scaly skin and a long dark green tail stretching away behind her. It looked like a rock lizard, or a fire gecko, yet somehow bigger than even Vlada. The tongue, which was almost as long as her forearm, wiggled in the air one last time and it made off behind the two men, running with two pairs of alternating legs. It scarpered up Kai's back and wrapped itself around him.

Kai's hand gently caressed the lizard's now dark green scales. "You're a jumpy one aren't you? But don't worry, Draiko won't bite. Well, unless you're bleeding. Are you? You look old enough to be." He winked.

Kyira spat at his feet. "I will make a coat out of it, or perhaps a new ankle sheath. Would it still change colour wrapped around my feet?" Draiko hissed and turned a deep brown.

Kai carefully helped the strange animal down from his back then tapped it on the rear end with his big toe, prompting it to scarper away into the shadows of a doorway.

"Ignore him," said Laeb, loudly. "I remember a time when Shipleader Kai would have welcomed a Sami to his ship." He shook his head. "Times long past."

Kai's expression was sour when he turned back. "Captain. I assume you have a reason for dropping by."

"I need ships," said Laeb.

"Yes," replied Kai. "For your *Tsiorc*."

"May we sit down?" asked Laeb.

"If you insist," said Kai. He stepped in through the same doorway Draiko had scampered through, and Laeb and Kyira followed.

Kyira reeled, the stench of rotting fish sticking in her throat. Beams of uneven light penetrated the dusty air through uneven shutters seemingly nailed shut on both sides of the wide room. Heavy blue velvet curtains took up the entire length of the far wall, behind a long table overflowing with gold. Coins carefully stacked into impossible shapes, gold plates, and goblets, even forged bars piled in pyramids. The wealth on this one table would see Kyira and her children's children living fat until they were dead.

"It's a sight, isn't it?" said Kai. "I always forget that there are those who do not live so." He flicked a shiny coin through the air. "A gift."

Kyira grabbed frantically, but the shiny yellow coin bounced off of her knuckle to the ground beneath a chair. She scrambled towards it and slammed a hand over it.

Something moved. Not near her, but in her peripherals, all around the room there were at least four or five independent movements. She stood, pocketing the coin.

Kai leaned across the table and pulled an urchin from a small gold-lined tank. "So, tell me, Laeb. Why did one of Sulitar's most talented watermen leave?"

"Our people have become fickle," he said. "They argue over the most meagre of possessions, spending entire lifetimes at each other's throats over the ownership of trinkets."

Kai scoffed. "Sulitar is a paradise! It is worth ten times that of any Ringland country. The brine in our veins brings with it a wildness of heart that no other nation can claim."

"Then why did you leave?" said Laeb.

"Itchy feet," said Kai, dismissively. "I could never sit still for long." One-by-one he pulled the spines out from the urchin, taking his time as though the exercise was incredibly boring.

Laeb stood with his feet apart like a man trying to convince another he was at ease. "I have near two thousand men I need to move down the Way. I counted twelve ships in the bay."

"Fourteen," said Kai.

"Excellent!" said Laeb. "Then we can just settle…"

Kai offered a sympathetic shake of the head. "Laeb—"

"Kai, time is against us."

"Against you, captain. Time is something I currently have in abundance. Even surrounded by gold, it is my most valuable asset."

"Then you are more a fool than I thought. Come on, Kyira."

"A fool!" snapped Kai. He jumped up from the table knocking over stacks of coins. "Tell me, captain. Who is the bigger fool, the man with fourteen holds filled with weed, china and steel ore, or the man with a broken army stuck upon the shore? What are your options without me? What are you plans without my fleet?"

"I have none."

"You have none." Kai sneered. "Why do you fight for these Ringlanders?" He motioned to Kyira blatantly, like she was just another object in this awful room. "What lies did they bewitch one of our own with?"

Kyira ignored the two men. Something was moving in the corner, and it was much bigger than the lizard that had crawled up Kai's back. She felt the coin one last time; imagine owning such wealth. It would be a shame to lose it.

She flicked it across the room, and it bounced against the creature hidden at the back of the room. It revealed itself, one line of black scales at a time, all the way down to a tail that stretched around the room and disappeared behind Kai. It was a lizard, but one ten times bigger than the one she had seen earlier. She blinked, trying to focus on its iridescent skin, then flinched as another appeared on its back. Then another by Laeb, and another by her feet. She jumped away as the little one snapped at her moccasins.

377

"What is this?" shouted Laeb, his sinuous sword held out at arm's length. "You're letting them breed?"

Kai bit into the urchin, then sucked out its innards and threw the shell to the large one. It arched backwards and snatched it out of the air with a set of jaws wide enough to take a young ox, then lazily gulped it down. "They do what they want, captain. Like their master."

"What are they?" asked Kyira, kicking the one near her feet.

"Tired," said Kai, "but mostly well fed." He winked, then leaned back and stroked the tail of the big one.

Laeb's hand hovered by his waist. "Kai, this abundance of time you claim to have is a delusion. New ships arrive every week from the Outer Reaches and beyond, who — unable to slow against the pull of the Way — find themselves desperately vying for protective bays to hole up in until Tyr's sanctions are released. Bays not unlike this one." He glanced around the room. "You've done a good job in hiding the scars of those battles. But perhaps not the spoils."

Kai's expression had grown more intense with every word, until it slipped away like a falling mask. "I grow tired, captain! Why are you here?"

"For passage," snapped Laeb. "Passage into Tyr."

"I will not go into Tyr," snapped Kai. "Not while those Bohr thieves steal from every ship that is forced by their doors. For the time being, our time is best spent here, and as you say, we seem to be doing alright."

"At the expense of every other passing ship," growled Laeb. "What happened to you, Kai? When did you become a pirate?"

"I am no pirate!"

"How many bows lie beneath us?" asked Laeb. "How many have you killed to protect this bay?"

Kai's bluster faltered. "We were here first, and should those other ships try and take it from us we will defend ourselves. We are no more pirates than you. Or this Sami."

"Have you actually met many Sami, Shipleader Kai?" Kyira reached behind to the rolled animal skin at her back, and approached the table, taking care to avoid the shimmering lizards watching her every move. Kai's eyes widened as she swept her forearm over the surface to create a space, knocking a pyramid of gold bars to the floor. The lizards hissed collectively. Kyira unrolled the skin slowly revealing the printed image of Tyr. With the faces on each side it was no longer a square, but the quadrants were clearly marked by a thick line beneath, showing the Kartta's words:

The Ways — Of Those — Who Shape The World — Shape Us All

"That is Tyr."

"It is," said Kyira.

"There is another way into the city?" croaked Kai.

"Would that information be worth something to you?" Kai made a grab for the map, but Kyira pulled it out of reach, and rolled it back into its protective skin. "You could finally sell your cargo. The cave is surrounded by high cliffs and only accessible from the Way, we need your ships to get us there."

"The new currency has made life difficult," added Laeb. "I bet Vasenfolk and Teräväens alike would pay double, or triple for what you have in your holds. You could actually get back to the seas again, along the inner coasts, as far as

Ge'Bat even."

"The Bohr's new currency has done more than make life difficult," said Kai, "There are riots in Terävä and Vasen."

Laeb glanced at Kyira. "Well, I'm sure there are still many rich patrons eager to stay fat. Besides, I can guarantee that no-one else is aware of this secret. You have nothing to lose here, Kai. If you sneak the Tsiorc into Tyr and we lose, the Tsiorc are wiped out and the Way reopens, and you will be first to trade to a city desperate for supplies. If we win, we open the back door for you, and let you partake in the spoils. Either way you avoid the tolls."

"Kyira, tell me, where did you get your map? I would like to learn how it was made."

Kyira slung the skin roll behind her. "Give our army passage, shipleader Kai, and I will show you."

Kai turned to the back wall and pulled a rope and the curtains split apart. Kyira gasped. Etched into the pale wood was a crude representation of not just Nord, but of the south, the Outer Isles, the Way, and in its centre, the vast Middle Sea.

"This is our world?" asked Kyira.

"Yes," said Kai. "As much as we know, but it is crude and inaccurate. The southern lands are more expansive and desolate than illustrated here, and the Outer Isles are not quite so big, but the shape is correct."

"A ring?"

Kai frowned. "Did you never wonder where the term Ringlander came from?"

Kyira couldn't believe it. Nord took up barely a tenth of the map, and barely a fifth of the land. "Nord is small."

"Nord is large," said Kai, brushing a hand over the carved

wood. "But the world is larger. Nord, Dali, Határ, Kemen across the disputed Northern Territories to Ge'Bat and up to our homeland Sulitar. A little further on over the Red Isles and back to you and yours in Nord completes the ring."

Laeb stared, equally as shocked. "I have never seen this version before. You made this?"

"My life's work," said Kai, scanning the board. "Don't let these scales fool you though." He placed a hand near the middle of Nord, near where the Laich might have been located. "This distance would take—"

"Thirty days," said Kyira. "To walk."

Kai grinned, then walked his fingers into the Middle Sea. "Or seven, if you have a good ship."

"And do we have good ships?" asked Kyira.

"The very best," said Kai. With a flick of the rope the map was hidden again. "Laeb, I will take your army to Tyr, even just to show you what it means to have brine in the blood. On the single condition that before you leave Kyira shows me how that map of Tyr was made."

Kyira stepped over the lizard's long tail and took Kai's hand. "We have a deal."

Unbreakable

The Tsiorc army was at least almost seventeen hundred strong, by Kyira's count. Spread over fourteen ships, that made almost one hundred and fifty souls per vessel, with two hundred in the lead ship, the Celsathar. The Makriliaens, now directed by Kavik, naturally chose to stay close to Laeb, so the Celsathar and its sister ship the Paliathar were filled from deck to hold with normal town people, clad in leather armour and brandishing newly forged swords taken from Kai's extensive armoury.

"It seems Makril is not so helpless after all." Laeb's voice made Kyira jump. "From the outside they may look a town of traders, but it is hard to ignore just how easy it comes to them."

Kyira watched as a tall dark-skinned sulitarian ran through some simple sword moves with an older man, moving together in almost perfect unison. "The effects of your people are far reaching."

"No, I don't think so," said Laeb. "There's something else there. My bet is that Makril was once part of a warring nation, and that blood is very much still present in the townspeople's veins."

The old man stopped to breathe and laughed with the

sulitarian guide. Abruptly, both men jerked as a deep clunk sounded within the hull. The ship ground to a halt and everyone not holding onto something was thrown two steps back.

"Laeb! What was that?"

The captain held up a hand. "Don't worry, it's normal. Watch."

Two sailors, gruff and uninterested, approached from behind, then shockingly climbed over the railing and out of sight. Kyira leant over, watching as they reached a narrow ledge just above the water then threw the end of a thick plaited rope to a pair waiting alongside in a rowboat. The pair in the rowboat rowed quickly to the Paliathar, much faster than Laeb and Kyira had moved, and handed the long rope over to the Paliathar's crew. It wasn't long before they had another rope and were on their way to the next ship.

"They're connecting the fleet?" asked Kyira.

Laeb nodded. "Suru is what we call the ropes, and they are made from Wallow fibres."

"The same lacquer used on the hull?"

"The very same. At high temperatures it can be spun as if it were a thread. Ropes made of wallow are near unbreakable."

Kyira took a deep breath. "As uncomfortable as it makes me, to think we'll be tied by an unbreakable tether to another ship, I have to say, captain, you played this well. Getting us here."

Laeb nodded away the compliment. "Always have a plan that no one else knows of, Kyira, and you will never go wrong. So, how long until we reach the cove, Navigator?"

"I'm not sure, exactly. I would say it is perhaps twelve leagues?"

"Be confident," chided Laeb. "Even if you're unsure. It will help win over the undecided, and by the eyes of Baeivi we have many of those."

"Then it is twelve leagues, Captain Laeb."

"Good!" He winked, and she found herself smiling back at him, then cursed herself for it.

"You did well with Kai," he added. "He was never an easy man, and near impossible to predict. You handled him, which is more than can be said for most others."

"Was any of what you said to him true?"

"About why I left Sulitar? Of course not! I left for the same reasons every young man does: to see the world and to get away from their father." His eyes widened suddenly. "Sorry. I... I. Sorry, Kyira."

"It's alright," she said, casting her eyes down. "What about Kai's pets? They are from your home?"

"The Ruffin?" said Laeb "They are, and they are a nuisance! Some sailors believe that they bring luck, but I'm yet to see any. They eat the rats, which makes them more tolerable. Otherwise I would throw the horrible creatures overboard."

Laeb leaned with her on the thick wooden side. "There's a myth that they are descended from Dagors. You would know them as dragons, from old tales. More myths. Who has time for stories, when the world is in such chaos."

"Then tell me more of the Tsiorc," asked Kyira. "How did you come to fight for them?"

Laeb studied her. "There were four of us, in the beginning. Duga, Feykir, Dia'slar and myself. We came here to make a life for ourselves. We each bought land from the Bohr, paid taxes, built and farmed, but it wasn't enough. There was... an incident, and Feykir's two wives were killed. That was nine cycles ago. I've been fighting ever since." Laeb gestured forward. "Look, the first clutch is departing."

Flanked on each side by black sandbanks, the first three ships drifted forward, side-by-side towards the edge of the stillwater, their bows pointing into the Way. The first ship crept forward, countering the swirling currents at the bay mouth, then turned sharply, pivoting around the sandbank and into the Way channel.

"I thought it would be smoother than that."

Laeb pressed his lips together. "That was smooth, Kyira."

The second and third ship, followed quickly in the wake, bobbing and chasing the slackness of their suru ropes along the choppy Way until all three ships had vanished beyond the high sides of the bay. The second and third clutches drifted towards the bay mouth, and with the same precision each ship lined up in the stillwater until the current dragged them all from sight. The forth clutch approached, but were not aligned.

Cries came from the townspeople rushing about the deck. "She's ran aground!"

"Oh, no! Stop them!"

"She's too far out," breathed Laeb. "There's a sandbank below — if they hit it, we'll lose them!"

"We have to help!" cried Kyira.

"There is nothing to do but watch."

Kai appeared suddenly from behind, roaring orders along the deck. "Tristan! Send in the next clutch! The old sailor who had been on their rowboat ran towards the main mast and rang a bell high up in the raeven's nest, but it was too late. The currents took the first ship, then as the second left the bay it turned against the current, and the deck tilted almost all the way into the water.

"She's capsizing!"

"Save them!"

Kyira's breath caught as the third ship drifted towards the sandbank, but the second-ship's manoeuvre had been entirely on purpose. The suru ropes all pulled taut and the combined momentum dragged all three ships out into a wide arc onto the Way as though they were made of nothing but paper.

A cheer burst out around the boat.

The bell rang again, and Kyira gripped Laeb's hand as the Celsathar and the Paliathar slid towards the Way. Laeb's grip tightened, and the Celsathar was tugged forward. The ship which had felt solid as ground when she stepped on it, now rocked and moved, throwing her from side to side, as the forces of speed clawed at her stomach.

"Hold on!" roared Laeb, above the wind.

Kyira's panic sharpened as the Celsathar accelerated, rolling with the eddies and waves. She took some solace from the sailors who milled about the ship quietly adjusting things, leaning opposite to every sway of the ship.

"Should they not be doing something?" shouted Kyira. "Tying ropes, or ringing bells or—"

Laeb shook his head, "The Way has us now, Kyira. There is nothing to do but ride the waves. Enjoy it!" he added, sounding more elated than a rational person should.

The Way

The blood of the Kartta pulsed in Kyira's veins, driving her pen over the parchment so that not a detail was lost. It rolled over the damp paper while she studied every inlet, every peninsula, laich and mountain range carved into the map on Kai's wall. She marvelled silently all the while at the shape of her land — Nord might have only been barely a fifth of the world, but at nearly a thousand leagues across and five thousand tall, its vastness was plain. She did not take down the names of those she had never seen before, they would remain etched as deeply into her mind as they were into the wood on the panelled wall. Nor did she add any colour, that would come later when she had fleshed out and polished the lines. For now she had to just capture it.

The nib caught on the canvas and spattered loudly. Her breath stopped. The blackness of the Shipleader's cabin was broken only by the shafts of light through the slanted shutters. Light that glimmered upon the scales of the sleeping Ruffin. Their bodies flashed through iridescence and camouflage along with their dreams, and while the spectacle was beautiful to behold they would kill her if they found her here. But what was gain without risk?

She held the pen completely still and as the heavy breathing of the large one resumed, so did the faster breaths of the others. Heart racing she traced the last few lines of the Red Isles, connecting the solid black line with that of Nord. The ink had barely dried when the ruffin's long tail whipped over her head, just missing an open box of pearls. There was another ruffin beneath the treasure-laden table, about the size of a dog. Crouching low, she squatted next to it, hiding like a hunted animal until eventually the thick sound of slumber echoed through the ruffin's barrel-sized chest barely a pace away. As gently as she could, she stood and rolled the map and eased it into the tube along with the map of Tyr. The pen went back into the spot between two large piles of gold coins — exactly where she had left it yesterday, and the day before that. The curtain rope, however, was now pressed hard up against the wall behind the largest sleeping Ruffin's thick, shimmering tail. Using the rolled canvas she inched a loop of the rope below around the Ruffin's flashing scales, then pivoted and padded out towards the door. There were a few extra urchin shells upon the floor, and Kyira picked one up, and tossed it smoothly towards the far end of the room. Before it had landed the door was open and closed and she was back on rear deck. A crashing sound indicated the Ruffin had jolted awake and knocked over the coins, and right after it came the thwump of a heavy curtain falling shut.

* * *

The north and south continents slid by on either side of the Celsathar, drifting in and out of the lazy har that marked the land. The constant rocking and jerking had made sleep impossible, so Kyira had remained on deck watching as the fleet organised themselves. It was a marvel of seafaring to witness, as the twinkling lights of twelve vessels spread out in a near perfect line leaving a gap for the Celsathar and Paliathar to sail through. The ships extended their water brakes together but staggered the release, so as Kai's lead ships took position at the front of the fleet the rest of the ships formed into a "V" shape, like a flock of migrating geese.

Kyira's ship was now in the lead clutch, navigating an entire fleet of sailors and soldiers towards a narrow cave mouth somewhere up ahead. She swallowed the panic down again, wondering if at some point she might just burst open all over the deck.

Kai appeared on the steps looking concerned. He had been moving tirelessly around the deck all night, waving flags, and shouting orders yet still somehow managed to find the time to check in with her. At first he seemed genuinely interested in the caves and cliffs on her map, but it was clear he was simply memorising it, as she had been memorising his.

Kai would do anything he could to get his hands on her map, and more specifically the Maelta itself, and she had no intention of giving either to him. Strangely, she was fine with lying to such a man. Perhaps lying in the name of a cause was more acceptable. Either way, it was done now.

"What's the matter?" she asked Kai.

Kai glanced at her from the railing, then turned back to the water. "We'll not be long."

"You know where we are?"

"I always know where we are, and where we're going." He

nudged her with his elbow. "It's good to know where you're going, wouldn't you say, navigator?"

"Not always," she said, lying again. A squawk drew her gaze upwards. The clouds were shrouded in thousands upon thousands of dark sea birds, moving as one in the opposite direction.

"They look like terns."

Kai didn't respond, nor was he even looking up. He was staring right at her. Through her. "It can't be," he whispered. "It's impossible."

The sound of banging footsteps broke the silence, as Laeb strode up the stairs. He stopped halfway up looking terrified.

"Kai, we're slowing," spluttered Laeb. "The water is slowing."

Suddenly Kyira felt it too. The heavy ship was leaning more, and the deck creaked and protested at the change in speed.

"Suffering souls," uttered Kai. "It's turning. The Way is turning. We need to get off now!" He started ringing the soundline frantically, then nodded for Kyira to carry it on. She took it and copied him, wincing as the shrill bell cut through the dewy morning air.

The deck exploded into action as sailors and soldiers alike filtered down into the guts of the ship. Kyira would never have believed they were the same men she had seen upon first boarding; they moved around with such purpose, like a kicked hornet nest.

"Kyira!" roared Laeb. "Follow me!"

They retreated into Kai's room below, and Laeb opened the heavy velvet curtains to reveal Kai's map.

"We're here, Kyira," said Laeb, pointing just along from

the symbol that marked Tyr. "Quick, the map."

Kyira unrolled her map and moved her finger along the parchment until it reached the secret cave that led beneath Tyr. "There," she said. "Captain, what is happening?"

"The tide is turning." He was scared.

"How?" The word trembled as it left her lips.

"I don't know how," snapped Laeb, "or why, but it's happening now, and if we don't get out of these currents…"

"But I don't understand—"

He took her by the shoulders. "Kyira I need you to stay by my side until I say you can leave. I need my map-reader."

"I am with you."

"Good. Now come on."

Back on the deck the number of sailors rushing back and forth between ropes and strange wooden pulleys had tripled. The movement was not the smooth precise action she had seen before, but panic. A group of Makriliaens had found their way above deck and were asking questions to anyone who got close.

"Shit," said Laeb, spotting them. "I don't have time for this! We need to go around." He sprinted around the main galley and ducked in through a tiny kitchen, all but dragging Kyira alongside. They emerged on the other side of the vessel near a huge wheel, that was being wrestled by two men.

Laeb grabbed the first sailor. "Tristan, I need a forty-degree turn."

"Forty?" growled the old sailor.

Laeb nodded. "I know it'll break the housings, but we have no choice now."

"You mean to leave the Paliathar to fend for themselves?" asked Tristan, pulling the pipe from his mouth.

"Yes," said Laeb. "Yes, I do."

Tristan shook his head. "Forty is still too wide — we'll be half way to the other shore."

"And on the wrong side," added Kyira. She held out her left hand. "The catacombs are only beneath Vasen on the Nord side."

Tristan scanned the cliffs on the left side, then turned back to them both, an incredulous look on his face. "You mean to swing us round into a cove that we cannot see?"

Laeb turned to Kyira. "Map-reader?"

"It's there, helmsman." She nodded at the huge wheel. "Do as the captain orders."

"Right," said Tristan, grabbing a brass horn with a long tube connected to it that disappeared into the wheel console. "I better be checking with Shipleader Kai."

"There's no time," said Laeb, gripping the wheel. "Listen to your navigator. She knows what she is about. Now, forty-degree turn, only when I say. You hear me?"

The two men looked at one another. Laeb was stronger and taller, but what the old sailor lacked in strength he more than made up for in stubbornness. Besides, the dents in his face were clearly more than just bad skin.

"Kai said you might try to intervene," sneered Tristan. "And if that were to happen, I was to use my better judgement."

Laeb's fingers twitched towards his waist.

"Helmsman," said Kyira, stepping between them both. "You must have felt the water slow."

The old sailor's frowned faltered. "I did."

"And seeing as you hail from the Outer Isles, where the mothers of storms themselves are born, you know the seas better than any other." Sensing Laeb's retreat, she stepped back to give herself more room. "Then you will have realised the seriousness of our loss of speed," said Kyira, delivering it as a statement rather than a question. "Tristan. There are times to act, and times to stay. This is a time to act. We are in danger."

Tristan's nostrils flared as he drew a deep breath. "Right, well you better be spot on with this one, or we'll be tongue kissin' the side of those cliffs, and that's the truth!"

Kyira followed the man's gesture to the black line of tall cliffs, sharp against the morning sky, their bases still a misty haze.

"Kyira," beckoned Laeb, standing a few paces away. He gestured her away from the wheel. "Thank you. Already I fear I cannot do without you." She suppressed her smile as she followed him to the mast pole, where he pulled a long blue flag from a bundle of others, all different colours. He let it unroll and began tying it to a thin rope against the mast. "Do you know *exactly* where the cave is?"

Kyira pictured the horseshoe shape or rocks surrounding the narrow inlet. "Yes. Exactly."

Laeb raised the flag up the mast. "Good. Do you know much about speed? Angles? Trajectory?"

Kyira shook her head. "On land, yes. But not on water."

"Then I will handle that part," he said, puffing, "but you need to update me from the bow, so we may correct our tangents. I need a measurement of how neat or loose our line is as we go. Do you understand?"

They were serious words, and the weight of them hung around her neck like a lead bell. She swallowed. "Of course, captain. I will not let you down."

"I know, Kyira."

"What does this mean?" she said, eager to change the subject.

The long blue flag was bouncing, but even with the speed they were travelling there was barely any wind. "It means the fleet needs to follow us."

She frowned. "What about the one in front? The Paliathar is out there!"

Laeb stepped away from the pulley rope, and grabbed her wrist, "Kyira, the tides of the Way haven't turned in a hundred generations: in fact, all that's known about the last time the currents reversed, is that they pulled everything on the surface down."

Kyira's stomach felt fit to explode. "Down…"

"To the bottom," added Laeb. "The Kanava currents have carved the Way into a fissure deeper than the Middle Sea and we are floating atop the deepest part." The flag rope suddenly jerked in his hand, indicating it had reached the top of the mast. "Are you ready? On your word, Tristan will turn us as sharply left as this ship can manage, and the fleet will follow. The angle should slingshot us into your cave, but I don't need to tell you that we only have one chance at this." Laeb led her towards the wheel, then veered left towards the stairs that led to the bow of the ship. "I will stand in between you and Tristan to relay. Do not let anything distract you." He turned to leave, then spun back towards her. "Remember that we are always moving forward with the water. That is the main difference between the land and water, your point of origin is variable, so what begins as a forty-degree turn will likely lessen. And our momentum is fading with every second. The Wallow will help us maintain our speed longer,

Kyira, but not the rest of the fleet. They need as much of a chance as we can give them before the wave comes."

"The wave?" spluttered Kyira.

It was too late. There was nothing else Kyira could do but watch as Laeb left her and climbed to the top of the stairs.

From the front of the ship she could see the Way laid out before her. The water once clear, had become a swirling soup of brown, mixed with a scum of roiling debris conjured up from the depths. Ahead the Paliathar was alive with activity, much like the deck behind her. The unbreakable suru rope that connected the Paliathar to the Celsathar was going slack as the Paliathar's speed waned.

She set her attention to the tops of the slow-moving cliffs, and pictured the lines of the map. Their horseshoe bay had the slightest of rises where the cliff above grew higher and a shade darker. She turned towards Laeb to shout to him that their course was true, but the words stayed locked in her mouth.

Kai was striding towards the captain, a look of rabid danger in his eyes. Laeb turned, but there was no stopping it. Kai's fist crashed into Laeb's face, knocking him to the floor. Laeb jumped up, pushing him away but Kai was not one to be so easily turned away from a fight and the two men locked together like embracing monkeys.

"Now!" roared Kyira. Men were such fools, fighting at a time when people's lives were at risk! She ran from the bow to the left side, leaving the two men wrestling, then whistled as loudly as she could. Tristan's head appeared from behind the huge wheel.

She moved her hands frantically over the signs, having to guess at how his unusual name might appear. *"Tristan!*

Now!"

The wheel spun hard, and the sails billowed as the face of the wind took them. Kyira peered over the edge to see the hull carving its way through the currents, and a thousand paces behind the closest ship had followed suit, trailing in their wake. Her stomach lurched as the ship swung left, throwing her and everything not bolted down to the deck. There was the sound of splintering wood and the Celsathar jerked upwards out of the water like a jumping fish. Kyira slid along the slick deck, and slammed into the far side of the bow. Without hesitation she jumped up as high as she could, flattening her body out like a table-top, and a barrel and an unfortunate soldier flew beneath her, bursting through the railing and vanishing over the edge.

Kyira landed heavily on her stomach with a slap. She grabbed hold of an unbroken section of railing reaching pointlessly at the air, but there was no sign of man nor barrel, just mist.

"Land!"

Her whole body tensed as the Celsathar entered the har. The cliff tops were fading but their shadow loomed. Closing her eyes, the image of the map synchronised with the cliff tops in Kyira's mind. The burst of speed from the sails had brought them in neat. They needed to change their angles, or they would miss the horseshoe bay and smash into the cliffs before it.

She turned to Tristan and whistled in Silbo. *"Too much! Too much!"* Mist rolled in over the deck, and Tristan's confused expression faded, then disappeared from view.

"Rocks!"

Thuds assaulted every side of the Celsathar's hull, drawing

panicked screams from around her. The shadow of the cliffs was growing darker every second as the Celsathar hurtled towards them.

Whatever line Tristan had given them was the line they had to hang their hopes on. With the har thick around them, there was nothing to see, or to gauge their position against. There was nothing to do but wait, and live, or die, while the Celsathar sped forwards, an unstoppable force. The cliffs would come, but even with all the people on this boat — the Makriliaens, Kai's sailors, the Tsiorc — it would be Kyira, daughter of Iqaluk and Thea, sister to Hasaan, navigator to the rebel army, standing upon the bow of the mother ship, who would die first.

Needles

The har ended. Walls appeared, so close Kyira could almost touch them. They were in a cave. The realisation travelled around the vessel like fire, as shouts and claps filled the air, rebounding off the cavern walls. Kyira closed her eyes to give her night vision a chance to adjust, and she sobbed in relief. Small points of light appeared as the ship drifted deeper into the cave, but there was no time to think on them. Sailors rushed around lighting lamps, their expressions still grim.

Kyira made her up way to the wheel deck and stopped at the wheel. "Tristan."

Tristan pointed his pipe at her. "Sami, it would seem I owe you an apology. You taught me a thing or two today, and I thank ye for it." He placed a gnarly hand upon her shoulder. "I mean it, girl, and that's the truth."

Laeb appeared at her side, his eye already blackening. His gaze drifted away from her as Kai sauntered over, looking worse. It looked as though Laeb had won. Fools.

As the mouth of the cave swallowed each ship they emerged from the curtain of mist like the vapour itself birthed them.

"The second clutch," said Kyira. "They made it."

Laeb's face stayed grim and something passed between he and Kai.

"What is it?" asked Kyira.

"The Paliathar," said Laeb. "We've lost her. There should just be enough time for the rest to get through but the deceleration of the tide gives a hint to the size of the wave that follows."

"Maybe they made it out, maybe they found another bay." Even as the words left Kyira's mouth, she knew them to be untrue. There was nothing on the map beyond the horseshoe bay to protect them.

Kai held her gaze, as though reading her thoughts. "By my reckoning, the Paliathar has a thirty-foot wave heading for them."

"Can't they just turn around?" asked Kyira? "Wouldn't the turning tide bring them this way anyway?"

Laeb shook his head. "But they don't have you, Kyira."

"We can't just leave them out there!"

"Believe me when I say," said Kai, "that there's nothing to be done. The Way currents are hard on the calmest of days, and today is not calm. The turning of the tides changes everything. Ships from the Outer Reaches will no longer be able to use the Way for travel to the Middle Sea. The Creator has, in a single moment, changed the fates of the entire world." He licked his split lip. "Tyr is finished. *We* are finished."

* * *

The cavern ceiling gradually drew closer, until it was so close the vessels had no choice but to berth near a narrow beach.

Pale crabs scuttled over every inch of rock, each one a little point of luminescence that filled the cavern like a night sky filled with stars. As beautiful as it was, Kyira couldn't find enjoyment in it, not when she had doomed Kai's fleet to be forever entombed within this cavern. She was picturing the faces of those poor people aboard the Paliathar when Laeb cleared his throat.

"Kyira," he said, gently. "The junction?"

"Yes. The tunnel off the beach connects with the sewer junction beneath Vasen, commander, but it is narrow. It will take us time to filter in." She traced the route under the city.

Laeb regarded the map and looked up slowly. He looked as bad as she felt. "There is time to be had."

He had been promoted after it had emerged the Tsiorc commander, a man named Suilven, had perished aboard the Paliathar. Kyira had no idea about how Laeb felt about it, other than the obvious hatred he harboured for the messenger, a smooth-looking man named Kilier.

"I have bought us time, but at what cost?"

"Without you, Kyira, an entire fleet would be far beneath the Way."

Kyira glanced over at Kai, who was ordering lines of men and women near the cave's narrow exit. "When all this is over, they cannot just leave and head back out to the Outer Reaches? It might not be the right direction but—"

"Kai likes drama, Kyira. That much is very obvious. He wears it as proudly as he wears his gold, but he has earned himself enemies. There are those in Anqamor who would pay a king's ransom to get hold of him and his fleet. As I understand they barely made it onto the Way in the first place. But the turning of the tides means he can only go back. They will be waiting for them. If the wave doesn't obliterate the island first, of course." He frowned at himself. "Don't worry about Kai, he is resourceful."

"Don't worry about him? Laeb, I have condemned him and his men to live in a cave!"

Laeb lowered his voice. "Well, he only really had two choices, this cave or the bay he had spent the past gods knows how long in. Besides, it will only make it easier to convince his men to come fight with us. They're strong and skilled." Laeb glanced sidelong at Kai. "I just need to convince you-know-who."

"This isn't their fight—"

Laeb's expression grew hard. "This is everyone's fight. Us and them. Humans against Bohr. Listen, Kai will be fine. The cold truth is that he will just have to get used to life on land. Thankfully, he has a very skilled navigator working for him."

Laeb's words encouraged Kyira, and they stayed with her as she and Laeb led the lines of the Tsiorc army through the tunnels. Over a thousand soldiers marching to war under the streets of Vasen. Her mission was to find Hasaan. Still, it did not hurt to have an army behind you, whatever your goal.

The pace slowed as the lines of soldiers trudged through the slow-moving, ankle-deep sewer, until overhead she saw a lantern hanging in the middle of the tunnel. Kyira stopped at the light, noticing a long rusty key dangling from the bottom.

"Here we are, then, commander. This junction takes us up to the street."

She pulled it off at Laeb's nod, and a few moments later

she was climbing a narrow stone staircase, slippery and green. When they reached the top, she gave several knocks on the hatch above their heads, and after a long wait, it creaked open. The sound of wind and rain battered the hollow building, the chill whistling through the holes in the bricked-up windows.

"In."

She jumped at a fearsome looking man lurking in the corner. The purple robe clinging to him showed a broad and muscled man, who looked quite unused to such derelict conditions. His pronounced features sat amongst a nest of thick dark curly beard, while a thatch of jet-black hair hung from the sides of his cowl.

"In," he said, again. "Now."

Kyira ducked in as fast as she could, almost tripping over a pile of rubble.

"Dia'slar," said Laeb, emerging from the hatch behind her. "I assume the hole in the wall leads to the building next door?"

"It does that, Laeb," boomed Dia'slar, over the din of an army entering the building two at a time. The line moved quickly, though. "The entire block is vacant," continued Dia'slar, "with holes to each terrace within. Plenty of room for your soldiers."

"Our soldiers," said Laeb.

"Of course," added Dia'slar, smoothly. "*Our* soldiers."

"I thank you, old friend. I imagine it took some influence to keep such a space free from demolition in a place like Vasen."

"And influence such as mine is hard to come by." Dia'slar had an unusual exoticness to his mannerisms that Kyira couldn't place. Along with his tanned skin, he was truly one of the more unique people she had met. "As is the money," he added, "but thankfully the Bohr have plenty of both for the taking." His gaze shifted back to Kyira.

"This is our map-reader," said Laeb. "Kyira, this is Councillor Dia'slar. Time is precious, old friend. Tell me what you know."

"The lord's army is camped on Mount Terävä."

Laeb's frown sharpened. "Mount Terävä? They are *outside* the city gates?"

Dia'slar nodded. "Why sacrifice your own men when you can wait for the rats to kill each other."

"The rioters? Yes, I have heard there is some dissent amongst the people within the city's walls."

"That is putting is lightly, Laeb." Dia'slar stepped closer as the room filled with soldiers. "And they are not rioters, they are organised. They're being led by the daughters of a shepherd who was recently killed by the Guardian of Tyr himself. A man called Erdal. I met the man. I even tried to stop the Pan Guard who sliced him in half. Alas, I was unable."

Laeb's eyes shone like a candle burning bright. "Taking on a Pan Guard in the name of justice? Dia'slar, I am glad that the Bohr's coffers had not blinded you to the hand of justice."

Dia'slar placed a hand upon Laeb's chest. "It is good to see you."

Kyira turned and left the two men to their gossip. The humid air was already warm with the smell of iron and leather, so thick she could almost taste it, as sailors, Makrili-aens, Sulitarians and Norduns shuffled around, looking for spaces to sharpen spears, oil daggers, or hammer shields. White triangles marked each item, painted roughly on rusted metal or chipped wood. She sidestepped over to the corner of the room and picked up a doll lying abandoned on the floor. The wooden child's face stared past her, its remaining glass eye hazy and a shade of what was probably once a very vivid amber.

"You'll be needing armour," said Dia'slar, appearing out of the throng of moving bodies. Over his arm was a set of leather. She took it and held it up, noting the flattened rivets that kept the overlapping plates in place. "One of the other women donated it. I guessed at your size." His hand moved towards her hip.

Kyira stepped aside. "I suppose I can make it fit. With some alterations. Thank you."

"And everyone should have a sword," said Dia'slar. He took one up from a pile on the floor and swung it around. "Here. This one is well-balanced."

Kyira took the blade with her poor hand. "Thank you. You are kind."

Dia'slar stepped into her again, but this time she had her knife ready, and she drew it lightly over the top of his wrist.

He snapped his hand back. "You dare cut me," he hissed.

"It was a scratch," she said, keeping the knife visible. She stepped towards him, as though the crowd of bodies behind had pushed her, and Dia'slar grinned as she drew so close that she could feel his heat. It took less than an eyeblink to cut through the thin silk at his side. Dia'slar shuddered as the flat of her knife pressed against his bare skin.

"In Nord," she whispered in his ear, "it is the woman who chooses the man, and no Nordun woman would ever let the likes of you near her." She stood back and allowed Dia'slar to step away.

He looked her up and down, as though weighing up his options, then offered a forced smile. "Fine. See you out there, Sami." He turned and melted back into the mass of soldiers.

She caught a glance of Laeb's red jacket and seizing a gap, followed after him. He disappeared into a room near the back of the long building. It was small, and aside from a single old table, it was completely bare. Standing around the table stood nine people, some she had never seen before and dressed in clothes like Dia'slar's. They were well tanned, and while they didn't have the brown skin of the Councillor they clearly had comfortable lives judging by their confident postures and distended stomachs.

"Kyira," said Laeb, catching her off guard. "Good timing. Can you bring out the map?"

"Yes," she said, fumbling for the parchment roll strapped to her back. "Here." She laid it on the table, and the circle closed in.

"The lord's army are camped on the Mount," Laeb pointed to the hatched hillside across the Way Bridge.

"Outside the city?" said Lyla. "You're sure?"

"Yes," said Dia'slar, joining the circle from behind, avoiding Kyira's glare. "My intelligence is reliable."

The Tyrians — two women and three men — removed their robes and began pulling on sets of heavy looking armour.

Lyla was shaking her head. "They're too big a force to take on head-to-head."

"Veterans and mercenaries," added Dia'slar.

"Either way," said Laeb, "we can't afford to split our numbers, and they outnumber us. Our attack must be focused and accurate. A needle. Here." He pointed to the Way Bridge. "There are tunnels beneath the main road, drains leading under the bridge itself. We sneak through the drains and take the gate."

"We lock them out?" A realisation washed over the table at Kilier's words as though he had uttered a secret that had not been spoken in a thousand cycles.

"We lock the lord's army out of their own city," said Laeb.

Kilier looked dumbstruck. "How then do we lead over a thousand men through Vasen without being seen?"

"It's obvious," said one of the Tyrian men, pointing at the map. "We draw them into the narrow streets."

His bare-chested friend with the top-knot nodded enthusiastically. "We keep the back solid. Then split our forces."

Lyla shook her head. "The streets will get the better of us."

Laeb nodded. "The natural compulsion of every system is to move to chaos. As the fights grows closer, so do the groups get smaller. We need to stay as one."

"Probability always favours the home team," added Kai.

"The weather is also very bad," said Lyla, "but if timed correctly, it should help us."

"Agreed," said Laeb. "The Sulitarians will take point, in case we meet any resistance. Thank you all. Go and organise your teams."

"And what about the Makriliaens?" said Kyira. "What should happen to them?"

Dia'slar scoffed as he walked away with the rest of the table of men and women leaving only Lyla and Laeb.

Laeb looked taken aback. "The lord's army are well trained

and vicious. I—"

"*You* have a responsibility to look after them," said Kyira. "As you said you would."

Lyla placed a hand on Kyira's arm. "Kyira, our responsibility is larger than a group of refugees."

Kyira pulled away. "The Makriliaens were a shining beacon when they rolled into your camp with Iqaluk and I. They would tip the scales in your favour, Laeb. Isn't that what Duga said? You took them in, trained with them, drew them into your fight."

"Our fight."

Kyira spoke, but she heard her father's words. "This is your fight, commander."

Laeb began pacing back and forward at the end of the table. "I knew it was a bad idea, bringing them in, but Duga convinced me to. He lied. He told Eoin that the event I witnessed above the lake was a weapon for the Bohr."

Lyla held a hand out to stop him. "Laeb. Are you saying that you knew it was not a weapon, yet you allowed Duga to manipulate the Makriliaens to join your cause?"

"It might have been a weapon," said Laeb, unconvincingly.

"You knew it was not!" snapped Kyira. "I saw one myself above a hill in Nord. A sphere of light that exploded, destroying the land and causing the sky to fall. I felt it stretch my very soul to breaking. It was the Gods themselves."

Laeb's eyes widened. "That is what I saw, but there is nothing to suggest it isn't a weapon."

"You twist words to suit yourself," she said, disgusted. "And now you send the Makriliaens to their deaths."

Laeb glared at her. "There will always be losses in war, Sami, and those who are strong enough to survive, will."

Kyira could not believe the words she was hearing. Whatever she had seen in this man had fallen away like loose rock. "You are a liar. You are no different to the Bohr themselves."

Commander Laeb leaned on the table, knuckles white and fingers over the map. When he spoke his voice trembled with barely-contained rage. "Understand that if we fail here, the lord's army will roll on through the Teräväen gates over the Way Bridge and out of the Vasen gates, and they will keep going until they meet Nord head on." His fist crashed down on the little table. "It will be the end for the Ringlander's way of life. Your life. Everyone's life. The Bohr want nothing less than total occupation. They are ruthless, Kyira, and they will stop at nothing until they spread upon Rengas like a cancer!" He turned and stormed out of the room.

"Laeb is a man of power facing down his nemesis," said Lyla. "He trusts you, Kyira, but you are standing between two unstoppable forces."

Kyira shook her head. The responsibility she felt to the Makriliaens was strong, but her bond to Hasaan was stronger. "Are you saying that I should just let this happen?"

A woman appeared in the doorway with Abika in her arms. The babe was strapped into some kind of armoured sling. Lyla nodded to the woman then took Kyira by the shoulders.

"No, Kyira. I'm saying we are standing upon the needle's point about to fall, and you must choose a side."

The Brink of Breath

Fia held up her cowl as the pair of Pan Guards marched by the iron fence at the end of the gardens. They stomped by, not sparing her or Keene a glance, until they were hidden by the branches of an old tree. Patrolling Pans could only mean Rathe's grip of Tyr had tightened. They were even calling him Guardian now. She shivered at what that would mean for the people of this poor city. The branches of the tree reached up to a bank of dark clouds, which were much thicker than they should have been for this time of year. She'd been in Tyr long enough to know—

"Shieldless!"

"Yes, alright!" With great effort Fia yanked the cadet's arrow from the wood.

"Jumpy, aren't you?" said the cadet, taking the arrow.

Fia gave a half-nod, hoping that would suffice. The cadet seemed far too confident with that bow on her back, and Fia knew the difference between confidence with skill and confidence without. If she tried to escape, she doubted she'd get as far as the garden gates before one of those arrows took her.

"You're going to have to be much quicker than this,

Shieldless. Sixty arrows per minute is the goal, and that was barely thirty."

"Are all the Kin as demanding as you?"

"Cadet Keene," added the girl. Her eye twitched a little.

Fia frowned. "What?"

"As Shieldless you are required to respect your Kin. Full title and name please."

"Sorry… Cadet Keene."

The cadet pulled two arrows from the ground and let them both loose at the same time. They thwacked into the trunk of the willow tree.

It was hard not to be impressed. "You're good with that."

"Yes," said Keene, tying her hair up. "I am."

"You should leave it down," said Fia. "Your hair is beautiful."

Keene pulled a long wooden needle from her fur boots and held it in her teeth. "It's not done for beauty. It's a sign of my people." When the bun was tight, she pushed the needle in and twisted it back on itself.

"Well," said Fia. "It's beautiful anyway."

"It's not as nice as yours," said Keene, standing and rubbing a lock of Fia's hair between her fingers. "Such deep colour. Where are you from?"

"Originally? Bakla. But I don't remember it much."

"Bakla?" frowned Keene. "In the Kemens?"

"Not quite," replied Fia. "Bakla, followed the disputed Northern Territories, and won its independence from the Bohr shortly after I was born. My mother and father were both fighters of freedom." She looked into the cadet's eyes, looking for some sign of feigned loyalty, some sign that the news Fia's parents were revolutionaries might be worthy of the cadet's superior officers. Maybe there was a promotion in it for her, or just maybe the cadet was actually a fierce supporter of a free Kemen, hearing the news brought in by raevens in whatever tiny tribe she happened to live in the frozen wastelands of Nord.

"My parents were fighters too," said Keene.

Fia blinked. "Who did they fight?"

"Anyone who threatened them. In the case of their deaths it was a band of the Tsiorc. I was out hunting with my mother, and we came upon the Tsiorc — three men sitting huddled around a fire — and they attacked us. It was my mother's idea to offer them some of our catch, and it earned her a crossbow bolt to the stomach. I ran, and they followed me back to our home and killed my father, my dog, and my pigs." She let out a resigned sigh. "That is why I am here." Fia reached out to her, but Keene shook her head and stepped back. "I have dealt with my demons, Kumpani. There is no need to feel sorry for me."

Fia's heart was racing. "I don't feel sorry for you, Cadet Keene. You are bold, and strong. Fearless. To know who you are, and where you come from is more than most can do." She smiled. "Hold on to it. Use it as a float when seas are rough. But don't hide it. Hold it dear. Without it, you would be someone else." There was long pause as the cadet stared at Fia. Had she gone too far? Where was she even trying to go?

"You are right, Kumpani. They are my demons."

"They are that, Keene. Clothe them. Feed them. Don't let them out of your sight."

Keene tilted her head. "One of the other Kin told me all Kemenese were dark skinned."

"Not all are dark skinned along the hot borders, but yes I am somewhat of an unusual sight, even in Bakla." Fia's cheeks grew warm. "I used to live here, in Tyr, and much of my time was spent in Vasen, pleasing the rich and powerful."

Keene's pupils dilated. "Really?"

"Really. That is the way of the Kumpani. Sought after by most, enjoyed by few."

"That sounds like a strange existence," said Keene, idly plucking her bowstring. "Being a pet for the wealthy."

"Oh no, it's not like that. The Kumpani are respected and revered. If I so chose, I could dismantle the life of any client who mistreated me." She clicked a finger. "Power, grace and beauty. Why? Would you be interested in becoming a Kumpani?"

"I doubt it." Keene nodded to the ground. "Arrow."

Fia chided herself for her cockiness, as she pulled one of the arrows from the wet grass and held it out.

Keene shot the arrow, then lowered her bow. "How does one become Kumpani?"

"Entrance into the Kumpani is by invite only, as a way of vetting new members," said Fia, plucking another arrow from the ground. "It doesn't happen often though — the traits of a Kumpani are hard to come by."

Keene went to take the arrow but Fia held it tighter. "You would learn skills," said Fia, stepping closer and softening her voice just so. "Skills that will be more useful to you than killing innocent people."

"Innocent? I'll show you innocent." She lifted her shirt. "The Tsiorc did this. Men. Hungry men. There was no innocence there."

Fia lightly traced the scar across the cadet's stomach and

412

around her side. "Men at war are all the same. All they care about are the spoils." She moved closer still, and the fresh smell of the cadet's skin drifted towards her. Fia let herself experience the moment, becoming acutely aware of her own body as if it were simply a tool she was holding. The cadet's cheeks bloomed, and her posture relaxed as Fia's hand moved down to the cadet's waist, resting upon the curve of her hip.

"I know what you're doing," breathed Keene.

"Tell me," said Fia. She loosened her grip on the cadet's bare skin and traced a finger up her back. "What am I doing?"

Keene shivered. "You are… toying with me."

"I am doing no such thing," breathed Fia. "The Kumpani do not just pick anyone to get close to." She stepped into Keene, pulling her close so that her own neck was but an inch from Keene's lips. "We choose those who are strong, who want, and desire and fight." The cadet's fingers found hers along the shaft of the arrow, trembling with feeling. She kissed Fia's neck. Pulses of excitement ran through Fia's body, and she closed her eyes and let herself be swept away in it. The cadet's hair tickled her face. It was as beautiful as Janike's hair, though perhaps not as thick. Keene's curves were less pronounced than Janike's too, but then Janike was a singular being. Fia had never met anyone like Janike before. Fia's heart thumped, aching for her lost friend, but this was no time to wish upon the dead.

Keene's breathing was heavy, as lust took over. Fia grabbed the cadet's free hand to stop it wandering and used it to pull her closer, so their bodies were pressed against each other. Their warmth spreading into each other. Here was another moment, a moment to treasure, to savour and to—

413

"Not interrupting, are we?" The rider Gorm and a familiar squat man with thick eyeglasses sauntered into the gardens.

Keene pushed Fia away. "No, of course not."

The incomers stepped onto the trimmed grass and pulled the gate closed. "Shame," said Gorm. "Shame, shame, shame. You've to come with us. Now."

Keene coughed. "Rider, I was just…we were just…"

"Just…"

Keene's face blushed furiously, as she looked for an honest way out. Of course, there was none.

Gorm turned to his companion and cackled loudly. "We're not here for you, cadet! We've come for your Shieldless."

Keene turned to Fia and shrugged. "Oh," she said, lowering her bow. She grabbed the remaining arrows and whispered close, "maybe next time, Kumpani."

Fia's stomach filled with butterflies as the cadet walked away. As Keene had had no way out, now suddenly neither had she. She turned to the two men. "Me?"

Gorm shook his head then patted his squat companion on the back. "Yes, you. And don't be using them wiles on me, or I'll knock 'em out of you. You know better than that. Right, well there you are, Seb. Make it quick. The Kin will be moving soon."

The squat man approached timidly, pulling a notebook from the pocket in his woollen coat. "You are the Kumpani?"

"Yes. What do you want?"

"Good! I am conducting a census of all the Shieldless who came in via Nord. I have your name recorded here as Atalfia?"

Fia blinked, then glanced at Cadet Keene and Gorm who were busy talking. "It's Fia."

The man looked her up and down, but not like most did. "I am Sebreth, Altinda'har to the Guardian of Tyr."

Fia's heart quickened — he was Rathe's man.

"I am told that a blue-eyes, that is, a Sulitarian fishman named Forn, of the vessel… the Ariathar, delivered you to the Kin near Makril? Is that correct?"

"That's right."

"Can you tell me of the firespiral?"

Fia frowned. "Sorry, I don't…what firespiral?"

Sebreth cocked his head. "You were in Makril, and you didn't see the fire tornado that destroyed the entire town?"

"I was in the water. Wait…The whole town? That is awful. What happened to the people?"

Sebreth was ignoring her. He looked up from the scrawled notes in confusion. "You weren't… there." He shook his head at his notes and drizzle started to fall.

"What happened to the people?"

"If you weren't there then you are of no use to me."

"Wait," said Fia. "Stop!"

A flash of light illuminated the gardens, and she glanced upward. A fork of lightning as black as nothingness itself burst out of the cloud and hung there, pulsing like the black veins of the Mother Baeivi. It flickered for a heartbeat then vanished, the clouds appearing bright in its absence. Then came the rain. The sound of raindrops on stone and grass growing so loud that she could barely hear herself talk.

Sebreth cupped his hands and a pool of blackening rainwater collected there. "The wrath of Baeivi produced a disc of swirling cloud so large it looked as though the night sky had taken on form and decided to touch the land, and the black rain that fell was the blood of the Forbringrs. A storm to end all storms. A storm on the brink of breath, a breath that held the focused power of life and death within it." Fia recognised the Forbringr's Scripture — there wasn't a Tyrian alive who hadn't been taught it at school.

"This storm is the beginning," said Sebreth, words almost lost to the rain. "The beginning of the end." His bug-eyes grew suddenly wider.

"Sebreth!" snapped Fia, losing patience. "Can *you* just focus please? What happened to the people of Makril?"

"Focus?" muttered Sebreth, as though he was unaware of all that was going on around him. "It has to be focus, like a magnet. There's no other explanation." He held a hand up to shield his eyes from the black rain. "The focus is upon the origin, but that means…it's here. And if it is here, I just can't send him through. I need someone else to go through first. A test." His gaze settled back on Fia.

Fia wiped the rain from her eyes. "What are you going on about you fool!"

Sebreth dropped his notebook and it splatted to the flooded grass. He grasped Fia's wrist. "I can grant your freedom! But you must come with me."

"Freedom?" gasped Fia. "Of course, but where?"

Sebreth pointed at the storm. "The centre of that supercell is hanging over the place like a magnet over a compass. That is where we'll find it, and we must find it, before it destroys us all!"

416

Hearthsalt

Kavik's shoulders were not made for small spaces. He didn't like them, and they didn't like him. The top of his head scraped against the drainpipe, forcing him down onto all-fours. He gagged and choked on the rancid raw sewage coating his hands and soaking through his breeks. He might have even sicked up. Except, he could think of nothing more than his daughter. Wishing was for lesser men, men who had gotten themselves deep in shit with no way out. They prayed to the Forbringr, the earth and to anything slightly bigger than themselves, as long as it might earn them a way out. But, he still couldn't help wishing for Janike's life to be returned to her. Even if it meant she'd never talk to him again, she would be alive. His palm squelched on something particularly solid and before he could stop it his elbow gave out, sending his face into the mud.

"Argh!" he spat, smashing his fist into the sludge, splattering it everywhere.

"Blooded fool!" hissed Kai, from in front. "Keep it down. We're in a fucking clay pipe beneath the docks and your idiot shouts will travel through them as quick as eels through a whale carcass!" He turned away and carried on, splashing

Kavik's face in the process.

Kavik kept his mouth shut, not for the fear of tasting someone else's old shit, but because he hadn't the strength to reply. No parent should have to outlive their child.

The end of the drainpipe was almost too narrow to get though by the end. Kavik stuck his head out, and gasped at the turbulent waters of the Way rushing by but ten feet below. He reached forward and shuffled himself out of the drainpipe, straining every muscle he had to keep from bending the wrong way and falling into the water. He hauled his mass out on to the sea wall, lifting himself up the side of the dock until he could grab the metal ring at the top. Then, quick as a cat, he grabbed Kai's forearm and lifted himself up.

"You alright big guy?" asked Kai.

Kavik nodded, then something caught his attention. "There's a horse nearby, I can smell it."

Kai nodded to a hidden alcove away from the gates, where are a cartwheel was just visible. "It's for us."

A fat drop of rain landed on Kavik's nose, then another. He looked up at the sky. "What an evil day."

Tristan's hand appeared at the edge, then his other hand, and finally the man himself leaping up from the drain pipe. He sat up against the tower wall and pulled a pipe from his inside coat pocket.

"You're bendier than you look," said Kavik.

"Aye," replied Tristan. "I am that. My wife used say the same."

Kai held out his hand to the old sailor. "The hearthsalt?"

Tristan tapped his pockets with a mock look of concern, then dug into his other inside pocket and pulled out a small wax paper bundle. "Safe and dry, for now at least."

"Good," said Kai, "but don't piss around, or I'll cut your thumbs off."

"What is it?" asked Kavik.

"Hearthsalt," said Kai.

"Sponsored by one of our great patrons," added Tristan. "Not that they'd miss it, and that's the truth. There's a half-ton of it back on the ship. Or at least, there was." He winked at Kavik. "Kai have you the sulphur?"

Kai produced a waxed envelope whose edges had been completely sealed shut. He gave it a little shake. "The wax has held."

"Fuck, it's the Kin!"

Tristan was right; there they were. The Kin had stepped off the Way Bridge onto the docks. Janike might have called them a short army; in truth, they were line after line of armed younglings marching straight for them.

"We should hide!" said Kavik.

"No!" snapped Kai. "We have a few minutes before they see us through the workers."

Kavik stared down at the empty dock. "What workers, Kai? Come on, we have to get out of here…" Even before he could finish, a bell rang out through the rain, and immediately the dock was filling with traffic. Dockers from the ships streaming one way, armfuls of fish, boxes and salt, and fresh-faced clean men and women from the other side, filed out of the warehouses and eateries towards the ships. The two crowds collided, merged and mingled in front of his eyes in a choreographed march.

Kai shook his head in disbelief. "Laeb might be a prick, but the man knows his work. Come on! They'll see us if we're

419

not quick." He opened the waxed paper to reveal a lump of silver rock, with cube-shaped crystals growing from the top.

"I ain't ever seen hearthsalt go so hard," said Tristan.

"It shouldn't have crystals," said Kai. "Not yet."

"Will it still work?" asked Kavik.

Kai shook his head at the advancing Kin. "Nothing for it, now." He tore the hearthsalt into five pieces, and handed some to Tristan. Tristan held the stuff like it was his first born.

"I know we haven't known each other long, Tristan. But you don't seem the sort to get nervous."

"Here," said Kai. "We've got to be quick now. Be quick, but by all that is good and holy, be gentle. Press your piece right into the lock, but wait until we have done ours, horse-master."

Tristan tip-toed over to where the gate was hinged to the mountainside, and began gently rolling and pressing the mysterious silver rock between his palms until it suddenly changed consistency, becoming like a grey putty. One of the cube-shaped crystals dropped from Tristan's lump, and hit the cobbles, where it cracked and fizzed. The cube melted into a tiny pool that smoked and charred the rock beneath.

"Cover your mouth," whispered Kai, from the gate's other hinge. "Don't breath it in. It will melt the lungs right out of you!"

Kavik stepped back, but Tristan stayed pinned between the rising, sparkling smoke and the iron gates behind him. The smoke subsided leaving the cobble charred and crumbling beneath.

Another bell rang out along the docks. "Quickly now,"

hissed Kai.

Kavik approached the lock, which looked as though it was made for a key thicker than his arm. He moulded the hearthsalt as Tristan had done, feeling the consistency change from rock to a soft ball of putty the size of his fist, then he pushed it all inside the keyhole.

"Forcing it into softness sets the timer," said Kai, appearing at his side. "But we need to hasten it along. That is what this is for." He upended the envelope he had been carrying and sprinkled the contents onto his palm.

"Sulphur?" asked Kavik.

"The very same," said Kai, pressing pinches of the yellow powder into the hearthsalt in the lock. "Tristan, you finished?"

"Aye," said Tristan, taking the envelope and sprinkling the last over his lumps of hearthsalt, now pressed into the hinges and creases of the huge iron doors.

Kavik turned back towards the dock. The Kin were easily visible now, marching towards them with intent, but Kai and Tristan were already moving, skulking away along the sides of the dripping Teräväen mountainside.

"Horse-master," hissed Kai. "Get to the cart!"

The three men sprinted towards the lines of Kin emerging from the mist, then veered off behind a ruined building where the horse and cart sat waiting. The sounds of footsteps marching along the cobbles were getting louder as they rounded upon a Tyrian with tied grey locs standing waiting with the horse.

"It's alright," he said, hands out. "Laeb sent for me. I'm a friend."

"Then speak the password, Tyrian!"

421

The stranger swallowed. "Vertfök."

Kai sheathed his knife, and both he and Tristan climbed in the back of the cart and under the canvas.

"Do you have a name?" asked Kavik, hopping up onto the cart.

The man sidestepped around and lifted the canvas for him. "Forbringr's blood! Just get in will you. The Kin are coming!"

"Password or no," growled Kavik. "I trust no man until I know his name. His true name."

"I am Allander, brother. Now get in!"

The Gates of Terävä

The sky was a chaotic mass of lesions and vapour, rolling around a hollow central eye above Vasen. The high stacks of cloud twisted upon each other, split by wide beams of fading sunlight that had briefly found a gap before being swallowed. It was the largest storm Hasaan had ever seen, dwarfing even the high razor peaks of the Teräväen mountain. A deep clap of thunder tore the air as though ripping the fabric of reality itself. The flash that followed leapt across his eye, leaving bright shapes against the dark sheets of rain.

The Kin marched over the central hump of the Way Bridge and the docks came into full view. From the elevated centre of the Way Bridge he had a full wrap-around view of the ocean. The grey water tipped back and forth, waves colliding with each other and throwing the moored vessels around like matchsticks. The warehouses sitting along the long stretch of dock, and where the gates of Terävä stood waiting, looked like they would flood soon, unable to cope with the overspill from the channel.

Their long procession marched on from the bridge and veered down the short steep hill. There was not even the slightest hesitation as the Kin's front lines turned onto the dock, and it wasn't long before his feet were soaking. Some of the squad leaders carried bows but almost everyone carried bundles of spears, baskets filled with swords, and one poor fat kid who was dragging a bag of cannon shot behind him.

A girl about his age with dark lines painted upon her cheeks and dressed in well-fitting armour, marched alongside him splashing delightedly with a younger man on her left. A middle-aged man with a horn walked on Hasaan's right at the end of the line, as stone-faced as surely he was himself.

"Nervous?" came a voice from behind.

Hasaan shook his head. "Nervous, Cailaen? Of course not. What reasons do I have to be nervous?"

Cailaen thumped his shoulder. "That's more like it!"

Hasaan gestured at the girl with the painted face. "A bit over the top isn't she, Cail?"

"I wouldn't say so, although she probably thinks she's off to war."

"Filling bags, hauling weapons, and making soup is hardly what I'd call war. Even if it is for the world's biggest army."

"You're right about something at least," said Cailaen, snidely. "My guess, dear squad leader, and something you should probably already know, is that the girl joined like us, and is excited to be doing something with her life. Hell, that armour was probably passed down from her daddy. Either that or she pinched it from the barracks. It does look like ours…"

"Hmm." Hasaan found himself wishing for Cailaen to leave him be. It was a feeling he'd had more than once since they'd arrived in Tyr.

"What I don't understand," said Cailaen, "is that we're dragging all of this stuff to the army, only to have to drag it all the way back again. Could we not have just walked to the gates, let them in, and picked up the supplies on the way through?"

Hasaan sighed, trying not to sound irritated. "It's a ritual, Cailaen. The Kin announce themselves to the lord's army, and lead them through the city crowds to sounds of applause."

Cailaen raised an eyebrow. "City crowds? Anyone who braves this bloody weather deserves an applause from us."

"Quiet," snapped Hasaan. "Look, we're stopping."

The lines of Kin came to an uneven stop at the foot of the gates. They must have weighed a few tons each, with no visible indication of how they opened. Peering around the cadets and their shieldless, Hasaan studied the cylindrical building and spotted a door near the bottom where Lor stood nearby talking to a group of older men giving orders.

"So," whispered Cailaen. "The lord's army are behind there? Just...waiting?"

"Not right behind," said Hasaan. "Lor told me it's pretty narrow between this mountain and the dockside. They're along the road."

"And they've been out there in this for a while now." Cailaen gestured upwards. "So I imagine they're keen to move north. What are we doing after we leave the city?"

"Heading north into Dali. That's all I know."

"And you have no problems fighting against your own countrymen?"

Hasaan leaned in and lowered his voice. "You said it yourself, Cailaen: minding the Paths for the rest of my days is no life for a young Sami. The Bohr will bring opportunity to Nord. Just imagine, cities like this one within the rolling mountains of Nord. Our homeland will become a powerhouse of strength. It's just a shame that not all see it that way." His voice trailed off, as he stretched up to see over the spears and heads in front. Lor was pointing up at the gates, and the narrow tower that stood beside it, ordering the senior officers this way and that.

"Let us hope we are on the right side then, dear friend." He tapped Hasaan on the shoulder and disappeared back into the rows behind.

The Horn's Call

L aeb leaned out of the front of the Vasen bridge tower. The long and narrow Way Bridge with its stone plinths and ancient cobbled road was beautiful, of that there was no doubt. Even the drains that ran along each side were worthy of description, their tunnel entrances as tall as he himself, solid and built to last. He fancied that he could hear the Tsiorc in there at this very second, breathing quietly as they stood, ankle deep in black water, waiting for his signal. Of course it was all in his mind — the roar of a tumultuous sea, the clapping of thunder, the random, melodic tune of ship bells drowned out all other sounds so that even his breath seemed a world away.

He glanced down, shielding his eyes from the sea spray and near horizontal rain. The bridge road below at the foot of the tower was clearly better maintained, while towards Terävä it was cracked and full of potholes. The Way Bridge may have been an iconic sculptural piece of architecture known around Rengas to represent the deep, solid roots of trade that Tyr controlled, but it was still a bridge, and if one side of it was allowed to fail, the other would soon follow. One side could not survive without the other.

Laeb did not care for the metaphor. Not when the lives

427

of thousands of innocent city folk were held in the balance — people living their lives, manning the docks, working the waters…paying their taxes, only to be dragged into a war that wasn't theirs to fight.

"It's the perfect bottleneck."

"Yes, said Laeb, "it is." He pulled himself back in, and Lyla wiped the black rain from his brow. "This is our moment, Commander. It will be sung about by our children and their children. They will recognise it as the changing of the tides, the taking, and the beginning of a new fight."

The babe slung to her Lyla's gurgled, and Laeb found himself struck by the weight of her words. Fia had often told him to cherish the moments in life, and yet he could do nothing but stand and watch them sail away. This might have been a moment to Lyla, and her child, and to everyone else who had squeezed into the bridge tower, but to Laeb moments were ships, and he was stuck on land watching them vanish off into the horizon. The creators of moments rarely had the luxury to stop and experience them.

He traced the lines of the babe's dark hair. "Let us hope so, for her sake."

"Look!" she whispered. "There it is." Two bright spots of light blossomed at the Teräväen gate, illuminating the entire mountainside for a few long seconds before dwindling down to a deep orange-red. "It seems Kai is not as incompetent as he looks."

Laeb turned. "Magister Firam, send in the back lines. I want them with the second and third regiments ready to flank from behind."

Firam nodded and crossed the tiny square room to the iron door.

"Wait," said Laeb. "Hold back three hundred Sulitarians."

Kilier gasped. "Three hundred? That's half of our best fighters!"

Firam also opened his mouth to speak, then rightly thought better of it. He gave a simple nod, then went to descend the tower ladder.

Laeb grabbed a horn leaning in the corner. "And Firam, take this. You have the honour of announcing that the rebel Tsiorc army has arrived in Tyr."

Firam took the horn, careful to keep the black Tsiorc flag from touching the floor. "I will, commander."

"Make sure it's loud."

Firam nodded. "It will be, commander."

"I thought he would have been happier," said Mihkil, after Firam had descended down the ladder to the Way Bridge.

Lyla tapped the young archer on the back. "Oh, I think he was. Firam is a private man."

"You would be, too," added Laeb. "If the Bohr had taken your lands and killed all of your blood within the space of a day."

Dia'slar chuckled darkly. "So, the man does have a soul after all."

Lyla's eyes narrowed. "I hardly think *you* are in a position to speak on Firam's soul. Besides, we all have souls. It is Commander Laeb's job to make sure we keep them."

"Mihkil," said Laeb, "are your archers in place?"

Mihkil nodded emphatically. "Awaiting your word, commander."

"Send them up."

"Right away, commander." Mihkil stepped over to the tower entrance and whistled out. There was a corresponding whistle from below and a group of archers climbed the tower ladder, lifting themselves and their tall longbows up onto the roof.

"The archers are quiet," said Dia'slar. "You would barely know they are there."

"And deadly," added Laeb. "You see how tall those bows are. They will devastate the Kin's front lines."

"That is not what I meant."

"What is it, old friend? You look like you have something to say."

"You know my allegiances, commander," said Dia'slar, as though he had been rehearsing the words.

"I do that," said Laeb.

"Then heed me. You have trained your people well, but it is clear to me that they are afraid. We should show our full hand now. The archers will do us proud but let us go one step further. Bring in the full ranks and show these Bohr who we are. Let us stand upon this bridge and bellow out our name in the Bohr's faces. Your men will thank you for it, and take solace from your confidence."

"What good would that do?" scoffed Lyla.

Laeb held out a hand to Lyla. "Dia'slar, you mean to include the ranks hiding within the drains as part of our first wave?"

"Absolutely! Their presence will strike fear into the hearts of the Kin. Let us throw our entire might behind that first blow." Dia'slar slammed his fist into his palm. "We can crush them!"

A murmur began to resonate through the stone floor, growing louder until the sound of Tsiorc soldiers marched by the tower bridge. Line after line of Sulitarians strode onto the Way Bridge, out in front of the tower's shuttered opening. Men, women, husbands, wives, mothers, father, grandparents, all armed and trained and ready to fight for the futures of their people and break the Bohr's stronghold over Tyr.

Lyla stepped forward and took Laeb's hand. "*Now* is my moment, Laeb. You and I."

Laeb gave the babe's head one last stroke. "For luck."

Lyla glanced sidelong at Dia'slar. "I shall leave him with you." Then turned to Kilier. "Luck to us all!" She descended the ladder and joined the lines of Sulitarians.

"Please, Laeb!" hissed Dia'slar. "Before it's too late. Add the final rank to the rear. Show these animals who we are!"

"Dia'slar. We have a plan, and I mean to stick to it. The only addition to the rear ranks will be you if you mention it again."

Dia'slar stepped back into the shadow of the tower room and Laeb turned his back on him.

The Tsiorc lines came to a stop a third of the way across the bridge, a short distance behind the entrances to the drains. One hundred lines of ten spread wide. A crack of lightning lit up the sky, and as though he were waiting for it, Magister Firam blew the Tsiorc's horn.

The tritone horn rang deep and pure, cutting through the wind and black rain like a hot blade through butter. Laeb relished the feeling as the sound cut right through him, as it would all who would hear it, and smiled at Firam's capacity to keep the horn ringing from the front lines. A long minute passed before the horn's call was eventually stolen away by the elements, and it seemed to Laeb that the whole of Tyr stood on the brink of breath, awaiting their fate, as he awaited his.

* * *

For the first time in an age, Lor's blood ran cold, but not from the smell of molten iron dripping steadily from the hinges of the Teräväen gates behind him, nor from the sound of that annoying little trumpet. His fear came from the sight of the Tsiorc — they had come from nowhere and taken the Way Bridge.

Taken might not have been the right word — *casually walked onto* may have been better, for it appeared that there had not been a single soul to stop them. "Where are the Pans?"

He back handed the new Sami squad leader across the face, forcing hushed silence from the senior officers nearby and the few lines of Kin who could see them. "Turn the lines."

The boy stared back at him almost defiantly. "Of course, Commander Lor."

Lor glared at him. By the damned shadows these Sami had hot blood. He watched proudly as the boy turned on his heel and began whipping the lines around to face the bridge. "That's right," he said. "Use it, boy."

The Kin would all die on the Way Bridge, as the first wave so often did, but it would give them time to open the gates for the lord's army. He rapped the iron with a knuckle, watching as droplets of black rain sizzled and sparked upon the ruined hinges. "Get the dock workers down here," said Lor, quietly to the remaining senior officers. "We need these gates open. Now."

* * *

Allander didn't seem phased by the horn. Kavik's heart, on the other hand, thumped as though it might burst from his chest. They were in an alleyway between two great warehouses, and the smell of raw fish was as strong as if he were holding one directly beneath his nose.

"Are we discovered?" whispered Tristan from underneath the canvas. "We can't see."

Kavik tore off the canvas from the cart. "By the tearing fucking skies, Tristan! They wouldn't blow no horn for finding three horseballs like us! The Tsiorc are in place on the bridge, you damned fool."

"So it worked?"

"The fuses were timed perfectly," said Allander, looking impressed. "The Kin were almost standing in front of the gates when the locks welded shut. What was it you used? Not sulphur?"

"Hearthsalt," said Kai. "And no, before you ask, we've none left." He looked around. "Where are we?"

Allander pointed to a white building that blocked the end of the alleyway. "Behind the Fiskar. My store."

"And who is she?" growled Kai.

Kavik snapped around, his hand reaching for the knife at his shin. How had he missed her? A slender woman with long, red-gold hair, high cheekbones and a fierce expression stood at the opposite end of the alleyway, tying and untying a knot. Her hands worked the sea rope as if that was all they had done since being able to clutch.

"*She* is Eris," said the woman, with a jerk of the rope. "Allander." Allander nodded obediently then stepped by the three men and stood at her side.

"Another new person?" muttered Tristan. "I feel like I've met most of bloody Tyr already."

"And who are you now?" asked Kavik.

Kai smiled as if he knew something everyone else didn't. "Eris. The Goddess of Discord and Strife, I do believe."

"I do not care for shipmen," replied Eris, before resuming her whispers with Allander.

"Then perhaps the docks are the wrong place for you."

Allander shook his head. "Kai, please. This is Erdal's daughter."

Kai straightened up. "Erdal's daughter? You are leading the riots?"

"Who the shit is Erdal?" said Tristan. "Another one. How are we supposed to remember all these people?"

Eris's eyes softened. "Erdal, in his name, was a shepherd, and he raised us after my mother died. Upon hearing my wishes to do something with my life," she said, clutching at the rope, "he sold his blood to the Guardian of Tyr, but rather than let him work it off, the Guardian murdered him where he stood."

"Erdal's death resonated deeply with the people of Terävä," added Allander. "The riots, as you call them, came soon after."

Kai took a step forward. "The riots are organised. You are creating dissent amongst the populace on purpose?"

Allander nodded. "Not organised. Orchestrated. Eris has reached into the heart of this city and found a new blood that will not so easily be spilled."

Eris's eyes grew fierce. "The people of Terävä will not put up with the Bohr any longer. We may appear weak to the

Bohr, but it will be that very miscalculation that sees their end."

"Are they ready?" asked Allander.

"Our people stand ready and waiting to strike."

"And who are these *people*?" asked Kavik.

For the first time Allander smiled. "My people, Kai's people, the people of Tyr and the Tsiorc. Your people."

Spears, Steel and Gold

The Kin army stared down at Kyira from the raised centre of the Way Bridge like they had come for her, like they were here only for her, and her alone. The wind roared past her ears, and a deep longing to be anywhere else settled in her stomach. Her muscles willed her to run, to leave this wretched city and never look back, but she didn't. She stood there, rooted to the ground like the mountain. Like the elder trees of the high north, like the God rocks, hard, and unyielding and…

"What are you doing here?" she muttered, for what felt like the hundredth time.

The Kin were better dressed than she, and most of the rest of the Tsiorc — their amour being mostly black and grey flecked with droplets of bright steel that glinted whenever a flash of lightning tore through the sky above. The dragonshead vigil of the Bohr stood sharp and black against burnished metal. There was no denying their young faces, but they were not the children Kyira had been expecting. A few more wrinkles here and there and they would have been indistinguishable from weathered veterans; nocked blades, scratched leather, shields. Steel. They looked eager to engage.

Breathe.

The Nordun warriors of the Tsiorc were clad in animals skins rather than armour, and their white-painted faces looked pallid with worry. Or perhaps fear. Even Kyira, who knew those faces so well, couldn't tell what they were feeling. It was the Sulitarians that stood out most, choosing only the brightest reds, yellows and blues to adorn their skin and leather armour with. They gave off the same waves of anticipation as the Kin, and it filled the air around them infusing the younger soldiers with battle-readiness. If they were to charge now, it might even last them into their first fight. Some had taken to wearing the petals of a yellow flower that seemed to litter every street, but each and every one of them wore a white triangle with a cross within it somewhere upon themselves. The stark symbol of the Tsiorc gracing every shield, leather chest plate and helmet alike.

Movement drew her eye as a bald head drifted forward along the side of the bridge, and the Magister, a man named Firam, strode by her carrying a horn in one hand and a flagpole in the other. He carried on until he reached the front of the Tsiorc lines then stopped there, waiting. Kyira had just begun to wonder what he was about when suddenly he thrust the Tsiorc flag high into the air and roared. The rest of the Tsiorc followed, bellowing and shouting a battle-cry that seemed to bounce between the clouds, the Way Bridge and the curtains of rain hanging around them. It was a statement. A reclamation. The red-headed woman who had been so good with the twine stood a few rows forward screaming, her chin held up to the sky and smoke leaving her mouth in a plume. Kyira felt the urge roll through her belly, building as all of the frustration and fear balled up and left her body all at once. She screamed as loud as she could, roaring at the heavens for her father, for her brother, her mother, for Vlada, for her life. For Nord. As her lungs were about to give out, a tearing screech cut through their voices, bolstering it and drawing it higher so that even the lightning was drowned out. Firam held the horn high as he blew, and the long note sang long and loud.

Finally it cut off, leaving only silence in its wake, but the Tsiorc were not done. The faces of the Sulitarians in the front lines contorted into wild expressions, and they reached up together as one, grabbing handfuls of air and pulling it back into themselves, as though taking energy from the storm itself, and focussing it on the Kin as an invisible weapon they could direct at will. The dance grew more intense but it was not for the Kin, nor even the lord's army trapped outside of the city beyond the harbour gates. It was a cry of ages, a cry of the people. Her people. Kyira, child of Iqaluk, of Nord, Pathwatcher and map-reader, tipped her head back and screamed as loud as she could. She was a Tsiorc and these enemies would feel her wrath.

* * *

Hasaan's guts turned to water as the horn blew again. He wanted to run and hide but he could not. He shuddered to think of what the consequence of such a thing might be.

"Kin!" he roared, banging his thick leather shield with his shortsword. "We are trained for this. These blue-eyes hold no magical powers. They are men. They are women. And they bleed like you or I. Cut them down as you would the tree, conquer them as you would the mountain." He nodded at the first officer of his Hand and lowered his voice. "Get ready."

Cailaen nodded meekly. Even the huge rider at his side looked unsure.

"Don't venture out from the groups," said Hasaan, trying to sound calm. "You're safer with others. Even if they're fighting for their lives. You hear me?"

The words seemed to distort, slowing. They weren't real. They couldn't be. He wanted to cry. He wanted to go home. He wanted to—

* * *

Lor paced back and forth at the back of the Kin. The elevated centre of the Way Bridge providing the perfect vantage point for everything that was happening, and it was all happening.

The Tsiorc had appeared from nowhere, somehow navigating through the streets of Vasen to the Way Bridge itself to stand before them like they owned this city. Fucking humans. Only luck had stopped them from marching straight to the docks and flanking them from behind. Lor fucking hated luck. The thought that someone might just let some almighty power decide upon their fate was enough to make him sick with disgust.

The black rain fell around him, slapping against the cobbles, heedless of his thoughts. The world would go on, past this day. Tyr would survive past this day. He would survive past this day.

He glanced back at the Teräväen gates, which were still sealed shut. It was a clever thing to lock Tyr's soldiers out of their own city, luck had definitely been on their side. Still, luck would only take you so far, and soon the gates would open and the lord's army would wash over this bridge like the Way currents themselves.

The Tsiorc horn blew again and the Kin roared in reply. Lor gave the squad leader a single nod then smiled as a sea of shining steel accused the sky. Finally, he was somewhere he knew.

* * *

"Stay by me!" came Cailaen's shout from somewhere, though Hasaan couldn't see where. He ran forward, the bodies around him a tide; hands grasping, steel flashing, grunts and breath and smoke and thick air. Was it the thick veil of fear that hung about them or was it the black rain? It drummed upon leather, clapped at wood and metal, in an assault of its own, soaking Hasaan and the rest of the Kin to their skin.

The Tsiorc rushed uphill towards those screaming, faces contorted with malice, and the distance between the two armies was abruptly reduced to nothing. The two forces came together like two hands clasping. Gaps opened up in the Tsiorc line as every second fighter slowed and slipped in behind the one to their left. The front rows of the Kin hesitated as they tried to evade the pointed ends of the Tsiorc's long spears filling those empty spaces.

"It's a trap!"

Hasaan tried to slow, but the rows behind drove him forward unheeding and unseeing. The first line of Tsiorc fighters shot by Hasaan's side, then the second, and third until he met a wall of bodies waiting for him, daggers and knives held out in front.

440

He had once seen a tradesman in Nord playing an instrument that produced a tune every time it was compressed, and it was that way now as the gaps between the Kin and the Tsiorc vanished, replaced with sweating fearful bodies, fighting for their lives. Bodies pressed into each other, one soldier the same as any another, too close for stabbing, fighting, shoving. Wails from those behind confirmed his fear: the first Tsiorc line had re-established, effectively trapping the Kin within the body of the Tsiorc soldiers. There was nothing to do now, but fight.

Hasaan focused on those in front, batting away the stabbing blades. He dodged, bending and twisting around sharp things, shoving his own forward in reply, until the strangest sensation made him gasp. He felt the resonance along the blade change as it found a mark. The pommel of his sword shaking as the meat around his blade struggled. The body he had stabbed was hidden in a throng of shadow and coloured cloth. Who was it? A man? A woman? Had they a family? A brother or sister? A father? He snapped his arm back, revealing a bloody smear along the blade, a half arm in length.

A hooked spear followed after his sword, and he barely managed to force it aside with an elbow. His hand fell upon the spear, and instinctively he grasped the wood and turned with it, the Tsiorc fighter on the other end snarled then pushed through the jostling wall straight for him. Hasaan lurched sideways through clutching limbs and hard heads, dragging the Tsiorc soldier into the gap Hasaan had left. The man hit the ground and disappeared under the feet of the advancing Kin, his scream cutting suddenly short.

Pockets of pitched fighting broke out as spaces began

441

to open up. Hasaan worked his way between the thickets, using the broken end of the spear to deflect Tsiorc and Kin weapons alike.

Streaks of arrow fire flew overhead so close he could feel the heat, disappearing into the main body of the Tsiorc. An older man with a white triangle painted across his face stumbled through a gap in front clutching at his throat, where a flaming arrow had taken him. A young Tsiorc boy appeared to Hasaan's left. He screamed and threw himself back from Keene's blade. She tripped forwards and the boy leapt on top of her, snarling and biting like a rabid monkey. Hasaan threw the broken spear into the boy's face, and Keene was able to wriggle free. She twisted and thrust a knife into the Tsiorc boy's side, then nodded a thanks to Hasaan before barrelling back into the fray.

* * *

Kyira hacked at anything that came too close with the sword Dia'slar had given her. It was indeed well-balanced, and had already relieved a few enemies of their limbs. She thrust it out, then stopped as the tip caught a young man in the shoulder. He was Sami. There was no doubt about it. His Lines spoke of barely six cycles since his Giving but by the Sisters of the Waning Crescent he looked to be about three times her own girth and all muscle, too.

She shook her head at him. "No, I am you. I am—"

The Sami danced towards her dipping between the other running bodies until he was by her side. Stone chips blew into Kyira's face as the soldier's curved hammer smashed into the stone.

442

"Come back here!"

The Sami threw the hammer out above his head in a wide arc, sailing past Kyira's stomach with a foot to spare. The weight of it spun the man around, dropping his red cowl over his eyes.

"Argh!"

Kyira jabbed with her shortsword, but met only hard armour. She pushed forward anyway, and the soldier stumbled back, his feet slipped out from under him and he tipped backwards over a low section of bridge wall. Just like that he was gone. Like Isak. Like Iqaluk.

She stepped towards the edge, but steel flashed in her peripherals. She sucked her stomach in, but bright pain blossomed beneath her ribs as a sword found a gap between her own leather chestplate.

A slow snarl formed on the Kin women's lips. "Killing your own? Don't worry, Sami. You'll be following him and no mind!"

Breathe.

Time slowed.

The Kin's sword rotated as her wrist readied the action and her arm began to swing back in answer. Kyira recognised the movement from the hundreds she had seen already in the clash. This Kin was an accomplished fighter, and her plan was to kill Kyira now, with this blow.

There was nowhere to go but forward. Kyira stepped in and elbowed the Kin hard in the face. The woman reeled back, pulling the sword with her. Kyira spun her own shortsword then swung it out. The motion felt true and honest, as though it had been written into the fates of the worlds. There was nothing else she could have done than be here at this second to perform this very act. The impact of the strike ran up her arm, but most of the energy had followed through and the sword bit deep in through the Kin's collar. The Kin woman looked surprised. She stumbled forward, pushing Kyira back and the bridge wall pressed against the back of Kyira's legs. She might have laughed to find herself in the same position as the Sami she had pushed over, ready to topple to the roiling swells below. Kyira didn't laugh; she did the only thing she could and let go of the sword and threw her arms around the Kin. The copper smell of blood filled her head, then the Kin's forehead cracked into her nose. The bone broke and tears filled Kyira's eyes, but she held on. She stepped up onto the low wall behind her and pushed against it as hard as she could, leaning in to Kin, snapping her head left and right to avoid the woman's wild heat butts. They stood locked together in an awkward embrace, while Kyira pressed her elbow down into the sword still sticking out of the Kin's shoulder. Eventually the Kin's wound got the better of her and Kyira overpowered her and pushed her away into the mass of fighting bodies behind. The woman's blonde-grey hair drifting away like driftwood upon the sea.

Then it all stopped.

An almighty roar, of bloody anguish itself cut through her, so terrible that Kyira, along with every other soldier upon the Way Bridge of Tyr, could do nothing but stop and turn towards the source: The TerävÃ¤en docks.

* * *

The Bohr king was twice, maybe thrice the height of the

444

men surrounding her. The creature was no surprise. The plan had always been to draw her out, but the sheer strength of her astonished Laeb as she rained blow after blow upon the heavy iron gates, tearing at the metal and pulling at the corners, dragging them further and further apart as though it had been built from sticks. The Teräväen gates leaned, screeching under the pressure, until the molten joints the Hearthsalt had done such a good job on finally snapped. The hinge on the mountainside gave, and the Bohr king pulled the whole door free from the housing, lifted it high above her head and tossed it into the rushing water of the Way. She back-handed the other swinging door, which tore away and dragged the gate tower crumbling over the dock edge into the raging water.

Laeb prided himself on his ability to remain unsurprised. It was a side-effect of observing every angle, imagining every possibility, but the nervousness creeping through his guts grew unbearable as the first shadows began to move in the dark space beyond the gate. Shadows that gradually resolved into wide, regimented lines of soldiers. Even without Duga by his side Laeb knew the game had changed, and not for the good. Upon meeting the hulking Bohr king, the lines of marching soldiers split into two streams like a river that had met an immovable object, flowing around either side. The Bohr king let loose another chilling roar, and Laeb drew a ragged breath.

"They're here. The lord's army have joined the fight."

* * *

Through bleary eyes Hasaan saw Keene pull her knife from

a Tsiorc girl's back. It looked like the cadet had taken her attacker through the kidney, so it would take some time for her to die. Keene shot him a look, a look that somehow seemed to read his thoughts, then she turned and stabbed again, and again, and again and the girl fell face first to the stone.

Hasaan had barely time to draw breath before two more Tsiorc rushed in, throwing wild arcs between he and Keene and roaring like lions. Keene danced between sword thrusts like a practiced veteran, slipping in between them until she reached the first Tsiorc, a bull of a man with bloody hair plastered to his face. Was it his own blood? There was no way to tell, nor time to consider it. The bull jabbed wildly at Keene, but the cadet rolled neatly underneath stopping at the second Tsiorc's feet before plunging her bloody knife into the man's guts. She held the blade in place as the Tsiorc slid off. There was no clutching, or grasping from this one, Keene had killed him dead with one lunge. The bull, still shocked by being so overlooked, picked up his companion's sword and spun them both.

"He's showboating," said Hasaan.

"You don't say," chided Keene, her hands mimicking and almost mocking the Tsiorc. Hasaan had seen it before at the Festival of life, where people would try to get their timing correct before jumping into the dancing circle, but this was no dance. The bull had had the same time to assess as much as Keene and Hasaan had, and when he tossed the sword spinning into the air, Keene's eye was drawn to it like a moth to a flame. The bull smashed his free fist into Keene's face, and she toppled back to the ground in a heap. With incredible skill the bull snatched the sword on its way back down and stepped forward.

Hasaan pulled his bow out, nocked and let fly. The arrow had barely wobbled before taking the man's hand and pinning it to his neck. Blood bubbled from his mouth and he fell in a heap over his friend.

"What you do that for?" growled Keene, spitting blood to the cobbles.

"I saved your life!"

Keene shook her head. "I am no Shieldless! I could have taken him."

Hasaan snarled. "You would have died you fool! He outfoxed you."

Keene snatched up her blade and wiped it on the dead Tsiorc's trouser leg. "I still think—"

"Do you have an extra joint in your leg that I am unaware of? Because that is the only way you could have avoided his sword had it come down." Keene stepped up to him, but said nothing. Hasaan stared back at her. "I saved your life, cadet."

"Then tell me, oh wise and learned leader." She nodded to the Tsiorc running up the Way Bridge behind him. "Tell me what good we are standing here, behind both forces?"

Hasaan spun on the spot. She was right. They had worked their way completely through the Tsiorc. He ducked. "Shit. Shit!"

Keene shook her head incredulously. "What? "They're getting to the real fight. The lords are over there. They need us—"

Thwump. It was a sound they both knew very well: the sound of an arrow hitting flesh. The bull had an arrow in his back. Another one sailed by Hasaan's face and clattered useless along the cobbles.

"Archers! Hide, Keene, hide!"

* * *

A girl with a painted face stared unseeing up at Kyira from the stinking entrance of the drain — hardly a fitting end for one so young. Her broken body a dam, slowly collecting the yellow petals that floated down on the black water. Bodies littered the entire width of the bridge, some still moving, but most not. The mass of soldiers had thankfully thinned, and it seemed the rest of the Tsiorc were largely ignoring the Kin and charging through them rather than engaging. The Kin were never really the enemy; Laeb was simply trying to push through them to get to the real threat that lay beyond — a stark realisation that filled her stomach with cold sickness.

At least Kyira was alive. It was a selfish thing to feel amongst so much death, but there it was. If she had changed when Iqaluk had died, then this had changed her again, and not for the better. Her eyes filled with tears as she imagined her father's expression at seeing her covered in the blood of so many innocents, surrounded by spirits of so many dead.

Dropping her sword, Kyira took the dead girl by her hooded skin coat and dragged her back on to the road. She thought of Iqaluk, of Isak, of the eleven men and six women whose lives she had taken since stepping on this bridge. Petals, drifting away, escaping down the drains to the sea. Away from this place. Forever.

* * *

Hasaan held himself tightly to the lintel.

"We should let fly," growled Keene, from further in. They had managed to secure themselves a hiding place from the archers in the tower, but the narrow depression had fast become a prison.

"Down!" hissed Hasaan, as another volley flew over their heads.

"Seven archers and eight arrows." She moved to set out for a better view and Hasaan grabbed her arm. "We can take them!" snapped Keene.

"No, we can't. The winds are too high, and they are too many. We wait…"

"For what? More archers? We are the only ones left, squad leader! The Kin have been trampled into the ground."

Hasaan glanced up at the centre of the bridge. Shouts and roars came from beyond its summit, as the Tsiorc battled unseen against the Lords. He wondered who was winning.

"If we take the tower," began Keene, "we'd be heroes…"

Her voice faded away as movement drew Hasaan's gaze down. A familiar shape was half-limping, half being dragged towards them across the far side of the bridge.

"Cailaen!" hissed Hasaan. "Get down!"

But Cailaen and the Kin carrying him stumbled forward, as though their exposed position and Hasaan's words were meaningless. Maybe they were. Arrows clattered around their feet, thwumped into the bodies lying strewn across the cobbles.

"What's he doing?" growled Keene. "Ander! Get out of there!"

Ander started, as though just seeing them for the first time. He threw up an arm and a heartbeat later it had been shot through. Ander stopped, studying the shaft. He had barely looked into Hasaan's eyes when a second arrow took him in the stomach, a third in the leg, a fourth in the shoulder carrying Cailaen. Cailaen flopped to the floor, and Ander pivoted, turning his body towards the tower of archers, his arms out protecting Cailaen from the deadly wind.

"No." Keene stepped out to give herself space to aim and a blur shot by her face, leaving a red line down her cheek. "Argh!"

The Tsiorc archers were baiting them, hoping to lure Hasaan and Keene from their hiding place. They were cats in a box, and it had to stop. He had to stop it. "Keene, can you see the lead?"

Keene stepped back just enough to peer beyond the wall. "Yes. The lead archer is inside the tower with some officers. I can just see his bow."

"What about the six on the roof? How many can you take?"

"Six."

Hasaan handed her one of his last two arrows. "You have seven chances. I will take the leader inside. Ready?"

Keene raised her nocked bow. "Yes."

Hasaan closed his eyes and puffed his cheeks out, breathing fast. His muscles willed him to stay where he was, but he fought them and both he and Keene stepped out together.

He drew.

His breath left with the arrow and both soared away on the wind. Keene's bowstring cracked three times, with two arrows each time, released as a death gust, fast and hard. Hasaan's arrow flew away from the tower, curving up with the wind as a force of nature. It reached its zenith, turned and dipped quietly in through the open side entrance of the tower. It struck the archer within the building a heartbeat after the five on the tower roof. Five.

"I missed one!" said Keene, pulling her last arrow.

The last archer ducked low on the roof, alive, but clearly injured. Keene hadn't missed. She never missed. Hasaan grabbed uselessly at his empty quiver behind him, but Keene had already nocked. The last archer kneeled up and pulled on his bowstring and both he and Keene let fly.

* * *

Laeb squatted down next to Mihkil's body. The boy was barely in his twentieth. Kilier cowered up against the iron tower door like a spider pushing himself into a corner. He had shut it the second after the Kin's arrow had sailed in through the side entrance, taking Mihkil through the ribs. Shortly after all six archers had fallen from the roof.

"We are unguarded!" whimpered Kilier.

"He can't have seen but a slither of open door from that angle," said Dia'slar, sounding more impressed than grieved. "How in Baeivi's name did he do that?"

Laeb pressed his head against the stone beneath the tower opening. He didn't know how to answer. It was an impossible shot.

"Commander?"

"What!"

"What are we to do next?" Dia'slar glanced over the edge of the window.

"Get down," snapped Kilier. "They'll send in another volley! I mean to live past this day, you fool!"

Dia'slar dropped low, his back to the stone. "Commander,

your people have done well to hold out so long, but they'll soon be driven back. Their graves are already written. Please, Laeb. This needs to stop."

"It has just begun," said Laeb. He stood, waiting for the pressure and sting of an arrow shaft. It never came. The two young Kin archers were rushing across the bridge to their friend, their quivers apparently empty. Laeb looked beyond them over the sea of spears and steel to the Terävaen side. The Bohr King was making her way towards Laeb's tower, parting the lord's army upon the bridge dwarfing the men around her.

"It is time to fight," said Laeb.

A fireball emerged from near the back of the Lords ranks and smashed into the front lines of Tsiorc leaving a flaming hole in the line. Burning soldiers from both sides leapt from the bridge into the tempestuous waters.

Laeb started as he realised Dia'slar stood at his side. "What a choice to have to make. Death by fire, or death by water."

"They have a Banéman," said Laeb, quietly.

"Kaliste. She is skilled, though not perhaps as skilled as Jagar. It will take her some time to recharge. Commander, the Tsiorc have dispensed quickly with the Kin, but the lords are a different story. They have already driven your fighters back to the centre of the bridge."

Laeb felt his eye twitch. "The lord's army numbers are working against them. They are so densely packed they can only fight one line at a time. That is their bottleneck."

Dia'slar shook his head. "A bottleneck made from glass. Laeb, we must leave before more of your people die.."

Laeb could take no more. "Then leave. Spy."

"Spy?"

452

"You heard me, *Councillor* Dia'slar."

The tall man took a step back. "Is this what we are come to, old friend? Bickering, and accusation? I thought you were better than that."

Laeb rounded on him. "You always considered me weak, Dia'slar. But you are wrong. Patience is not weakness."

"I fight for what is right, brother. I fight for us. Every day I speak in those halls is a day I act in the name of our people."

Laeb scoffed. "So, you do have a people?"

"Of course," said Dia'slar. "Your people. Our people. We hail from the same land, Laeb. These petty Ringlanders may fight all they want, but it is Sulitarian blood, our blood, that will reign. It is us that will emerge victorious in this game."

Laeb shook his head. "Game? There are no games here. Only people's lives!" Sadness swept over him. "If Duga was here, he would have warned me off you, from the very minute I stepped out of the Vasen sewers. He would tell me your allegiances have switched, Dia'slar. That you are no longer on our side. That everything you have uttered since we have met has been designed to confuse and misdirect. He would tell me not to trust you, to cast you aside and leave you to die in the gutters of your city. A city that clasped its fingers around you and drew you in to nuzzle at its breast. And nuzzle you did, Dia'slar. You burrowed in and made a home and let this place infect you. You are not Sulitarian! You are a thief ousted, and you have NO people."

Dia'slar shook his head. "No, Laeb. Please. I am faithful to you. To the Tsiorc. I swear it!"

Laeb pulled his blue steel sword out. "Leave, now, or you will join the graves of *your people*."

The man looked taken aback, but his expression cooled

quickly. "You call it spying. I call it surviving."

Laeb felt his lip curl up. "Then go back and die with them. Either that or die here. Now."

Dia'slar inclined his head. "Commander Laeb, it's been an honour."

Kilier pulled the door open and hid behind it, cowering, and Dia'slar walked to the opening. He gave a final slippery smile then descended down the ladder.

"Consul," said Laeb, taking the door and holding it open against Kilier's very clear wish to see it closed. "The Bohr king is on his way to us. Go and tell the men we kept behind that it is time to fight."

* * *

Cailaen's face was deathly pale, made worse by the crimson smear under his eye where he had rubbed his cheek with bloody hands.

"It looks clean," said Keene, studying Cailaen's leg. "Just the meat."

"See?" added Hasaan. "There you are. Clean."

"The meat?" said Cailaen, with a frown. Hasaan shook his head to quiet his friend and Cailaen's eyes widened. At least Cailaen knew when to keep his mouth shut.

Keene tapped the shaft drawing a hiss from Cailaen's teeth. "The meat. The thigh heels well. Well, mine do. These skinny things may take longer."

"How did you do?" asked Hasaan.

"Out there?" Cailaen rubbed his forehead with a shaky hand. "Well, I'm still here, Squad Leader."

As if of one mind they all turned to look at Ander's body.

He was their age. He might not have looked it sure enough, but Hasaan had always gotten on well with him, even after he had made Squad Leader. "I'm no squad leader, Cail. We're friends. Brothers, and we are more than all of this. Come on, friend. Let's get you up."

Then everything happened too quickly to understand. Cailaen was tugged from Hasaan's arms and dragged sideways as a flash of leather and fur rushed by them. Keene stumbled and landed upon Cailaen, and the Tsiorc soldier side-stepped left towards Hasaan.

Steel.

Hasaan threw himself back to the lintel to give himself time. The Tsiorc soldier swiped her blade through where Hasaan had just been standing, her blade already crimson red. His feet caught on something and he blocked wildly hoping to use his bow as a shield, but her shortsword found the bow's curve and slid along it forcing it clattering to the cobbles.

Hasaan stumbled back as the Tsiorc woman advanced. For what he could see above the cowl she was southern-skinned with dark, painted brown eyes. The fur coat she wore looked too big for her frame, but clearly it wasn't restricting her. Keene rose, and leapt over Cailaen who was lying on his back. The two women fought like animals, tearing and scratching, each landing devastating punches to each other's heads and bodies. The Tsiorc feigned left and right and...

Cailaen was dead.

The Tsiorc woman had opened him up at the stomach like a fish. His eyes stared up, glassy and vacant to a sky he would never see again. He uttered his friend's name under his breath, knowing that he would not reply.

"The meat!" roared Keene. The Tsiorc woman leapt forwards, spreading her arms in mid-air to confuse, then knocked Keene sideways with a jab that came from nowhere. The Tsiorc landed lightly and struck Keene again in the face following the fist with an elbow. She retreated as Keene swung wildly to fend her off, but the woman was outmatching her and each blow pushed her back further and further.

"Meat—" The next punch took Keene in the mouth and she staggered back, her lips and teeth broken.

The meat.

Hasaan grabbed the shaft in Cailaen's leg and yanked it free, then he took up his bow and let fly. The arrow took the Tsiorc woman deep through the side of her chest plate.

* * *

Kyira ran as fast she could, but Lyla was dead before she hit the ground. She slowed as the Uigur girl pushed herself up holding Lyla's shortsword out, then stumbled, barely able to see from eyes that were already bruised and swelling.

"She deserved more than you," said Kyira through her teeth, and pulled her own sword.

The girl lunged and Kyira stepped aside to let her tumble to the road. Something knocked into Kyira's side and she fell sprawling to the Uigur girl's side. Kyira rolled herself away, grabbed her blade and jumped back to her feet to meet the next. How he would pay for his sneakiness! She pulled Iqaluk's blade from her belt and readied herself, and all at once her world ceased to exist. The rolling clouds, the chalk-white buildings of Vasen, the perfectly even cobbles, the grey

456

sea spray reaching over the wall towards the battling armies, the bodies, the blood. None of it existed anymore.

"Hasaan?"

A man stared back at her, the sword in his hand shaking. He wore her brother's face, but it could not be him. It was not Hasaan. Kyira had witnessed this man, covered in blood, standing upon the body of another, blood streaming from a wound in his shoulder where a knife was still lodged, she had witnessed him kill Lyla from barely ten paces away. He was a murderer. The bow in his other hand looked as natural on him as if it had always been there, and it had. Hasaan had been barely two when he picked up their father's hunting bow, making a game of plucking the string and laughing at the music it made.

"Kyira?"

A hundred questions, but which to ask. What to say to this imposter. "You are hurt."

The man glanced at his shoulder, looking surprised to find a blade sticking out from it. He went to touch it then stopped. He knew that blade, and he knew it well. He had been there the day Kyira had been gifted it by their father. The wonderful twist to the bone handle that helped it rest perfectly in the palm, and the dark mottled pattern on the steel. It was a sturdy, simple blade, but it was beautiful, and she had loved it until the day she had given it to Lyla.

"Kyira, why did she have your weapon?"

"It may be a weapon to you, Hasaan, but to me it was a tool."

"You gave her your knife. Why?"

Her throat was so tight she could barely speak. "To rebalance. Hasaan what are you doing here?" Her streaming gaze fell to the body at her brother's feet. "Is that Cailaen? Hasaan, what have you done?" She held up her shortsword, and the tears came freely. "Did you kill him too?"

Hasaan motioned to the heap of rags upon the road. "She attacked us! What was I to do?" He moved towards her, heedless of the shortsword in her hand, and Kyira found herself backing off. This was her brother. He would not hurt her.

"Stay back, Hasaan."

Kyira stepped sideways in a wide circle, keeping her sword and Iqaluk's knife pointing at her brother the whole way. He moved with her and bent down to the Uigur girl as she reached Lyla.

Kyira dropped the knife and pulled at Lyla's coat. It had been pinned to her side. Just maybe then, it had provided enough padding.

"Stay back!"

Hasaan raised his hands and took another step. "Kyira, please, I want to help."

Kyira reached in behind Lyla's back. There. The sword was too long to cut through the coat so Kyira turned the blade against the arrow. The shaft was buried half in Lyla's side just below the armpit. A heart shot from ten paces.

The arrow snapped and Kyira pulled the coat over it, peeling back the sling. There was no movement.

"What are you doing?" said Hasaan. "You cannot be here. Kyira, please."

"I do not know you," she said, tugging the sling away from Lyla's body. "So do not... talk to me... like you do." Kyira grabbed Iqaluk's blade and pressed it lightly into the sling. The tight cloth tore and the babe's foot fell out from between the folds.

Hasaan drew back. "A babe? Kyira, why would she do that? Why would she take a babe into battle?"

"Shquad leader!" The Uigur's urgent tone made Kyira's head turn. "We have to go, the Tshiorc are shending in more men. We will get caught between them if we do not leave."

Kyira lifted Abika free from Lyla's body and held her close. She was sleeping deeply. Drugged, most likely.

"There are drains beneath us," said Kyira. "*That* is how I and the Tsiorc army got here."

Hasaan looked Kyira and the babe up and down, his face pale. He walked back to Cailaen's body and took off his friend's black and red jacket — the colours of his army — and held it over him, ready to hide Cailaen's face. The seconds became minutes, but it was only when the Uigur coughed that Hasaan let the coat fall.

He turned towards them. There was no emotion in his expression, nor regret, just cold, stark realisation that this was where his quest for a new life had taken him — the path he had chosen. He walked straight by Kyira and the Uigur girl to the drain entrance and disappeared into the dark tunnel.

Greeting the Earth

asaan stepped out into a deserted narrow street that curved out of sight with tall houses lining each side. He gently pushed the broken gate back over the entrance to the tunnel as though the entire Tsiorc army might suddenly emerge behind him, then padded over to the blind corner. Nothing but more houses and corners.

Crowds of people rushed by the end of the alleyway, their coloured silk garments billowing out behind them, dragging trunks, cases and livestock — their lifelong possessions — as far away from the Way Bridge as they could.

"They're headed to the gates," said Kyira. "And we should join them."

"No." A twinge at his shoulder made him look down. The hilt of Kyira's blade was still lodged there. He pulled it out smoothly, wincing as the sharp blade sliced him anew.

"Here."

Kyira shook her head. "Keep it. Maybe it will change your fortunes."

Hasaan stepped back from her. The fact she stood beside him still confused him, and he would not have believed it but for the very real, visceral way she had appeared. The babe in her arms had started moving, screwing its eyes up tightly in fitful sleep. Its soft skin looked completely out of place against Kyira's blood-stained armour.

"How did you know?" he uttered.

Kyira rubbed the child's back through her minksin. "I knew Lyla. I watched as this babe was strapped to her back."

Hasaan flicked the blade with a fingernail. "No mother I have met would have brought a child into a fight like that."

"You have not met any mothers then," said Kyira. "We need to go. Before the battle breaks out into the city."

"Kyira wait—"

They both stopped at the sight of Keene carefully puncturing the swollen bruises above her eye. Blood burst from the hole and gradually the swelling reduced, revealing the menacing whites of her eyes. "We're going nowhere, Sami. We're not here to escape. Squad leader, my suggestion is that we use the drains to sneak back in behind the lord's army, either that or we flank the fighters and do what we can from behind."

"I don't think the drains connect up on the bridge, cadet. And if we attacked from the rear they would only have to turn around and beat us down."

"Then what? We provide archery support. With enough arrows…"

"Arrows?" said Kyira. "You mean to attack the Tsiorc from behind? Like cowards?"

Keene rounded on her. "I don't know who you are Sami, but quiet down or I will end you here. Baby and all."

Kyira's eyes burned fiercely. "I should like to see you try."

"Stop it," snapped Hasaan. "Both of you. There has been enough death today."

Kyira looked at him, holding the same look of disgust he

461

felt in his guts. "What Iqaluk would say to see you now. To see you like this, standing at the end of a path you should not be on. It is a dead end. A decoy. There is still time to back track before you are completely lost."

Keene shook her head vigorously. "If we cannot take the drains, and an attack from the rear will leave us exposed, we'll need to find another means of crossing the Way. What about her? She got here, she must know something."

Kyira looked down. "I know nothing." She looked up when Hasaan hadn't replied, and her stare grew cold, as though she was somehow able to see his thoughts.

"You were never a good liar."

Keene shook her head. "Who are you—"

"Orsila!" A portly man holding his folded silk hak around him barrelled by, almost knocking them from the entrance. "Wait for me! Orsila!" he shouted, pulling a child's trailer loaded with items clattering along behind him.

The man's partner was running up the hill ahead of him in a cascade of pink silk, having clearly abandoned him to their possessions. One of the trailer's wheels caught on the wall sending numerous clay pots to the cobbles, scattering gold coins around Hasaan, Kyira and Keene's feet. A few others glanced at the pile, but none tried to pick them up.

The owner eyeballed them and tugged at the unwilling cart, then left it where it was and rushed up the hill behind his wife.

"Look," said Keene, nodding as the man and his wife stopped by a large group near the brow of the hill. "What are they looking at?"

Hasaan stepped out into the main street, almost slipping on the coins, and jogged up the hill, stopping alongside the group of Vasenfolk. The view of the bay was much the same he had seen when he first arrived in this city: the bridge leading to the docks, the favelas and the long staircase, and the mountain itself. Except all was shrouded in black rain The sea was a turbulent mass of monstrous waves that broke against the bridge, sending long streams of foam sliding down the Way, the bridge above was a ruined mess of bodies and fighting — the main body of the Tsiorc forces had been reduced to a single knot at the bridge's centre, and the lord's army, which had also taken heavy losses, was surrounding them to finish them off.

A lump formed in his throat as he spoke. "Kyira, how did you get into Tyr?"

His sister hesitated, but the gravity of this moment — as the last hundred of her people were rounded up to die — was enough to loosen her tongue. "There are ships hidden in the catacombs below Vasen. Kai's ships made it in through a secret entrance, just as the Way's tide turned then we travelled underground through the city until a contact let us in to an old orphanage. There we waited, and tooled up before taking back to the drains."

Keene snorted. "So, that's how they did it. Fucking drains. Vasen is a rabbit warren of drains and tunnels."

Hasaan shook his head in disbelief. "An orphanage? What state are the ships in?"

"You may be a good climber and passable archer, Hasaan, but you are no sailor!"

"Answer him!" growled Keene, looking even more vicious now her eyes had opened up.

"I will not! Those are our ships, not yours. Men and women who—"

463

Keene grabbed Kyira by the neck, and snatched her only free hand, raising it in the air. "I was not lying when I said I would end you, Sami! Squad leader are you hearing this? We should cut her down and leave her to die." The Vasenfolk standing around stepped back to give the three of them a wide berth, watching them as much as they were watching the Lords and remaining Tsiorc engaging upon the Way Bridge far below.

Hasaan looked down at the blade. *A change in fortunes.* "Cadet, put her down."

Keene looked surprised. "Squad leader…"

"Kyira, where is our father?"

The cadet let Kyira's hand fall. "Hasaan…She is your sister?"

"My only sister," said Hasaan. "Where is Iqaluk, Kyira?"

"I think you know, brother. He greeted the earth."

"No… no," The swelling rose in his stomach like hot tsampa bread, ready to burst out of him. "How?"

Kyira wept freely. "At the hand of a Banéman named Jagar." Hasaan listened intently as Kyira recounted his father's death.

The knife in his hands suddenly made sense. "Rebalance." It all made sense. He glanced down at Kyira's belt and there was Iqaluk's belt blade. It was exactly how he remembered it, the twine sheath lovingly made by their mother before either he or Kyira had been born. The bone handle looked charred.

"He gave his life for mine." She swallowed. "So that I may… I may find you."

The image of Iqaluk's face was torn from Hasaan's mind as the crowd began gasping and pointing. Across the Way the Teräväen favelas were alive with motion as streams of people trickled out from the foot of the shanties, filling the long staircase and streets around the docks. Men, women and children ran at the lord's army soldiers, wielding sticks, forks, swords, and rocks until soon the trickle had become a torrent of thousands of people, appearing out of the homes and streets of Terävä like ants from an anthill. The streams drew together like a great river, following the gesticulations of five people standing on a cart in between, to pour onto the bridge and slam into the back lines of the lord's army in a clash of metal and bodies.

"Why are the Teräväeans attacking us?" came a voice from behind. "We are one nation!"

"They're attacking their own people!"

"They're mad! All of them, mad!"

The Teräväeans mowed down the lines of hastily formed lord's army soldiers with almost incomprehensible ease, drawing them back away from the Way Bridge and onto the docks, filling its length in pitched fighting. Lines of fire spread amongst the lord's army lines like stubborn dandelions blooming through cracks in a rock.

The Teräväeans pulled back, leaving the Lords caught between fire on one side and the furious Way currents on the other.

Keene looked up at Hasaan, wide-eyed. "They've oiled the docks!"

More people appeared, attacking those fleeing from the flames, and soon the lord's army soldiers were throwing themselves into the rushing water, disappearing beneath the surface.

"Where is this orphanage, Kyira?"

"No!" snapped Keene. "There is still time! We can still add to this fight."

Hasaan sighed. "Keene, the Tsiorc are chasing the lords! Look!" He pointed at the knot of Tsiorc men barely reduced in numbers and chasing down the few remaining bands of black armoured lord's army soldiers. "We are lost!"

Keene pushed him and he fell to the road stunned. "You are a Squad leader, Hasaan!" she roared. "Act like it!"

Hasaan was perplexed. She was right, but how could he live with himself? Cailaen, Iqaluk. "How many more have to die, Keene? This is a battle of fools." He took off his bow.

Keene shook her head. "Don't you dare!"

Hasaan pushed the bow into her hands. "Cadet Keene, I promote you to squad leader."

Keene snatched it from him and smashed it, splintering over her knee. The bow string pulled the torn wood apart and Keene threw the bow broken to the cobbles. Her shoulder flinched, as though she wanted to hit him, but Hasaan didn't move.

"Coward," was all she said before she turned and sprinted away. She skidded to a halt at the street littered with gold coins and glanced back at them like a trapped animal set free. She adjusted her armour, and stormed off towards the drain entrance.

Stones and Strategy

"Steady!" roared Laeb. "Straighten up!"

The front lines of Tsiorc, composed of mostly Sulitarians, took Laeb's direction and pushed forward almost as one, their swords disappearing between the layers of black armour ahead, felling the lords like they were but a field of saplings and producing a fresh chorus of screams. The method was a simple one. Step in, stab diagonally to the left then pull back. Take a step back and roar obscenities. Point at the space between, rapidly filling with the dead and await as the anguish and anger took over before repeating. Alternating between simple left and right would have been too easy to predict, so Laeb had devised another: left, right, left, left, then right, left, right, right — a simple pattern that most of the Sulitarians remembered with ease. Perhaps it was so easy to remember because the rhythm of a thousand generations coursed through their veins, or perhaps there was something intrinsic within the pattern itself. Either way, the lord's army were completely unable to predict which way the Tsiorc would jab next.

"And out!" roared Laeb. "Switch on three!"

The front line of the lord's army slumped forward, forcing the men to scramble over the dead bodies to even get close enough to use their swords. Meanwhile the first and second lines of the Tsiorc switched places smoothly, and the Sulitarian third line stepped in second to await their turn. Fresh soldiers entered the fray, Makriliaen and Daliaen steel met leather, met skin, met bone, as frenetic blows rained down upon the lord's army. Nothing could stop them; the Tsiorc's blood was red with fury — their homes fired, their people murdered, and the lord's army, the protectors of Tyr, the Great Hand of the Bohr, in their way. Two styles of fighting against an army whose only loyalty was to the coin.

The wrath of the Tsiorc would conjure fear within the lord's army ranks and the fight would grow even easier. The bottleneck would hold, as Laeb knew it would.

"All back one!" he roared, and the Tsiorc stepped back. The bodies piled up in front of the lords were already four high. "And ROAR!" The Tsiorc erupted in rapturous screams. This was their fight, and theirs alone. Steel cracked against leather bound chest, against shield and stone.

Firam stepped out of the back line. His bruised face had a fresh laceration along his jaw, but it didn't seem to be bothering him. If anything, he looked ten cycles younger. "The lords have led their soldiers into a meat grinder!" he shouted, gleeful. "The dragons will fall!"

Laeb checked his environment. The counterpoint could come at any time, and it never did well to overlook the setting of your fight. The clouds seemed to move with purpose, against the wind, as though they were tethered to something much larger. The wind may simply have been travelling in a different direction higher up, but Laeb doubted it.

"Why do you always look so worried, Commander?"

roared Firam.

"Prepared, Magister. Nothing more."

Firam cackled. It was a sound unlike anything Laeb had heard the man make before. "The Forbringrs are here with us, Commander. They're here to witness this day! The fight to end all fights! The end of the Bohr! The fight to…"

Laeb followed Firam's drawn gaze back down to the soldiers upon the Way Bridge. The Bohr king was storming through the centre of the lord's army throwing men and women around like children's dolls. A line of Pan Guards followed in the King's deathly wake, standing upon those unfortunate enough to be in their way.

This was it. The counterpoint. He had to get this right. He waited as long as he dared, until the Bohr King had almost made it to the Tsiorc lines. Three lines, two lines, one…

"ZUVERI!" roared Laeb. The Tsiorc lines pulled back into two halves, one half each against their own side along the walls of the Way Bridge. The Bohr King tumbled forward into the unexpected gap almost falling. "NOW!" roared Laeb.

The decimated front lines of the lord's army could do nothing but watch over a wall of dead bodies as the gap closed in, and nigh on three hundred Sulitarian fighters leapt upon the Bohr King, stabbing and fighting.

Laeb jumped from the Way Bridge wall and ran forward with all of his might, his bluesteel sword out in front, and the Bohr King's head mere steps away. Three steps, two steps, one…

The Bohr king rose up, tearing the soldiers off her back like they were only annoying biting insects. Laeb hesitated. Her golden eyes were fixed upon Laeb. Far away he had known she was large, but up close he realised how wrong that approximation was. She was the largest being who had ever lived. The Mother of all Bohr.

Laeb skidded to a stop at her feet, and she pulled off the few rebels hanging on with her huge hands, then squeezed them to death. Blue blood dripped from cuts all over her body, and then suddenly she was just no longer there. The decimated line of the lord's army was all there was, until two Pan Guards stepped into the new space ready to cleave him in half. They had the same animalistic features as the King, but one had long horns that curled down like a ram while the other guards were smaller, like a young deer. They both loped towards him on their reversed ankles, twice as tall as any man. The ram got to him first and raising its jagged sword, leapt forward. Laeb dove sideways and the monstrous weapon cut deep into the stone where he had been standing, barbs and all. Laeb took stock of the bridge, but the king was gone. She had moved faster than he could account for, faster than his eye could see. Faster than logic could...

The ram tore the sword free, and Laeb rolled. It wasn't elegant, but it was enough as the other Pan crashed into the ram in a tangle of heavy limbs and rolling, clanking metal. The back lines of the Tsiorc engaged, tearing past Laeb and beating at the Pans, stabbing frantically at anything not clad in armour, but even in their greater numbers they were simply no match for these things. Laeb's fingers twitched. He had to show his men that they could be killed.

He threw himself forward, shoving through the gaps of his own soldiers, reciting Kavik's words over and over. "Ankles, groin and eyes. Ankles, groin and eyes."

The ram loomed over him. "Ankles!" His blue steel sword sliced through tendon and muscle alike and the ram's balance faltered. "Groin!" The sword found the softness beneath the Pan's simple groin covering, and the ram squealed, bending over double. "Eyes!" Laeb drove his sword up and into the eye of the ram's head, the curve of the metal pulling the blade up through the only soft part of its skull and tearing out the other side. Both the Tsiorc and Pans stopped fighting and stared at the body at Laeb's feet in a moment of peace that seemed to go on forever. The sound of a turbulent sea, and rumbling thunder were the only sounds.

The remaining Pan Guard snarled and dropped to all fours, bounding towards him like a tigre, mouth foaming, and locs flying out behind it.

Laeb set his feet and held his sword out, aiming for the head. The tip of his sword held still in waiting as though somehow the world and all of its contents were born from that single origin point, rotating around it. If he was to die here and now, this Pan would be coming with hi...

The Pan skidded to a halt well short of the end of Laeb's sword. Its animal eyes were fearful and wide. A crushing grip took hold of Laeb from behind and the bridge and sky spun away. When he stopped moving the Bohr king's face was in front of him.

When she spoke it was the sound of the mountain and thunder. "Laeb. Finally we meet." Hot, stinking breath washed over him. The deer Pan Guard stood below him looking up, uncertain and afraid.

"Glad... to meet you, Zuveri," he said, croaking through the pain.

Her huge hand tightened around his torso and something inside him broke. He wanted to scream, as warm searing pain spread through him, but he did not. He would not.

"You see the damage you have done," she said, turning him to face towards Terävä.

The lord's army had been decimated. There was a clean path of black stone still visible all the way along the Way Bridge to the Teräväen docks on the other side. The remaining Tsiorc had clumped together; there couldn't have been more than sixty left.

"Yes," said Laeb. "Nothing like killing your own kind."

"They are not my kind!" growled the Bohr king. The warmth spreading throughout Laeb's insides halted as the sheer force of the king's grip stemmed the flow, stopped his blood from moving, extending what short time he had left. The thought made him smile.

"Humans are a scourge," growled the Bohr king. "It doesn't matter how they die. And you *will* all die. You however, Captain Laeb, are fortunate enough to be one of the few who meets their end at the hands of the Bohr king."

Laeb snorted. "Human I may be, but I still drew you to me. I set out the bait, and you took it, like any other animal."

"You did not lure me here, human. I came here of my own volition, to end you. I wanted to see the look upon your face as your puny soul leaves you."

A familiar cart appeared at the Teräväen end of the bridge, with five figures standing upon it. Even at this distance Laeb could see Kavik's awkward and massive shape surveying the carnage, his hand held up against the onslaught of black rain still pelting down. Kavik and Kai's presence was a sign of victory, but it was bittersweet. They were too late for him.

Laeb wished suddenly to be with Kavik, standing next to him, upon another landscape, in another life with Fia at his side, their friends and neighbours enjoying a glass of rice ale, and their children and grandchildren chasing each other amongst the long, dappled shadows while the sun set behind them. Another life perhaps, but one he had the power of bestowing upon others, and more besides.

He shifted painfully towards the Bohr King. "You might have been the motion, Zuveri, but it was I who placed the pieces." The King's wide mouth split into a silent snarl at the use of her name, and Laeb threw his head back and laughed. He couldn't help it. He let the laughter rise up through him like a force outside of his control. His greatest plan, his last plan had come together as simply as if it had been written on paper. As simple as a story to be read. The Bohr King squeezed again, but this time much harder. He choked as blood bubbled from his lips, forced up from his wounded, broken body. His insides contracted, his body spasmed, and his heart hammered above it all, yet still he smiled.

Firam stood at the entrance of the drain at the centre of the bridge. The horn of the Tsiorc in one hand, and a flaming torch in the other. He nodded towards Laeb, and Laeb nodded back.

Zuveri turned as Firam vanished into the dark tunnels, and her snarl faded.

"I'm ready to die for my people, Zuveri. Are you ready to die for yours?"

Deep creases appeared around those animal eyes, so close he could see her pupils dilate.

"I thought not."

The hearthsalt hidden within the drainage tunnels of

the Way Bridge caught immediately as Firam's torch made contact with it. A handful could burn through the thick iron Teräväen gates, so then what would a half-ton do? Laeb had asked each of the three hundred Sulitarians fighters to take a handful and lace the drains with it, and had been waiting with palpable excitement to find out exactly what would happen. Well, now was that moment. Light burst from the bridge road, from every pothole, between every crack in every cobble, burning stone, and bone to cinder. The tower behind exploded, sending a blast of searing heat towards them where they stood.

Zuveri ducked and cowered, but no matter how fast she could move, she would not outrun this.

The golden fields and dappled shadows melted away. The children's joyful screams now distant echoes. Fia's sunlit features grew dim, replaced with black, replaced with pressure so intense...

Safe Harbour

"Let me see it."

"No," said Kyira, sheathing Iqaluk's blade. "You do not deserve to touch it."

Hasaan paused, unsure of how to shape the words stuck in his throat. He had to try — she was all he had left. "I'm sorry, Kyira."

Kyira turned her back to the bay and rounded on him. "You are no longer my brother, Hasaan. Abika and I are all that matter now. You can keep your apologies."

"I'm sorry for the pain I've caused you. And Aki."

"Don't call him that! How would he feel to see you here? Killing your friends, your people in the name of the Bohr? What would he say to you?"

The guilt burned a pit in Hasaan's stomach. He had so much to make up for, so much to repair. He should leave her and the babe to themselves, but something inside of him wouldn't allow it. He decided right then and there that he would follow her until she forgave him.

"Kyira, please listen, I—"

The ground beneath shook and the few Vasenfolk who had stayed behind suddenly gasped in horror. A ball of white light exploded out from the Way Bridge down in the bay. There was the smallest of delays and a shockwave tore through the air, the sound of a muffled tear that cracked through Hasaan's very soul. The white fire changed hue to yellow and orange, loosening as the bridge was reduced to stones blown apart into the Way channel. Chunks of rock, carts, bodies flew flaming into the air.

"Oh, lords!"

"By the blood of…"

The archway piles that held up the bridge crumbled and the Way Bridge was no more. Vasen and Terävä were two cities spread across two continents. The remaining Kin and the lord's that had been on the bridge were all just… gone. The remaining Sulitarians too. The Pans, the Bohr king…

A roar blew in on the wind, but it was not the Bohr king. The crowds in Terävä were exalting. Cheering. A cart sat in the centre of the crowd, and even from here Hasaan could see the joy upon their faces as the five standing upon it hugged each other. He watched transfixed as they were picked up by the crowds and carried like kings, like champions away into the favelas.

"The storymakers of kings," said Hasaan. Kyira and the babe locked eyes with him. "Come, sister. It's over. Let's go home."

* * *

Kyira wondered what the chalk white streets of Vasen had been made to accommodate, because they looked too narrow for everything but the smallest of carts. The narrow streets were not the main reason though that she and Hasaan stayed single file — she was not quite ready to walk at his side yet,

476

if she ever would be ready at all.

The winding roads led gradually downhill, sometimes revealing a brief glance of a hillside between the high buildings, or even a view of the remains of the Way Bridge and the waves breaking over it. The weather above seemed to echo the fear in her heart, as lightforks as black as a week-old firepit tore at the sky, holding for an unnatural length of time, only to burst apart without touching the ground. Abika jumped at the thunderclap and Kyira pulled her closer.

"You are certain you know the way, sister?"

Kyira flinched. "Do not call me that. I am not your sister."

"Kyira, I—"

"I said do not call me that!" She exhaled the rest of her anger and tried to quiet Abika's sobs, but it was no use. "The effects of her sleep are wearing off."

Hasaan had drawn close. He looked as though he wanted to take the child and hold her, but there was no chance of Kyira ever letting Abika go, especially not to him. She held the babe closer and Hasaan drew back, rubbing his forehead.

"The Sulitarians are proud fighters," he said. "I see it now. My bow was my most prized possession, and I took it into battle, it makes sense that a mother would take her child."

"Her name was Lyla."

Creases appeared on Hasaan's forehead, worry lines like Iqaluk used to get.

"She had no home. There was no one…" She swallowed, feeling the words catch in her mouth. "There was no one else left to look after Abika. What else was she to do? Who else would she leave her most *prized possession* to?"

Hasaan looked to his feet, then up at the roiling sky, just as their father did when he was feeling downtrodden. Was he crying? She couldn't tell. His gaze locked onto something behind Kyira and she spun towards it. There was no danger, at least nothing immediate. A grey square had appeared at the bottom of the street. The Way rushed by, churning muddy and grey with debris and wood. A partial bow stood out briefly from the surface before bumping into the remains of the jetty and rolling away taking some of the wood with it. In front of the jetty there sat a lake of standing water that was creeping up towards a bright red crane which lay on its side at the end of the road, and to which one small rowboat was tied.

"The Vasen dock," said Hasaan. "Or what is left of it." He nodded his head at the long buildings stretching away in every direction. "Well, which way is it? The orphanage?"

Kyira shrugged. "I don't know." The babe squirmed again. "All I remember was the street, which was very tight."

"That does not help us," said Hasaan. "There's so many buildings. How on earth are we supposed to know which one the Tsiorc hid in?"

"These are all too small." Kyira turned on the spot scanning the landscape, trying to match their journey to that which the Tsiorc army had taken through the underground tunnels to the Way Bridge. "It is too hard. I have never been underground before."

Hasaan didn't speak. He was cocking his head sideways like a hound might, staring at the lines of buildings and frowning. "This hill is unlike anything I have ever seen. It does not move with the earth like the ones in Nord do, it seems like it was... created somehow."

Kyira followed his outstretched hand. He was right. How had she not seen it before? There was an unusual quality

478

to the land. "The hill does not make sense because…" She stopped.

Hasaan turned to her, a knowing smile forming at his lips. "Because of the catacombs beneath Vasen."

Kyira shook her head. "I don't know why I didn't see it before. It's so clear. We need to get higher." She took off down one of the streets running parallel with the Way and veered off left up a steep rise that looked like a dead end.

The street ended in a circle with houses all around. Strange square gardens with perfectly short green grass, yet every home was as empty as the rest. Holding Abika close she vaulted onto one of the low walls, on to the roof of an outhouse then lifted herself up onto a short balcony.

"Vasen curves like it was built upon a rolling wave of hillside," said Hasaan from below. "Like a swell of land preparing to break over the sea. Tyr might be ancient, but it was built by humans, before it was stolen by the Bohr…" He bent down to the foot of a wall and lifted an iron grate and took a deep breath. "This drain is a run off, and run offs like this one must channel the water down."

Kyira nodded. "But they cannot go too deep because of the catacombs, so they follow the shallow contour of the hillside. That was why the flow within the tunnels was so slow."

They stared at each other. They had both come to the same conclusions because they were both Sami. They were both their father, and he was with them.

The Orphanage

The long grey building was clearly vacant from its neglected appearance. The roof wasn't flat like the other Vasen buildings, but sloped and sunken in places with curved, once-orange tiles now a dingy moss covered green. Hasaan might have even overlooked it, for it looked like several buildings linked together, rather than one long building. An iron weathervane depicting a woman cradling a child sat upon the only chimney still standing.

Hasaan pressed himself tight against the wall as curtains of black rain assaulted the cobbled street.

"It might be guarded," roared Hasaan, belying the trepidation currently watering down his insides.

Kyira nodded, doing her best to hold her arm over the babe strapped to her chest. She looked more and more like a mother hen protecting her chick. "Laeb is clever," she said. "He may have left a man or two behind. Hasaan, we have to get out of this. It is getting cold. Abika will freeze."

"And what of this Kai?"

She shook her head. "They sabotaged the gate. They won't be able to get back until…"

Hasaan swallowed. "Until the lord's army and the Kin are all dead." He pulled Kyira's blade from his belt and tapped the sticky blade against his palm. "Then we must be ready. We must do what needs to be done."

Kyira frowned at him. "You are not who I thought you were."

Hasaan nodded to the child. "That makes two of us then."

Suddenly the door to the building burst open, and a blond boy tumbled out and sprinted away down the street.

"Glynn!" Kyira burst forward onto the street, and the boy stopped and turned. He barely had time to hold up an arm before a bright light exploded around him, searing him into cinder. The flash was followed by a surge of heat that blew Kyira back into Hasaan. He barely caught her.

"Shiach!" said Hasaan. "Are you alright?"

"What was that?" yelled Kyira.

Hasaan blinked away the blue forked lines burned into his retinas. "Was that lightning?"

"Glynn!"

Ahead of them, where the boy had been standing there was nothing but a charred hole, with cobbles around the edges of the crater still glowing bright, hissing as water poured in.

"Hasaan, what in the Lands is going on?!"

Hasaan tried to rub the ringing from his ears, but it was no use. The sky was a thick mass of black cloud that stretched out in all directions. Swirling spikes of vapour grew outwards from it, twisting down towards the ground, and inside, flashes and veins of black pumped with energy and light, filling the sky with cloud.

The street behind them flashed and the babe let out a terrified scream. Another hole, burnt out of the ground from a lightning strike almost too fast to see. The tendrils of cloud, began twisting, and turning faster and faster, forming into spinning vortexes of wind, each one burgeoning and quivering, eager to roll across the Vasen hills and suck the city up into oblivion. Another flash exploded behind them and the building with the balcony was reduced to rubble and mortar.

Kyira grabbed Hasaan's hand. "Come on, Hasaan! We need to get into the catacombs! We need to get underground!"

The narrow street cracked and split as they leapt over the charred holes towards the door of the orphanage. The Forbringrs were here, but they didn't want just Hasaan, Kyira and this child. They wanted all of Tyr.

Landfall

asaan leapt over the hole where Glynn had been standing and crashed through the orphanage door in a clutter of broken wood. His heart hammered, but only once, the next beat coming an age later, and instead of the floor greeting him, he hung suspended unable to fall, unable to stand, unable to do anything but stare ahead.

Beyond the splintered door the orphanage room was a scene frozen in time, as three individuals held motionless like a painting in front of them. Guardian Rathe and a squat man in a black cloak stood over a prisoner. Fia. Her eyes were bright with tears, her cheeks dirty and bruised, her red hair tangled and unkempt.

Blue bars of light inched through the air between them, showing that time had not stopped, but was moving very slowly, and Hasaan seemed to be stuck between the force that pulled him down and something unseen from above, holding him silently in limbo. Gaps began to appear in the building walls as the mortar that held them together drifted apart. The floor, the walls, even the very air looked like they were no longer a part of reality, and were gradually being reclaimed back by the creators themselves. What if it tried to reclaim him? What if the pieces that made him, and

Kyira, and the child were reclaimed? He couldn't let that happen. He turned his head, willing his strength to fight the forces that held him fast, and he saw Kyira behind him, her expression stuck between surprise and fear, her body half way through the door, her hand holding onto his breeches. The baby blinked at him, and they all crashed to the floor.

* * *

Wind. That was the first thing Kyira felt after things returned to normal. Not the cool, bracing wind that rushed along the Nord vales, but a harsh bitter wind filled with dust and sand and splinters. These were the same forces that she had encountered on the hilltop with Iqaluk. But something was different. This time it was not just a random hill in Nord that would bear the awesome power of the Forbringrs, it was she.

* * *

Hasaan scrambled up and Fia's wide eyes stared back at him, bound and gagged and barely ten paces away. She jerked her head upwards towards Guardian Rathe, and he looked down at her. He shook off the effects of the time change, and he saw Hasaan.

"Fia!"

Hasaan pulled his blade, Kyira's blade, from his belt and hurled it through the air.

* * *

Rathe couldn't believe his eyes. The once-solid walls, old stone walls that should have held fast instead floated apart, releasing the mortar holding them together into a fine sand that orbited the room. The stones themselves broke apart, as the effects of the tunnel tore at their constituent parts, rendering them into a fine dust. It was a wondrous thing to behold, and he had Seb to thank for leading him here to witness it. The Banémen possessed power, but he doubted Kaliste or even Jagar had ever seen anything like this. A tunnel from one world to another, and all he had to do was wait for the door between realities to open, and he would finally be free of this forsaken world. He would begin again in a new world, and they would worship him as a king. First of all though he had to appease the creators of this world. He lifted his blade high above his head, ready to sacrifice the Kumpani at his feet. He had never believed in the Gods before, but it was hard to deny their presence now, and it was always best to be sure. Wasn't it?

* * *

It began as a spot of light, a trick of the eye yet as real as Kyira herself. The pulsing flame floated six feet from the floor in the centre of the room, between him, the Bohr, and her brother. The dust in the air drifted towards that single point, orbiting it, feeding it, and it grew to the size of a grape, jerking and eager to break free from whatever held it.

Hasaan tossed his blade and the woman at the Bohr's feet caught it with her bound hands and threw herself back. The Bohr tried to move but his hesitation had already written his fate.

The woman pushed the knife into the Bohr's groin drawing a scream that warbled from his throat and distorted the air. He stumbled forward, and the point of light that was a tear between realities passed without resistance through his strapped breastplate and into his chest. Every muscle in his body tightened all at once, drawing his shoulders back and standing out high from his neck. The scar on his head burst open, then was sucked back in. His face grew hollow and his head and chest shrunk, as the hole in reality consumed him from the inside. His mouth opened in silent protest and he was sucked completely into the hovering ball of light. There was no time to think on it, a rock whipped by, before disappearing fizzing and spluttering into the tear. It grew again, morphing through impossible shapes and glowing like burnished gold all the while. It was the single source of power for all that existed, a point of origin from which everything would be born or die. The evaporating walls thrummed in time with it straining against the tear's pull, jostling inwards, breaking into powder. The floor followed, cracking into planks, then splinters, then dust. Blue light burst in as the building became nothing but a nebulous cloud of matter with Kyira and Hasaan floating amongst it. Kyira reached forward, tried to push the air away, tried to find a way to escape the pull of the tear before it consumed her, Abika and Hasaan.

* * *

Fia reached out as far as she could, but the Kin's hand drifted away from her. She screamed, roared in frustration, but the sound came out muted, stolen away by the fighting forces.

486

There was nothing to grab, or use for purchase, it might have even been funny to see them bobbing around like flotsam if it weren't for the imminent threat of that glowing eye. Hasaan drifted upwards with her, a look of absolute terror on his face grasping for the girl with the baby. Unable to hold himself steady, he grabbed for them but tumbled left and let go sending them off on a wider orbit around the eye. The girl floated by Fia, clinging tight to the child all the while.

Hasaan mouthed something, but the words wouldn't form. She floated back around, her arms and legs kicking uselessly, towards the glowing eye that had already taken Rathe — easily the strongest man she had ever met, but there was nothing she could do but scream as loudly as she could at it.

"Argh!"

As her trajectory took her along its side it seemed to glow brighter, anticipating its next meal. The heat pulsed off of it in waves, searing her skin as she floated closer and closer to it, then at the last second she curled her body and sucked in her stomach, missing the thing by barely a hair's breadth. She sailed past it, and was flung out wide.

Sebreth, the bastard who had led her to this place on the promise of freedom, had somehow dropped outside of the eye's influence and was floating down to the floor, which was now fifty paces below them.

"Sebreth!"

The fool man had his eyes closed and here she was floating back around towards the eye again, and she knew this time she would not be so lucky. She needed an anchor. She tore off her hak and twisted the cloth, tying a knot in the fabric. Then with all she had she threw the knot at the fat little man.

487

Sebreth rolled helplessly on his axis and came to focus on the naked form waving wildly for his attention, then clocked the makeshift rope. He reached for it but the knot hurtled by him and drifted away. Fia reeled in the hak as fast as she could. This was it — the last roll of the dice.

* * *

Hasaan tumbled back as something big knocked into his back, knocking him onto a new path around the tear. Fires raged in the distance around Vasen, and the white buildings of the rich crumbled, only to be picked up again by the whirling winds whipping through the remains of the city. A deep rumble drew his gaze down, and through the haze a deep crack split the earth like breaking ice, moving up and out into the street, and growing wider, swallowing the cobbled road they had just walked upon, the crater that was the remains of the blond boy Glynn, the balcony, the drains. All of it was being swallowed by the crack. It continued out through Vasen, swallowing homes, and streets and gardens all the way to the Domst square. The sun clock monuments that Fia had pointed out when they entered the city split and fell like matchsticks in the distance as the crack reached the Domst and Justice Courts. Both fell unceremoniously, and quietly, vanishing into the catacombs below.

Hasaan watched helpless as the crack grew into a yawning abyss that opened up beneath his feet pulling the whole Vasen hillside away as massive chunks of land and rubble into its depths. The thrashing water of the Way broke through, rushing in as a torrent, tearing the mouth of the Way open deep into the Vasen hillside.

Hasaan hung above it all, caught between forces and waiting for his turn to die as Rathe had. He squinted at the shining orb in front of him, but his eyes refused to focus on it. Round like a ball and glassy, Kyira was the only one of them reflected on its surface. It wanted her. It wanted the child. Her reflection, which at first was a dull smear of dirty colour, grew sharper as she spiralled around the tear until it showed her in her full glory, spinning in the air, dark hair whipping around, her face streaming with black rain. He shouted his sister's name, screaming as loud as he could. Again, and again, and again...

* * *

Clumps of earth and stone rushed by Kyira, slamming into the glowing tear now barely ten paces away and itself two paces wide, big enough to swallow her. The woman who had thrown off her hak was pulling the other man closer to her, and at once Kyira saw that she was using the man's weight to pull herself away from the tear's influence. But they were so much lower than she was, further from the epicentre. They had a chance that Kyira and Abika didn't. That Hasaan didn't. At least, not yet.

Kyira looked down into Abika's eyes blinking through the stinging rain, clinging on to her. *The only way to move forward is to leave something behind.*

"Kyira!" Her name drifted on the wind, quiet, the voice unmistakable.

"Iqaluk?"

It wasn't her father. Hasaan was twisting below her, scrambling against the unseen forces. He was shouting, yelling, stretching his arm desperately towards her, and Kyira reached towards him, shifting and tilting as her centre rolled around. It was barely a pace!

"Hasaan!" She stretched further, willing the space to close, willing her brother to come closer, but it was too far. She couldn't reach him. She was being pulled into orbit again.

And if she was, then Abika would be too.

That meant there was a chance.

The only way to move forward is to leave something behind.

Kyira tore the sling, and lifted the bundle, babe and all, over her head and let it all go.

* * *

Fia felt the eye call her. Her reflection appeared on the surface, a streak of skin against the black waters below. She groaned as the force of the eye pulled her upwards, while the weight of the fat man pulled her down, her skin stretching as gravity was denied her weight — two opponents fighting for her. She and Sebreth both began to rise slowly upwards towards the glowing eye. End game. She had lost.

* * *

Hasaan's expression was wild as he fumbled for Kyira's hands, wet and slipping in the rain. Fat globules of water splashed against them as they orbited the tear, but they were moving steadily together. She clutched at his dark Kin jacket, and pulled him into her chest, holding him close, so that they were now a single object with a new centre. The sky roiled above them, the clouds spinning with immeasurable

490

force. If she was to die here, she would die with Hasaan.

As Kyira had expected, the floating bundle of cloth hurled around towards them after a full orbit around the tear.

"Here she comes!" she roared, into nothingness.

Kyira stretched up as far as she could, lifting away from Hasaan and standing upon his thighs. "Hasaan, we are too low!"

He stared up at her, knowing what she must do, willing her to do it.

The only way to move forward is to leave something behind.

She took Hasaan's head in her hands. The seconds lingered into an age as they looked upon each other, his eyes the same green as Iqaluk's. She hated him, but she loved him. He was a part of her, as she was a part of him. He deserved a second chance, and at last she knew how to give it to him. She crouched low and kissed his forehead, feeling the warmth of his skin, the taste of his salt sweat upon her lips then planted her feet into his chest and pushed away as hard as she could. The effect was immediate, he dropped low, beyond the pull of the raging tear, speeding up as the forces of this world reclaimed him, falling towards the dark churning waters of the Way channel far below while she flew upward into the bundle of rags that was Abika. She grasped at the cloth, clutching it to herself as she had her brother, but her trajectory was taking her closer to the tear. Into the tear.

The sphere's outer ring enveloped Kyira's hand, and black fire crackled up her arms, at first a tingle then burning her skin. She tried to push back but the tear had her. Black lightforks snapped towards her, their energy crackling through the air, hungry for her being. She roared, fearful for her life, for Abika's life. Lives that meant something, but the fingers of night sought her out inexorably. The reflection burst apart and the sphere split open like an overfilled waterskin. Fresh air poured in from it, wonderfully clean, and Kyira's pores reached out for the healing breeze, embracing it. Then black lightning penetrated her body.

Immediately it sought out her mind, and words formed in her head. *Let go. Let go. Let go.*

"NO!"

The tendrils of light grew sharper, delving deeper; thousands of needles penetrating the inside of her head.

Kyira tightened her grip.

Let go.

Salt blood filled her mouth. "I WILL NOT!"

Let go.

A vibration moved along her chest, and down her arm. She felt her fingers loosen as the tear wrestled her for control of her own hand. It was trying to steal Abika.

She glanced down at Abika and dug down deep within herself, to places of darkness she wished she would never see again.

Breathe.

Her heartbeat slowed, but her body raged as the fire searched through her for a way in, a way to take over, a way to own her. It raped, and coursed and attacked the corners of her mind. Her memories, Iqaluk. Hasaan. Her mother.

Breathe.

Let go.

The Dark

Kyira dove deeper into the void, concentrating as hard as she could, feeling the heat of the light behind her, as the tear's lightning followed her down into the depths of her own self. She knew this place well. It was a place she retreated to when things became too much, a place for hiding things.

Then she saw it.

It looked like the beginning of another tear — a single point of light but within the frame of her mind. She moved towards it and a sound like steel upon steel tore through her, but it was outside her body. The tear was screaming.

She willed herself forward again and the point of light grew bigger, showing the space, highlighting its own existence. The lightning behind her tugged, but this place was hers. The breath in her body, the beating in her chest. This place was hers. In here, she was God.

She willed the lightning off, and the tugging ceased. She turned and willed it to vanish, and the blue forks vanished into mist.

A tortured scream echoed outside the darkness. Numbly, she was aware of pain in her ears, but it didn't matter. Nothing mattered anymore. She reached out and pulled the point of light inside and she felt the tear outside close.

Oranges

The soft smell of flowers and fruit drifted in on the wind. Warmth. Sunlight. Birds called to one another, but not any songs that Kyira recognised. The leaves rustled gently in the breeze, bringing new scents. Soil, water, plants.

No. Nord was her home. Ice and clear water, the smell of fish and oiled leather, burning lamp oil, goats, dew.

There were orange fruits hanging in lines all around her. She looked along her line noticing that the groves were tied with twine in places. Cultivated land. People. She held Abika closer and stood just high enough so that she could see above the plants. There were people here, moving down the lines methodically testing the fruits, taking some, leaving others. They wore wide hats that hid their faces, but they looked like any other farmer Kyira had seen. Farmers were safe, they could be trusted.

Still, this place was not hers.

She sat back down, noticing the thrumming which was less of a noise and more of a feeling. The tear shone, reflecting everything around her, all except her or Abika. It was smaller now, and barely wide enough for a person to crawl through. One or two of the stalks had been severed where it had opened, but the plants had yet to fall. Kyira pulled an orange fruit from one and tossed it at the shining orb. It hit the surface and bounced off, landing on the dry mud below. The skin grew lighter, yellow then brown then through to black as the insides shrivelled and dried. Then it was no more than a husk, and as she watched, it fell apart as dust and was blown away with the wind.

The tear began to shrink and Kyira stayed with it until it was no bigger than the size of an orange itself. It held for the briefest of moments, hovering above the ground like it would deny all that had happened: the destruction of Tyr, the violent death of a Bohr sucked into it from the inside out…What might it do now? Was it still dangerous?

The glassy orb that was a door between places began to fade, revealing the twigs and stalks behind, becoming clearer as this world took back the space the tear had stolen. Finally, a cool breath blew out from it and it was gone.

The air in its place shimmered, holding onto the memory of an ungodly thing. She frowned. The holes in the world were as natural as the hills, the ground, even herself and Abika, which meant of course that it had just died, yet this did not feel like its end.

Kyira reached out to the severed plants and pulled on the twine which came away with a sharp tug — the farmers in this place used the same knot she used for holding taimen to her back, a life that seemed further away than even Kai's maps could account for.

She tied the twine around Abika's delicate wrist careful not to chafe the skin. The last two fruits from the broken plant were pulled and dropped into her waist bag. The leather armour that Dia'slar had given Kyira came off over her head as easily as it had gone on. The man had been right about her size in the end. She dropped it over the shimmering air. It didn't turn to dust as the orange had, but there was just enough power lurking there to break down the intricate links and hoops into a clinking pile of rust and fibre that smoked in quiet indignation.

The memory of the armour, of the war, of a land she called home slipped away as she stood. Beyond the groves there was a line of trees, but no hills. It was so flat she couldn't see beyond the end of the field. There could be anything out there. Her feet took her on, down the line past the sweet floral scents and the quiet rustling of browning leaves in a summer wind.

This place might not be hers, but then perhaps it could be.

She stroked Abika's delicate hair. Her soft features were already proud like her mother's. Abika's focus drifted beyond Kyira's head then back, and her smile blossomed like an opening flower.

"Let us find somewhere to rest, dear Abika." Kyira ran a finger over the babe's head, brushing away a loose strand of her soft hair. "Daughter."

THE END

Thank you for reading my book and supporting my work. If I can beg you further to leave a review on Amazon or Goodreads you'll help me reach more people. Even better, if you know someone who likes fantasy give them this book to read.

Wasted

An extract from **Fallen Shards, Book 2 of the Ringlander Series.**

The sinew strings of Vasta's guitar rolled off the end of his fingertips releasing sound out into the warm evening air. The music notes flattened out becoming one with the thin smoke of his crackling fire, joining a chorus of lapping waves from the nearby lake, the soft cawing from the duskgulls, and the rustling of new spring leaves hanging from the birch tree behind. It was a song that tied Vasta to the world with a tether of natural music. He chuckled softly at the metaphor — it seemed even his unconscious mind refused to let go of the past.

He set his mind purposefully back to the strings and relaxed into it. He had no particular tune in mind, just an idea of which notes should join with which. He kept the chords major, but that was the extent of his purpose; he was merely a conduit for this section of the piece, and this newly crafted guitar was his medium. The sound had yet to bed in, the strings and wood still strangers, but come the moonrise they would be lovers, intimate in ways that only the two could be.

His fingers seemed they were no longer a part of him as he played. The memory of years of scientific experimentation running through his carpals had clearly not dulled despite his tendency to think otherwise. His hands were his most prized tools, capable of dropping even the smallest drop of mercura, or separating hair filaments of hearthsalt from iron. As far as he knew he had been the only scientist in Kemen capable of doing so, yet now a smattering of musical notes were the extent of their successes.

The tune calmed his soul sending his thoughts towards the faces of his four children who he could see as clearly as if they were sitting across the fire at this very moment. Children he would never see again. Meha and Frela were smiling as they always were, their identical features scrunching up whenever he called either of their names. Mical, the in-between child, not planned but not unwanted either, with his strong nose that might have overpowered the features of any other. Then, of course, there was Strev, the oldest, with his wide smile and keen eyes. Those that didn't know him called him insolent, Vasta called him resourceful, not to mention he had a singing voice which was among the most beautiful Vasta had ever heard, as biased as a father's opinion was. They were all beautiful, and what's more, they each possessed qualities of his own he hadn't known until they were mirrored in them.

He shook his head at the sadness of it, and his mind settled upon the image of Colees. His fingers stumbled at her disappointed expression — that was all he remembered now, even after so long. He wondered how the years had treated her, and whether the cruel lines of time had softened her scorn.

He had stopped playing, his fist tight before him. He splayed his fingers, hoping to diffuse the tension, but the

498

lightness had gone. He had wasted it, as he had wasted all else. The evening air seemed no longer a symphony of sound but rather oppressive — a cage with the lake on one side and the hills behind. Anger caught in his throat, too deep to ignore. It could be quelled, because it was only anger at his own foolish choices, but one must not quell the natural forces of these worlds. Not again.

He stood up and lifted the guitar above his head, and it bumped into the low branches of the birch tree and fell behind him, dropping awkwardly over the uneven ground with the unmistakable sound of cracking wood.

"Fool," he whispered, with a shake of the head. He lifted it carefully, but the tension of the strings pulled the damaged neck splintering away from the body. It was time to go home.

Glossary

A glossary of terms and pronunciations used in this book:

Alamar: A cross between a camel and llama.

Altinda'har: *[All-tin-dar]* An under rank below the Kael, a secretary of sorts that acts an emissary between the merchants, traders, unions and workhouse owners.

Anqamor: A large island west of Határ.

Atacru: *[At-ay-roo]* Prayer time (starts at 6am ends at 7am).

Avere: *[Av-ee-yer]* Children who are raised by a village, rather than a single set of parents.

Bakla: An independent city in the south. Fia's birthplace.

Banéman: *[Ba-nay-man]* Ancient assassins interbred for their abilities.

Baeivi: *[Bee-yay-vee]* Mother Nature herself, personified as a God. *"Be confident!" chided Laeb. "Even if you're unsure! It will help win over the undecided. And by the eyes of Baeivi we have many of those."*

Blue eyes: Referring to someone from Sulitar, often used as slang for someone who is foreign or an immigrant, doesn't belong, or is just stupid (depending on class of speaker) *"Are your eyes blue? Such a thing dishonours us."*

Captain Laeb: Captain and tactician of the Tsiorc, originally from Sulitar.

Celsathar: *[sells-a-thar]* Kai's ship. Hewn from one single tree trunk in Sulitar.

Charn: The absolute best charsand that is dredged up from the way mouth itself. It is particularly fine and is exported to make black clay for ornaments in palaces.

Charsalt: Precious white veins of salt within the black cliffs of Tyr.

Charsand: The black sand of Tyr.

Child of the Bohr: A half-blood Bohr, like Rathe.

Chinaes: *[Chin-ay-us]* A game of stones, a cross between Backgammon and Go

Common Nordish: The main language of Nord.

Culdè: *[K-yoo-l-de]* Of the Sami, one who doesn't follow the aspirational Lines tattooed upon their face. They are often considered lost souls.

Cycle: A year.

Dagors: The Sulitarian word for Dragons. *"There's a myth that they are descended from Dagors. You would know them as dragons, from old tales. More myths. Who has time for stories, when the world is in such chaos."*

Dali: Large western country of hills and valleys where the Tsiorc retreated back to after Drakemyre. North of the Way.

Dearg Twins: Two twins who caused havoc for both Kyira and Hasaan separately in Nord whilst they were growing up

Dia'slar: Councillor and friend of Laeb who came from Sulitar.

Domst: A church, or place of worship.

Drakemyre: The location of the Battle that was Lost

Dreki Wars: A time of unrest in which the Bohr gained a larger presence within the human cities of upper Rengas.

Eris: Erdal's first daughter, and leader of the Teräväen rebellion.

Fairsky: An island to the east of Tyr which can usually be seen clearly in good weather.

Farram: A messenger.

Feast of Moons: A spring festival. In Tyr, a fertility celebration for young singles, who don the moonflower upon themselves when it blooms.

Firewine: Highly alcoholic wine from a poisonous grape. *Kavik nodded slow. "Aye, some nice aged firewine. I'd even take a seete these days, although I always thought it smelled better than it tasted."*

Forbringr: *[For-bring-err]* A term that literally means "God".

Futhark: *[F-yoo-tha-rk]* The runes the Bohr use to write with. (Omitted through drafts).

Ge'Bat: An island to the far east with two emperors, who reign peacefully, one in the spring and summer and one in the autumn and winter. *Ge'Bat owned the shipping lines for almost the entire Eastern side of the world. Or so those who travelled west would say. Rathe snorted. "Well, who wouldn't want to shit on gold, Sebreth?"*

Giant's Teeth Mountains: A mountain range just beyond Fairsky island.

Gnarlnut: A big nut that grows underground.

Goahti: A type of Sami hut, build for a nomadic life.

Greyt root: *[Gr-ay-et]* A sweet orange root, dug up from the ground in Nord.

Hak: A kimono-like dress worn by men and women alike.

Hallam: A scientist that Seb refers to. *"There are theories," began Seb, "particularly by Hallam and his research with precious* *metals, that suggest infinite realities, in infinite variety, and indeed when one considers that one reality can exist, the door opens, so to speak, to many more."*

Harkko: *[Har-ko]* A standard unit of currency in Tyr.

Határ: *[Hat-arr]* Is the central border country in which Tyr resides.

Hauwi: *[How-wee]* A place in Sulitar famed for its warriors. *He paused while the soldiers moved through a synchronised manoeuvre. "At least these ones look like they are improving. Although a few good Hauwi fighters would have had them carved from wood."*

Hav: The Tyrian word for fishy air. *The Tyrians called the stink, hav, as though such a trivial thing deserved a special name, Rathe called it a nuisance.*

Hearthsalt: *[Har-th-salt]* An element like magnesium that looks like a silver bubble or polished smelt cast offs, until pressure is applied, then it becomes like grey putty. Added with sulphur it burns at extremely high temperatures.

Highlands: Everything above the Way

Kael: High Advisor/High Justice Chief.

Kaldi: A hot beverage made from a kaldi seed. Kaldi seeds are loaded with caffeine and hold many calories and offer lots of energy to weary travellers.

Kaleb: Keeper of horses for the Kin.

Kaliste: One of the Banémen.

Kanava: The currents of the Way, particularly the ones that extend out into the Middle Sea.

Kartta: An ancient clan of Sami who sought to pass on their knowledge of the lands by encoding information in Maeltas, boxes that can be opened to reveal a map.

Kaem'aor Sea: *[Kay-my-or]* The Sea of the Dead, a

landlocked sea located in the Kemen Empire.

Kemen Empire: A hot country in the south where the Bohr originally came from.

Kemenese: The common language of Kemen. *"Really?" said Kai. "Tur dalla mur fin ma de'a?" He stood waiting for a response. "Ah, so you don't know Kemenese."*

Lopal: Liquid Opal.

Lowlands: Everything below the Way.

Maelta: *[May-al-ta]* A the Kartta used to encode maps. They often contained maps that had been made specifically to deceive, when the true map was hidden within the folds and mechanism of the box. Each section of the box can be opened and used as a printing block, the sections are placed together in a specific pattern to reveal the map.

Makril: A town in Nord.

Makriliaen: *[Mak-ril-ian]* Someone who comes from Makril.

Mark: A standard unit of currency in Tyr, smaller than a Harkko.

Muta: The Sulitarian word for Chinaes.

Nara: A large horse sized deer. They are clever, strong and fast.

Nord: The highest and most mountainous country in Rengas, where Kyira is from.

Nortun: A settlement near where Kyira's, Hasaan and Iqaluk had camped.

Ortaxe: A short heavy curved axe.

Outer Reaches: The Outer Ring of Rengas.

Paliathar: The Celsathar's sister ship.

Pantheon: A God that originates in Sulitar. *"Oh, how I remember the smell of that awful stuff. Acrid enough to wake*

Pantheon himself."

Pipegreen/smokeleaf: Tobacco

Plumfruit: A hairy plum with purple segmented fruits.

Raeven: *[Ray-van]* A breed of eagle of varying sizes used for sending messages in the south. In Nord, they are much larger and are used for hunting. Vlada is one such raeven.

Redula: A trade language used chiefly in the Red Isle. *"Alright, how about Redula then? Thäehiänmernin dräwh mært'lerr?" Strange clicks came from his lips between each word."*

Rengas: The world.

Ringlander: Someone who lives on the mainland, though the term is really only used by foreigners, as most who live in Rengas don't know their world is ring-shaped.

Samian: The language of the Sami.

Scrabs: Black beetles.

Seete: *[Seet]* A very alcoholic drink made from rice and mixed with seaweed that can be drunk hot or cold.

Seòmar: *[Sayo-mar]* Idle words with no substance. Often spoke in the council halls to distract from real topics. *The result was that Sofek's speeches were often referred to as Seòmar, or chamber chat. Hollow words from a hollow man.* (Omitted through drafts).

Shieldless: A prisoner of the Kin, that can be trained into a Kin after surviving a certain number of engagements. They're often used for reloading and messaging.

Silbo: The language of the raevens. A type of warbled whistling that the Sami use to communicate with some animals, namely raevens. Some of the more isolated Sami tribes use it to communicate with each other too.

Sister: What Kyira refers to as a hill or mountain in Nord.

Stallo: A sky demon that killed Baeivi.

Stoytree: A slow-growing tree that produces a particularly dense wood. The alternating rings create a chequered pattern when cut are used for Chinaes boards.

Sulitar: *[S-yool-itar]* Is the Outer Islands name for the largest island to the east, usually spoken by a native.

Suru: *[Soo-roo]* Unbreakable ropes made from spun Wallow fibres.

Taegr: *[Ty-gur]* The line that marks the upper circle of the world.

Takiagh: *[Ta-cai]* The language of the sea spoken by Kai and the sailors. *"And who is this that does not understand Takiagh — the language of the sea. A Ringlander?".*

Tallo: A large hall.

Taraunteen: *[Ta-rawn-teen]* An island of the Outer Isles that sees particularly rough weather. *"It was... unbelievable. I've never seen such raw power, not even in Taraunteen, where the hurricanes of this world are born.".*

Terävä: *[Ter-ah-vah]* Tyr's poor side, so named after the razor mountain the favelas are built into.

Teräväen: *[Ter-ah-vah-ian]* Someone from Terävä.

The Eye of Pantheon/Pantheon's Window: A huge hole in the top of the Domst. (Omitted through drafts).

The Kin: The name of the conscripted arm of the Lord's Army that Hasaan and Cailaen join.

The Laich: *[Lay-c-h]* A Samian name for a large body of water.

The Lord's Army: An army or mercenaries stationed in Tyr.

The Red Isles: An island in the Outer Isles to the north east. Astir's home.

Tomha: *[Tom-ha]* A hallucinogenic medicinal tuber root

dried and pounded into powder, carried by peddlers to treat wounds and long nights. *Nordun peddlers harvested the root for exactly that reason, drying and pounding it into powder to extend its life. They called it Tomha and used it to treat wounds and long nights alike.*

Torv: *[Torv-e]* Peat.

Tristan - The old sailor who takes Laeb and Kyira to the Celsathar

Tsiorc: *[Ss-yor-ck]* The rebel army led by Commander Suilven.

Tyr: *[Te-er]* The city that sits at the mouth of the Way, and largely controlled by the Bohr.

Tyrian: *[Te-er-ian]* Someone from Tyr.

Vasen: Tyr's rich side, where Rathe lives and sits in a very narrow part of Határ.

Wallow: *[Wo-ll-ow]* A special lacquer applied to the Celsathar that repels water and makes it faster through the water.

Zuveri: *[Z-yoo-veer-ee]* The Bohr King.

THE PATH AND THE WAY

RINGLANDER

MICHAEL S. JACKSON

mjackson.co.uk | @mikestepjack

About the Author

Michael reads, he writes, he designs, he codes and he drums. He lives in Manchester with his wife and three children.

You can connect with me on:
- https://mjackson.co.uk
- https://twitter.com/mikestepjack
- https://facebook.com/mikestepjack

Subscribe to my newsletter:
- https://mjackson.co.uk/signup?src=book1

Printed in Great Britain
by Amazon

62685822R00312